THE GHOST OF US

ALSO BY
JAMES L. SUTTER

Darkhearts

THE
GHOST
OF US

—

JAMES L. SUTTER

WEDNESDAY BOOKS
NEW YORK

First published in the United States by Wednesday Books,
an imprint of St. Martin's Publishing Group

THE GHOST OF US. Copyright © 2024 by James L. Sutter. All rights
reserved. Printed in the United States of America. For information, address
St. Martin's Publishing Group, 120 Broadway, New York, NY 10271.

www.wednesdaybooks.com

The Library of Congress Cataloging-in-Publication Data
is available upon request.

ISBN 978-1-250-86976-0 (hardcover)

ISBN 978-1-250-86977-7 (ebook)

Our books may be purchased in bulk for promotional, educational, or
business use. Please contact your local bookseller or the Macmillan
Corporate and Premium Sales Department at 1-800-221-7945, extension
5442, or by email at MacmillanSpecialMarkets@macmillan.com.

First Edition: 2024

10   9   8   7   6   5   4   3   2   1

For my father, Jim Sutter—
the guy you want around in the apocalypse.

THE GHOST OF US

1

CHAIN-LINK CLAWED AT clothes as we ducked through the hole in the fence. Ahead, the old factory cast late-afternoon shadows across an overgrown field, broken windows yawning with glass teeth. Wind-waved grass turned the building's stillness into threat—a predator waiting to pounce.

"Oh, *hells* yes." I rested the collapsed tripod against the ground and got some B-roll.

"It sure *looks* haunted." Holly's agreement came with noticeably less enthusiasm.

I pointed to a patch of buckled pavement shot through with lines of dandelions. "We'll do the intro over there."

Holly frowned. "Why not here?"

"Wrong angle." I pointed at the sun, then at my nose.

Holly rolled her eyes so hard her whole head lolled back. "Your nose looks *great*, Cara."

"'Great' as in 'Great Wall of China': Massive. Astonishing. Visible from space."

"Fact check: the Great Wall is not, in fact, visible from space."

"Unlike my nose."

Holly sighed but followed. Around us, the paper mill sprawled like a box of dumped LEGOs, all smokestacks and boilers and crumbling warehouses. Off to the right, pilings held part of it out over the burbling Snoqualmie River.

"Perfect." I framed the scene, checked the sun again, then stepped in front, leaving room for Holly in the shot. "See? Much better."

Holly leaned in to check Camera One, which was really just my dad's old smartphone. "Your nose looks exactly the same."

"Like a tanker ship, and twice as oily. But now less obvious! Gotta get the shadows right."

"You gotta get *therapy*."

Easy for her to say—Holly's flat nose fit her face perfectly, completing her whole round-cheeked pixie thing. Plus, she had the luchador mask.

"Just roll camera," I said.

"Not until you agree I'm right." Holly's Bantering Face softened into the giant puppy eyes of Concerned Face. "Seriously, Cara. You look like Robin from *Stranger Things*."

"So I look like the weird one?"

"You said she was the *hot* one!"

"Also true." I'd let Maya Hawke explore my Upside Down any day. And I *did* kind of look like a redheaded version of her. In the right light. If you forgot your glasses.

Holly gave a triumphant grin. "So you admit you're a total snack."

There was no stopping Holly in Mom Mode. The wrestling mask wasn't just a disguise—she was merciless in her friendship, taking you apart in the Emotional Support Octagon.

"Okay, fine! I'm gorgeous and confident and *definitely* don't have a giant zit I'm gonna edit out in post. Now will you *please* hit record?"

Holly gave me one last evaluating look, then pulled on her mask. She tapped the screen and ran over to stand next to me.

The thing is, I *was* proud—mostly, at least. While only sociopaths are *completely* proud of themselves, at eighteen, I'd spent plenty of years learning the hard way not to give a shit what anyone else thought of me. And while I might not love my nose, my outfit today was as snatched as always: a form-fitting maroon coverall that matched my cherry Docs, unzipped to the waist to flaunt a black-and-white-checked top and a black bandana. Plus my signature white shorty moto jacket.

I might not be the best ghost hunter on YouTube, but I was damn sure the best-*dressed*. I gave the camera a wide smile.

"Hey there, hunters! Welcome back to *Caranormal Activity*. I'm your host, Cara. And with me as always, ready to provide spiritual security, is the Catholic commando herself—the one and only Masked Exorcist!"

Holly grinned through red-and-gold polyester and did a bicep curl with her Bible.

"Today we're at the old Stossel Paper Mill. Founded in 1926, it was shut down in the eighties. While it was operating, the mill was a nightmare of acid burns, dust explosions, crushings by giant logs— all the sorts of traumatic deaths primed to generate hauntings."

I made my face go somber.

"Sadly, not all the deaths are historical. A little over a year ago, local high school senior Aiden Reyes lost his life in one of these buildings, leading to renewed calls for the site to be torn down." I paused respectfully, then grinned. "Which is why we're investigating while we still can! Now let's go find some ghosts!"

I held the pose, giving myself padding for the edit, then relaxed.

Holly ran back to the phone. "Got it!"

"All right, let's move in." I slid my backpack off my shoulder.

Holly picked up the tripod and grimaced. "Do we *have* to go inside?"

"Um, yes . . . ? Obviously?" I pulled out my Maglite. A headlamp would leave my hands free, but it was literally impossible to look cool in a headlamp.

"Yeah, okay." Holly still didn't sound happy.

I took a closer look at her. "You're scared."

"No!" She made an offended face, then snorted. "I mean, okay— *yes*. It's just . . . that guy *died* here."

"Yeah, and if it turns out he's an angry ghost, you can go all Matthew, Mark, and Luke on his ass. Just not until I've recorded it."

I wasn't *quite* as cavalier as I sounded about tromping through somebody's tragedy. It was one of two reasons I'd agreed to put off hunting in the mill for this long, despite its convenient location.

But then yesterday I'd gotten the letter.

> Dear Cara,
> The admissions committee has reviewed your application, and
> unfortunately . . .

That had clinched it. Finding a ghost was now officially my only
ticket out of Stossel's suburban purgatory, and there was no time to
waste. If that meant dancing on some upperclassman's grave, then
lace up my fucking pointe shoes.

Holly wouldn't want to hear that, of course. A part of me wanted
to tell her anyway—to remind her that this wasn't just a hobby for
me, that *some* people didn't have their perfect life all laid out and
humming along, ready to carry them away after graduation.

Instead, I looped an arm around her shoulder.

"Besides," I said, "wouldn't laying his spirit to rest be a good deed?"

She wrinkled her nose. "Yeah, because that's *totally* why we're out
here. Your subscriber numbers have nothing to do with it."

I spread my arms. "It's a virtuous cycle."

Holly crossed her own arms, still holding the tripod. "Whatever.
I'm not worried about *ghosts*. I'm worried about *becoming* one—
falling through the floor into some rusty chemical vat. Nobody
even knows we're out here."

"Again: obviously." I softened. "Look, people hang out here all the
time. We'll just take a peek, okay?" I tapped her arm gently with the
flashlight. "Besides, what're the odds we'll *both* fall into a rusty vat?"

"You're so comforting." But she began walking toward the factory, using the tripod as a makeshift Steadicam.

A tromped-down path through the grass skirted the big buildings with their concrete foundations and yellow-brown brick.
Glassless windows with rotting frames offered glimpses of arcane
machinery—tangled pipes and mysterious tanks squatting in darkness. I shoved my phone inside to capture what I could. It might
not be ghosts, but it was still atmospheric as *shit*.

Next to a particularly moody section, I raised a hand. "Hold up—let's get a wide shot of us in front of this."

Holly dutifully hauled the tripod out into the field, then ran over to stand next to me. The two of us clowned for the camera, me pretending to try to climb through one of the windows while Holly held me back.

And that's when the other reason I avoided the factory came sauntering around the corner.

Sophia was *supposed* to be at track practice. I hated that I still memorized her schedule every year, but it made it easier to avoid her—except for today, apparently. Two boys and a girl followed, weed stench rolling off them like a roadkill skunk.

Sophia froze at the sight of us, a Disney-villain smile spreading catlike across angelic features.

"Making more videos, Cara?" Her words oozed false innocence.

I ran for the camera, but they were closer—stupid wide-angle shot. Sophia grabbed the tripod, tossing it back to her boyfriend. Brandon Hamm might be a barely sentient sack of creatine, but you didn't need to be a National Merit Scholar to play flying monkey to Sophia's wicked witch. He lifted the tripod up over his head, miles out of reach. "Oh," he crooned, "did you want this?"

I stopped short, refusing to give them the satisfaction of watching me jump for it. "Give it back." A distant part of me took pride in managing to keep the whine out of my voice.

It didn't matter. The sharks smelled blood and spread out, circling me.

"Dance for us, Scarf Girl!"

"Release the kraken!"

"Don't get too close now—she's feisty!"

My hands clenched into fists at my sides, but there were four of them, and Crony Girl had her phone out, meaning anything I did now would be all over school tomorrow. Nothing to do but stand there, watching Sophia's poison smile while her pet meat-mountain looked to her with a doglike hunger for approval.

Holly came running over, yanking off the luchador mask. "Knock it off!"

Sophia did an exaggerated double take, as if noticing her for the first time. "*Holly . . . ?* What are you *wearing?*" As if she hadn't hate-watched my channel plenty. When it came to researching your enemies, Sun Tzu had nothing on Sophia Franklin.

Holly ignored her, focusing instead on the Auxiliary Jock, a less beef-tastic dude with spiky hair. "Noah! Is *this* who you are? What would Cammy think?"

Noah the Arkless Wonder shrank under Holly's flood of disapproval, but Holly was already rounding on the other girl. "And Madeline—you want your mom to find out you're smoking weed?"

"I didn't!" the girl protested, but she took a step back.

Sophia squared up to Holly. "Nobody would believe you."

Holly crossed her arms. "Wanna find out?"

The two stared each other down—the popular girl vs. the girl people actually liked.

At last Sophia gave a sniff and reached back without looking. Brandon deposited the camera in her hand.

"Here." She handed it over, tossing a final smirky side-eye my direction. "It's nice you're here to chaperone, Hol. We wouldn't want Scarf Girl recording anything . . . *inappropriate.*"

"Don't call her that!" Holly snapped.

But Sophia was already flouncing away, douchey ducklings trailing behind her.

Holly waited till they'd disappeared back along the trail, leaving me my pride, then put a hand on my arm. "You okay?"

My stomach quivered, muscles spasming with the strain of containing my shame. Hot tears pricked at the backs of my eyes, but I refused to let them fall. Not for Sophia. Never again.

Holly squeezed. "We could come back a different day—"

"*No.*" The word came out sharp, but I couldn't help it. Holly didn't *get* it. Perfect, lovable Holly, who always came so quickly to my defense—she didn't understand. We didn't have *time.*

Because in four months she'd be gone.

And I'd still be right here.

"Sorry." I turned back toward the factory, blinking with purpose, scrubbing my eyes dry by force of will. "Just keep recording."

Holly still looked concerned, but she pulled her mask back on and followed, camera at the ready.

The trail came to an entrance, its door long gone save for a single rusty hinge. I took a deep breath, then forced a cheerful smile and turned, giving a thumbs-up for the camera as we headed inside.

The ceiling here had collapsed, sunlight illuminating a carpet of splintered wood and broken bottles. Graffiti covered the walls in a thousand shades of dick: Big spray-painted dicks. Small Sharpie-scrawled dicks. Dicks with pitchforks, dicks with faces, dicks proclaiming that Trump won or all cops are bastards.

"I'm sensing a theme," Holly deadpanned.

"Welcome to the Phallus Palace." I looked into the camera. "I've gotta say, I'm disappointed. Half of these are barely recognizable." I motioned for Holly to zoom in on a particularly underwhelming example. "Like, what is this? A sad elephant?"

"It kinda looks like a croquet mallet," she offered.

"There we go, then. Gentlemen, if you're gonna draw a dong, take some pride in your craft."

"You'd think a bunch of guys getting together to draw genitals would be less homophobic, too." Holly leaned in to examine a scrawled message. "They didn't even spell 'Leviticus' right."

"Do better, people." I moved through an archway guarded by a long, serpentine penis with scales and wings. *Dongles & Dragons.*

The next few rooms were all stained concrete floors studded with asymmetrical platforms and rusted bolts. Eventually we found ourselves in a chamber with its ceiling still intact. A row of small windows sloped rays of light like a Renaissance painting down onto a stained mattress ringed by burger wrappers and empty forty bottles. *Still Life with Crabs.*

I swept my hand out dramatically. "And here we have the honeymoon suite. Complete with bottle service."

Holly covered the nose of her mask. "Please tell me that smell is *animal* pee."

"Humans are animals." A doorway at the other end led on into darkness, and I shined my flashlight through onto a stout tree of ductwork. It would have made for a creepier backdrop, but Holly was already clearly uncomfortable. I waved to a spot beneath the windows. "Let's set up here."

With the tripod positioned, I handed Holly our compass, then addressed the camera, holding up my own phone to display its screen.

"The Masked Exorcist will now use this compass to look for magnetic anomalies, while I scan for abnormal electromagnetic frequencies. You can see here I've got the EMF Detective app, but there are plenty of others out there—hint hint, sponsors!"

We set to work. After several minutes of nothing, I turned back to the camera.

"Okay, no anomalies yet. But don't get discouraged! While unexplained electromagnetic phenomena can indicate a haunting, EM fields can *also* cause hallucinations. So a normal EMF reading just means that if you *do* see a ghost, at least you know you're not trippin' balls."

I traded my phone for my spirit box and began scanning the static between stations, looking for spectral murmurs. Across the room, Holly stared down at the gross mattress with equal parts disgust and fascination. "You think people really sleep here?"

"I think they do more than sleep." My traitorous mind immediately pulled up images of Sophia and her boyfriend. Thanks, brain.

"Ew." Holly wrinkled her nose.

"What, you don't wanna lose your virginity in an abandoned paper mill, surrounded by decaying Arby's bags?" I held the radio up to my ear.

"How'd you know my wedding theme?"

We should really have been doing this in silence, but I figured banter was part of the channel's appeal. Maybe the entire appeal, given that we'd never actually, you know, *found* a ghost.

Holly was still frowning at the mattress. "It just seems so *sad*."

"Some people get off on sad." I clicked the radio off. "They do not, however, get off on twenty minutes of static. Come on, let's try the scope."

I pulled out the plastic case and popped the latch, revealing a battered thermal imaging scope nestled in molded foam. Dad had been so excited when I'd asked for it for my birthday, even if I hadn't wanted a rifle to go with it.

"Can I use it this time?" Holly asked.

"Sure." I grabbed the tripod.

Holly put the scope to her eye and walked slowly through the rooms, scanning back and forth. I followed, trying for a nice action shot, then got distracted by some rare non-phallic graffiti of a Satanic goat head. I thought it might make for a good closing image: I could fade out until it was just—

"*Cara.*"

Holly stood frozen midstep like a deer, scope trained on the doorway to the unlit sections.

"There's something in there."

I sprinted over and snatched the scope, shoving the tripod into her hands. Through the digital lens, the concrete walls around us were cool purples, broken by the vibrant orange squares of windows. The lightless room beyond the doorway lit up just as bright, a rainbow of temperature gradients.

At the far end, half-blocked by rusting metal, a cold spot danced, blue-black against the warmer background. Maybe two feet wide and six feet tall.

Exactly the right size for a person.

Finally! I yanked out my phone and started recording, holding it up to the scope's eyepiece. I widened my eyes insistently at Holly, who'd totally forgotten about the main camera. When she pointed it at me, I whispered, "Localized drops in temperature can indicate the presence of spirits." I jerked my head toward the dark room. "Set up the tripod and give me some light."

She hesitated. "Maybe—"

"I can't hold the flashlight, Hol—I mean, Exorcist. Come on." I didn't take my eyes off my phone screen.

Behind me, the tripod's feet clicked into position. A flashlight beam shot past me into the gloom.

I followed it in. The floor here switched from concrete to wood, the old gray boards creaking. I placed each foot carefully, ready to leap backward at the first sound of splintering.

On my phone, the cold spot flickered like an inverted flame.

The flashlight beam bounced and jittered as Holly did her best to angle it from the door's entrance. I felt a burst of irritation that she wasn't following me in—followed immediately by guilt. She was just doing the responsible thing. As usual.

The cold spot was on the other side of what looked like an old boiler. I ducked beneath a flaking pipe . . .

. . . and my heart sank.

There was a hole in the floor beneath my "ghost," leading down several feet into some sort of access space. I put my hand out and felt the breeze blowing up from it, cooled by its subterranean passage.

"It's just a draft." I got a few seconds of it through the scope, then flipped to the front camera and smiled. "And *that*, hunters and haunters, is why we investigate."

I ended the recording, my phone popping up a notification that my battery was almost dead. I shoved it back into my pocket and stared down at the hole.

So close. So close to a new identity as the wunderkind investigator who proved ghosts were real. A new life far from people like Sophia. From best friends who left you behind.

As if triggered by my self-pity, my mind flashed to the boy who'd died here—and how he'd maybe fallen through a hole just like this one.

Okay, so things *could* be worse. Barely.

Holly called from the doorway: "You okay?"

I sighed. "Yeah. Coming."

Out in the mattress room, the light from the windows climbed the walls, warm with impending sunset.

"Think we've got enough?" Holly asked.

Of course not, I wanted to snarl. It wouldn't be *enough* until I found a damn *ghost.* And the factory was huge—you could search for days and not cover it all. I wanted to go into the collapsed sections. To spend the night here, listening to it creak and groan. To read out lists of everyone who'd ever died here, calling out to their spirits.

But I couldn't snap at Holly—especially after what she'd just done. After *everything* she'd done for me. She'd never cared about ghost hunting, and I could tell from the way she was fidgeting with her phone's Keroppi PopSocket that she'd exhausted any actual enthusiasm and was now burning pure, unleaded friendship. I could always trust her to back me up, but that didn't mean I needed to abuse the privilege.

Especially when I wouldn't have it for long.

"Sure, okay." I put the scope away and pulled my secret weapon out of my backpack's laptop pocket. "Lemme finish up real quick?"

"Cool." Holly smiled in relief and scampered back toward the Gallery O' Schlongs. "I'll wait outside."

I let her go and laid my secret weapon out reverently on the floor.

Somebody who didn't know better would probably have called it a Ouija board, but that's like the people who call all soda "Coke." This was no mass-produced cardboard novelty. Its double-stacked letters arched in beautiful calligraphy across a smooth sheet of lacquered cherrywood. Beneath the alphabet ran a line of numbers and the words "yes," "no," and "goodbye." It came with a matching planchette—a little heart-shaped piece on rollers, burned with the image of a winged skull. It looked like a relic from the Salem Witch Trials. A blasphemous treasure from the Vatican's secret vaults.

I'd gotten it off Etsy.

I made sure the camera was properly framing things, then sat down cross-legged and put both hands on the planchette. I took a deep breath, trying to clear my mind and open myself.

The way talking boards worked—in theory, at least—was that ghosts could use the planchette like a cursor, rolling it around to point at letters and spell words. It worked best with multiple people,

but while Holly's Catholic conscience was cool with helping me
ghost hunt, she drew the line at attempts to actually summon the
dead.

Which was fine, honestly. The thing that turned talking boards
into a party game was that multiple hands touching the planchette
made it easy to nudge without being sure who was moving it. Using the board by myself meant that, if it moved, I'd know for sure
whether it was me or something else.

Without Holly, the room was silent. I soaked it in, then murmured, "If any spirits be present, please reveal yourselves."

And I waited.

Around me, the building ticked and sighed in the breeze. In the
distance, Holly's phone dinged.

Nothing.

It didn't really matter—not to the channel, anyway. I could point
to the winning lottery numbers, and people would still never believe
I'd actually communicated with the dead. This part was just for me.
So far, I'd done it in a dozen different places, and never moved the
planchette except for one time when I'd sneezed. Pollen: 1, Polter-
geists: 0.

But still . . .

Feeling simultaneously glad and guilty that Holly wasn't here
to disapprove, I called, "Aiden Reyes. If you're here, please make
yourself known."

More waiting. A plane rumbled past overhead. Somewhere in
the distance, a car stereo subwoofed its overcompensation.

All at once, the tears I'd managed to hold off earlier came rushing back, burning up out of my ducts and boiling down across my
cheeks. Not for Sophia—*fuck* Sophia. These were for Holly, and the
letter, and the future that should have been mine.

I scrubbed a fist angrily across my cheek and gripped the planchette. "Come on, Aiden, you fucker," I husked. "I *need* this."

A puff of cold air brushed across my damp cheek.

I jerked upright, jolted out of my misery as the hairs on the back
of my neck rose.

"Hello?" I stretched out with my senses, straining to take everything in. I forced my fingers to unclench, resting them lightly on the planchette, ready to help it move. *Begging* it to. "Aiden?"

I held my breath, willing the breeze to come again.

But everything remained still.

Outside, birds sang to the impending sunset. In my pocket, my phone gave an answering chirp that meant *Okay, but seriously, though, you need to charge me, like,* now.

"Goddammit." I stood and turned off the camera.

You'd think failing every time would make it hurt less.

But you'd be an idiot. Failure is *failure.* You never get used to it. Ask me how I know.

2

THE WATERBROOK HOUSING development had three house designs, in four approved shades of beige—you could walk into any neighbor's home and know immediately where everything was. Only the gleaming rectangles of solar panels set our roof apart in the looping maze of McHouses winding up the hill.

Holly pulled Van Morrison up to the curb. "Tomorrow we work on my channel, yeah?"

"Bet." I slid the minivan's door open to get the tripod out of the back. "Send me your files when you get home?"

"Of course." She hesitated. "Hey—some of the orchestra kids are hitting up the outdoor movie in Marymoor on Wednesday, if you wanna come?" Her voice turned up hopefully at the end. "They're playing *Ghostbusters: Afterlife*."

"Nah, I'm good." As hot as Mckenna Grace in a proton pack had looked to me at fifteen, not even she could make me voluntarily spend time among the trolls and vipers of Stossel's student body.

Holly looked disappointed but unsurprised. "All right, then. Later, lady."

"Later."

I watched her drive away—signaling carefully even in our empty roundabout—and felt an uncomfortable twinge of resentment. I knew it wasn't fair to begrudge Holly an evening with her other friends. But it's hard to be charitable when you're broke, and Holly Time was now a rapidly dwindling resource.

I slunk up the driveway, past Mom's Prius and Dad's electric pickup with the ARMED LIBERAL bumper sticker. Inside, Dad stood at the kitchen counter wearing lab goggles to chop onions, while Mom dug around in our overstuffed freezer.

"Hey, Cara-bear! How was the hunt?" Dad's cheerful delivery had the staleness of lines prepared in advance.

"Ghostless." I kicked off my boots, leaving them in the pile next to the empty shoe rack.

"You'll bag 'em next time. Where'd you go?"

"I'd like to plead the Fifth."

That got a laugh from him, while Mom straightened and said, "Excuse me?"

"I respectfully decline to answer, on the grounds that it may incriminate me."

Dad grinned, looking a little more like his usual self, but Mom crossed her arms, a bag of shrimp dangling ominously from one hand.

"Oh, *I* see the confusion—you think the Constitution applies to you." She gestured with the shrimp. "But as soon as you walked through that door, you entered the Independent Dictatorship of Weaveria, where I'm Supreme Dictator for Life."

"Co-dictator," Dad noted.

"Co-dictator," she conceded, eyes not leaving mine. "So where were you?"

"You sure you don't want plausible deniability?"

Dad snorted in admiration. "Jesus, kiddo, how many bodies we burying?"

"I don't want *deniability*," Mom said. "I want to know where my daughter is."

"Home, obviously."

"Cara." Mom's voice lost all playfulness.

I hadn't really expected it to work, but I did *try* not to lie to my parents. Especially when there was video evidence.

"We were at the old mill."

"The *paper mill*? Where that boy *died*?" Mom's eyes went wide, nostrils flaring. If she were a lion, this would be the last thing a gazelle saw.

"Relax, Mom. We didn't even go inside." I paused. "I mean, not far."

"You could have been hurt! Or arrested for trespassing."

"I had Holly with me. And people go there all the time."

"Oh? And what kind of people are those?"

Not the best line of inquiry. "Mom! We were totally safe."

"By what metric? Do you *want* me to ground you?"

"Us," Dad reminded.

"*Really? Ground* me?" I pulled up short, taking a breath and twisting my tone back into place like an off-center bike seat. "Mom. I'm eighteen."

"And still living under my roof."

"Right." My smile was a window frame painted shut.

They both winced as Mom's words glanced off the elephant in the room. Score one for the depressed girl.

Dad put on his Serious Smile—the one that said *I'm in a good mood, and you'd be wise to keep it that way.* "You know you can't post that video, though, right? That mill's private property."

"Dad, it's condemned. Nobody cares."

"Whoever's paying taxes on it does. And they could be liable if something happened. They might nail you to the wall just to make an example."

"They won't," I insisted.

"But they *could.*" Dad pressed a finger authoritatively down on the cutting board. "Especially after what happened to that other kid. Now, I appreciate you telling the truth, so you're not in trouble"—he looked sideways to check with Mom, who threw up her hands—"but in the future, keep the hunts to public areas. And be smart about it, all right? Nothing that'll have us paying bail or checking the morgue."

"Fine." I slumped.

"And no posting that footage. Your mother has enough cases without taking on *Cara v. The Consequences of Her Actions.*"

"*Okay,* guys, I get it! It's not like we found anything anyway." I looked to the stairs. "Can I go?"

"No way, bucko. It's Family Night."

"*Again?*" I gave them an incredulous look. "We just had one last week!"

"And we're declaring another," Mom said. "Dictators' prerogative."

"Oh my god." As if this were what I needed today.

It was obvious why they were doing it. Unconditional, nonconsensual emotional support, just like Holly. I wondered if they'd go so far as to actually *address* our Room Elephant, or just let it keep standing around, shitting up the place.

Dad forced cheer back into his voice as he waggled the pasta box. "We're making Tasteful Noods."

"I wish you'd stop calling it that."

"Never!"

The Weaver Family Togetherness Death March ground onward, like Conan shackled to the Wheel of Pain. Both Mom and Dad did their best to keep things light, continuing to avoid the reason for the evening. But as the credits of *Cabin in the Woods* scrolled past and I finished my bowl of Ben & Jerry's Thick Mint, Dad went for it.

"See?" he said. "Living at home isn't so bad."

"*Dad.*"

"We know you're disappointed, honey." Mom squeezed my shoulder. "But actually, the class sizes at community college are *better.* And you can transfer after a year or two, with way smaller loans."

"It's really not the end of the world," Dad agreed.

I leaned my head back against the couch and closed my eyes. I loved my parents—I really did. And I didn't even mind living with them, most of the time. But the idea of another year in this town made me want to gouge my eyes out with my ice cream spoon.

"Are we done?" I asked.

"Almost." I opened my eyes again to see Dad holding out his arms. He pumped a fist. "Choo choo! All aboard the Hug Train!"

"Oh my god. You're such a dork." But I moved into his hug. He smelled like onion, and warm flannel, and the sour, weedy hops of the brewery where he worked.

Mom joined us, kissing the top of my head. "He's indeed a dork. But you've got half his genes, so . . ."

Dad made a wavery ghost voice. *"It'll happen to youuuuu . . ."*

We broke apart, and at long last I escaped upstairs to my bedroom.

One nice thing about my parents' brand of lefty libertarianism: my room was mine to decorate however I wanted. String lights illuminated walls covered in tarot cards (which I didn't believe in) and a vintage *X-Files* poster claiming the truth was out there (which I absolutely did). Woodcut prints from old-timey occult texts hung interspersed with a photo of my grandmother and another of me and Holly investigating the abandoned Northern State Mental Hospital. There was a shelf full of reference books and horror novels, and a cloth tapestry of the sephiroth—the tree of life from Jewish mysticism, not the Final Fantasy character.

Holly once told me that the first time she'd seen my room, she'd been afraid I wouldn't want to be friends with a Christian. But really, it was the opposite: my room was a monument to the search for answers. I might not be convinced by hers, but who was I to say they were wrong?

I sat down at the tiny desk beneath my window, and my phone gave a grateful beep as I plugged it into my laptop and began transferring files to clear space. While the videos trudged over like lazy ants, I opened a browser tab.

The MyUW icon stabbed out at me from the bookmark bar. A tiny purple badge of shame.

The University of Washington hadn't been the only college I'd applied to. There'd been schools in other cities—New York, London, Edinburgh—but those had been long shots, arrows fired into the air just to see what happened. Their rejections hadn't hurt. But UW was my in-state school. UW was supposed to be *safe*. With Holly already accepted into Bible college on the other side of the country, the prospect of reinventing myself in the anonymity of a big-city university had been the only thing making the future seem bearable.

Emphasis on *had been*. I dragged the little icon to the trash and tabbed over to YouTube to finish watching the most recent episode of *Ghoul Scout*.

For my money—which was exactly two dollars a month on Patreon—*Ghoul Scout* was the best ghost-hunting show around. The host, Carson Keene, was a normal-looking guy in his thirties, with blond hair, glasses, and an impressive collection of meme T-shirts. The way he combined the hunt for ghosts with education and motivational monologues had been the primary inspiration for my own show. Plus he was local to Seattle.

When I'd been fifteen, Dad had taken me to one of Carson's book signings downtown. I'd been so nervous I could barely speak, but when Dad did the most mortifying thing possible and mentioned that *I* was a ghost hunter as well, Carson hadn't rolled his eyes. Instead, he'd made everybody else wait while he chatted with me about strategy. Here was one of the most famous paranormal investigators around, with over a million YouTube subscribers, and he talked to *me* like a colleague. After Dad had taken a picture of us—which currently hung in the place of honor above my bed—Carson had given me his card and told me to drop him a line if I ever needed advice.

I'd never done it, of course. I knew he didn't *actually* want to mentor some rando fan. But the card still sat in the edge of the picture frame.

His current video series, "Notes from the Underground," was him in the part of the Seattle Underground you couldn't access on the normal tour, a spider-clogged maze that wove between the concrete foundations of downtown skyscrapers. He hadn't found anything, but you'd never know it from his grin.

"Well! *That* was gross!" He plucked cobwebs from his face. "But whether you're dealing with a mouth full of spiders or a bunch of closed-minded skeptics, an investigator's job is to do whatever it takes to find the truth. So until next time—search hard, stay open, and remember that your weirdness is your superpower!"

Eight-bit outro music played. I leaned back, grabbing my plush ghost from the Mario games and kneading him like a stress ball.

"Someday, Boo." I stared at the list of top patrons scrolling past. "Someday, when I find a ghost, those'll be *my* fans. And Stossel will just be a dead link on my Wikipedia page."

In my ear, a voice said, *"Yeah, good luck with that."*

I lurched to my feet, tripping over my desk chair as I spun.

The room was empty.

"Wait," the voice said—male, young. *"You can hear me?!"*

"Who said that?!" I raised Boo like a club, turning in circles.

My eyes fell on the computer.

Of course. The credits were still playing, but maybe a glitching pop-up ad? Malware hijacking the speakers? I thought of some neckbeard taking control of the camera and slammed the lid closed.

"Oh holy balls!" The voice still sounded as close as if I were wearing earbuds. *"Finally! FINALLY!"*

I backed away until my shoulder blades jabbed into drywall, thumbtacks digging into my back. "What's happening?" I tried and failed to keep my voice from shaking. "Who's talking?"

The voice laughed delightedly, still an inch from my ear.

"Who do you think, genius? I'm Aiden Reyes—the dead kid from the factory."

3

EVEN AFTER YEARS spent searching for a ghost, my first thought was that I had definitely misplaced my marbles.

"Don't worry," the voice said quickly. *"You're not hallucinating."*

"Oh good—because *that's* not exactly what a hallucination would say." And on that same note—"Did you just read my mind?"

"No, you just kinda had that look. Still do, actually." He gave a manic laugh. *"Holy shit. Holy* shit*! Do you have* any idea *how long I've been waiting for this?!"* The laughter caught, shifting into something closer to sobs.

Some crucial neurons finally got their shit together and I dove for my phone, nearly yanking my laptop off the desk by the connector cable. I turned the camera in a slow circle, recording the empty room. "Hey, sorry, but—can you say something?"

"Like what?"

"I don't care! Anything!"

"Um . . . you're kinda putting me on the spot?" But the distraction seemed to be grounding him. *"Mic check, one, two, one, two?"*

I stopped the recording and played it back.

My voice, speaking to an empty room. Then silence.

"Why can't it hear you?" I demanded.

"How should I know?! This is my first time being dead!"

"Right. Okay." Stop. *Think.* What would Carson Keene do?

First, he would definitely *not* waste his shot at a genuine ghost encounter by freaking out. I sat down on the edge of the bed and took a deep breath.

Step one: determine the parameters of the phenomenon.

"Aiden," I said, calmly—or at least, calm*er*, forcing down the rising tide of excitement. "Hi. Sorry, you startled me. Can you make yourself visible?"

"No, sorry." Then, less certain: *"I mean, I don't* thiiiiink *so? But I've also never been able to talk to anyone before, so . . ."* He still sounded breathless, off-balance.

"Can you try? To manifest, I mean?"

"How?"

A reasonable point. "How about . . . visualize yourself standing in the room. Just imagine yourself as hard as you can." I squinted, shifting my focus around in case it worked better with peripheral vision. "Are you doing it?"

"Yes . . . ? Maybe . . . ?"

The room remained empty.

My face must have shown it, because he gave that slightly unhinged laugh again. *"Guess your connection to the afterlife is audio only. Low-bandwidth warning. Please try turning me off and on again."*

"So, wait—" I struggled to think. "You can't talk to anyone else?"

"Nobody!" His voice sounded pained. *"I've been floating around for a fucking* year. *I spent, like, the first month screaming in people's ears, trying to write on mirrors or poltergeist objects around—all that ghost shit. But none of it works! I'm just . . . here."*

I imagined myself in his position—invisible, unable to talk to Holly or my parents—and my stomach clenched sympathetically. "So why now?"

"You tell me! Maybe because you did the Ouija board thing?"

"That's not how those work." I realized I was correcting a ghost on how to talk to ghosts. Ghostsplaining.

And still quite possibly hallucinating. Could that factory have had a bunch of chemicals still floating around?

I grabbed for my desk drawer. Beneath loose pens and a hopeless snarl of ribbon, I found two ten-sided dice—relics of a short-lived roleplaying phase with Dad. I sat on the floor and held my phone out.

"I'm going to throw these dice," I said into the camera. "Aiden, you tell me what we get." Then I closed my eyes and tossed the dice behind me.

The ghost huffed. *"Seriously? That's what we're doing right now?"*

"Just read me the numbers." I kept my eyes closed.

"Fine—seventy-five. Or fifty-seven."

"Seven and five," I repeated for the camera, then opened my eyes and turned toward the dice, letting the phone record the whole thing.

One seven.

One five.

"Okay." I fought to control the rising tide of excitement threatening to burst up through my sternum and closed my eyes again. "One more."

"Dude, come on!"

"Please!" I threw the dice. "For science."

A sigh. *"Thirty-two."*

With two ten-sided dice, there was a one percent chance of guessing correctly—two, if you read the number forward and backward. To guess correctly twice in a row . . .

I checked the dice.

Three and two.

Ding ding ding. We have a winner.

"You're real," I breathed.

"Yes, okay, we've established *that!"*

"Sorry, it's just—wow. Okay." My heart was a dubstep stutter, but in a good way. "Um, my name's Cara Weaver. Nice to meet you. I have so many questions."

"You and me both, sister." He paused. *"Wait—why do I know your name?"*

"Umm . . . because I'm the only ghost hunter in Stossel?" There was only one other reason an older boy might know my name, and if that was going to be my first conversation with a ghost, I might as well swallow my dice and choke to death right now.

"Yeah, I guess . . ." But he still sounded thoughtful.

I hurried onward, looking around the still-empty room. "Where are you, from your perspective? You sound like you're right next to me."

"Oh, um—now I'm over by your desk?" His voice stayed the same volume.

I looked at the toppled chair, the desk totally undisturbed. "Can you touch anything? Levitate something?"

"That's a negative, Ghost Rider." His words strung together in a hectic rush. *"I can fly, though. And float through walls. All the standard ghost tricks, as long as they don't involve, you know, actually* doing *anything."* Another laugh. *"So you're a real ghost hunter?"*

"Yeah." Then, more honestly: "I mean, I *want* to be. I've never actually found one." An idea arose. "You said I'm the only living person who can hear you—what about other ghosts? Can you talk to them?" I pictured myself interviewing a whole stream of spirits, with Aiden as my interpreter. I could call the series *Hello from the Other Side,* and use that Adele song for the intro . . .

"Nope, sorry. I don't even know if there are *other ghosts."*

So much for my undead talk show. "What about other supernatural beings? Angels? Demons?" Suspicion narrowed my eyes. "How do I know you're really Aiden Reyes, and not a demon trying to trick me?"

"Jesus! Trust issues much?"

"It's called being scientific," I bristled.

"Yeah, well, I left my ID in my other pants—the ones on my corpse.*"*

"Just a sec." I opened my phone and did a search for "Aiden Reyes Stossel."

A *Seattle Times* article about his death was the top hit, complete with a photo that had to have been his senior picture.

He was handsome, with a smile that said he knew it. A tight button-up showed off muscular shoulders on an otherwise slender build, a black crystal pendant hanging in the open collar. Warm brown skin glowed beneath an upswept wave of dark hair bleached light at the tips. Clearly a jock—you didn't get pecs like that in chess club—and there was a second pic of him wearing a plastic homecoming king crown, which should have been all I needed to file him immediately in my giant folder of People Who Suck. But there was something about his eyes that softened it—that said he knew what you were thinking, and he was in on the joke. No wonder he'd been popular.

I put my face right up to the phone, holding my hands around it to shield it from ghostly eyes. "What're your parents' names?"

"Luis and Katherine. Why?"

I scrolled quickly through the article, verifying. "What sport did you play?"

"Water polo. Look, while I enjoy answering security questions as much as the next ghost, don't you think if demons were real, they'd have Google?"

"Uh. Fair." The growing irritation in his tone told me to ramp back the interrogation. Aiden was officially my most important discovery since the massaging showerhead. I couldn't afford to annoy him.

Too bad making friends wasn't exactly my strong suit. How did you small-talk a ghost? "So you were a senior at Stossel?"

"Yeah." A half laugh. *"Maybe I still am? Do they graduate you if you're dead?"*

"I heard about it. When you died, I mean." There had been precious few details, but that hadn't stopped folks from talking. "What actually happened?"

"What happened is I was stupid." He sighed again. Now that the initial rush of emotion was giving way, dude sounded *tired*. But also clearly relieved to finally be talking to someone. *"You know my sister? Meredith?"*

"Not really." Of course I knew *of* her—we were both seniors, and her brother's death had made her briefly famous by association. But Stossel was a big school for a small town, pulling kids from miles around. All I had was a fuzzy image of a quiet, dark-haired girl—a fellow high school cockroach, scurrying beneath the notice of the social elite.

"Not surprising," Aiden said dryly. *"Meredith doesn't really do 'people.' Anyway, we used to go exploring together—logging roads, abandoned buildings. It was kind of our thing. But that night I was alone."* He hesitated, long enough to make me think there was more there. *"Anyway. I was climbing through an upper story of one of the mill buildings, and the whole floor collapsed. I fell, and a beam came down on top of me. Pretty much pulped my organs."* He laughed uncomfortably. *"Get it? Paper mill? Pulped?"*

I winced.

"Yeah. Good times. I couldn't lift it off, and my phone was smushed in with the pudding of my torso, so I just laid there and yelled for help." Another pause. *"It took a while."*

"God." You don't become a ghost hunter without reading a lot of tragic death stories, but it was something else entirely to hear one straight from the victim. I was suddenly ashamed of how eagerly I'd devoured accounts like his from the safe distance of a phone or laptop.

Still, a professional would be writing this down. I opened a notes app. "So, when you died . . . What happened then?"

"You mean, was there harp music and dead relatives? Nah, nothing like that. It just hurt, and after a while it stopped hurting and was just . . . dark. But then I did feel something."

"Yeah?" I swipe-typed as quickly as I could.

"It was like . . . a magnetic pull, but toward everywhere. Like I was a balloon being blown up—expanding in every direction. But also floating upward. Does that make sense?"

"Death . . . equals . . . balloon . . ." I made a show of typing it out. "Sure, what could be clearer?"

He snorted. *"Okay, try this: Imagine when you first get in a hot tub. At the start, it's too hot, and you're all tense. But then there's that moment when your body gives up and relaxes, and you just kind of . . . let go. Release."*

"*Ohhhhhhhh!*" I nodded sagely. "So you're saying death is like peeing in the pool."

That startled a laugh out of him—a real one this time. It was a warm sound, rich and full. The kind of laugh that made you want to immediately repeat whatever you'd done to make it happen.

"*Exactly!*" he said. "*The forbidden thrill! And there was this light everywhere. But then, just as I was starting to let go, everything reversed. Like a vacuum was sucking me back together. I opened my eyes, and I was floating above my body. And that pull I'd been feeling condensed down into two directions—toward my body, and toward somewhere else. When trying to get back into my body didn't work, I followed the other one, and it led me back home. To Meredith.*" His voice turned bitter. "*Which is when I realized that nobody could see or hear me. It didn't matter, though, because by the next morning, Mer had figured out something was wrong and told our parents. The cops found my body later that day.*"

"Shit."

"*Yeah. Watching Mer and my parents go through that . . .*" He trailed off.

His obvious pain pulled at something in my chest, but I needed to keep him talking. "What about after that? You said you spent the first month trying to talk to people. What've you been doing since then?"

"*Oh. Um . . .*" He sounded embarrassed. "*Netflix, mostly?*"

"Netflix?!" I couldn't tell if he was joking.

"*I mean, it's not like I have a subscription. I just wander through people's houses until I find someone watching something fun. This one neighbor lady and I have been binging* Love Island Australia—*those dudes have* no *game.*"

"You've been granted life after death, and you're watching *dating shows?*" I scrunched my face incredulously.

"*Hey, what am I supposed to do? I'm a* floating eyeball *here, remember?*"

"Right, sorry." I held up my hands. "But still—why stay in *Stossel?* If I had ghost powers, I'd be out of here in a *second.*" Hell, if I'd had my own *credit card.*

"It's not my call!" Aiden's frustration grew. *"I can go wherever I want, but as soon as I stop concentrating, I get pulled back toward the factory or Meredith."* He paused. *"Or you now, apparently."*

I inhaled sharply, nearly choking on a lungful of surprise-spit. "Me?"

"Ever since you did your bit at the factory. That's how I followed you home."

That was both incredibly fortunate and deeply disconcerting—I'd wanted a ghost, not a stalker. I managed to cough away my startle-drool and asked, "So, are you still being pulled toward the other places?"

"I mean, I can feel what direction they're in. But whenever I'm with one of them—one of you—it feels . . . stable? Anyway, it's my turn to ask questions. First up: Why the hell can you hear me?!"

"In my professional opinion?" I tapped the corner of my phone against my bottom lip. "Fucked if I know. All my research suggests ghosts form for a reason—some unfinished business they're supposed to complete before they can pass on. But without knowing yours, I've got no idea how I factor in."

"Oh, I know why *I'm a ghost."* He said it as if it were the most obvious thing in the world.

My phone jarred painfully against my teeth. "You do?"

"It's pretty much the only thing I do *know. It's Meredith. She . . . hasn't exactly been doing great since I died."*

I raised an eyebrow. "And this is surprising?"

"I mean—no, obviously. But you don't get it. Mer's kind of a tragic loner. And by 'kind of,' I mean 'completely, indisputably, perpetually.'"

"Okay . . ." She could join the club. High school was a shit sandwich with double mayo. If not for Holly, I'd have begged my parents for a GED evac long ago.

"When I was alive, we would hang out, or I'd drag her along with my friends. But ever since I shuffled off this mortal coil, she's become a total shut-in—just gets high and works out in her room. It's like she's in prison. I'd hoped she'd work through it, but . . ." He sounded frustrated.

"And you think that's your unfinished business? Helping her?"

"*Obviously. That pull I talked about? It's not to home, it's to* her. *At first, I thought it might just be about who I was closest to. Mer and I were like age-gapped twins. We were—*" He coughed self-consciously at the sudden catch in his voice. "*She was my best friend.*"

"I'm sorry." Pitifully inadequate, but what else was I going to say?

"*It's fine. So yeah, the more I watch her collapse in on herself, the more certain I am that she's why I'm here. I need to help her be happy again. I can't explain* how *I know, I just do. Maybe that's part of how all this works?*" A forced laugh. "*I know that sounds nuts, but what about this isn't, right?*"

"Right." I felt a peculiar mix of relief and disappointment that this part of the mystery was already solved. "But if you know what you're supposed to do . . . what are you doing about it?"

"*Nothing!*" The word punched out of him like a broken bone through skin. "*That's* the problem! *I know* what *I'm supposed to fix, but I don't know* how*! I can't talk to her, can't hug her, can't send her a note— can't do anything except watch her get worse.*" He paused, and his voice got small. "*I wondered for a while if this was Hell.*"

His naked pain wormed its way into my withered apple of a heart. Sure, in life, he'd been a popular kid, which meant he was probably an asshole—in the royal court that was high school, you didn't ascend the throne without leaving bodies in your wake.

But whoever he'd been, he'd loved his sister.

"Damn," I murmured.

"*Yeah.*" He took another long breath—a fact that suddenly struck me as bizarre. Why would a ghost need to breathe?

"Any*way,*" he said, pulling himself together. "*Now there's you. You've gotta be part of the puzzle, right? Whatever I'm supposed to do to help Meredith, it clearly involves you.*"

"But I don't even know her!"

"*I know, but plenty of people hang out at the factory, and none of them have ever heard me. It's gotta be something about you in particular.*" I felt the weight of his unseen gaze. "*So what's your deal, Cara Weaver?*"

Danger—evasive action required. "You already know about the ghost hunting," I dodged. "That's my only interesting thing."

"I'll be the judge of that."

The casual confidence with which he said it was both irritating and kind of endearing. I rolled my eyes. "Fine. But let's run more tests as we talk."

I made him repeat the dice experiment, hiding them under increasingly dense objects to learn what he could stick his spectral head through. (Answer: everything, though he still needed light to see.) Then it was time for the thermal scope, which stubbornly refused to show anything, and the talking board, which failed similarly.

As we went, I gave him a carefully sanitized version of my life: only child, homeschooled by my grandmother up into middle school, aspiring YouTuber—all the little details I could paint in around the edges, hoping he wouldn't notice the glaring omission at the center.

An angry, rational part of me wondered why I was even trying. All he'd have to do was follow me to school to learn that Cara Weaver, soon-to-be-famous ghost hunter, was actually Cara Weaver, teenage pariah. And since when did I give a flying dildo what some popular boy thought of me, anyway? Let alone a dead one.

Still, for all my disdain, I found myself wanting to delay that revelation, even if just for a night.

"Cara?"

I blinked, jerking my head up. "What?"

"You tired?"

"No, I'm—" A traitorous yawn swallowed the end of the word. "I'm good."

"Right." He sounded amused. *"It's just that this is the second time you've fallen asleep midsentence."*

"Shit." I blushed. "Sorry."

"Don't be. Honestly, it's kind of adorable—you're like one of those fainting goats."

I made a face. "Wow."

"It's a compliment. But seriously—I don't sleep anymore, but you seem wiped."

He was right, but still—how could I literally sleep on this opportunity? This was the single most important moment of my life. Wasn't it my scientific duty to stay up all night?

But it was hard to think of good experiments when I could barely keep my eyes open. With another curse for my disobedient meatbag of a body, I asked, "If I sleep, will you still be here in the morning?"

Aiden laughed. *"Are you kidding? You're the first person I've talked to in a year. You couldn't make me leave."*

My shoulders relaxed. "Okay, great." I looked around. "So, uh . . . where do you want to hang out while I sleep?"

"Oh. Um . . . wherever, I guess?" His voice shrank, and in that sudden vulnerability I could hear all the nights he must have spent alone in the silent factory, or watching lives he couldn't be a part of. Holly might call me a misanthrope, but at least I had her and my parents. Aiden had gone a year without human contact.

The thought of forcing that on him for another night was unbearable, even for me. "You could stay in here, if you want."

"Yeah?" He perked up, sounding almost comically excited.

"Sure. I can stream something for you on my laptop. It'll have to be on headphones, but . . ."

"No, that's great! Slumber party! Excellent."

The relief in his voice gave me a warm glow. *See?* I told Imaginary Holly. *I can be friendly. Even to popular kids.*

With him piloting over my shoulder, I scrolled through a list of garbage reality series, getting him set up with a show called *FBoy Island*. (Why are dating shows always on islands?) Then I killed the lights, got into bed, and changed clothes under the covers, palming my nightguard rather than putting it in where he could see. (Some things were just too dorky to risk.)

"Well," I said, "good night."

"G'night."

Silence.

Then, softly: *"Cara?"*

"Yeah?"

"Thanks." His voice was as open as that laugh had been. *"It's really nice to have someone to talk to."*

"You too." To my surprise, I meant it. For all that this dude was my ticket to fame, he was also on an extremely short list of people I'd had actual conversations with recently. We had that much in common.

That thought swirled through my head alongside visions of Carson Keene interviewing me on his channel as I tried to force myself to sleep. I'd almost drifted off when Aiden shouted, *"Wait!"*

I jerked upright. "What?! What's wrong?"

On the laptop, a bunch of roided-out dudes were attempting to dance, with varying degrees of success.

"Wait wait wait," he continued, laughing. *"I finally remembered why I know your name!"*

Oh please no. Cautiously, I asked, "You did?"

"You're Scarf Girl!" he crowed.

Fuck. I shrank backward against the headboard, pulling the blanket up to my chin. "I think you've got me confused with—"

"No way—I remember now! I was already in high school, but Meredith told me about it." He chuckled. *"But don't you see? This is* perfect! *Everything makes sense, now that I know you're gay!"*

"Bi," I corrected automatically. Then: "Wait, what does that have to do with anything?"

"This is why the pull led me to you! Meredith is gay, too. And what better way to get her out of her funk than a girlfriend?"

My jaw dropped. Never mind that I hadn't known Meredith was gay—it didn't matter, because we were absolutely *not* having this conversation. "I'm not gonna *date* your sister!"

"Why not? Oh shit—you're not dating somebody already, are you? Is it that wrestler girl?"

"What? No." Holly was as straight as a Kansas highway. "Holly's just a friend."

"Then what's the problem? Meredith's awesome, and you're totally her type: Cute. Femme. Little bit morbid."

My brain caught on the word *cute* like jeans on a barbed-wire fence, but I tore free. "Do you *realize* how offensive that is? To assume that just because your sister and I are both queer, we'd want to date each other?"

"Yeah, okay, it's not perfect. But it's not like I'm really in a position to comparison shop, here. If you were a ten-foot-tall green hamster, I'd still try to hook you two up."

"Wow." Had I really been starting to feel sympathetic toward this asshole? "I can't believe you found a way to dig the hole deeper."

"It's called 'being a good wingman.' But the fact that you both like girls has *to mean something, right? It's fate! And don't worry, I know she'll be into you. I've seen her browser history."*

"I'm not *worried*," I spat. "I'm *pissed*. And what makes you think Meredith needs a relationship? Why can't I just, like ... be her friend?"

"Yeeeeeah, no." He laughed, and the sound wasn't nearly as charming this time around. *"Like I said, Mer isn't good at friends. Besides, boobs fix everything. They're the original antidepressant."*

Here, then, was the brotastic Neanderthal I'd expected from a homecoming king. I pulled the comforter tighter around me. "I'm not a *prostitute*."

"Oh, but I *am?"*

"What are you *talking* about?"

"I heard you fantasizing to your stuffed ghost. You wanna pimp me out—lead me around on a leash, show me off and get famous. Well, guess what, Ghostbuster? I don't have to be here. You need me as much as I need you."

My righteous rage stumbled to a halt.

He was right—the recordings I had wouldn't look like anything to a skeptic. I'd need verified testing under actual lab conditions if I wanted out of my current life and into a new one as a pro ghost hunter. I'd just assumed he'd *want* to help me.

"This isn't about me," I sputtered. "It's about *science*."

"Yeah? Well, I don't give a squirty shart about science. I care about Meredith. *And what* she *needs is a cute girl to ask her out."*

There was that word "cute" again—only now it tasted like the transaction it was. Something people said to get what they wanted.

I shoved past it, ladling on as much scorn as I could muster. "So, what—if I don't do what you want, you'll hide? Rob the entire world of this discovery?"

"The world was doing just fine without me," he shot back. *"Or, you know—not. But that's not my problem anymore."*

I glared at the air. The idea that someone could have answers to the biggest questions in human history and refuse to share them . . . How could anyone be that selfish? That *shallow?*

When he spoke again, it was gentler. Conciliatory. *"Look . . . I'm sorry. I didn't mean to come on so strong."*

"Is *that* what you call it?"

"I get why you're mad. But this just feels *right—the same way I know that Meredith is why I'm still here. So let's make a deal: You don't have to sleep with her, or anything like that. Just . . . take her to prom, all right? Do that, and I'll be your science experiment for as long as you need. We both get what we want."*

There were so many problems with that, I didn't even know where to start. But what my mouth said was, "I don't go to dances."

"Neither does she—that's the point." A spectral sigh. *"I just want her to have one night that feels, like,* magical, *you know? So take her to prom, show her a good time, and we'll call it even. Deal?"*

My pride wanted to tell him to go float through a septic tank—to haunt the ass end of a diarrheic raccoon. But underneath it, the mercenary part of my brain was doing the math.

Holly had been trying for years to get me to go to a dance with her and her boyfriend. Standing around being judged by a bunch of overdressed kids humping in a gymnasium sounded like a very specific circle of Hell—especially when one of them was Sophia. But how long was a dance, really? Three hours? I'd just jealously watched Carson Keene crawl through mud and spiders, and he hadn't even come out with a ghost. What was this in comparison?

"What if she says no?" I asked.

"Leave that to me. I've got the inside intel." He was all cheerful confidence again. *"Plus, I was kiiiind of an expert at asking girls out."*

Oh good—Casper the Fuckboy Ghost as my personal dating coach. "Glad to see being dead hasn't hurt your ego."

"I'd toot my own horn, but it got squashed under that beam."

"Gross." But at least he still had his sense of humor. The last thing I needed was a sulky ghost.

"Welcome to being dead, sister. So are we good or what?" He paused. *"You can't see it, but I'm holding out my hand to shake."*

I hesitated—but what choice did I have, really? All my dreams hinged on finding a ghost, and now I had. Without him, I was nothing. Would *continue* being nothing.

And it was like Carson said: ghost hunting meant doing whatever it took to find the truth. Now I knew what it would take.

I put out a hand and palmed the air.

"Fine," I said. "You've got a deal."

4

WHEN CHRIS STAPLETON'S "You Should Probably Leave" dragged me up out of sleep the next morning, there was a terrible moment when I was sure it had all been a dream. Everything seemed too normal: the washed-out light of an overcast sky, the frantic jangle of keys against travel mugs as my parents ran for their cars.

Then Aiden's voice said, *"Morning, Sunshine."*

My eyes shot open.

"Do your parents always leave the house like they're fleeing a bomb threat?" He paused, then in an amused tone said, *"Nice mouthguard."*

My hand flew to my mouth. *Dammit.* I pointed to the door. "Out."

"Aww, don't be embarrassed! It gives you a whole Mike Tyson vibe."

"Out!"

"Okay, fine, I'm going! Let no one say I'm not a gentleman."

I got dressed under the covers again—who knew if I could trust Mr. Floating Eyeball not to perv on me—then raced through the rest of my morning routine, being sure to chuck the dice in my bag. As I tied my hair back, I said, "You're coming with me, right? So I can prove you're real to Holly?"

"Are you sure that's wise?"

"Yes . . . ?" This was both my ticket to fame and a major scientific breakthrough. Did he think I was going to keep it to myself?

"I'm just saying, you're the only person I can talk to. If you get thrown in a mental hospital, that's a problem."

"Not gonna happen." But he had a point—maybe it wasn't the best idea to go spreading my news around until I'd gathered more concrete evidence.

But Holly was my best friend *and* my ghost-hunting partner. I couldn't keep this from her.

"I'm telling Holly," I said slowly, "and probably her boyfriend, Elvis, just so she doesn't spontaneously combust trying to keep the secret. But *just* them. For now."

"Do you trust them?"

I snorted. "If we were starving in a life raft, Holly would cut off her own leg and grill it for me."

"That's . . . graphic."

"I spend a lot of time reading about death. Point is, Holly's the most honorable person who's ever lived. She's like Jesus and Malala had a baby. And Elvis does whatever she says. Don't worry."

Aiden hesitated, then said, *"Okay, but nobody else for now. And especially not Meredith."*

I laughed darkly. "No worries there." I could just imagine how that would go down. "She's gonna find out when we publish, though." Along with the whole world, hopefully.

"Yeah, but this whole prom plan only works if she doesn't know about me. Promise you won't tell her. Not until I say it's time." His voice rose anxiously.

"Okay, I promise! Calm your tits." I rolled my bike out of the garage and strapped on my helmet, only to realize I'd forgotten something important. "Crap—how fast can you go? Can you . . . I dunno, ride on my handlebars?"

"As delightful as that image is, I can fly faster than you can pedal."

"So you say *now*." I keyed the garage door closed, then swung into the saddle.

Most mornings, Holly picked me up—just another way she put the "best" in "best friend"—but on Tuesdays and Thursdays she had to go in early for select orchestra. That was fine, though. Cool April wind pulled tears from my eyes as I swooped down our development's long asphalt curves.

Growing up, I'd spent hours biking around backroads with my grandmother, much to the terror of my parents. With its heart-bursting hills and narrow shoulders, Stossel wasn't exactly bike-friendly, and drivers loved to curse you out for cycling on *their* road. But Nana had refused to be cowed, so I wasn't, either.

Gravel crunched as I turned onto the valley bike trail and up-shifted, building speed.

"You bike *all the way to school?"* Aiden sounded incredulous.

"No, I turn around halfway." Now that I was fully awake, I was remembering what a dick he'd been the previous night.

"What if it rains?"

"Then it rains." I'd almost said *then I get wet,* but caught myself in time. Dead boys were still boys.

But Aiden said only, *"Wow. Hardcore."* I searched for mockery, but he seemed genuinely impressed.

I put my head down and pumped. Up in the hills, houses caught the morning light in bright signal flashes, but down here by the river, wetlands flowed past, split by dense green rows of strawberry fields.

Stossel had started life as a farm town, and was still the sort of place where granges sold feed and seed unironically. Since then, however, Seattle's suburban sprawl had pushed relentlessly eastward, rolling up each little town in its wave of commuters. Downtown Stossel still only had the one commercial street—kitschy restaurants and antique shops squashed between big box stores—but now an ever-widening ring of housing developments spread out from it.

I'd spent my entire life in that ring, which felt more like a hamster wheel. I couldn't believe that, of all the places they could have chosen, my parents came here—or, in Dad's case, *back* here. But he'd wanted the independence of a rural homestead, while Mom had wanted the culture and community of the city. So they'd compromised on Stossel, which had neither. *Thanks a lot, guys.*

I hit the edge of town and popped smoothly up onto the street. I loved how powerful my body felt like this—the way I could lock in and become one with the bike. Driving was terrifying, and running should be outlawed by the Geneva Conventions, but biking—biking was freedom.

I shot through an intersection right as the light changed, earning a honk from a truck trying to turn right. I gave it a jaunty one-finger salute.

"Jesus!" Aiden's laugh was both startled and delighted. *"You don't take any shit, do you?"*

"Nope." I wasn't about to fake humility. But I also couldn't deny a rush of satisfaction. I hadn't forgotten how he'd held my discovery for ransom, or the patronizing way he'd talked about his sister. But it was hard to stay mad at someone who kept paying you compliments.

No wonder so many people made stupid decisions.

⌖

Lunch at Stossel High took place in the Commons, a two-story glass atrium where the school's wings joined together. The overall atmosphere was that of a mall food court, if your food court had exactly one terrible restaurant. But at least the convoluted floor plan made it easy to hide.

I made my way through the line and bought a square slice of bready cafeteria pizza and a basket of fries that somehow smelled like both chicken and fish.

"French fries!" Aiden moaned with pornographic longing. *"God's most perfect food. I can almost smell them."*

I'd spent all morning interviewing him, writing him questions under the guise of taking notes. Not being able to focus on him exclusively was infuriating—especially given how little school mattered in comparison—and if not for the need to see Holly, I would have happily faked sick to stay home. Distracted by my own thoughts, I responded automatically. "You can't smell?"

"No taste, no smell, no touch. The world is basically a movie."

"Bummer." I popped a fry ostentatiously into my mouth.

"Your sympathy is overwhelming."

"Talking to yourself, Scarfy?"

My shoulders clenched, and I turned to find Sophia and two of her beta bitches blocking my way.

"Guess somebody's got to," Sophia continued philosophically, "since nobody else will."

"Where's your babysitter?" one of the cronies asked.

"Do your parents pay her to take you for walks?" That was Madeline, the secret pothead from the factory.

"Holly's just doing her Christian duty," Sophia crooned. "Ministering to the leper."

The sting of it was, they weren't entirely wrong. Holly had been a Popular Girl once, before proximity to me dragged her down. She still made friends wherever she went, everyone eager to be in her group projects or inviting her to birthdays. She could gossip with the drama club, party (chastely and soberly) with the jocks, or play Smash Bros. for Jesus with the Young Life kids. She could have sat at a different lunch table every day, if she weren't so loyal to me.

The reminder always made me excruciatingly jealous. Not of Holly—she would have gleefully hauled me along into the septic soup of high school socialization. I was jealous of everyone *else*, for thinking they had a right to her. The cretins in this school didn't deserve her, she was simply too kindhearted to accept it.

She was going to do great at college.

I felt warmth on my hand and realized I'd made a fist, sticking my thumb right through my slice of pizza. "Fuck off, Sophia."

"Careful." Sophia waggled her head from side to side. "You don't want to get suspended again."

I was blushing furiously now. Sophia was bad enough on a normal day, but to have Aiden see it . . . I put my head down and shoved past them. "Eat my ass."

"Only in your fantasies," Sophia called, to a chorus of cackles.

I hurried up the stairs to the wide, balcony-like second floor.

"I see Sophia is still as charming as ever," Aiden observed. *"What's her beef with you?"*

"I don't want to talk about it."

"And why did you get suspended?"

"I *said* I don't want to talk about it!"

I made it to our regular table, a small round one overlooking the parking lot. Holly and Elvis were already there, sides touching at every conceivable point, chairs squeezed so close together that the plastic threatened to fuse.

Elvis was Vietnamese American, same as Holly, with chunky rectangular glasses, green zip-off tech pants, and a faded blue NASA shirt. True to his name, his hair was greased up in its trademark rockabilly quiff. Holly had met him two years ago in their church worship band—her on violin, him on guitar—and the two had immediately become inseparable. I tried not to mind—Elvis was a good guy, and he adored Holly. But it didn't change the fact that every lunch period with them was a gelatinous lump of congealed sexual tension.

Holly extracted her hand from Elvis's long enough to wave, kicking a chair out for me. "Hola, chica! What are the haps?"

"A lot, actually." I sat.

"Yeah?" She leaned forward eagerly.

"Um." Now that the moment had come, I felt surprisingly shy. I trusted Holly completely, and Elvis by extension, but . . .

"Last chance to turn back," Aiden murmured.

I smiled in something that was almost embarrassment.

"I kinda . . . found a ghost?"

Holly's eyes shot cartoonishly wide. "You *what*? Where? When? How?"

"That pretty much covers it," Aiden observed.

"Last night. After you dropped me off. And, uh." I took a deep breath. "He's here right now."

"Surprise!" Aiden's voice strongly implied jazz hands.

"What?" This time the word came out flatter. Holly cocked her head.

"It's Aiden Reyes. The boy from the factory." I waved vaguely, then remembered I had no idea where he was, exactly. I could be grabbing a handful of ghost ass. I yanked my hand back. "He's invisible, and can't interact with the world. I'm the only one who can hear him."

"O . . . *kaaaaayyyy,* yeah, great!" Holly drew out the words, managing to eventually stumble back into her normal enthusiasm, but that hesitation broke my heart a little.

Elvis, as usual, was blunter. "Do you have evidence?"

"Oh good," Aiden deadpanned. *"Another scientist."*

I ran them through Aiden's story and the previous night's discoveries, then showed them the dice experiment. Elvis insisted on running it several times, then upped the ante by walking out of sight, writing out random words, and having Aiden read them and report back to me.

"Well," he said, after Aiden had begrudgingly repeated *squid, trapeze,* and *peanut butter,* "there's definitely *something* strange going on."

"Yes, thank you, Doctor Obvious. Glad we cleared that up."

I had to agree with Aiden. While I respected Elvis's dedication to rationalism, his whole wannabe-Vulcan refusal to get excited could be a real buzzkill.

Fortunately, Holly contained enough enthusiasm for two people. Or two hundred.

"Do you realize what this *means*?!" She squeezed Elvis's bicep insistently with one hand, as her other was already busy holding his. "This is the biggest theological revelation since Jesus left the cave! Cara, you *have* to let me share this on my channel—after you do, I mean. People are gonna be *way* more open to the Word if we've got proof!"

I frowned. "Aren't you always saying the whole point of faith is that it *doesn't* require proof?"

"Yeah, but that's because I *already* believe. For people who don't, this could be *huge.*"

"Assuming there's really a ghost," Elvis cautioned. "A lot of folks are gonna call bull. We don't have a lot to work with here."

"I could say the same," Aiden sniped back.

Holly gripped Elvis tighter, looking at him anxiously. "But *you* believe, right?" Good ol' Holly, always campaigning for me.

Elvis's gaze flicked back and forth between us. He held up a hand.

"On the one hand, as Carl Sagan said, extraordinary claims require extraordinary evidence." He raised the other, still holding Holly's. "On the other, Sherlock Holmes said that once you've eliminated everything impossible, whatever's left, however improbable, has to be the truth." He shrugged and let his hands drop. "The Holmes thing is a fallacy, as there are probably explanations that *aren't* a ghost—but since I don't think any of them are necessarily more believable, we might as well move forward with this one."

From Elvis, it was a parade-worthy endorsement.

"Oh my *gee*." Holly grabbed Elvis's head in both hands. "The fact that you can just drop quotes like that is so. Dang. *Hot*." She opened her mouth and buried her face in his hair, miming biting at his skull.

"Those two need to get a room," Aiden observed, half-admiringly.

"Tell me about it," I muttered.

Elvis, looking both embarrassed and a little out of breath from Holly's brain-devouring attack, said, "So how *are* you going to prove it?" He gestured toward the dice. "Anything on video is too easy to fake. Even in-person is gonna be hard—people will assume everyone except them is a plant. It's classic stage magic."

Holly looked suddenly chagrined. "Is it rude that we're talking about Aiden in front of him?"

"No, please," Aiden said dryly. *"I love being a zoo specimen."*

"He says it's fine," I said.

"Hi, Aiden." Holly waved at the air next to me. "Nice to meet you. Sorry about"—she gestured vaguely—"everything."

"Thanks." Aiden sounded both surprised and mollified. Apparently not even the undead were immune to Holly's charms.

"We could try interviewing him," Elvis suggested. "Have him reveal things only he would know. Maybe his passwords?"

"That's a hard no from me, boss. My browser history dies with me."

I shook my head. "People will assume we hacked his accounts, or that his family is being conned. That's how scam séances work, or fortune-tellers and horoscopes—the marks want so badly to believe that they make things fit, and overlook the parts that don't." I popped my knuckles with my thumb. "The only way this'll work is to get a bunch of experts together in a lab and show them."

"How?" Elvis asked.

"I'll figure something out. Maybe if I can publish enough convincing footage, they'll come to us, even if only to debunk it. We just need to get them here. Aiden can do the rest."

Elvis nodded slowly, lips pursed to one side. "That could work."

"Awesomesauce!" Holly was grinning again. "So we shoot a video, yeah?"

I chewed at a hangnail, thinking fast. "I think we start *documenting* now, but hold off on publishing. Make sure our first video collects all our most compelling evidence. We might only get one shot."

"Good call," Elvis said. "If people can easily explain your first video, they're not gonna come back for more."

"Exactly. The plan only works if things go viral, so whatever we put out has to be self-contained—one giant thermonuclear truth bomb." I frowned. "Until then, this has to stay between the three of us."

Holly's face turned instantly serious. She held out her hand, dragging Elvis's along with it, and extended her pinky. "Your secret's safe with us."

"Loose lips sink ships," Elvis agreed.

"*Friend*-ships!" Holly added.

"*This is simultaneously the sweetest and dorkiest thing I have ever seen,*" Aiden noted.

"Hundred percent," I agreed, hooking Holly's pinky with my own. "You guys are the best."

Aiden cleared his nonexistent throat. "*As much as I hate to interrupt the friendship circle, aren't you forgetting an important aspect of this story?*"

"Right." I sucked on my teeth. "So, there's one more *minor* complication . . ."

I explained the Meredith deal. By the time I finished, Holly was all Concerned Face.

"You agreed to take her to prom?"

"Yeah, I know." I grimaced and made a *what can you do* gesture. "But it's one dance. I'll live."

"That's not what I meant." Holly pressed her lips together. "Doesn't that seem kind of ... dishonest?"

"Oh, for fuck's sake," Aiden groaned.

"I'm just taking her to a dance!" I protested.

"But you don't even like her!"

"So? People go to dances with friends all the time. You're always trying to get me to go with *you.*"

"That's different. You said yourself that Aiden wants it to be a date. Pretending to have romantic intentions when you don't is leading her on."

"But isn't that why people *go* on dates? To find out if they like each other?"

"Exactly!" Aiden agreed.

Holly looked unconvinced.

Most of the time, being friends with the kindest, sweetest girl in the whole world was easy.

This was not one of those times. I looked to Elvis, but he was leaned as far back in his chair as possible, distancing himself from the argument like a sensible coward.

"Look," I tried, "are *blind dates* dishonest? By definition, neither person is interested yet. If you set me up with one of your church friends, would that be lying? Because that's all Aiden's doing here. Setting us up."

I saw the point hit home. Holly bit her lower lip. "But you have ulterior motives."

"Everyone goes into dates with ulterior motives. And I'm not even trying to get into her pants. Aiden just loves his sister and wants her to be happy—how could that be wrong?"

"Booyah!" Aiden crowed. *"Mic: dropped!"* I found myself thinking I could get used to having my own invisible hype man.

Holly crossed her arms without letting go of Elvis's hand, dragging him bodily back into the discussion. "Okay, maybe the date isn't wrong, but doesn't she have a right to know Aiden's alive? I mean, not *alive*, but ..."

I rolled my eyes. "Right. Because she's *totally* gonna buy that. 'Hi, you don't know me, but I've been chatting with the ghost of your dead brother, and he thinks we'd look *real* cute together.'" I took a breath and forced myself to ramp back the snark. "We'll tell her eventually, I promise. Right, Aiden?"

"I mean ..."

"He says 'Of course, we just need to wait for the right time.' You know, build up trust."

"Hey!"

I was talking as fast as I could think—like running downhill, just falling and hoping your legs can keep up. "In the meantime, I can hold up my side of the bargain, and maybe help her have some fun. She's been through so much—doesn't she deserve that?"

Holly's pathological soft spot for underdogs was her biggest weakness—and the entire genesis of our friendship. In eighth grade, we'd both briefly been part of the same after-school youth group— her for the interdenominational Christian fellowship, me because they played laser tag. When the group turned on me after the Scarf Girl incident, convincing the chaperones to drive away and leave me standing alone in the church parking lot, it hadn't mattered that Holly barely knew my name. She'd been so furious that she'd stayed behind with me, declaring herself my new best friend.

It was the greatest thing that had ever happened to me.

Her skepticism held out for one more moment, then broke like a dam. She sighed. "Fine."

"*Thank* you." I turned to Elvis. "Good by you, King?"

"Hey, don't look at me. Dating etiquette is way outside my knowledge base. I'd still be trying to figure out how to introduce myself to Holly if she hadn't grabbed me by the hair like an absolute cavewoman."

Holly dug fond fingers possessively into his pompadour. *"Mine."*

"See?" He made the sign of the cross. "Go with God, my child. Get your sapphic mack on."

"Great." I took a deep breath and stood. "In that case, I need to go ask a girl about a dance."

"Wait—now?!" I'd clearly caught Aiden off guard.

"No time like the present. Prom is in, what, a month?"

Holly looked equally unsettled, but was physically incapable of not being supportive. "Go get her, lady!" She gave me two thumbs up. "Eye of the tiger!"

"Thanks." I pushed my lunch toward her. "Watch my pizza."

"You're just gonna walk up and ask her?"

I headed for the stairs. "Yes . . . ?"

"I don't think that's a great idea." Aiden sounded genuinely nervous. *"Why don't you wait, and I can coach you?"*

My shoulders rose defensively. "I don't need *coaching*. You wanted me to ask, so shut your ghost-hole and let me ask." I stomped down the stairs and onto the logoed linoleum of the Commons's main floor.

In truth, I didn't feel quite that confident. Asking people out wasn't something I did, especially not after becoming Scarf Girl. But that hadn't really been a problem, since there was nobody in this festering cesspool worth asking out anyway. I'd always figured that once I was off to college and nobody knew who I was, *then* I could worry about romance. Until then, there was nothing to do but turtle up in my room and read *Owl House* slashfic.

But Aiden wasn't giving me that option. Which was fine, really— there was no reason to be nervous, because I had nothing to lose. Meredith and I didn't even know each other. Better to get it over with quickly so Aiden and I could move on to more important things.

I found her sitting alone at a table sized for five, tucked away near an emergency exit. She wore an ash-gray denim jacket that might have come that way, or else been loved down from true black into the lunar dust of a half-burned charcoal briquette. Ripped black jeans and a light gray hoodie gave her the color scheme of an old movie, accentuated by perfectly straight black hair parted artlessly down the middle and tucked behind her ears. Against that monochrome palette, her skin blazed golden brown, punctured by the white dots of earbuds. She sat with her back to the door, eating a wheat-bread sandwich and staring with blank eyes at a banner for a canned food drive.

She maintained her stare as I approached, not turning to look until I was a foot from the table. When she did, the cold intensity of those eyes—so dark they were almost black—was like a sledgehammer to the sternum.

I'd seen plenty of mean eyes: the petty viciousness of bullies, roosters, and purse-sized dogs. These weren't those. Her eyes were *heavy*—a physical weight that bore down on you. I took a step backward before catching myself.

"Um. Hi." I gave a limp wave.

One thick black eyebrow rose. "Hi . . . ?"

"I'm Cara Weaver."

"Okay."

Silence.

When it was clear no more would be forthcoming, I gestured to her earbuds. "What are you listening to?"

"Music . . . ?" Now the corner of her mouth quirked up as well—not a smile, but the sort of puzzled expression that said *you can't possibly be as stupid as you look, can you?*

"Right," I said. "Cool."

"My god," Aiden whispered. *"You really have no idea what you're doing, do you?"*

I grimaced.

"So, umm . . ." I wished we had some classes together, anything. Short of asking about her sandwich, which even *I* could see was pathetic, I'd used up all the obvious conversation starters.

Then again, she clearly didn't do small talk. Might as well go all in.

"I was wondering if you'd want to go to prom with me."

That got a reaction. Both eyebrows went up now, and she blinked.

She set her sandwich carefully down atop her lunch bag and pulled out her earbuds. "What did you say?"

"*Sweet fuckity Christ,*" Aiden moaned.

"I asked if you wanted to go to prom with me."

She stared. After an uncomfortably long moment, she asked, "Why?"

A damn good point. But it was too late to back out now. Blood rushed hot to my cheeks. "I just thought it might be fun. You know. To go. Together."

"*I can't watch,*" Aiden continued. "*God, why can't I cover my eyes?! Curse these invisible hands!*"

Meredith continued to stare. She had a way of holding her face almost perfectly still, each movement animatronically precise and deliberate. Those eyes were abandoned mine shafts you could fall down and no one would ever find you.

At last, she put me out of my misery.

"I don't know you." She enunciated each word clearly, her voice neither friendly nor cruel. An adult explaining to a lost child that she was not, in fact, their mommy.

"Yeah, no, I know." I realized I was picking nervously at my thumbnail and forced myself to stop.

Her eyes narrowed. "Why would I go to prom with someone I don't know? How is that fun?" Simple statements of fact.

It was too much. My face burned, announcing my shame to everyone.

"Good point," I said, spicing it up with some finger guns.

And I fled.

5

"**THAT WAS PHYSICALLY** *painful,*" Aiden observed. *"Like watching a puppy get hit by a car. On loop."*

My skin itched under the stares of the lunchroom as I retreated. It was like I'd suddenly forgotten how to walk, my body further betraying me. How fast did people normally walk? Should I swing my arms? Straighten my spine? I felt like a mall-walking grandma, or one of those Boston Dynamics robots that are always falling over. ShameBot 5000.

You did the thing, I reassured myself. *That's all that matters.* Yet my stomach churned so hard I thought I might actually vomit as I ducked into a hallway. I wasn't ready to go back and face Holly and Elvis, but I had to get out of the Commons—even if I was pulling off Casual Nondescript Walking, my flaming cheeks were too obvious. Embarrassment in a high school is blood in the water.

"Seriously," Aiden continued. *"It was like one of those nature documentaries where you see the orca circling the baby seal, but you're powerless to stop it."*

"Yes, okay, *thank you.*" I found a bench and sat down, pretending to dig through my bag as an excuse to hide my face. Fear sweat slicked my armpits, already seeping through my shirt. My brain tried to comfort me with the reminder that this still wasn't my *worst* public humiliation, which was exactly as helpful as it sounded.

"*Sorry,*" Aiden said, finally sounding sympathetic. "*Don't take it too hard.*"

"Yeah?" I laughed angrily. "Exactly how hard *should* I take it? It wasn't even like she was trying to be mean—more like I wasn't worth the energy. Like I was a pop-up ad she was swiping away."

"*I* did *warn you,*" Aiden reminded, then sighed. "*That's why we need to train you up before next time.*"

"*Next* time?"The thought of those pitiless eyes watching me like a bug in a jar squeezed my stomach into a fist. "Why would there be a *next* time? I said I'd ask her, and I did. She said no. Mission accomplished."

"*Uh—yeah, no. We agreed you'd take* her to prom.*"

"I can't take her if she doesn't want to go!"

"*Sure you can. You just need to try harder. Apply a little game. A little* strategy.*"

"I don't play games," I muttered. "And no offense, but your sister super sucks."

"*I know you just got beat with the rejection stick, so I'm gonna pretend I didn't hear that. But the deal's the deal. No date, no ghost.*"

"That's not fair!"

"*Neither is dying alone in an abandoned paper mill. Suck it up, buttercup.*"

"Buttercup? Really? Are you a football coach now?" I rested my forehead atop my backpack.

"*Look,*" he said, sounding exasperated. "*It's not you, okay? I've only known you a day, but you seem cool. She's just a hard nut to crack.*"

"That's an understatement." But I couldn't help but thaw a little.

"*Meredith's like M&M's: hard on the outside, sweet on the inside. You'll see.*"

In my pocket, my phone buzzed—Holly, no doubt, having watched my retreat from the balcony.

I sighed. "If you say so." Then I picked up my bag, smoothed down my hair, and headed back out to face the punishing comfort of Holly's support.

⌣

"Will you put that down? We need to focus."

I waved Mom's voltage meter in Aiden's general vicinity one last time—still nothing—then flopped down on my bed in surrender. "*Fine.* Meredith Reyes, round two. Hit me with your brilliant strategy, Fearless Leader."

"That's more like it!" In my imagination, Aiden paced around the room like Admiral Ackbar briefing the rebels. *"The thing about Meredith is that you can't come straight at her or she'll retreat. She was shy before, but now she's full-on wounded animal, snapping at anything that gets close. You gotta find some treat to tempt her out of her cage."*

I made a face. "You talk about her like she's a dog."

"Whatever, she loves dogs. We used to volunteer at a shelter together."

"Oh, so she *does* have a heart. Alert the authorities."

"Dude, her heart is like—" He made an exasperated noise. *"You can't see it, but my arms are way far apart."*

"Phantom limbs for an actual phantom." I stared up at the Judgment tarot card on my wall, with its angel blowing a trumpet over a crowd of people. "So why just Meredith?"

"What do you mean?"

I waved at the card. "I know you're her guardian angel, or whatever, but you had like a million friends. You were fucking *homecoming king.* So why aren't we sending messages or doing stuff for them, too? Or your parents?"

He sighed. *"I thought about it, trust me. I must have composed a thousand notes over the last year, imagining exactly what I'd say if I got the chance. But, like . . . most of my friends have moved on, and my parents . . . assuming we could even get them to listen to you, would it be right to reopen those wounds? What could I even do for them?"*

"You could let them know you're okay."

"Exactly how is this okay?"

"You know what I mean."

"Yeah, but I'm not gonna be around like this forever, right?" He

sounded both scared and hopeful at the prospect. *"I could try to reassure them that I'm happy in the afterlife, but honestly, being dead fucking sucks. And talking to them now would just mean they'd have to lose me twice."* His voice steadied. "Meredith *I can actually* help. *I love her to death, but socially, the girl's a garbage fire. She* needs *me."*

After the brick wall she'd presented me with today, I could see that. Still, his casual dismissal of her grated. "For somebody who supposedly cares so much, you sure like talking shit about her."

"I'm not talking shit! I'm planning an intervention. Meredith is amazing, she just has no idea how to present herself to the world. I did what I could to showcase her when I was alive, but she was always so afraid of people. And it's only gotten worse since I've been gone." His voice went tight and quiet. *"She's just given up on everyone."*

Once again, I marveled at how quickly Aiden bounced between bombastic snark and barely contained grief. I wondered if he'd always been this open, or if a year in isolation had scraped away his protective coating. Being myself a creature of barbs and wit, his sudden blasts of sincerity were disconcerting.

He drew a breath. *"Anyway, I messed everything up for her by dying, so I need to fix it. And you're gonna help me."*

"Lucky me."

"Today you got flustered. But trust me—deep down, she wants *someone like you to drag her out of her shell."*

I snorted.

"It's true! She's got a secret romantic side, she just needs somebody to sweep her off her feet. All you have to do is stay calm and take charge. Refuse to take no for an answer."

I raised an eyebrow. "Isn't 'refusing to take no' the definition of harassment?"

"The difference between flirting and harassment is whether it works."

"Spoken like a grade A incel."

"Hey, which of us has dated more girls? The point is, she was right that it's weird to go to prom with a stranger. We need to work our way up to it. Which is why we need to find a different activity the two of you can do together."

"Wait—*another* activity? I only agreed to take her to the dance!"

"Yes, and we're using one to get to the other. Try to keep up." His tone turned hopeful. *"You don't rock climb, do you?"*

"No . . . ?"

"Damn. That's her main thing—or used to be. I guess there's always movies, but 'Netflix and chill' isn't really first-date material . . ."

"It's not a date," I said, but without much heat. I'd already agreed to Aiden's plan, so why fight it? I remembered her earbuds. "What about a concert?"

"Yes! Concert! Perfect!" He clucked his tongue thoughtfully. *"I know all her favorite bands. We'll find one playing Seattle, and you tell her you've got an extra ticket. How could she say no?"*

She didn't strike me as lacking in that department, but I opened my laptop and found a site of all-ages concert listings. "What does she like?"

"Neo-soul, hot blues . . . Stuff that sounds old but isn't."

"I don't know either of those."

"Me either, until she showed me. Not really my thing, but it's okay."

"So what *is* your thing?" I couldn't help but be a little curious about this mystery boy who'd shown up in my ear. Besides, any information you could collect about a ghost was part of the job, right? "Who's your favorite band?"

"Oh, Darkhearts. All the way."

I snorted. "The cringe vampire guy?"

"Chance Kain is not cringe!"

"Dude always looks like he's about to recite sad poetry."

"Okay, one: girls love sad poetry—this is a clear example of why you need me. And two, dude's voice is, like, pure sex. Listen to 'Asleep at the Altar' and tell me you aren't snail-trailing your panties."

I winced. "You're disgusting."

"Filters are for the living, girlfriend. But okay, Ms. Judgey—what music do you listen to?"

I shrugged. "Country, mostly."

He laughed incredulously. *"And you call Darkhearts cringe?!"*

"Country isn't cringe!"

"A bunch of dudes who've never been more than a mile from a Star-bucks, wearing cowboy hats they bought off Amazon?"

"At least they don't pretend to sleep in a coffin!"

Aiden affected an atrocious twang and began to sing:

> *"Well, my horse broke down*
> *and he stole my truck,*
> *so my little woman left me*
> *and I'm down on my luck . . ."*

"That is *not* what country sounds like!" But I couldn't help laughing.

"It totally is. I've spent my whole life in this town—if there's one thing I can spot, it's city people pretending to be cowboys. But actually, that's a perfect fit—country is just blues for white people."

"Ex*cuse* me?!"

"Show me the lie. Anyway, keep scrolling, let's see if there's anything I recognize."

I returned my attention to the laptop. All-ages shows on the Eastside were limited to a handful of teen centers, but Seattle had some proper clubs. Halfway down the page, Aiden said, *"Stop! That's perfect!"*

"Which one?"

"Sly Gaze. And they're playing Saturday!"

I clicked through to the club's website. "Oof! Are concert tickets always this expensive?"

"Gotta pay to play, baby. I'd help, but I doubt my accounts still work."

"And you're sure this is the only way?"

"Definitely. Concerts are fun! People! Loud music! Everybody full of energy!"

It was sounding worse by the moment, but at least it was soon. Better to get it over with so I could get back to the real mission. I signed into my PayPal, but my finger hovered over the purchase button. "Maybe we should wait to buy them. Just in case she says no."

"That's loser talk. If you leave yourself an out, you'll take it. Dating is like sports—you gotta commit*!"*

"God, please no sports metaphors." But I clenched my teeth and clicked.

"There we go*! Commitment!"*

"Rah. Go team." I leaned back in my chair, exhausted. "Can we get back to ghost stuff now?"

"Almost." He sounded so genuinely happy that I nearly forget my annoyance. *"You've got a plan, you've got the date, you've got* me—*but you're still missing the most important element."*

Jesus Christ—we'd barely even made a dent in the list of experiments I'd thought up, and more questions were popping up all the time. What was his top speed? How high could he fly? Were there ways to block the magnetic pull he described, or strengthen it? Did his observation affect the world at a quantum level—and was there any way to test it for cheap in a bedroom? There was just so much we didn't *know.*

But I'd already come this far. I sighed. "What? What more could you *possibly* want from me?"

I could hear the smile in his voice.

"Swagger."

6

HOLLY STOOD BESIDE me as I waited in the school parking lot.

"You sure you want to do this?" she asked.

"No. But I don't have a choice."

"Quit complaining," Aiden said. *"This is gonna be great."*

Holly's face scrunched up in protective indignation. "You *always* have a choice. Ghost or no ghost, you don't have to do anything you don't want to. If Aiden doesn't understand that, he can go French himself."

"Wow," Aiden drawled. *"Busting out the big guns, huh?"*

I sighed. Being in the middle of an argument was bad enough when the two sides could hear each other. "It's fine, Holly. I—"

"There she is!"

A low blue sedan with tinted windows split off from the line of cars snaking through the entrance and made for the farthest corner of the lot, where we stood near the fence overlooking the retaining pond.

"That's my car," Aiden said proudly. *"I installed the spoiler myself."*

"And I'm sure it makes it much faster."

"Whatever. At least I had a car."

I squeezed Holly's shoulder. "You should go."

"You sure?"

"I'm sure." The last thing I needed was an audience.

She gave me one last supportive look, then scampered off, backpack charms jingling.

Meredith had the front windows down, even though it was still cold enough for jackets. Thick, syrupy bass slithered out as she pulled into the most remote parking spot.

"You've got this," Aiden whispered. *"Remember: confidence! Don't panic and run like last time."*

"I didn't *panic*," I muttered, stalking toward the car. "I made a *strategic retreat.*"

"And nearly threw up all over yourself. Strategically."

"A time-honored distraction tactic. Turkey vultures would be proud. Now shut up and let me work my mojo."

Meredith stepped out of the car. She was wearing the same outfit as yesterday, only this time beneath the denim jacket was a yellow T with a mammoth logo, the neck chopped out and revealing a little black crystal pendant identical to Aiden's. She stopped as she saw me, leaning on the open door to watch me approach. Her look of casual indifference would have been devastatingly cool if it weren't aimed at me. As it was, it was mostly just devastating.

"You again." She sounded only mildly curious.

"Me again."

A breeze rolled a discarded Red Bull can across the pavement. My brain whistled the theme from *The Good, the Bad and the Ugly.*

"Confidence!" Aiden howled.

I shoved my hands into my pockets. I was wearing my best high-rise boyfriend jeans—blue, to pop against my Docs—leaving just a narrow stripe of midriff below a gray crop top, all overlaid with a plaid flannel and my white moto jacket. A pair of oversized white Audrey Hepburn sunglasses finished it off, minimizing Mount Proboscis while providing a one-way shield of smoked glass to hide behind.

That last bit was crucial. Dad had taught me that when encountering dangerous animals, it's important not to let them see fear. Meredith seemed like she qualified.

I stuck out my chin, meeting her flat look with my own.

"Let's try this again," I said. "My name's Cara Weaver, and I've got two tickets to the Sly Gaze show on Saturday. Wanna come?"

Dark eyebrows rose. "How'd you know I like them?"

"I hear you playing them sometimes when you drive in." I was pleased by how smoothly the prepared answer flowed. "While I'm out locking up my bike."

"Oh." Meredith finally looked disconcerted, expression flickering between suspicion and something that might have been pleasure before settling on the former. She glanced around, as if looking for who might be filming. "I thought you wanted to take me to prom." It came out as an accusation.

"Yeah, well, *somebody* told me you weren't interested in going with someone you didn't know. So again: hi, I'm Cara. This is your chance to get to know me."

She stared at me with that zombie-blank expression. Blinked once. Twice.

And then she smiled.

Her whole face transformed. Cheeks that had been sharp and severe softened, folding up the corners of those raptor eyes. Where Aiden's photograph grin was easy and practiced, Meredith's seemed artless, coltish—a newborn deer. It was like someone had pulled the blinds to let in the sun . . .

. . . and then slammed them down again. The smile vanished, face reassembling into its statuesque planes.

"*You* don't know *me*," she said. "So why would you want to go with me?"

"Oh, Jesus *fuck*." I pulled the ticket printouts from my pocket and held them up. "This isn't rocket surgery, all right? We like the same band, and I've got an extra ticket." I rolled one of them up and poked it through a link in the fence, holding it there. "Now, do you want to go with me, or should I just chuck this straight into the pond?"

"Maybe a little too *confident,"* Aiden murmured.

But Meredith just stared, arms crossed over the top of the door. "Well?" I demanded.

The corner of her mouth turned up. She bobbed her head. "Okay."

Relief flooded through me, threatening to cut my marionette

strings, but I forced myself to stay standing tall. *Show no fear*, I reminded myself. *Not even in retrospect.* I pulled the printout back through the fence and held out my empty hand. "Cool. Gimme your phone."

Another suspicious look. "Why?"

"Because you're gonna need my address to pick me up on Saturday."

"Okay, now that *was smooth."* Aiden sounded legitimately impressed.

Meredith still looked wary, but slowly unlocked her phone and handed it over.

I entered my number in her contacts, then put my address into Google Maps and saved it before handing the phone back. "Seven o'clock?"

She stared at the phone as if it were an alien artifact, then slid it back into her pocket. "Sure."

"Cool."

And I turned and walked away like an action hero, refusing to look back at the explosion behind me.

Aiden whistled. *"Damn, Cara! That was straight-up* sexy.*"*

A warm glow spread outward from my stomach, but I just smiled. "I know."

7

SATURDAY NIGHT ARRIVED drizzly and dark. I sat by the front window, watching for Meredith so my parents wouldn't have a chance to intercept her.

Dad wandered past—not for the first time. "So! First concert in the big city!"

"Yup."

He took a sip of his La Croix and stared out the window with me. "You know, when I was a kid, Seattle had a law called the Teen Dance Ordinance. You could only have all-ages shows at teen centers, and they couldn't go late."

"Well, yeah," I said. "You had to get the buggy home before the horse got sleepy."

"*Oof!*" He thumped a fist against his chest, then yelled into the kitchen. "Erica! Your daughter's giving me a midlife crisis again!"

Mom walked in, holding her open laptop. "Honey, stop owning your father." She kissed the top of his head. "You know his old-man heart can't take it." She closed the laptop and turned to me. "Who's this girl you're going with?"

"Meredith. A friend from school."

"And Holly isn't going with you?"

"No, just us."

"Mmm." She tried to hide a smile and failed utterly.

"*Mom.*"

"I didn't say anything." But the smile only widened.

Outside, Meredith's car rumbled into the cul-de-sac, announcing itself with one of those unnecessarily loud exhausts Dad called "fart cans."

"Gotta go!" I grabbed my jacket and hugged both parents perfunctorily.

"Have fun!" Mom said, while Dad called, "Make good choices!" Then I was out the door.

"All right, game time," Aiden whispered excitedly in my ear. *"Just do everything like we discussed, and you'll be great. Remember, I'm your cheat code. I'll be right beside you the whole time."*

"Joy of joys." I opened the passenger door.

Since I didn't exactly go to concerts every day, I'd let Aiden talk me into pulling out all the stops in the wardrobe department. I'd kept my Docs (the only decent shoes I owned without bike cleats), but beneath the moto jacket I had my best top—a teal half-sleeve thing with printed birds that looked modest on the hanger but clung tight and somehow added a cup size. On the bottom were what I thought of as my Bondage Jeans, whose black lace-up sides showed *way* too much skin for school—or anywhere, really. I'd never actually had the guts to wear them in public, not wanting to deal with the attention they'd bring. But even Holly had agreed that they looked too good on me to *not* buy them.

Meredith, for her part, was dressed the same as always, the only difference a new color of T-shirt. She looked me over as I sat down, expression impassive.

Judging by Aiden's wolf whistle when I'd shown him, my outfit achieved its intended effect. Yet now, in the face of Meredith's stony stare and casual clothes, I felt suddenly ridiculous. Who was I trying to fool? I was a nerd from the suburbs—I'd never been up in a club in my life, nor to a concert that didn't feature cowboy boots and my parents. And what was I doing getting all sexied up for Meredith, anyway? This whole thing was about fulfilling my promise to Aiden, not seducing a gender-flipped Oscar the Grouch who hadn't said ten words to me.

Still, it felt like I should have gotten *some* reaction. Part of me wished she'd mock me, just to have it out in the open. Anything other than this blank wax-statue stare. I wanted to curl in on myself like a dead bug.

But no—*fuck* that. And fuck her. Let her think what she wanted. I was here for *me*.

I squared my shoulders and put on my best smile. *You're the predator*, I reminded myself. *Smiles are threats. Show her your teeth.*

"Hey," I said.

She nodded, still staring. "Hey."

"Compliment the car." Aiden's stage whisper was far too loud. *"Everyone loves talking about their car."*

"Cool car," I said, obligingly.

Meredith's blank expression cracked, brows lowering.

"It's my brother's."

"Oh." My reply came out quieter than I wanted, betraying that I knew what that meant.

Meredith turned and pulled away from the curb, tapping her phone. Something slinky with horns and a thumping bassline flooded the silence.

"That's okay," Aiden said, sounding rattled. *"I should have thought of that, but it's fine. Go to the concert questions. Remember: questions and compliments, that's all you need."*

I reached for an excited voice, trying to gloss over the awkward moment. "This is cool, huh? I haven't been to a concert in forever. What's the best concert you've been to?"

Aiden had told me what her answer would be: the time he'd taken her downtown to see a Darkhearts benefit show. He'd made me read about it online, so I'd be ready to discuss it coherently.

But her jaw remained clenched, eyes hard as they watched the road. "Dunno."

"What the hell?" Aiden groused, still way louder than necessary. *"That show was awesome!"*

"I, uh." It was hard to concentrate on the conversation with his voice braying in my ear. "I guess mine was the Chicks. With my dad." I laughed self-consciously. "Pretty cringe, huh?"

Meredith shrugged and turned out onto the highway.

"Don't self-neg," Aiden admonished. *"It looks weak—you want her to* respect *you. Ask another question!"*

A current of cold air made me shiver, and I turned the vents away from my overly exposed legs. Meredith apparently liked her cars as frigid as her personality.

"Anyway," I said quickly, "I'm glad we're going to see Sly Gaze tonight. What's your favorite of their stuff?"

"Good. Keep it light."

Meredith inhaled, nostrils flaring, and finally relaxed a little. "Probably *Don't Linger.*"

The name sounded familiar, but it wasn't one of the songs Aiden had made me listen to—her tastes must have evolved over the last year. But I nodded enthusiastically. "Hell yeah—I love that song!"

She glanced sideways at me, a tiny wrinkle appearing between her brows. "That's the album."

"Oh! Right!" I laughed self-consciously, feeling sweat start to prickle in my armpits. "I'm awful at song names." Shit. Self-negating again.

"Confidence!" Aiden whisper-shouted. Did he really think that was helpful? Would he have water poloed better if I'd been there screaming *Score a goal!* in his ear?

Meredith pursed her lips, gaze darting back and forth between me and the road. "What about you?"

"Definitely 'Make Me Mean It,'" I said, glad to finally have a prepared answer. According to Aiden, that *should* be her favorite song.

She nodded sideways. "Good choice."

"Finally!" Aiden sounded relieved.

We crossed the river, then began climbing Novelty Hill Road—a steep, squiggly forest tunnel that was an absolute death wish on a bicycle, the metal guardrail dented from a thousand bumper kisses.

Meredith took the turns with casual grace, leaned back with one hand on the wheel, car purring excitedly beneath us. After two years of riding with Holly, who drove like a Victorian governess giving a posture lesson, I couldn't help but find her self-assurance a little mesmerizing.

"Don't go quiet," Aiden urged. *"Keep her talking! You're supposed to be drawing her out, remember?"*

I gritted my teeth, but he was right. "So. What do you do for fun?"

She shrugged.

"Ask about her favorite show."

Of course, Aiden had already made me memorize her favorite shows, as well as her favorite books, movies, and a whole cornucopia of other random Meredith trivia. Because apparently in His Homecoming Highness's mind, the only way I could *possibly* survive a date was with Cold War levels of espionage.

I did as instructed. Meredith gave it a moment of thought, then said, *"Ted Lasso."*

I hadn't seen it—Mom and Dad refused to pay for multiple streaming services, and I watched more YouTube than TV anyway. But Aiden had, and that was all that mattered.

"Okay, perfect!" he gushed. *"Now repeat after me: 'That show is great! I love how it's all about the characters growing as people and dealing with their issues. That ending with Roy and Jamie was perfect.'"*

That sounded a little corny to me—I preferred my moral lessons via final girls and ironic but inevitable dismemberment. And I *really* wasn't loving this whole line-by-line force-feeding. But I wasn't the one driving the Romance Express. I dutifully parroted him.

"Yeah?" Meredith glanced over, finally sounding interested. Points for the ghost, I supposed.

"Now say: 'Yeah, but Rebecca and Sam should have stayed together.'"

I did.

Meredith frowned, but nodded. "Totally."

"Who's your favorite character?"

It was like I wasn't even here—just a tube Aiden was speaking through. A human echo.

Without hesitation, Meredith responded, "Roy."

"Ha!" Aiden said. *"Figures."*

"Ha!" I repeated. "Figures."

"Shit, no, don't say that part!"

Across the front seat, Meredith's eyes narrowed. "Why?"

"Oh, umm . . ." I had no idea who any of these people were, and no way to chew Aiden out for getting me into this.

"Shit, shit! Roy's just like her—he's grumpy, but a secret softie, with huge eyebrows. But you can't say any of that. Say, uh . . . 'Because you don't talk much.'"

I followed instructions.

She was still giving me the side-eye. "Right."

"Okay, new plan," Aiden announced. *"Before each line you need to repeat, I'll say 'line.' So it'll be like 'Line: I thought Roy and Keeley's relationship was so cute,' and you—"*

I turned to the window, hiding my face as I whispered, *"Stop. Talking."*

"What?"

Across the car, Meredith muttered, "Good idea."

Great. So now she thought I talked to myself, too.

I leaned against the door, trying to collect my thoughts as roads widened and turned to freeway. Aiden kept jabbering, suggesting conversational openings, but I was done with his little puppet show.

Meredith's phone was the first to break the silence, helpfully informing us that we needed to merge immediately across three lanes of traffic. Meredith swore, head whipping back and forth over her shoulder as she muscled her way in, almost missing the exit. She let out a breath as we finally made it onto the interchange, but her knuckles remained white on the steering wheel.

"Don't drive into the city often?" I observed.

She glared. *"You* could have driven us."

"Not unless you wanna ride in a bike trailer."

She gave me an incredulous look. "You don't drive?"

"Nope."

"How?" She waved at the traffic around us. "You can't get anywhere without a car!"

"You can if you want it bad enough."

"But *why*?"

"Passenger cars produced three billion tons of CO_2 last year. I refuse to add to the problem." Which sounded better than the truth: that after years of almost getting squashed on a bike, the responsibility of piloting a multiton death machine was too terrifying to contemplate.

"So you're getting *me* to drive you instead?" Meredith studied me from beneath arched brows—they really *were* impressively full. "How is that different?"

"You were already going to the concert. I'm just riding along."

"I'm only going because *you* invited me!"

I shrugged. "Details."

Meredith shook her head, but at least we'd broken some of the ice. I decided to press my advantage.

"What's your car's name?"

Now she turned her head all the way to stare at me. "Why would my car have a name?"

"Why *wouldn't* it?"

"Because . . . it's a car . . . ?" She yanked her gaze back to the road.

"Wow—way to make it feel special. What kind of barbarian doesn't name things?" I stroked the dashboard's pebbled plastic. "It's okay, Car. She doesn't mean it."

"What're you doing?" Aiden demanded. *"Stop being weird!"*

But Meredith looked intrigued. "You name your stuff?"

"Only the important things."

"Like what?"

I held up my phone. "Meredith, meet Alfred. Alfred, Meredith."

"Alfred?"

"Like Batman's butler. Because he knows everything and does whatever I ask."

Her sideways smirk couldn't decide if it was friendly or not. "So you're Batman?"

"It's not about me. Besides, it was either that or Smithers, and I'm sure as hell not Mr. Burns."

Meredith snorted, but she was talking. "What else?"

"Umm . . ." I tapped my lip. "My dad's got an electric pickup named Dumps—as in 'dumps like a truck'—and my mom's Prius Prime is Optimus, for obvious reasons. My laptop is Macklemore M. Book, Second of His Name. The best is my friend Holly's minivan, which is named Morrison, because—"

"Van Morrison." Meredith smiled.

"Exactly!" I leaned back against the door to get a better look at her. "Names are important. Good thing for you I'm here to help. So let's see . . ." I hummed. "The car's blue, so . . . how about Dash? Like Rainbow Dash."

Aiden squawked indignantly. *"You can't name my car after My Little Pony!"*

Meredith's face matched his tone. "Too childish."

"So Blue's Cruise is also out?"

She snorted again, but there was that flashbulb pop of a grin.

"Blueberry," I said. "Or Muffin."

"MUFFIN?!" Aiden sounded like he might have an aneurysm.

"These are all too cutesy," Meredith said.

"Chunks. Like 'Blue Chunks.' It's a homophone."

"Ew."

"You wanted less cute. Gonzo."

"No."

"Yancey."

Meredith glanced over in confusion. "Why Yancey?"

"I dunno, I'm out of blue stuff."

"Why are you doing this to me?" Aiden moaned.

Meredith shook her head.

"The Reyes Car, like 'racecar.' Or Meredith's Good-Time Fun-Wagon."

"No!" But she was fighting a smirk.

"Mr. Puttington."

"Mr. Puttington!" Meredith's laugh exploded out of her, full and loud. She leaned over the steering wheel, a lock of hair falling

down into her face. She pushed it back behind her ear, gasping for breath. *"Oh my god."*

"Lord Puttington, of the Stossel Puttingtons. A dapper chap, if a trifle brooding. Total BDE—big Darcy energy." I grinned. "Do we have a winner?"

"No. Absolutely not." She looked over at me again, grinning, this time with a bit of wonder. "Seriously, though, why does it need a name? I've only got one car."

"So? What if your parents were like, 'Why does she need a name, we've only got one kid?'"

I realized what I'd said a second too late.

"Daughter," I corrected quickly. "If they only had one *daughter.*"

But Meredith's face fell like a portcullis descending. She stared straight out the windshield.

"Nice," Aiden observed. *"Truly top-notch work. Good thing you didn't let anybody help you."*

"Sorry," I said, not knowing who I was talking to.

"It's fine," Meredith said, but she didn't look at me.

We sailed on in silence, through suburbs grown into cities, then out over Lake Washington. The towers of Seattle rose up before us in the sunset.

In the city proper, things got complicated. Prompted by Siri, who seemed to be actively orchestrating our deaths, Meredith changed off one freeway and onto another, only to have to immediately dodge across three *more* lanes of traffic for a left-hand exit. I held my breath as she wove us through, earning a deafening blat from a semi.

"Jesus Christ!" she yelled.

"Who designed these roads?" I agreed. "M. C. Escher?"

Off the freeway, things were no better. One-way streets forced us in circles, some of them up hills so steep you couldn't see the intersection as you waited for the light. Rain spattered onto the windshield. Meredith merged out of a bus-only lane, only to miss a turn, her phone rerouting with a chipper suggestion that she get her shit together.

At last, I spotted the club's neon marquee. "There it is!"

Just past the entrance, a second sign with a giant finger and the word PARKING pointed down at a cramped lot between two tall buildings.

And right beneath it, a smaller sign: LOT FULL.

"*Full?*" Meredith sounded panicked. "How can it be *full*? It's a *parking lot*!"

"It's okay," I said. "Maybe there's another one."

"This city is *batshit*."

We circled the block. Then another. Rows of parked cars lined the street on either side, thick as legs on a millipede. The minutes dragged on as we crawled slowly down dumpster-filled alleys, or started to turn into the hidden mouths of subterranean parking garages, only to have to back precariously out again as signs proclaimed MONTHLY PASS HOLDERS ONLY.

"The show's already started," Meredith moaned.

"It'll be fine," I said. "There are openers. Look, there's a space!"

Meredith managed to parallel park in only two tries, as an Uber driver honked angrily. Before I could congratulate her, though, Aiden said, "*White curb.*"

"What?" I opened my door to reveal a curb indeed painted white. Next to it, a little sign said THREE-MINUTE PASSENGER LOAD ONLY.

"*Fuuuuuuuck.*" Meredith grabbed a handful of her hair, pulling hard. "We're gonna have to turn around and go home, and all because there's no fucking *parking*." She glared over at me, as if I'd personally filled up the parking lot.

I stomped down on my temper, forcing myself to remember that, as stressful as this was as a passenger, it was worse for her. Instead, I said, "You've got this. Let's just keep looking."

Meredith grunted, but we pulled back out. Two blocks later, Aiden shouted, "*There! On the right!*" I echoed him.

"It says 'No Parking'!" Meredith snapped.

"Yeah, until eight! It's past eight!"

Meredith slammed on the brakes, earning more honks. We ignored them as she wedged herself into the spot.

"Are we good?" she asked.

I peered out at the logic puzzle of overlapping street signs on the lamppost. "You're good."

"Oh thank fuck." She leaned her forehead onto the steering wheel.

"Nice work."

Meredith angled her head to see if I was mocking her, peering out from beneath a curtain of hair. When it was clear I wasn't, she mumbled a grudging "Thanks." Then she took a deep, shuddering breath and straightened. "*Ho*-kay. Let's go see some music."

Inspiration struck. "Wait! We need to commemorate this achievement."

"What?"

Outside my door, easily twenty different vinyl stickers covered the steel trunk of the streetlight. I picked one the size of my hand—a crude cartoon figure with a butcher knife and the word BLOODBATH, all spattered with droplets of red paint. I slipped my nails under its edge, peeling it carefully free. Then I slid back into the car and slapped it onto the dashboard.

"*Hey!*" Aiden yelled.

Meredith looked almost as shocked. "What're you doing?"

"Claiming your territory." I smoothed it down against the leather-textured plastic, making sure it adhered, then sat back and looked Meredith in the eye. "This *used* to be your brother's car. But you drove it into the most bananapants traffic in a thousand miles. You navigated a labyrinth of one-way streets and battled the Parking Minotaur, and came out alive." I gestured to the sticker. "So celebrate your victory. Take the wrapper off this thing and make it yours."

"*She doesn't need a dumb sticker,*" Aiden grumbled. "*It's gonna get the dashboard all sticky!*"

Meredith stared at me, expressionless.

It occurred to me that perhaps I'd overstepped. That I had, in fact, desecrated her dead brother's car. She had every right to tell me to walk home.

To my shock, she bit her lower lip uncertainly. She looked at the sticker, then back at me, eyebrows raised. "Bloodbath, huh?" The tiniest hint of a smile. "Real vote of confidence in my driving."

"There we go!" I laughed with relief. "That's your car's name now! Bloodbath."

"Oh my god." Meredith laughed as well, and my body lit up at the sound. Not just because it was infectious—though it was, uncontrolled and volcanic, on the verge of snorting. But because I'd made it happen. Me, on my own, without any of Aiden's coaching or inside info. *I'd* made this silent, stony girl crack up. I felt like a superhero discovering her power.

"We can't call it Bloodbath," Meredith insisted.

We. I liked the sound of that.

"Too late," I countered. "The best names choose you. It's already done. Meredith, meet Bloodbath. Bloodbath, Meredith. I'm sure you'll be very happy together."

Meredith shook her head, but she was still smiling. She unbuckled and opened her door.

"Come on," she said. "Let's get this party started."

8

IT WAS SEVERAL blocks to the club, the rain pattering down on our heads and kicking up the paradoxically dry smell of asphalt and exhaust.

"Okay, fine," Aiden conceded as we walked. *"Nice save with the sticker. I'll even forgive you for messing up my car. This time."*

I snorted softly to show what I thought of his generosity.

The Continuum wasn't much to look at from the outside: just a two-story concrete box wedged between taller buildings. A bank of thick, black-painted metal doors ran beneath a neon sign in the shape of an ouroboros, pink tubes flashing between two different configurations so that the snake seemed to circle as it ate its own tail.

Inside, the lobby was sparsely populated, mostly wristbanded adults standing in line for the bar. A few musician-looking types stood behind tables of T-shirts and vinyl, staring at their phones. We headed up a wide ramp to another line of doors, through which bass boomed like cannon fire.

A wave of hot, humid air smacked us as we passed through into the club proper. In the half dark, moving bodies had turned drizzle-damp clothes to clouds of steam that rose, catching the lights in bright streamers. The opening band looked to be closing out their set, given that the lead singer appeared to be pouring alcohol directly onto his piano.

"Damn," I shouted, "it's hot in here!" I shrugged out of my coat, already feeling sweat threatening in my pits.

Next to me, Meredith did the same. It was the first time I'd seen her without that jacket, and my mouth spoke before my brain could catch up. "Holy shit!"

Meredith jumped back. "What?"

"You're jacked!" Wide shoulders strained against her T-shirt, tugging the outer edges of the sleeves upward. Beneath smooth skin, contours of muscle revealed themselves subtly with every movement—the pop of a bicep, the subtle bulge of a tricep. Did I even *have* triceps? If so, they'd never bothered showing themselves.

"Okay, good compliment," Aiden observed, *"but you might want to tone it down a little."*

Meredith looked embarrassed, crossing her arms and tugging at her sleeves, which only drew attention to the flutter of tendons in her wiry forearms. "I guess."

"No, it's awesome!" Her awkwardness immediately became my own. I of all people, with my big ol' *Sex and the City* nose, ought to know that you don't randomly comment on strangers' bodies. I tried to cover by putting on an Eastern European accent and making a fist. "Stronk like bull!" *Oh god, now you literally just called her a cow. Shut up, Cara.*

"I . . . don't think that made it better," Aiden agreed.

Fortunately, the opener chose that moment for their big finish, setting the piano ablaze and letting the roar of the crowd mercifully drown out whichever foot I might have put in my mouth next. The band walked off, and the house lights came up, accompanied by Amy Winehouse making questionable decisions about rehab.

I seized both the opportunity and Meredith's arm—which was just as firm as it looked. "C'mon, let's get rid of our coats."

Upon learning the jaw-dropping price of coat check—thank you, tech salaries—I instead found a corner at the back of the club where a bunch of tables and chairs had been stacked. I shoved our folded-up jackets beneath them.

"They'll be safe here," I said, with absolutely nothing to back it up. "I mean, those prices were nuts, right? What are they doing back there, giving each coat a massage?"

"*Careful,*" Aiden warned. "*You don't want to seem cheap. You already let her drive you*—you're *taking* her *out, remember?*"

Meredith just shrugged. "Sure." She kicked our jackets deeper into the shadows. "You work?"

It took me a second to realize what she meant. "Oh—not really." I blushed. "In the summer, my parents pay me to volunteer." The Weaver party line was that we had enough money, and I should leave entry-level jobs for people who needed them and give back to the community instead. Which was fine in theory, though in practice *us* having enough money didn't always translate to *me* having enough money. Now, though, it just made me sound spoiled. "You?"

"I used to scoop ice cream at Shorty's." Something about the way she said "used to" made me think I knew exactly when that had stopped.

"That makes sense." Those arms could scoop a lot of cones. I couldn't stop staring at them. Not that the rest of her wasn't equally appealing—the fabric of her T-shirt clung delightfully, showing the diagonal lines of her bra cups, the little bulge of her crystal pendant—but I had plenty of practice not looking directly at girls' boobs. Her arms, on the other hand, or the dramatic taper of her torso—those were novel viruses, to which I had no immunity.

Meredith raised an eyebrow. "Why does that make sense?"

"Um." *Come on, Cara—concentrate.* "I just mean, I think I remember seeing you there. Do you get free ice cream? That would be cool. I could eat ice cream every day. I'm a strict waffle cone girl, though—cake cones are Styrofoam, sugar cones are made of compressed disappointment, and people who get bowls for a single scoop are already dead inside." I cut off my babbling with a laugh that sounded nervous, even to me. The fact that I knew Aiden must be cringing only made it worse.

Meredith's mouth turned sideways. "Trust me, it gets old."

"Not for me. One time, when I was ten, I ate so much ice cream that I freezer burned my tongue. The skin peeled off in long strips."

"Gross!" Meredith's nose wrinkled—but she smiled, too.

Aiden groaned. *"Jesus, Cara! We're trying for* mystique, *remember?"*

He was probably right. As pickup lines went, "this one time I pulled off bits of my skin" was pretty tough to get behind. But also . . . she'd smiled, hadn't she? Wasn't that what mattered? After all, it didn't matter if *Aiden* thought something was cute. He wasn't the target audience.

"You okay?" Meredith's head cocked sideways, and I realized I'd spaced out.

"Head in the game, Weaver!"

Enough. Time to adjust the plan. "Wait here a sec."

Meredith frowned. "Where are you going?"

"Gotta race like a pisshorse."

"What?!" She laughed with the force of a sneeze.

I grinned. Underneath her glower, Meredith was proving a pretty reliable straight man. "Bathroom. BRB."

I escaped before she could decide to come with, moving quickly back out into the lobby and down the stairs marked RESTROOMS. I stopped short of going in—anyone forced to poop at a concert had enough problems without Aiden perving on them. Instead, I stood outside and put my phone to my ear. "Aiden?"

"Yeah?" It still weirded me out how he always sounded so *close.* The phone helped make things feel more normal, as well as hiding the fact that I was definitely talking to myself.

"I can't do this with you hanging around. It's too distracting."

"Okay, okay—I'll be quiet."

"It's not just that. It's hard enough talking to Meredith—I don't need you watching over my shoulder like the Simon Cowell of romance. It's like . . ." My eyes flicked to bathrooms. "Like trying to pee when someone's listening."

"You're talking to somebody who's had to use trough urinals."

"I don't know what those are."

"Consider yourself fortunate."

"Look, my condolences to your wiener, but that doesn't change my point."

"Come on, you need *me! I'm the inside info!"*

"Yeah, and that's fine when we're planning. But now that we're actually *here,* I need you to back off and give me space."

"So what am I *supposed to do?"* He was full-on whining now. *"Do you have any idea how* boring *it is being dead?"*

"Dude, you're at a *concert!* Watch the show! Go backstage! Float around and look down girls' shirts, or whatever it is you normally do."

I'd meant it as an insult, but he hummed thoughtfully. Teenage boys: evolution made them cute so you didn't strangle them before they could reproduce.

"Just leave us alone until I get home, all right?"

"Until you get home? *What, you want me to ride in the trunk?"*

"Great idea. You can pretend we've kidnapped you."

"That's not fair!"

"*Fair?* The only reason I'm *here* is because *you* decided to hold all of science hostage! You wanted me to take your sister out, so I'm doing it. But I'm not putting on a show for you—I've already got enough performance anxiety with one Reyes." I paused, basking in my own righteous glow, then took pity. "I'll tell you everything afterward, I promise."

He groaned. *"Bluhhhhhh. FINE."*

"You promise? No spying on us?"

"If I'm trusting you, you need to trust me."

It wasn't like I'd be able to tell if he cheated anyway. "Okay."

"Great. Then get back up there before she thinks you've had some sort of ass disaster."

I ascended the stairs and found Meredith looking over the albums on one of the merch tables.

I waved toward them. "Isn't it weird that records are popular again? I mean, you can stream any song you want—who wants to pay thirty bucks for a slab of vinyl you have to flip like a pancake?"

Meredith shrugged. "I think they're cool."

"Oh." Maybe Aiden was more useful than I thought. But I doubled down. "Are you into cuneiform, too? Do you have a big rotary phone

in your bedroom?" I stepped back and framed her with my fingers, director-style. "No, wait—you're more a top-hat-and-penny-
farthing girl, aren't you?"

It was the right play. She smirked and moved away from the
table. "You're the one who still rides a bike."

As we returned to the show floor, the house music cut off and
the lights went down, the crowd bellowing its approval. The energy
of it thrummed through me—the tectonic rumble of so many
people's excitement. I grinned over at Meredith and found her
smiling back, the pull of the mob irresistible even for her. Without
thinking, I grabbed her hand and dragged her forward. "Come on,
let's try to get close!"

We made it within four rows of the stage before the mass of
bodies grew too tight to keep moving. The pressure squeezed us
together, the bare skin of her arm pressing up against mine, surprisingly cool. I was suddenly conscious of how gross and sweaty I
must be in comparison—not to mention the comparative softness
of my overcooked-noodle arms.

Shadows walked out onstage, to the rowdy cheers of the crowd.
Then the stage lights came up, revealing an eclectic group rang-
ing from a young Black keyboardist with facial tattoos to a lumpy
white drummer who looked ready to teach third-period physics.
But all eyes were on the woman who sauntered up to the mic.

She couldn't have been more than a few years older than us, but
the stage made her a thousand feet tall, as ageless as an elven queen.
She wore a strappy halter that zigzagged across her chest, offering
triangular slices of deep brown skin and a taut line of bare midriff
above wide, striped flares. Her perfect Afro caught the light, giving
her a halo as she casually palmed the old-timey mic—then bent
double in a James Brown scream.

"WELLLLLLL just *say* your *piece* al-*read*-y . . ."

The other instruments burst into action, pumping a bass-heavy
groove straight into our chests. The singer unfolded with a grin,
swiveling perfect hips as she extended a finger that felt pointed
straight at us. She sang like she moved, sinuous and sultry, growl-

ing melodies that arched your back and hooked you low, dragging you into motion.

I glanced over at Meredith, who'd lost any trace of her usual detachment as she stared open-mouthed at the goddess onstage.

I elbowed her and shouted into her ear, "Is it just me, or is that the sexiest woman on the planet?"

"Oh my god, *yes*." Meredith laughed with relief.

That laugh was intoxicating. I wanted to keep pushing—to say something salacious, just to see what she would do. Would she blush? Would she *agree*?

But it was one thing to shock Holly by talking like that. Holly was safe. Meredith . . . Meredith was anything but safe.

And the last thing I needed was to remind her she was here with Scarf Girl.

I turned back to the stage, letting myself be swept up in the music and the animal energy of the crowd.

I'd been to concerts with my parents, but they were always big-name country acts, in stadiums with assigned seating, or else at places like the Puyallup Fair, where you watched while eating elephant ears and smelling livestock.

This was nothing like that. The songs I'd played on my phone bore only a passing resemblance to the pulsating waves that lifted us up, the bass buzzing in my bones as the singer poured out her soul ten feet from my face. Her voice was incandescent, a fire that lit you up and refused to be put out. I found myself jumping and swaying, not so much moving as being moved, like the wave pool at a water park, carried along with the crowd.

I looked over and saw Meredith dancing as well, hair swinging around her face, chopping it into single frames like a strobe light. She was smiling—a smile meant only for herself, distant but happy. Again, I was struck by how much it reshaped her face, melting away the hard edges. She looked . . . nice. Like someone you could relax around.

But the magic was already beginning to give way to other concerns. The longer the band played, the tighter the crowd squished, everyone driven together by the urgency of those behind us. I didn't mind being smashed up against Meredith on one side—didn't mind at all, actually, her hip against mine, the side of her breast a soft pressure against my arm. But I was getting entirely too acquainted with the armpit of the giant guy on the other side of me, and the sweat soaking my shirt was no longer strictly my own. And the longer we stayed here, the less easily I could ignore the occasional hand brushing my ass.

"Hey!" I shouted. "Can we move back?"

"What?" She angled her ear toward me.

"Back." I managed to get an arm free enough to point.

A disappointed look flashed across her face, but she buried it quickly and nodded.

Temperature and decibels both dropped significantly as we retreated out of the human petri dish and away from the massive speaker cabinets.

Unfortunately, so did Meredith's mood. By the time we were clear, standing among the scattered hipsters who nodded along coolly, she looked like her normal self again: walled off and disillusioned.

"Sorry," I said sheepishly.

"No problem," she said. "You can see better from back here anyway." But I could tell she didn't mean it. Her hips, which had given in so naturally to the power of the stage-front scrum, now barely twitched to the beat, shifting like a kid who needed to pee. Her arms crossed protectively over her chest.

It was a crime to draw her out of that escape, to nail her back onto the cross of the world. And it wasn't what Aiden would want.

But Aiden wasn't watching us.

Nobody was watching us.

With a start, I realized that I was anonymous—truly anonymous, in a way I never was in Stossel. Right here, in this city, in this *moment*, nobody knew me. Not even Meredith.

I didn't have to be Cara the Weirdo. Cara the Scarf Girl. Cara of Snapchat infamy. I could be anyone.

So who did I want to be?

Up onstage, the obvious answer undulated, doing a body roll with the mic stand. A figure of pure, liquid confidence, unbound by laws of gods or men.

I turned to Meredith and held out my hand.

"Come on. Let's dance."

Meredith's eyes shot wide, and she took a half step back. "I don't dance."

"So? Neither do I."

She hugged herself tighter, jaw setting in what would have looked like scorn, had I not just seen the fear there. "You go. I'm good."

The old Cara—Normal Cara—would have left it at that. Would have taken the rejection and retreated to lick her wounds, comfortable in her resentment and the knowledge that this was the natural order of things.

But this wasn't a normal night. And I wanted to see Meredith with that look again—that loss of herself in sweet abandon.

"No way." I grabbed her hand, breaking her defensive stance and pulling her back toward the crowd.

"But I don't know *how*!" All Meredith's posturing fell away now, face revealing the same naked terror I lived with every day—the fear of other people's opinions.

She hadn't yet realized what I had: that tonight, in this place, we were invulnerable.

"Of course you do," I said. "PE made everyone do that stupid dance unit in middle school."

She laughed incredulously. "Yeah, for *line dancing*!"

"And swing." We reached the edge of the crush, where there was still that mob energy but with room to move. I turned to face her, then lifted my arm up over her head. She followed instinctively, swinging out, then rolled back in as I whipped her back, grabbing her other hand.

Her eyes were still wide, but surprise replaced the fear. A ghost of a grin snuck past her guard.

But she still said, "I don't even remember the basic steps!"

"Then make 'em up, dummy!" And I demonstrated.

It was like I was possessed—like a new spirit had come down to ride my body, like the lwa in Haitian Vodou. I bobbed my shoulders from side to side, letting my hips follow in a wave. A simple motion, but I could feel Meredith's eyes on me—admiring, jealous, scared. The combination was intoxicating. I stretched my arms wide, still holding her hands, forcing her in close. Her chest brushed mine, electric and unignorable. I raised my hands and spun her out again.

This wasn't me. I wasn't the sort of person who could grab a pretty girl and make her dance. And yet here I was. Her hands moved in mine, rougher and stronger than I would have thought. And warm. Very warm.

I tried to lead her through a half-remembered move called the Dishrag. I hadn't gotten to lead much in school, and we missed grabbing hands behind our backs, stumbling roughly apart. But when I turned back, she was laughing.

"See?" I beamed. "Dancing!"

"Dancing," she agreed—then threw back her head and shrieked. *"Dancing!"*

We let the beat take us. This was no *Dancing with the Stars,* no let's-see-who's-watching high school humpfest. We let the music in, and our bodies followed. There were no moves, only movement, making things up on the fly, coming together and breaking apart. I stretched my hands over my head and swayed like a snake, thrilling at how powerful it made me feel—Cleopatra and the serpent both. Meredith went low, shoulders down like she might charge in and tackle me, and I didn't hate the idea. Hands moved in arcane patterns. Colored light glistened along the sweat-glazed expanse of her arms, shadows carving the lines of muscle, accenting the inverted triangle of her shoulders, the secret parenthetical of her hips. Her long hair fell in her face, and she whipped it backward, fanning it out in a flat plane.

The whole time, her eyes never left me. They burned above a savage grin as we circled each other like fighters. I held her stare until the pressure grew too great, and then I closed my eyes, feeling her attention like hands on me. Every time I regained the courage to look, she was watching. Not the musicians. *Me.*

All around us, people screamed for the band, but here in this place we were a binary system—two burning stars, orbiting something invisible between us. We spun and careened, grazing each other's surface, tearing off pieces and leaning into that gravity.

No one would call us talented. But no one was calling us anything.

We belonged to the beat, and we were beautiful.

9

ALL TOO QUICKLY, it was over, the band taking their final bows and flinging drumsticks and water bottles into the crowd.

Meredith straightened, face flushed dark, strokes of ink-black hair plastered across her forehead. Sweat soaked her shirt in patches, red cotton painted onto her lean frame, the string of her pendant diving insolently down beneath her collar as if daring me to follow. An inch of bared skin blazed out across the top of her jeans, catching my eye like a fishhook, and it felt like something might tear as I forced myself to look up and meet her gaze.

"Wow," she gasped.

"Yeah." Despite all my biking, the dancing had left me breathing hard, muscles wobbly.

"I think I'm gonna pass out." Her grin could have put the club's spotlights to shame.

We stumbled back to our coats, then to the packed bathroom, passing up overpriced Dasani to drink from cupped hands and timed faucets, our faces glowing back from sticker-crusted mirrors. Then we were spilling out onto the street with the rest of the crowd, the cold spring air stabbing welcome knives deep into wet clothes.

Meredith spread her arms, radiating heat. "I've never danced like that before."

I leaned gratefully against the cool brick of a neighboring bank. "Imagine if they taught *that* in PE."

Meredith laughed, and the sound came easily—the ripple of the river in summer. My stomach warmed.

"God." Meredith closed her eyes and tilted her face up to the night sky. "I don't wanna stop. I just want to run out into the city and let it swallow me."

I felt it too—the euphoria of exhaustion, of being out too late in a foreign land. I could picture the two of us running through empty avenues, hand in hand, lit by stars and streetlights.

"That could be arranged," I said.

She looked over in surprise. "Yeah?"

The crowd around us had thinned with remarkable speed, everyone disappearing into Ubers and around corners, leaving us alone on the sidewalk as the club doors clicked closed behind us.

Somewhere nearby, a siren wailed. Across the street, an old man muttering to himself in the awning of a darkened restaurant dropped his pants and began taking a dump on the sidewalk.

"On second thought," Meredith said carefully, "let's go home."

"Absolutely."

Back in the car, I saw her glance at the sticker on the dashboard, a little smile playing across her face. She turned the key, but this time didn't bother synching her phone, the only sound the gentle growl of the engine and the soft squeak of tires on wet pavement.

"Thanks for driving," I said.

She gave an exaggerated shrug. "Oh, you know—it was no big deal."

We both laughed. We'd danced away our defenses, and suddenly everything was 1:00 A.M. funny.

We pulled out onto the now blessedly empty street. The rain had stopped, and sewer grates sent up plumes of fog that caught the lights of empty skyscrapers, making fairy sculptures in the air.

As we sat at a stoplight, Meredith nodded to one of the roiling wisps. "It's so pretty."

"It's literally poo gas, Meredith."

She laughed again.

"It *is* kind of poetic, though," I mused. "All the farts of the city, every race and gender, all coming together."

"World peace through sewer stank."

The light changed, and we drove on.

Meredith headed for the freeway, and I felt another twitch low in my gut at the easy, confident way she drove, swiveling to check her blind spot as the car glided along. Long hair slid smooth across denim-clad shoulders, daring me to reach out and tuck it back behind her ear.

And the city. My heart ached at every paint-tagged overpass, at the cranes of the distant port rising like long-necked dinosaurs. My long-awaited salvation, receding into the rearview.

Maybe it was the dreamy space of being out late, damp and exhausted as someone else took responsibility for getting me home. I had a flash of being carried out of swim lessons as a child: warm inside, cold outside, half-asleep on Nana's shoulder. That quiet spot of safety.

Whatever the feeling was, it demanded confession.

"I didn't get into college," I blurted.

Meredith looked over in confusion. "What?"

I waved out the window. "I was supposed to be here next year. At UW. But I didn't get in."

"Oh." Meredith looked unsure what to do with this information.

"This was supposed to be my escape. My way out. But now I'm going to have to live at home and go to fucking *community college.*"

Meredith looked away, carefully checking her sideview mirror. "That's what I'm doing."

My armpits tingled with embarrassed sweat. "I mean, no shade to community college—I just really, really need to get out of Stossel."

"Why?"

I gave her a disbelieving look. "Are you *joking*? Stossel is a trash fire wrapped in a dumpster fire, stuffed inside the Hindenburg. It's a turducken of suck. Tursucken."

A ghost of a smile tugged at her cheek. "It's not that bad."

"Maybe not for *you.*" I leaned my head against the cool window glass. "I just wanna live somewhere where everyone doesn't already hate me."

She frowned. "People don't hate you."

"Fine—some of them hate me, the rest just *disdain* me." I spun a finger in the air. "Everybody needs someone to look down on, and once you're unpopular, it's self-perpetuating. Same with the popular kids—sometimes they're hot or fun, but mostly they just get anointed, and then they're popular *because* they're popular, like bargain-bin Kardashians. It's a fucking caste system, and it only works if somebody's on the bottom." I spread my hands. "And that's me."

"I'm sorry." Meredith sounded like she meant it.

"It's not your fault." I popped my knuckles against the dashboard, trying to get back that weightless feeling from the concert. "Do *you* get shit from people?"

"Nah. People don't hate me." She stared into the distance, mouth a thin line. "They don't think about me at all."

The bitterness in me couldn't help but respond with, "Sounds nice."

"I guess." She gripped the steering wheel, still not looking at me. "So how did it happen?"

I looked over. "What do you mean?"

"The whole Scarf Girl thing."

I jerked, banging my head painfully against the window.

I'd known she knew. *Everyone* knew. But hearing that name from her mouth . . .

Meredith saw it and winced. "Sorry—I mean, I know what *happened,* I just—" She bit the words off. "Sorry."

"It's fine." It was tempting to let her embarrassment bury it again. There was no reason to pick that scab. Not in front of this girl I barely knew.

But the night was too dark and wide for secrets. The lights strobing past pulled me open, shining inside and commanding me to speak. I could feel the weight of the story massed up inside me, like water behind a dam.

I sighed and leaned back in my seat, staring at the upholstered ceiling.

"When I was in eighth grade," I said, "I did the stupidest thing I've ever done.

"I fell in love with Sophia Franklin."

10

IT HADN'T SEEMED stupid at the time. It was eighth grade, and the other girls at Cedar Mountain Middle School were still sharpening their claws, having only recently discovered the art of rising up by punching down.

Sophia and I sat next to each other in band, and I'd immediately become obsessed with her: The perfect straightness of her brown hair, gelled into a stylish pixie cut that looked impossibly grown-up. The graceful curl of long, smooth fingers around the trombone's slide brace. Spaghetti-strap camis showing off pale shoulders and cleavage that could have skipped a few grades.

The thing was, she seemed to like me, too. She laughed at my jokes, and if her own jokes had an edge, at least they were funny when they weren't pointed at *you*. It was easy enough to overlook any bitchy tendencies when she was blinding you with that smile, all impish cheeks and brazen eye contact.

Then she told me to download Snapchat, and everything changed. Where at school she graced me with the same cursory attention she paid everyone in her court of sycophants, on Snapchat she was all compliments: how much she loved my red hair, how cute I looked in whatever I was wearing. She only ever messaged me at night, and almost immediately her questions turned flirty: Did I think she was pretty? Did I like girls? Did I ever fantasize about kissing them?

The answer was always yes.

If I'd been crushing before, I was now full-on *wild* with freshly minted hormones. With Sophia in the driver's seat, our chats got more graphic: talking about what turned us on, or describing porn we'd seen in lurid detail, always under the guise of jokes and *can you believe it?* Sophia was adamant that our conversations had to stay secret, but that was fine—having been homeschooled until the year before, I didn't have anyone to tell anyway. And she made it seem fun. Like we were secret agents.

Sure, it was hard to not get that same attention from her in public. Here I was, falling in love with her, and I'd never even been over to her house. But if it wasn't a fairy-tale romance, it was still worth it to crawl into bed every night, legs crossed and aching, waiting to see what she might type.

And then, a couple weeks in, she dared me to send her a video.

Just a short one, she said. I didn't even have to get fully naked. She just wanted to see me. It would be fun. It would be hot.

It was a terrifying proposition. But there was also nothing in the world that I wanted more than for Sophia Franklin to think I was hot. And as she assured me, Snapchat deleted everything as soon as you viewed it anyway.

So I changed out of my pj's and into my sexiest underwear. On a whim, I grabbed my blue Seattle Kraken scarf as well, wrapping it around myself like a bandage dress.

Then I propped my phone up on my desk, turned on Lady A's "Need You Now" . . .

And I danced.

It was only ten seconds—just long enough for me to unwind the scarf and attempt to seductively straddle my desk chair. I didn't have a lot to offer, in either dancing ability or physical assets, but her flood of overheated-face emojis made it all worth it. And if Sophia was too shy to reciprocate with a video of her own—well, wasn't it nice to be the daring one, for once?

That word—*daring*—was still in my mind the next day at school. And I knew, I *knew,* that the video had changed something between us. We'd crossed a line.

So standing in the hall after band, after I'd just said something to make her laugh—I took the plunge and laced my fingers through hers.

She jerked backward, yanking free as if burned. She took a quick, panicked glance around at the other girls, who were mostly watching in confusion.

"You lost your mommy, Cara?" Sophia laughed, but her eyes were an accusation. "Need me to help you cross the street?"

My heart sank. I knew I'd messed up, and tried to laugh it off with the rest of them, playing like it had all been some weird joke.

That night, she didn't respond on Snapchat. I tried telling myself she just needed time, but I knew the truth: that this whole thing had been a fairy tale, and as in all fairy tales, I'd gotten greedy and broken the rules. This silence was my punishment.

If only.

As soon as I arrived at school the next day, I could tell something was wrong. Eyes followed me. People pointed me out to their friends.

It wasn't until I heard the word "scarf" that my stomach really dropped. I marched up to the snickering boys and demanded to know what was so funny. One of them—the bravest or the most sympathetic—showed me his phone.

There I was, humping skinny hips on my desk chair.

The nightmare unfolded from there. Apparently, it was actually trivial to save something from Snapchat—something anyone who wasn't a naive homeschool kid would have known. And Sophia had done so, posting the video anonymously on an image-hosting site. She'd sent the link to her friends, who'd sent it to *their* friends, until the entire school rang with the soulful twang of my humiliation.

I ambushed Sophia before band, desperate to be told it was all a mistake—that someone had stolen her phone, that she'd been hacked.

But the Sophia I'd thought I'd known was gone. She eyed me with such contempt, dismissed my appeals to our secret relationship with such a derisive sniff, that I almost wondered if I'd fantasized the whole thing.

I responded by hyperventilating in the instrument storage closet.

The school made me call my parents, which was when shit really hit the fan. Mom went straight to threatening both criminal charges and civil suits if the school didn't fix this *now*. There was an emergency parent-teacher meeting, and I got to tell my story again to both them and the principal, an experience even more excruciating than the video itself. Various students were questioned. Eventually Sophia herself was dragged in.

With eyes as dead as a shark's, Sophia explained that yes, she'd seen the video, and had indeed messaged with friends about it. But she didn't know who'd posted it originally. As far as she knew, I'd posted it myself as a way to get attention.

By this point, I was begging Mom to just let it go and hoping people forgot. The principal agreed. Yes, he said, even with my underwear on—his mouth twisted in distaste at the words—this could still possibly be considered child pornography. But were we really going to charge dozens of students with a life-destroying crime over a moment of poor judgment? (The way he said it left no question of *whose* poor judgment.) As far as disciplining Sophia went, without any sort of digital trail—because of course my phone had deleted everything as promised—my accusation was purely a matter of "she-said, she-said." The principal said this last line with a thin little smile, and I thought Mom might actually punch him.

But that was the end of things, as far as the administration was concerned. The school sent home a handout about the dangers of sexting and a notice that any student found disseminating such material would be suspended.

Yet the damage was done. To the teens of Stossel, Cara Weaver had ceased to exist. There was only Scarf Girl.

It wasn't just about the nudity. Within a year, there would be more explicit nudes, traded from boy to boy like pornographic Pokémon. It wasn't even just that I was the first.

The thing that kept people coming back to Scarf Girl was the horrifying, hilarious *earnestness* of it. The obviousness of my need. Nothing chummed the water like vulnerability.

And Sophia—she never moved on. Having successfully evaded punishment, she told anyone who'd listen how I'd sent her the video out of the blue. An "unsolicited tit pic." One by one, she peeled away my few friendly acquaintances, advising them that being around me was unhealthy for their own social standing. Her cronies emptied spit valves into my backpack, knocked sodas onto my lunch tray, texted me pictures of my face with my nose warped to grotesque proportions—all the classics.

Each time, no one laughed louder than Sophia. After a while, everything that had come before started to feel like a dream—like she'd always been dedicated to my destruction. It didn't even really feel like hate. Sophia tormented me in the way waiters are nice to you: with that thinking-of-something-else detachment of someone just doing a job.

I told Meredith all of this, proud of how level my voice stayed. When I finished, she shook her head.

"That's fucked up."

"Pretty much," I agreed.

"I knew it must have been bad, but . . ." She shook her head again. "She must have been scared of being outed."

"Maybe? Or maybe the whole thing was just for the lulz. Maybe she needed a human sacrifice to ascend to the popular-girl pantheon. Either way, it had the same effect."

"Yeah." Meredith set her jaw. "Whatever her reason, Sophia's garbage. She can fuck off into the sun."

"Thanks." As much as it stung to tell my story, it felt good to see Meredith mad on my behalf.

"And *nobody* stuck up for you?"

I leaned my face back against the window, angled up toward the passing night. "Nobody except my family. I didn't even meet Holly until afterward."

Outside, the silent towers flowed past. Thousands of lit windows, full of people whose names we'd never know, and who'd never know ours. Who'd never know anything about us except what we told them.

Paradise.

"It doesn't matter what I do," I finished. I thought again of dancing at the show, of the sweet thrill of anonymity. "The only answer is to get out of Stossel and start fresh. Become someone new."

Meredith shook her head with sudden violence. "*You're* not the one who needs to change. If people don't like you—fuck 'em."

Again, her anger warmed me. But still . . . "It's not that easy."

"It could be." She looked over as we passed into the I-90 tunnel, orange lights chasing the dark across her face. "If you're already unpopular, then you've got nothing to lose, right? You can be whoever you want. Right now." Flashes of her set jaw, pursed lips. "I think you're already pretty cool, though."

Any lingering trace of exhaustion evaporated. When Meredith Reyes looked at you—*really* looked at you—it was like grabbing an electric fence. The kind that locked your muscles so you couldn't let go, even as it cooked you from the inside out.

I swallowed.

"Thanks," I managed. "You're cool, too."

Side by side, we shot out of the tunnel, crossing the bridge into somewhere new.

11

"SEE? I TOLD *you we'd be great at this!"*

"What's this 'we' shit? Last I checked, things only started going well once *I* made you back off."

I was seated fully clothed on the toilet lid, phone blasting music so it wouldn't be quite so obvious I was talking to myself in the bathroom.

"Sure, sure." Aiden's voice held no trace of humility. *"You're the player, I'm the coach—I train you up, game time is all you. The point is, we* won*! When you fell asleep last night, I flew over and checked on Meredith. She was* singing."

"That's good?"

"Mer sings to herself when she's happy. She'd kill me again for telling you, but I used to catch her doing it all the time. Anyway, she's been as silent as an Easter Island head since I died. Last night totally made a difference."

The words buzzed pleasurably around my chest. A part of me wondered at that visceral response: Was it from succeeding at the mission? Or was it the memory of Meredith dancing, all wild smile and unguarded eyes?

"She any good?" I asked.

"Not even a little. The girl couldn't carry a tune with a forklift. It's like two coyotes fighting."

That just made the image more adorable. I couldn't help but

smile at the thought of her dancing around her bedroom like an off-key cartoon princess.

"So I've just got a couple of notes—" Aiden continued.

I snapped out of my reverie. "I thought you said I did great!"

"That doesn't mean you can't do better. *Standard post-game analysis, so you can shore up your weak points. Haven't you ever played sports?"*

Team sports were my personal vision of Hell, but I said only, "Sounds like a blast, Coach, but we're working on *my* part of the deal now, remember? It's time we weighed your soul."

"You mean, like, am I weighed down by sin, or . . . ?"

"I'm sure the weight of your sins could open a black hole, but that's not what I mean." I leaned forward, elbows on knees. "In 1907, Dr. Duncan MacDougall tried to prove the existence of the soul by measuring the change in mass at the moment of death. He pegged the weight lost at twenty-one grams. Scientists have tried to replicate his experiments with varying results, but the basic idea is that if you're here, you must have *some* sort of mass or energy." I gestured to the bathroom scale. "So hop on."

"You know I can't touch anything."

"And until last week, you *knew* you couldn't talk to anyone. Just concentrate on pushing down as hard as you can."

"Okay . . ." He still sounded skeptical.

I waited. The scale's digital readout remained at 0.0.

Immediately I realized my mistake. "Shit—this doesn't go low enough. One sec."

Downstairs in the kitchen, Dad stood scrolling Instagram in his bathrobe, half-eaten toast forgotten in front of him. He looked up as I ran in. "There she is! How was the concert?"

"Good! Really good. Hey, do you know where your kitchen scale is?"

"That depends." He leaned back against the counter, slurping loudly from his THICC DAD coffee mug. "Are you selling drugs?"

"What?! No!"

"Are you sure? The nanny state comes down hard on dealers."

"Dad, seriously. It's, um—" I scrambled, "—for a science experiment." Technically true. "A take-home lab."

"Right." He winked. *"Experimentation."* He opened a cupboard and pulled out the scale. "Just as long as you're doing it in a safe environment."

"Please stop."

"And remember that goes double for hallucinogens. One time at Burning Man, I did shrooms with your uncle Patrick and woke up in the middle of the playa with nothing but a velvet top hat and a sunburned—"

"Okay-that's-plenty-thank-you!" I grabbed the scale and fled.

"Is it just me," Aiden asked, *"or is your dad weirdly awesome?"*

"Don't get me started," I grumbled.

Back in the bathroom, I cranked the shower onto maximum heat and set the scale down on the counter. "Try this one."

The scale was rated down to a tenth of a gram, but again, the readout refused to budge.

"Harder!" I snapped. "Come on, push!"

"What are you, my Lamaze coach?" His voice sounded strained. *"I'm pushing like a goddamn constipated elephant!"*

Still the scale stayed dark.

"Okay, fine," I conceded. "We'll try a different test. Hold on."

Steam was quickly turning the bathroom into a sauna, fogging the mirror. I was committing three of the bigger sins in the Weaver household: wasting water, wasting energy, and doing both without running the fan. Dad had tried to raise me on two-minute "survivalist showers"—shaking yourself dry like a dog afterward so your towel dried faster—but around twelve I'd learned that the words "period migraine" were a cheat code unlocking unlimited shower time. Dad was a self-proclaimed feminist, but he'd still rather let me run hot water till the heat death of the universe than discuss his daughter's menstrual cycle. If your crimson tide didn't star Denzel Washington, Dad didn't want to hear about it.

Clearly noticing the strategic toilet paper reserve standing in its plastic-wrapped mountain, Aiden asked, *"You ever wonder why toilet paper companies advertise their social media accounts?"*

"I have not, in fact, ever wondered that."

"This one invites us to 'join the conversation.' Like, how exactly do they expect that to go? Who's posting 'After eating @TacoBell, my ass was a black bean crime scene, but @Charmin got it handled!'?"

I laughed, then pulled out my phone to check. "Maybe one of their eighty-three thousand followers?"

Aiden choked. *"How is it fair that eighty-three thousand people follow a* toilet paper company, *but* I'm *the one who's dead?!"*

"The universe has a weird sense of humor." I waved my phone, testing the steam that now hung thick around my face. "Okay, I think we're good."

"For what?"

The idea had come to me on the drive home last night. "I figure steam is the lightest, easiest-to-manipulate thing we've got. Plus ghosts and fog have a long connection in literature."

"And here I thought you'd invited me in for a steamy rendezvous. So, what—I should just . . . wave my arms around?"

"To start."

"Okay . . ."

I squinted at the steam. "Are you moving?"

"I'm twerking furiously."

"Really?"

"Prove me wrong."

The steam continued its lazy wafting.

"Okay, try drawing something on the mirror. Or concentrate and *will* the mist to take a shape."

"Roger that."

I waited.

"Do you see anything?"

I was staring so hard I was getting a headache, trying to pick out shapes in the mist. "See what?"

He snickered. *"You'd know."*

Ah, boys. I wondered which scribble in the Phallus Palace had been his.

I sighed and slumped back on the toilet. "Okay, so much for fog."

"So what now?"

"Now you get out of here so I can shower for real. I smell like a dozen armpits, only two of which are mine."

"Wow. You really know how to suck the mystique out of a shower fantasy."

"Yeahhhh, sorry not sorry." I pointed to the door. "Begone, spirit."

"As you command . . ."

I showered quickly, aware for the millionth time that I was putting a lot of trust in Aiden not to peep, and equally aware that there was nothing to be done about it. As I slipped into fresh clothes, I saw that I had a new text.

From Meredith.

Saw your videos.

Shit. I sprinted back to my bedroom. "She found my channel! Meredith!"

"So . . . ?"

"So don't you think she's gonna be suspicious? I'm a ghost hunter, you're dead . . . it doesn't exactly take Hercule Poirot to put it together!"

"Who?"

I threw a pillow. "Fuck!"

"Calm down. She probably just googled you."

"But what if she figures out I'm only doing this *because* of you?"

"Right. Because her first thought is definitely *gonna be that her dead brother's playing matchmaker."*

"She could still think I'm trying to investigate you!"

"So convince her you're not. Regardless, there's nothing we can do about that."

He had a point, but still. I covered my eyes. "But what do I *say?*"

"Just act normal."

As if *that* was a skill I'd ever had. I bent over, burying my face in the bed.

"C'mon, don't leave her hanging."

Normal. Okay. What would a *normal* person say when her pet ghost's little sister found out she was a paranormal investigator?

Still upside down, I typed: What did you think?

I stared at the words for a full thirty seconds, then hit send and let the duvet muffle my scream.

Even if she hadn't guessed the truth, the idea of Meredith watching my videos twisted my stomach like a carnie spinning cotton candy. Sure, I *wanted* her to see them—I wanted *everyone* to see them. But somehow knowing she was watching my amateur Scooby-Doo routine was suddenly the most excruciating thing in the world.

. . . Right up until the pulsing dots of her reply appeared, at which point *they* became the most excruciating thing in the world. They resolved into words.

Want to take me hunting?

The fresh deodorant in my armpits coughed once and expired, sending up its own fragrant little phantoms.

"Okay, *now* what do I say?" I thought of what Holly would do. "Should I help her 'find' you?" I made finger quotes. "Then you two could actually talk."

"No way! The plan is the plan. And look—it's working! She's initiating *hangouts! You're totally rocking this."*

"I guess." Somehow his praise puffed me up without reducing my panic.

"Just take her on a standard hunt. Whatever you did before you met me."

"Right." I stared at my phone, and took way too long to respond with: Sure. When?

My phone dinged.

Now?

"Perfect!" Aiden crowed.

"It's not perfect!" For the concert, I'd had time to prepare for all the different ways things could go wrong. Sure, it had worked out, but just because you pulled off a trick once didn't mean you were ready to perform without a net. "We've got, like, ten more experiments to get through today!"

"*Later. You gotta strike while the iron is hot.*" I could hear the grin in his voice as he added, "*And her iron is* definitely *hot for* you."

"Shut up." I blushed, unsure whether it was at the innuendo or because a part of me wanted it to be true. "Also, aren't you supposed to wait, like, three days after a date before texting?" Had it even *been* a date? I'd asked her to a concert, she'd accepted, we'd gone together. But did *Meredith* see it that way? My body simultaneously thrilled and rebelled at the idea.

"*Since when do you care about 'supposed to'? Tell her to come get us.*"

That got my attention. "She's not getting *us.*"

"*Of course she is. I only gave you space last night because you were freaking out.*"

"I'm *still* freaking out!"

"*Too bad—you've proved you're a champion. Deal with it.*"

As much as I felt unprepared for another date, it would be even worse with an undead Cyrano de Bergerac shouting tips in my ear. I straightened, kneeling on the bed and glaring at the air. "If I'm a champion, then I don't need you there."

"*But it's my* mission!"

"Yeah, and if you wanna pull a Lannister and seduce your sister, go right on ahead. But if you want *me* to do the job, then we play by my rules. And Rule Number One is that you let me do the dates *my* way. *Alone.*" I locked eyes with the empty air.

Maybe it was a bluff—both of us needed each other too much to walk away. But honestly, last night with Meredith had felt good— *really* good. And I wasn't about to let the paranormal peanut gallery mess it up.

I waited. At last there came a ghostly sigh.

"*Whatever,*" he grumbled. "*I expect a full report when you get back.*"

I felt a little thrill of victory, but covered it with a mocking salute. "You got it, Coach." Then, before I could let nerves get the better of me again, I slumped back against the wall and typed out my reply.

Now is good.

12

I SLID INTO Meredith's passenger seat half an hour later, noticing with a rush of satisfaction that the BLOODBATH sticker was still in place.

As we exchanged town for trees, the lumpy billboard of Glory Rock loomed up beside the road, plastered with fresh graffiti. Where the last few weeks it had read GO WOLVES!, along with its usual patchwork of heart-wrapped initials and analog shitposts, one whole face of the rock now advocated HANNAH BRADY 4 PROM QUEEN!

I snorted. Meredith shot me inquiring eyebrows.

"Just that." I waved at the rock. "Popular kids marking their territory. Pissing on the same tree." As if the world needed more reminders of who was winning.

Meredith considered that. Then she said, "I used to help Aiden and his friends paint it."

Great. Now I'd insulted her *and* her dead brother. When was I gonna learn to keep my mouth shut? "I mean, sometimes it's cool," I finished weakly.

She frowned. "No, you're right. It's dumb. It's always the same people."

"Ex*act*ly!" The word whooshed out in a relieved rush. "I mean, compensating much? Who needs their name on a rock?"

"Right."

There was something off in her tone. I turned to look closer at her. "Would *you* want your name up there?"

"No!" But her head sank defensively between her shoulders.

Sawhill Cemetery was as old as Stossel itself, dividing the sprawl of town from the green carpet of timberland stretching out into the Cascades. A clump of dark-clothed mourners clustered like penguins at the edge of the parking lot, while more casually dressed visitors picked their way through bright headstones.

I watched Meredith's gaze turn toward the funeral, and wondered briefly if a cemetery had been a bad decision. But there weren't a lot of places to go hunting on short notice, and I'd made sure Aiden hadn't been buried here. Plus, you couldn't exactly look for ghosts without some reminders of, you know, *death.*

I parked and led us uphill, into the graveyard's older section, where our hunt would be less likely to ruffle feathers. While the whole place was open to the public in daylight hours—most folks treated it like a park that just happened to contain corpses—there are few places so public that teens can't get kicked out if an adult gets a bee up their ass.

Maybe it was strange to find a graveyard relaxing, but Sawhill was one of my favorite places. Not in some gothy Wednesday Addams, Mary-Shelley-losing-her-virginity-on-her-mother's-grave sense. (Okay, maybe a little bit.) But there was an air of mystery to it. The oldest pioneer markers, wiped blank by weather, could have been anyone's. Above us, a murmuration of starlings so thick and dark it looked like billowing fabric alighted in one of the trees, their clicks and whistles sounding like R2-D2 throwing a rave.

I cut us off the gravel path, through the forest of headstones. Down below, graves stood in neat rows, but up here settlers had planted people wherever they damned well pleased, most facing west out over the valley. The markers themselves grew more creative, too: death's heads, sculpted tree stumps, obelisks like tiny Washington Monuments.

"This is one of my favorites." I tapped a stone that just said JAMES HERSH—STRUCK BY LIGHTNING. I thought about that sometimes: how a person could live an entire life, only to be remembered for their last moment. Aiden could probably relate.

Meredith gave me a sidelong look. "You have favorite graves?"

"Doesn't everybody?"

Meredith bent to read the inscription on a neighboring stone. "'Ezekiel Tibbets and Wife—Our Names Live On In Memory.'" She grimaced. "Except for hers, apparently."

"Yeah. Guess ol' Zeke had the money for an epitaph, but her name was just too much." I jerked my chin toward another stone. "Look—that one just says 'sister.'"

Meredith's lips thinned. "I know the feeling."

Right. I sat down on a broad, squared-off headstone and dug into my backpack. "We'll start with this." I pulled out one of the little hand-crank radios Dad had gotten us all two Christmases ago.

Meredith frowned. "Ghosts use radios?"

"We call them spirit boxes. You use them to scan for EVPs—electronic voice phenomena." I turned the radio on and was rewarded with a blast of crackly music. I thumbed the dial until it faded to static.

I motioned, and she sat down next to me on the stone. There wasn't a ton of room, and I was suddenly extremely aware of the warmth of her thigh through her jeans, the gentle pressure of her shoulder. I swallowed and held the squawking radio out so she could see.

"The key is to scan around, but to try to stay *between* stations— just the static. Ghosts have an easier time coming through if they're not competing with Rihanna."

"In theory," Meredith half asked.

"In theory," I agreed.

I scanned slowly through, listening for any voice that didn't resolve into a DJ or Burger King ad. This close, I could smell Meredith's hair—coconut with a trace of citrus. It seemed too gentle for her.

After a few cycles through the spectrum, Meredith asked, "So how exactly does this detect ghosts?"

"It depends who you ask." I was glad to slip into the safety of

Lecture Mode. "Some people think ghosts can straight-up manipulate radio waves, but I think if that were true, we'd hear from them
a lot more. More people think it's the white noise that's important.
Their idea is that ghosts can shape the noise *just enough* to form
words—like how some people who've had throat cancer can talk
by holding an electronic larynx to their neck."

"And that's what you think?" Her voice had the too-casual tone
of someone treading carefully.

I shrugged. "Maybe? It's just as possible that any communica-
tion takes place entirely in the brain—that the white noise is just
a focus, allowing us to tap into an innate ability to hear the spirit
world. But that wouldn't really account for recordings, so . . ." I
shrugged again. The coarse weave of her jacket whisked against my
smooth one.

"Right." Meredith looked uncomfortable. She reached into her
jacket and pulled out a metal ballpoint pen and a sandwich baggie
dusted green. "You mind?"

That probably shouldn't have been a surprise, but somehow it
was. I didn't have anything against weed in *theory*, but given that
Holly wouldn't even drink kombucha due to the trace alcohol, I
didn't exactly have a lot of opportunities to experiment. I was sure
I could smoke with my parents if I asked—it was exactly the sort
of antiauthority bonding moment Dad lived for—but getting high
with them sounded as awkward as their offer to buy me ethically
produced porn.

"Oh, uh—no, go for it."

Meredith unscrewed the pen and removed the ink cartridge,
leaving just the hollow metal tube, then packed and lit. She held
the smoke, offering me the makeshift pipe and lighter.

"Um, no thanks." I held up my hands. "I don't like lighters."

She laughed a cloud. "You can just say you don't smoke."

"No, really!" I knew millions of dollars had been spent trying
to convince me it was cool to say no to drugs, but all those bill-
boards saying 75% OF TEENS HAVEN'T USED MARIJUANA IN THE
LAST MONTH! just made me think, *Wow, a lot of people get high.* I

didn't care about it either way, but it was suddenly very important that Meredith not think I was a prude. "Seriously—having a flame that close to my thumb just freaks me out."

Meredith cocked her head. "You want me to light it for you?"

Oh. Well then. "Uhhhh . . . sure . . . ?"

Before I could reach for it, she leaned over and held the pipe to my lips. To have her touch me there, even through the proxy of the pipe, felt shockingly intimate. I was immediately aware of how her own lips had wrapped around the metal just moments before. A trace of secondhand Carmex prickled my nose.

Meredith held the lighter flame to the pen's tip. I took a tiny puff, not so much inhaling as holding the hot smoke in my mouth.

Meredith watched, no doubt seeing straight through my act. After a moment, she sat back, reclaiming the pen. I blew the smoke out slowly, trying to make it seem like I'd taken more than I had. I didn't want to seem ungrateful. And despite the burning skunk-cloud coating my mouth, there was still that faint taste of her . . .

She took another deep toke, then looked away, shaking her head. "Sorry, but . . . this all sounds like bullshit."

I nodded. "Oh, totally."

"Wait—what?" Her head whipped back around, face suddenly very close to mine.

"Yeah, um—" Her lips were wide, and surprisingly soft-looking for such a hard face. Must be all that lip balm. I looked quickly out toward the valley, scrambling to reboard my train of thought. "I mean, a lot of the science around ghost hunting is pretty fringe." I waggled the radio. "You know about pareidolia?"

"No?"

"It means seeing patterns that aren't really there. Like when you look at a cloud and see a rabbit. Or Jesus' face on toast."

"Or constellations?"

"Yes, exactly!" I jabbed the air with the radio. "The fact that somebody looked at a couple dots in the sky and said 'that's *totally* a crab' is one hundred percent pareidolia." I shrugged. "Anyway, that's the most likely explanation for EVP—people hearing what they want to hear."

Meredith squinted. "So you *don't* think it's real."

"I think it doesn't *matter* what I think. To be a ghost hunter—a *good* one—you have to be a skeptic. Or at least act like one. Otherwise you'll never prove anything."

She pointed her pen-pipe at the radio. "So why are we doing this, if you don't think it'll work?"

"Because it *might*." I clicked the radio off, letting the rustle of breeze on grass rush in to fill the silence. "If we had tools that worked reliably, the question would already be answered. Instead, we've got stuff like this. I use it all, in hopes it'll point me toward something I can verify." I leaned back, hands curled around the edge of the stone, and looked out over the valley. "A lot of important scientific discoveries start with hunches, or myths, or accidents. Microwaves were discovered when a dude working on radar accidentally melted the candy bar in his pocket. The only reason we can mass-produce penicillin is because two scientists stumbled across the right moldy cantaloupe. Science has to end clean, but it can start anywhere."

Meredith remained silent. I looked over and found her staring at me.

The bottom dropped out of my stomach. Beneath the spotlight of her gaze, I could hear how I must sound—the same half-assed nods to the scientific process as any crystal aura psychic or QAnon conspiracy theorist. Or maybe she was just distracted by the oil field of blocked pores on my face, my nose a mountainous, cratered landscape. It was impossible not to contrast myself with her own flawless complexion.

How could her eyes be so big, yet give nothing away? Every instinct screamed to pull back, to look anywhere else, but it was too late—there was no way to do either without *looking* like I was. The only option was to stare back, like a highway deer in the moment before it's mowed down.

She nodded slowly, a little sideways bob. "That's really cool."

A wave of relief, immediately boiled away by the heat of a blush. "Yeah?"

"Yeah." She smiled with half her mouth. "When I asked to come out with you . . . I didn't really know what to think. But I'm glad I came."

"Yeah?" I realized I was repeating myself. "I mean—yeah, cool. I'm glad, too. That you came, I mean." Oh my god, *stop talking*.

Meredith cartwheeled the pen through her fingers, legs stretched out in front of her, looking like an album cover. She tapped a heel against the grass. "Why ghost hunting?"

"What do you mean?"

She waved at the gravestones. "You've clearly put a lot of time into it. Why?"

"Oh. Um." I trapped my upper lip between my teeth, then realized what I was doing and stopped. Meredith was cool, but . . . "It's kinda personal?"

"Oh." Something hardened around her mouth. "Gotcha." She tapped out the dead weed and stuck the pen back in her pocket.

The thought of Meredith disappointed—disappointed in *me*— felt catastrophic. In a rush, I said, "But also, death's the last great mystery, right?"

Only as the words left my mouth did I realize how insensitive they were. Again, the suggestion of emotion behind her eyes—a shadow rolling past beneath the water's surface. She leaned forward, elbows on knees, and I could see the weight pressing down on her. The faint dimples above her brows. The hollowness in her cheeks. Cored out from the inside, like a building eaten by fire, until only the facade remained.

"I guess so," she said quietly.

And suddenly I wanted to tell her everything. About Aiden, and how he loved her so much he'd come back from the dead just to make sure she was okay. Anything to take away that survivor stare.

But no—what did I think I'd accomplish by spilling everything? Meredith and I had hung out exactly twice. She wasn't going to believe I was the press secretary for her dead brother—especially if he refused to play along. All I'd do is piss them both off, nuking my own future in the process.

Meredith was watching me again, and I realized the silence had stretched too long. I needed to say *some*thing.

"I wanted to find my grandmother," I blurted.

Meredith cocked her head.

"She died when I was thirteen." My limbs felt jittery. I crossed my arms. "That's why I first got into ghost hunting. Because I missed her."

Meredith thawed a little. "You two were close?"

"That's . . . kind of an understatement." I rubbed the back of my neck. "Nana homeschooled me up into middle school. She lived way out in the hills, so there weren't really other kids around. We spent every day riding bikes, or researching stuff, or doing experiments in the creek. She was . . . kinda my only friend." I laughed self-consciously.

"She sounds great." The casual way Meredith said it—no raised eyebrows, no barely concealed sneer—was a life ring in the ocean.

"She was. Nana was . . ." How to even describe her? "She was one of those people who feels too big for real life, you know? Like, she was this total backwoods pioneer lady. She could butcher a deer and fix a car and sew her own clothes. But she'd also worked on archaeological digs, and knew about genetics and robotics and just . . . everything."

"Wow." Meredith looked genuinely interested.

"Yeah. She was a total badass, too." I knew I was rambling, but it felt good to talk about her. "My dad never knew his dad, but there was a shitty stepdad around for a while. Apparently one night the dude got drunk and hit him, and Nana picked up a beer bottle and smashed it against his teeth. Then she held the broken bottle under his jaw and said that since he loved drinking so much, she could make it so he drank all his meals going forward. Dad never saw him again."

"Seriously?" Meredith's eyes were wide.

"I know, right?" I sighed. "Anyway. When I was twelve, my parents made me start going to regular school. Six months later, Nana was gone." Even after all this time, my eyes still burned at the words. "I was kind of a mess."

Meredith's mouth twitched up knowingly.

"I just kept wishing I could *talk* with her again, you know?" I angled my face away, clamping down on the lump in my throat. It wasn't fair to get this emotional when Meredith's loss was so much more recent. I forced a laugh. "I remember watching *The Muppet Christmas Carol* and wishing I were Scrooge so she could be one of my ghosts. And then I thought about how she always said you could learn anything on YouTube, so I started researching the afterlife, and . . ." I spread my hands. "Thus did I become the weirdo you see today."

Meredith's forehead wrinkled. "I don't think you're weird."

Her words curled up in my stomach, soft and warm as a kitten. "That's because you're a woman of culture and discernment." I grimaced. "Unfortunately, most people don't share your enlightened sensibilities."

Down the hill, the funeral group started singing a hymn, their voices blending smoothly. People always sounded better from a distance.

Meredith bounced knuckles against the headstone. "I've never been popular, either. But I always had Aiden."

"That must've been nice." I tried and failed to keep the jealousy out of my voice.

"Yeah, it was." She ran her tongue beneath her top lip, like a brawler checking for damage. "It was also *fucking* annoying."

I blinked. "What?"

She snorted. "You don't have siblings, do you?"

"No."

She stared down toward the singing mourners. "The thing about being Aiden's little sister is that you're never first. Every sport, every grade, everyone's always saying what a superstar Aiden is—and that you, by comparison, are not." A muscle in her check twitched.

"Everyone your age is either crushing on him or wanting to *be* him. And they're nice to you, but only because they like *him*. Because he's a good big brother and always brings you along. You're a package deal—the 'free gift' that nobody actually wants."

I wanted to protest, but it occurred to me that Aiden was the reason *I* was talking to her as well.

She bent over, ripping up a tuft of grass. "You know what the worst part is?"

"What?"

Her face stayed as still as ever, but I could see the water reflecting in her eyes, like an overfull glass refusing to spill over.

"The worst part is that they're *right*. Aiden was great. Like, yeah, I hated being runner-up. And the way he was always trying to give me advice was condescending as fuck. But I still loved him more than anybody."

Her arm snapped out, flinging the grass sideways.

"And he *fucking* died on me."

She scraped her jacket sleeve angrily across her eyes, leaving the skin red.

"So now, not only have I lost the *one* person who actually *gave* a shit about me, I also get to go from being 'Aiden's little sister' to 'the girl whose brother died.'" She barked an angry laugh. "My parents can barely look at each other since he died—but they can still talk about *him*. All day, every day. *His* stock just keeps going up. Never mind that he's the one who wrecked our family—those little fuckups get glossed over when you die young. So now he's gone full JFK—perfect forever. And I'm just the disappointing sister who will never, ever measure up." She shook her head. "He ruined my life *and* I miss him so bad I wanna throw up. How's that for fucked?"

"Pretty fucked," I agreed.

She glanced over, mouth twisting into a bitter smile. "Guess I sound pretty self-absorbed, huh?"

"No," I said quickly.

"Anyway." Her tone was a door slamming closed. She flipped

a leaf over with the toe of her Converse. "You really think there might be an afterlife?"

I realized I'd turned my entire torso toward her, my knee pressing hard into hers. Now she did the same, denim jacket falling open, tiny horizontal ripples where her T-shirt pulled taut across her chest. I could see the unfilled dots of piercings in her earlobes.

"I think," I said slowly, "that being scientific means constantly revising what we believe about the world. The only thing I know for sure is that there's still more out there waiting to be discovered."

She watched me. I stared back, refusing to break eye contact. Letting my face show my conviction.

She looked away first, shaking her head. "I wish I could believe that."

This girl. So hard, yet so fragile.

I bumped her shoulder with mine. "You will."

She looked back, raising an eyebrow. "You think?"

It was all there in her face: the desperate desire to hope, and the fear that wouldn't let her. That stillness she cultivated, the way she constantly kept her expression blank—it wasn't disdain. It was the stillness of a house of cards, the fear that the slightest movement would bring her crashing down.

I wanted to cup her cheek. To show her she didn't have to hold herself apart just to hold herself together. I wanted to see her shields come down, the way they had when she danced. To see her get carried away. To carry her there myself.

Fuck Aiden's mission. This was for me now.

I smiled.

"I don't think," I told her. "I know."

13

IF MY BEDROOM was an occult supply store, Holly's was a cupcake truck crashed into a pet shop. Everything was soft, puffy, and pastel, from the fluffy white duvet to a crane-game's worth of plushies. A portrait of Jesus gazed down from one wall, chaperoning a photo of Holly and Elvis playing music in church, both in the scarved uniforms of the Vietnamese Eucharistic Youth Society, their eyes locked with an intensity that could have set his thorny crown on fire. A framed poster of Fray Tormenta, the luchador priest, hung incongruous among the cotton-candy cuteness.

"It looks like Willy Wonka's kitten factory in here," Aiden had said when we arrived. *"Everything is either fuzzy or a marshmallow. With a side of Jesus."* Which was honestly a pretty good description of Holly herself.

The marshmallow in question currently stood beneath the Jesus portrait, having exchanged the wrestling mask she wore on my channel for a cute skirt-and-sweater combo—the sort of modest but fashionable outfit that flaunted by concealing, saying you were so hot, you didn't *need* to show skin. I'd never been able to make it work, but Holly was the queen of Sunday Style. I'd never minded before— our contrasting fashion senses had always felt like a fun quirk—but nowadays every little detail made a treacherous part of my brain whisper *Bible college.*

"I still can't believe Meredith resents me," Aiden whined, continuing in the same vein he'd been monologuing since I gave him a

recap of this morning's graveyard date. *"All I ever did was try to help her! Now I come back from the* literal dead *just to fix things for her, and all she can do is complain about me? What the* shit?*"*

I flicked a hand, trying to wave him to silence.

Holly broke off mid-take. "What?"

"Sorry. Was trying to get Aiden to shut up." I glanced down at the laptop she was using as a teleprompter. "Take it from 'in conclusion'?"

"Okay." Holly took a deep breath, centering herself, then beamed that nuclear-powered smile.

"So in conclusion, we can see that the Bible actually gives us a bunch of reasons to *support* queer and trans people. Yes, Paul says it's against nature—but he also says in 1 Corinthians that men having *long hair* is against nature, and I challenge anyone to look at Jason Momoa and tell me that's not the Lord's work." She gave the camera a look so perfectly deadpan that I had to bite my cheek to hold in a laugh.

"The Bible was written by men of a particular time and place. But reading scripture is about looking beyond the words to see the *point,* and it's on all of us to keep advancing Jesus' mission of kindness and acceptance. Remember Matthew 7:16: good trees bear good fruit, and bad trees bear bad fruit. A religion should be judged by the impact it has on the world." She frowned. "And we've all seen the suffering caused by a Christianity that rejects LGBTQ+ folks."

Then she smiled again, and it was like the sun coming out. "So let's fix it! As always, you may not agree with me on everything—and that's okay! Here on *No Judgment,* we don't believe in purity tests. If I can only sell you on one percent of Christ's teachings—well, that's one more percent than you had before. So thanks for coming with me again this week, as we all try to be"—she raised her arms as if hugging the world—*"a little bit better."*

"And cut!" I tapped the phone.

Holly deflated, blowing out her cheeks. "Oy. Did that sound even *mildly* natural?"

"You were *great.*"

"Really?" She looked hopeful.

No Judgment: Jesus for Ordinary People was Holly's own YouTube channel: a progressive, big-tent take on Catholicism designed to help her become a world-famous theological influencer, and eventually the Catholic Church's first ordained female priest. (Nobody ever accused Holly Pham of thinking small.)

I came around the camera and bear-hugged her, oscillating her rapidly back and forth. "You-were-great-and-it-was-great-and-the-shaking-will-continue-until-you-agree!"

Holly squirmed, but not unhappily. "It wasn't too preachy?"

"It's literally preaching, Hol."

"But it can't *sound* preachy! That's the whole point!" Holly wriggled free and flopped down on her bed.

"It sounded like you always sound, but with more citations."

"Seemed convincing to me," Aiden agreed.

Holly's face lit up as I passed the compliment along, which brought a twinge of irritation—*my* compliment wasn't enough to reassure her, but some undead boy she barely knew . . . ?

"You know, I was thinking last night about his—" She looked guiltily into the empty space next to me. "Sorry, *your* description of how dying felt, and what it might mean. Like, if it was *just* dispersal in all directions, that could be like Obi-Wan becoming one with the Force. But that sense of being pulled *up*—that's *gotta* be your soul being pulled to Heaven, right?"

"Or Valhalla," I protested. "Or any other afterlife. There's no reason it has to be Catholic Heaven."

Holly waved dismissively. "That doesn't matter."

"You don't care if your team wins?" Aiden sounded intrigued. I sighed at the distraction but parroted him for Holly's benefit.

"It's not about winning," Holly explained. "It's just proof that *a* religion is right. We've already won Pascal's wager—proof of an afterlife will draw people to religion in general. Not all of them will pick mine, but at least they'll pick *something.*"

Personally, I had my doubts, but Aiden said, *"So religions are like*

Pepsi vs. Coke—you might fight over customers, but you all need to get them to the soda aisle."

"Exactly!" Holly grinned impishly. "That's what I'm trying to do with my channel—a Coke Zero version of Catholicism. All the Christ, none of the carbs." Her eyebrows rose. "Hey! Maybe that dissipating feeling was your sins being shed, and the upward part was your purified soul ascending!"

I snorted.

"Hey!" Aiden squawked. *"I'm pure!"*

"Like a sewage treatment plant," I muttered.

"Maybe part of him gets to move on, and the other part stays until Judgment Day?" Holly tapped a nail against her teeth. "Or maybe going to Heaven just *feels* like expanding, because you're growing spiritually?"

"See? Holly gets it. Tell her my soul is engorged with virtue. The girthiest of spirits."

"Definitely not purified," I noted.

"What—her entire religion is based on Mary rawdogging the Holy Ghost, but I'm the naughty one?"

"Oh my god, *stop.*" But I couldn't stifle a laugh.

"Seriously. You never wondered why the Pope wears a hat that makes him look like a giant penis?"

Holly gave me a questioning look.

"You don't want to know," I said.

"If you aren't going to translate my profound theological insights, then can we please *get back to brainstorming the prom proposal?"*

I rolled my eyes. "Prom isn't for weeks. We've got plenty of time."

"In that case, we can go over my post-date analyses. First note: You're talking too much. Girls like questions, *not monologues."*

"Dude! You weren't even *there!*"

"You told me enough. I'm making an educated guess. Next up: Aiden's Rules of Flirtatious Touching—you might wanna narrate this part, so Holly can learn, too."

"Right. Prom time." I sat down cross-legged on the bed. "This thing ain't gonna brainstorm itself."

"Already?" Holly squirmed. "Maybe I should do another take."

"No way. You nailed that one." I reached out and grabbed her arm. "Hey—you're not still upset about me asking Meredith to prom, are you?"

Holly looked away.

"Holly." I squeezed, making no effort to hide my need. "Promise you're not mad." I could shrug off basically anyone's opinion, but not Holly's.

"I just don't think you should be planning some big romantic proposal if you don't like her."

"I don't *not* like her," I countered. Which was something of an understatement. Thoughts of Meredith dancing in the club, or leaned up against a gravestone like an art-school angel, had been playing on loop all afternoon.

Holly pressed her lips tight. "I'm just saying. You shouldn't lie to her."

"Jesus, Hol, it's not *lying*! It's just not *telling*. So prom was Aiden's idea—so what? Meredith doesn't need to know the reasons for everything I do. I mean, if you had to bail on a date with Elvis because you had horrible period shits, would you tell him?"

"Cara!" Holly's eyes bulged, but she laughed.

"See? There're some things people don't need to know, *even* when it affects them." I grabbed a stuffed lizard and waggled it, as if it was talking for me. "I'll tell her about Aiden as soon as I can. We just need to get some things figured out first, so I don't seem totally unhinged."

"You won't seem unhinged," Holly huffed, but I could see that I'd won.

"So you don't think I'm a jerk?" I needed to hear it.

She sighed heavily. "You're not a jerk." She pursed her lips. "And it *is* nice to see you finally going on dates."

"See?" Aiden prodded. *"Even* she *thinks this is a good idea."*

I grimaced. In the same way that Holly was always trying to get me to hang out with people, she was also always pulling for me to meet somebody. Not because she thought there was anything

wrong with being single, but she was ecstatic in her own relationship, and too generous not to want that for me.

What she never understood was that most people weren't like
Elvis. It wasn't that nobody ever asked me out—even with my
oversized nose, I was solidly cute, and the average high school boy
would fuck a wide variety of produce if you put a hole in it. The
problem was that, high school being what it was, everyone knew
about Scarf Girl. When the whole world's decided you're a slut, the
only folks who approach you are the ones excited by that prospect.

Guys who asked me out inevitably fell into two categories:
self-proclaimed "nice guys" who were themselves deeply unpopular (sometimes for good reason) and who hoped my own lack
of popularity put me on their level, or else skeezy popular dudes
who assumed I'd blow them out of gratitude. As for the queer girls
and enbies: Stossel might be only thirty miles from Seattle, but
there still weren't many of either, and half of those seemed more
interested in claiming the sapphic label than actually dating girls.
Altogether, there'd never been anyone worth my time.

Until now.

"I thought we just established that this isn't a real date," I protested weakly.

Holly caught something in my tone and snapped into focus. She
leaned forward, searching my face. "Wait. You said the concert was
fun, yeah?"

"Yeah," I admitted.

"And then she texted you *the next morning* to hang out. And you
liked that, too?"

"Yeah."

Holly grinned, starting to catch the spirit. "*And* you think she's
cute."

"I mean . . ." I blushed. It wasn't a fair question. Even in her aggro
mode, Meredith was beautiful in the way a statue was beautiful—
elegant and impenetrable, all that black hair framing a fuck-off
stare that was as mesmerizing as it was eviscerating. But seeing her
dance, that damp T-shirt hugging the tight lines of her . . .

"So you *do* like her! Which means the romance part isn't lying!" Holly grabbed my hand, all joyful sincerity. "Cara—this is wonderful! I'm so happy to see you finally opening up. And this whole miracle with Aiden . . . maybe it's part of God's plan for you. Maybe he's trying to show you it's okay to let somebody in."

"She has a pooooiiiint." Aiden drew the words out musically, enjoying my discomfort.

"Okay, slow your roll, Reverend." I pulled gently free of Holly's grip. The way she could ambush you with therapy was simultaneously the best and worst part of being her friend. "I think God—*if* he exists—has bigger concerns than my love life."

"Every sparrow that falls," Holly shot back serenely. "God's got time for you, Cara."

"Oh snap!" Aiden did a sports-announcer voice. *"And it's another point for the God Squad!"* He made crowd-cheering noises.

"Okay, okay." I held up my hands. "Maybe Jesus is building me a Tinder profile. Or maybe I'm just humoring a weirdly obsessive ghost. Either way, can we please *focus*? Meredith's already shot down the prom idea once—if I'm gonna do a full-on promposal, it has to be bulletproof."

"Sure," Aiden agreed, as if this weren't all his idea. *"But first, I've got a question."*

I leaned back against the wall, sharing a long-suffering gaze with the painting of Jesus. "What?"

Aiden paused dramatically, then asked, in a too-casual voice:

"Are period shits really a thing?"

14

I FOUND MEREDITH where I'd met her, at the lonely table by the fire exit. Only this time she was standing, lunch bag in hand.

"Ready?" I gestured with my basket of soggy fries.

"Yeah." Her face was blank—the expression I was already coming to think of as Shields Up—but beneath it I could sense her tension: The stillness of a bullet waiting to be fired. Or an egg waiting to hatch.

Holly and Elvis waited at our usual table. As Meredith and I approached, I could feel myself absorbing her anxiety, producing my own in a chain reaction.

In a weird way, this was bigger than the concert or the cemetery. Those had just been me and Meredith, safely cordoned off from the rest of my life. This was Holly and Elvis. I didn't know which scared me more: that they wouldn't like her . . . or that they would.

Of course, the question was moot, given that Holly, the human golden retriever, was a one-woman friendship factory. She radiated glee as we approached, wagging her nonexistent tail at the prospect of finally adding another member to our crew.

Before I could even make introductions, Meredith pointed to Elvis's T-shirt, with its honeycomb pattern of golden hexagons. "James Webb Space Telescope?"

Elvis blinked. "You like space?"

Meredith gave him an incredulous look. "It's *space.*"

The two immediately fell to arguing about the privatization of spaceflight.

"I didn't realize you came with a space nerd," Aiden whispered approvingly. *"Bonus."*

Across the table, Holly gave me a grin that screamed: *Look! Our significant others made friends!*

To which I smiled back more reservedly, meaning: *Yeah, but she's not my significant other.*

To which Holly waggled carefully penciled eyebrows, meaning: *Are you suuuuuuuure?*

This facial semaphore might have continued, except that at that moment the absolute last voice I wanted to hear said, "Meredith Reyes!"

I turned to find Sophia, accompanied once again by her boyfriend, Brandon, the latter squeezed sausage-like into his letterman jacket like an eighties sitcom villain.

"Oh good," Aiden grunted. *"Her again."*

Sophia made a show of surprise, glossy pout forming a perfect sex-doll O. "You must be hard up for company to hang out *here*." She gestured at me. "Or has Holly recruited you to volunteer with her charity case?"

I gritted my teeth, but Meredith wasn't fazed. She stared back at Sophia with those impassive eyes. "What's your problem, Sophia?"

"No problem." Sophia oozed fake compassion. "You've just already suffered so *much*. I hate to see you add to it like this."

"What a trash bag," Aiden muttered. *"I can't believe Brandon's still dating her."*

I hunched, shoulders rising. Maybe if I got up, I could draw Sophia away from the rest of them, like a mama bird leading predators from the nest. But my chair was blocked by the appropriately named meat-wall of Brandon Hamm.

Meredith, however, didn't cower. She returned Sophia's fake concern with a look of cool disgust. "God, you're a real catch, aren't you?" Her gaze shifted to Brandon. "And *you*—way to pick a keeper,

Hambone. But I'm guessing it's less about what comes out of her mouth than what comes in it, huh?"

I scooted my chair sideways, far enough to catch Brandon's shocked expression.

Sophia's lips formed a tight little cat-butt asterisk. "Looks like you *do* belong up here," she said icily. "You know the only reason anyone ever talked to you was because of your brother, right? Without him, you're nobody."

Trust Sophia to know exactly where to stab. Meredith went perfectly still.

"Fuck that!" Aiden snarled. "Do *something, Cara!"*

As if I could. My fingers curled to fists. "Fuck off, Sophia."

I said it loud. Around us, neighboring tables quieted, kids turning to watch.

Sophia grinned triumphantly. "I'm just saying what everybody knows."

I opened my mouth, but Meredith cut me off.

"What everybody knows," she agreed calmly. "Just like everybody knows about the time you shat your pants at soccer practice."

Sophia's mouth dropped open. *"What?"*

Aiden cackled in delight.

"Come on, you were how old—six?" Meredith shook her head. "Plenty old enough to remember. *I* sure do."

Sophia took a step back—only one, but it said everything. She looked around, suddenly noticing our audience. "You're a liar."

"Am I?" Meredith laughed easily. "There were other girls on that field, Soph. You tried to play it off like it was mud, but everyone could smell you."

"Yes!" Aiden crowed. *"Fuck her up, Mer!"*

"You shut your goddamned mouth!" Sophia was turning as pink as her lip gloss, body winding tighter with each word.

"Hey now, don't lose your shit." Meredith rolled a finger. "You know—again."

Brandon stepped around the table toward Meredith, sensing an opportunity to play white knight. "You need to shut up."

"Why?" Meredith stood slowly. She was a full six inches shorter than him, and probably a hundred pounds lighter, but I'd never seen a real person look so lazily dangerous. She cocked her head. "I'm not judging. If you wanna plow the back forty with Princess Muddy Buddy, that's between you two."

Someone at a neighboring table brayed a laugh.

Brandon's face darkened. He loomed over her, fists clenched. "Don't talk about her."

"Or *what*, Hammy?" Meredith lifted her chin. "You wanna take a swing? Go right ahead."

"Cara." Aiden sounded suddenly nervous. *"Go get a teacher. Right now."*

But Brandon hesitated, glancing around at everyone watching. "I'm not gonna hit a girl."

"Why not? Afraid to get your ass kicked by someone half your size?"

Brandon's face continued to redden, turning his thick, squared-off head into something between a tomato and a LEGO man. "You fucking dyke," he growled, backing off a step. "If it wasn't for Aiden—"

"If it wasn't for my dead brother, you wouldn't have an excuse to walk away right now. Luckily for you." She smiled, then nodded over at Sophia. "So go change your girl's diaper before you both get a rash."

"You're *nobody*." Sophia dug desperately for that same pressure point as she backed away, Brandon in tow. *"Nobody."*

"If you're the alternative," Meredith said lightly, "then nobody is fine by me."

Then they were gone. Meredith sat back down again, not even breathing hard.

"Holy *shit*," I whispered.

"Hundred percent," Elvis agreed.

Meredith shot me a sideways smirk, somewhere between proud and embarrassed, and took a casual sip from her water bottle. My heart flipped over inside my chest.

"Did she really . . . ?" Elvis stopped short of actually saying it, glancing at Holly.

Meredith made a face. "Does it matter? She was *six*. I wouldn't have brought it up if she wasn't being such a bitch."

Holly went for the more important question, looking worried. "Would you really have fought that guy?"

Meredith shrugged. "Honestly, Brandon's not a bad guy. Aiden used to hang out with him sometimes, when they both did water polo. But that was before Sophia started leading him around by the dick." She looked over at me. "People do stupid stuff for the girls they like."

My heart was now officially spinning like a turbine.

Which was stupid. I'd dealt with Sophia on my own for years. I wasn't some damsel in distress—didn't need this girl swooping in and offering to fight for me.

But *fuck* if it wasn't hot.

"Violence over words is never the right choice," Holly said primly. Then she broke into a huge smile. ". . . but that was *totally* bad-A!"

Meredith snorted, but her smile was friendly as she asked, "'Bad-A'? Really?"

I rolled my eyes. "Holly doesn't swear."

"But 'ass' isn't even a swear word," Meredith pressed.

"That's what *I* always say!" I leaned across the table eagerly. "Besides, I'm pretty sure the Bible says Jesus rode an ass."

Meredith smirked. "Hot."

"Stop," Holly said, but she was laughing.

I flushed with pleasure. "I mean, really, if anyone deserved to ride a fine ass, it was Jesus, right? Seems like the least we could do."

Now Aiden was laughing, too, his relieved chuckle blending with the group.

"Really, *stop*," Holly said. "That kind of ass is different, and you know it."

"Okay, okay." Meredith held up a hand. "Can you substitute 'donkey'? Like, 'that guy's a donkey-hole.'"

"Kiss my donkey," I added.

She grinned at me. "Your donkey looks *amazing* in those jeans."

Elvis cocked his head. "I think you just retro-engineered the etymology of 'badonkadonk.'"

And with that, Meredith was one of us. It felt natural to see her there, holding down her quarter of the table. She looked different, too—cheeks softening, arms spreading out as her body loosened. She laughed with the energy of a dog let off a leash.

It looked good on her. *Really* good.

As Meredith asked Elvis the usual question about his name, Holly turned to me, eyebrows high and best-friend telepathy beaming. *Still sure she's not your girlfriend?*

My blush answered for me.

15

SUNDAY WAS MY parents' annual disaster-preparedness party. From all across the neighborhood, the paranoid, the curious, and the lonely crowded into our house to eat chips and hear about all the ways they could die slowly. Several children ran loose, leaving Dorito-orange handprints along the walls, but fortunately no other parents had forced their teenagers to attend.

Mom and Dad were in their element. Dad wore a sleeveless shirt with RIGHT TO BARE ARMS over crossed bear paws holding revolvers, and positively glowed as he walked people through long-term food storage, first aid, and of course basic firearm safety. Mom covered things like go bags and evacuation plans, mutual aid, and how to shut off your house's gas and water. Whether the disaster was earthquakes, nuclear war, or the inevitable Mount Rainier eruption, my parents had you covered.

"We should have invited Meredith," Aiden griped.

"Are you kidding? She probably thinks I'm weird enough already." I would normally have made Holly keep me company, but she and Elvis were at a post-Mass event with their VEYS group.

"Meredith loves weird shit," Aiden countered. *"It's why you two are perfect together."*

"Dude. It's been two dates." But the flush rising up my neck agreed with him.

I was under house arrest for the duration of the party, banned from leaving or escaping to my room, but given that my childhood had been one long master class on the apocalypse, I was allowed to skip the presentations. I hid in our front room, backed into a corner with my phone out and earbuds in so it would look like I was on a call.

Mom passed through leading a tour, gesturing cheerfully at me with a pipe wrench. "To your left, you'll see the elusive Redheaded Grumble-Teen. You're really getting a treat, folks—she normally only emerges from her den at feeding times."

I shook my fist at her in what my Italian grandfather called a *che vuoi*, fingers pinched together in exasperation. She grinned and made it back at me. People laughed.

"Cara here is the cyclist of the family. Mountain bikes are excellent in disasters—all it takes is one big accident, and a freeway becomes a parking lot . . ." She continued on into the garage.

"Your parents seem strangely happy about the possibility of Armageddon," Aiden noted.

"Tell me about it. It's not that they *want* society to collapse, they just really like planning for it. They met on a disaster-preparedness forum."

"That's both dorky and adorable."

"Adorkable." I leaned my head back against the chair. "Honestly, I kinda envy them."

"Why?"

I hadn't meant to say anything, but talking to Aiden was a little too much like talking to myself—it had a dangerous way of slipping past my filters. "They know exactly how weird they are, and they just *do not give a shit.*"

"Aren't you kinda the same way?"

"No." The curse of my life was that despite everything, I still *wanted* people to like me. Mom and Dad were little islands unto themselves, occasionally bumping into other islands and forming flotillas of like-minded islands, but fundamentally content with their individual island status. (Okay, maybe islands wasn't the best metaphor.)

My grandmother had been that independence on steroids. It was a matter of principle for Nana to never censor herself, never let herself be bullied or guilted. She wasn't a jerk—she'd supported charities and causes, and listened to me in a way few adults did. But in the end, the only approval she'd needed was her own. It had rubbed plenty of people the wrong way, but that was fine by her. She was an outsider by choice.

I would have loved to feel that self-assured—to never crave anybody else's validation. Instead, I was like an emotional diabetic: dying for lack of something other people somehow manufactured inside themselves.

"*Confidence is key,*" Aiden agreed. "*I was always trying to explain that to Meredith.*"

I snorted. "Uh, Earth to Ghost: she's got *plenty* of confidence. Did you forget her offer to kick Brandon's ass?"

"*Well, yeah, okay,* physical *confidence. Mer's never been afraid to throw hands.*" He chuckled. "*In fact—pull up my Instagram.*"

I did so, producing a little grid of smiling Aidens.

"*Damn,*" he said wistfully. "*I was such a smokeshow.*"

"And humble, too."

"*Oh, come on—I'm* literally *dirt these days. Nobody's jumping these bones except earthworms. Let me pour one out for my body, all right?*"

I scrolled through his photos. Water polo. Mirror selfies. A river float with friends, chilling on an inner tube—seriously, did the dude *ever* wear a shirt? The little crystal pendant he wore only served to emphasize his partial nudity.

"*You're bi, right? So you like guys, too?*"

I nodded sideways. "In theory."

"*In theory?*"

"In practice, most boys are walking gonads who should be confined to a prison island until they're twenty-five. But yes, when they can shut up and stop being immature assholes for two minutes—guys can be hot."

"*Do you think* I'm *hot?*"

"Which of those conditions do you think you're fulfilling?"

He laughed. "*You're such a hater, Cara.*"

"Just honest." I shook the phone to draw his attention. "Did you have a point? Or were we just pulling this up so you could ogle yourself?"

"You say that like it's a bad thing. But yeah, like I was saying—Mer's never been afraid to scrap. See that scar on my eyebrow?"

I zoomed in on the current picture. There was indeed a little chunk missing from his left eyebrow. "That was her?"

"Clocked me with my own baseball trophy."

"Why? Other than all the obvious reasons, I mean."

"Thanks," he deadpanned. Then his voice turned embarrassed. *"I, uh . . . may have told her that girl sports don't count . . ."*

"So you deserved it."

"I was eight! 'The patriarchy' hadn't yet entered my vocabulary! But that's also just how we were—Mom always said if we weren't playing we were fighting, and half the time she wasn't sure which was which."

I raised an eyebrow. "You *fought* your little sister?"

"Hey, which of us has a facial scar?" He sighed. *"Anyway. That stopped a long time ago."*

He sounded so suddenly weary that I had to ask. "Why?"

The ensuing silence went on long enough that I thought he might not tell me. Then he sighed again and said, *"One of the reasons we fought so much was that Mer always wanted to hang out with my friends."*

"Really?" Never mind what she'd already told me about him always dragging her along—it was hard enough to visualize Meredith hanging out with Aiden's royal court under duress, let alone *wanting* to.

"The thing about Mer is that she doesn't actually want *to be a loner. She makes this big show of rejecting parties, and popularity, and all the traditional high school stuff, but whenever it was her turn to pick for our movie nights, it was always* Clueless *or* She's All That *or* Ten Things I Hate About You. *And anything with a big, over-the-top romantic gesture turns her into a total marshmallow. That's why I'm so all in on prom—because deep down, she* craves *that Hollywood teen experience."*

I thought about her response to the painting of Glory Rock. "I can see that."

"*Yeah. For some reason, she's convinced she can't have any of it—by high school, I had to guilt her hard to get her to go to football games with me, or anything with other people. But when we were kids, she was like my shadow. Most of our knock-down, drag-out fights were when I tried to do something without her.*" He paused guiltily. "*Usually it wasn't even that I didn't want her there. It was just to show I could, you know? To keep something for myself. Does that make sense?*"

"Sure," I lied. I tried to imagine feeling so loved that you had to run away just to get out from under it.

"*Anyway, the summer I was twelve, our neighbor Michael Watanabe got a pool. And one day, some of us noticed that the patio roof sloped almost all the way out to the water. If you climbed out the second-story window, you could run down it, jump, and clear the five feet of cement to land in the pool.*"

"That sounds like the world's stupidest idea."

"*Remember how I said we were twelve? Anyway, the guys were all daring each other to do it, and one by one we did. And it was terrifying but fine. But then Meredith wanted to do it. And we were stupid, but we weren't stupid—nobody was gonna let my kid sister bash her brains out. So of course she got pissed and ran home.*

"*. . . Or so we thought. Ten minutes later, I look up and see she's snuck out onto the roof. I yell for her to get down, but she just grins and jumps.*

"*And she doesn't make it.*"

My hand went to my mouth. "Oh my god."

"*Three days in the hospital, then bed for two weeks.*" He tried to keep his tone light, but I could hear the pain behind it. "*Mer never blamed me, and Mom and Dad tried to pretend they didn't, but everybody knew it was my fault.*"

"But you tried to *stop* her!"

"*Yeah.*" His voice was flat. "*And I should have tried harder. I'm her older brother. That's the job.*"

I tried to think of an argument that could punch through his guilt, but before I could, he forced himself back into a more casual tone. "*Anyway . . . Meredith and I never fought after that. I mean, she'd still come at me sometimes—the girl's a fucking bobcat—but I refused to fight back. Eventually she grew out of it."*

"Clearly not all the way, if she was gonna take on Brandon."

"Yeah, and his balls would have been marmalade. She fights dirty."

I snorted. "Sounds like my grandma. Nana always told me, 'Cara, never fight. But if you *do* have to fight, fight like you're going to jail in the morning.'"

Aiden laughed, for real this time. *"Your grandma sounds awesome."*

I smiled. "Yeah. She was kind of a superhero."

"So have you ever gotten in a fight?"

He saw my hesitation.

"Oh man, you totally have!"

I considered saying nothing, but it was surprisingly hard to stay quiet when Aiden asked you a direct question. Even invisible, the intensity with which he listened cracked you open like a pistachio.

"Just once," I said slowly. "And it wasn't a *fight.*" I sank deeper into the armchair, lowering my voice even though there was nobody nearby. "So . . . you know about the Scarf Girl thing . . ."

"Yeah?"

"Well . . . afterward . . . one of Sophia's favorite tricks was to wait by the band room. When I'd go to pick up my trombone after last period, she and her friends would hold the door closed, trapping me inside until I almost missed my bus."

"Shit. What'd you do?"

"Cried, mostly. There were always several of them—I could see them through that little wire-reinforced window in the door. After the second time, I didn't even try to push out or yell, just waited until they left or a teacher came by." I remembered the faces, the laughter. Some of the girls I'd thought of as friends. Others hadn't even known me. I wasn't their enemy—I was a team-building exercise.

"Then one day, as I was trapped in there wishing I was still home-schooled, I thought about what Nana would do. So I went to the closet and got a music stand—one of those heavy black metal ones. And I chopped it through the door's window like a fucking battle-axe."

"*What?!*" Aiden sounded both shocked and delighted. "*No way!*"

"I didn't hit any of them," I clarified. "But I got a two-week suspension."

"*I'll bet!*" He laughed. "*That's awesome!*"

"I guess."

"*You* guess?"

How to explain? "I mean, yeah, Sophia and her pack backed off some, at least physically. But that's when people *really* started avoiding me."

"*But* she *was the bully! You're a hero!*"

"In a movie, maybe. In real life, she was popular. And once you put a music stand through a window, everybody starts seeing you as dangerously unbalanced."

"*That's bullshit!*"

"That's life." I could still feel the first time I noticed people subtly leaning away from me, drawing back like the fronds of a touch-sensitive plant.

"*It was worth it, though, right?*" Aiden sounded like he needed to believe.

I shrugged. "It taught me that when push comes to shove, most people would rather hurt you than risk slipping off their rung of the social ladder. Being an outcast is an efficient sorting system." Better one loyal friend like Holly than a hundred who would throw me under the bus.

"*Well,* I *think it's cool as hell,*" Aiden insisted. "*You went full* Braveheart! *Swinging that music stand like 'FREEEEEDOOMMMM'!*"

I laughed. "It wasn't *exactly* like that."

"*Too late. It's in my head like that forever now. Painted face and everything.*"

"I can live with that."

"*Seriously, though.*" His voice softened. "*You say you're not confident like your parents, but I never would have had the courage to stand up to everyone like that. You give the whole world the finger and do your own thing. That takes guts."*

A warm glow filled my chest. There it was—that approval I didn't want to need. Aiden might have his annoying moments, but he had Holly's same gift of knowing exactly what you needed to hear. No wonder Meredith missed him.

"It's not really a choice," I demurred. "Everybody already avoids me anyway. I just figure if I'm gonna be lonely, I'd rather be alone."

"But you're not alone," Aiden noted. *"Not anymore."*

I hadn't really thought of it in those terms before. Holly might be leaving soon, but Aiden . . .

Aiden would still be right here with me.

Something in my shoulders unclenched. Slowly, I shook my head.

"No," I agreed. "Not anymore."

16

IT WAS SHOCKING how easily Meredith slid into my life. Suddenly it was as if she'd always been there at our lunch table, or waiting for me by the bike rack before school. Holly beamed so hard over my induction into the secret society of People with Crushes that she looked poised to go up like a Roman candle.

Meredith, for her part, seemed to take everything in stride. She'd float along so cool and detached as to make you wonder if she was even listening, then suddenly cut in with an insightful observation and heart-stopping smirk, turning my organs to liquid honey.

We'd even begun texting a little, though that part was more complicated. The written word and I had never been particularly friendly, and the constant memes and emojis Holly and I exchanged felt childish with someone as solid and serious as Meredith. She seemed built for *important* conversations—the sort of deep revelations that felt natural in late nights or graveyards but pretentious when typed on a phone. Having Aiden reading over my shoulder didn't help: while he'd agreed to stay quiet when Meredith was around, the privacy of my bedroom allowed no such excuses. Between his "expert coaching" and Meredith's taciturn responses, it seemed safer to keep things in person.

Now it was 11:00 A.M. on one of those random half days the school bizarrely called "in-service days." I waited by Meredith's car in the parking lot, anxiously watching her approach.

"It's gonna be fine," Aiden whispered.

"Says the guy who fell to his death," I muttered back.

I had reason to be nervous. As we'd left school the previous afternoon, Meredith had turned to me out of nowhere and said, "You free tomorrow?"

I hadn't been—Holly and I had a shared history presentation to prepare—but from behind Meredith, she'd given me a double thumbs-up. Let it never be said Holly Pham was less than a perfect wingwoman.

"What's up?" I'd asked.

"Wanna go rock climbing?"

As if a concert in the city hadn't been intimidating enough. But Aiden's cheer had told me what my answer had to be.

"You don't get it," he'd insisted later. *"This is huge!"*

"Yeah, a huge *mistake.*"

"Don't you see? The graveyard thing could have been platonic, but this? This is a genuine, no-cap date. Meredith just asked you out! She's never done that for anyone before!" He laughed delightedly. *"Honestly, I didn't think she had the balls. Er—ovaries? Whatever."*

I grimaced. "I don't like heights."

"So don't look down. You'll be on a rope the whole time. But look—" His voice turned serious. *"You have to let me come along."*

I jerked my head back, scowling. "That's not the deal!"

"Just this once! Please—you don't understand. Climbing is the thing that makes Meredith happiest, and she hasn't done it since I died. That was me—I took that away from her. And I just . . ." His voice shook with emotion. *"I just really need to see her climb again, okay? Please."*

Ugh. Earnestness: my only weakness. Say what you will about Aiden, but the boy begged well.

"Fine," I groaned. "But you can't say *anything.* And keep your distance, okay? I don't want you breathing down my neck."

"You'll never even know I'm there," he promised.

Now here I was, ghost in tow, wearing black bike pants and a pink REI pullover. I thought it looked pretty all right—the artificial fabric hugged my body in a way that was flattering without trying too hard—but as Meredith approached, she frowned down at my feet.

"I forgot to bring you shoes," she said. "We'll have to swing by my house." Her obvious lack of enthusiasm about the prospect did nothing to assuage my nerves.

Meredith was quieter than usual as she drove—which was really saying something—and I got the feeling she was watching the road mostly to avoid looking at me. She was wearing a hazard-yellow puffy and salmon capris, and it felt strange to see her so colorful. Like a crow dressed up as a parrot.

We drove east, taking one of the endless roads winding up into the hills. It never ceased to amaze me how Stossel seemed to sit right on the edge of the map: one minute you'd be driving past housing developments with Teslas in the driveway and Starbucks in the cupholders, and the next it was goats grazing between half-disassembled trucks.

Trees screened Meredith's house from the road, the driveway two gravel lines curving back through a moat of gold-green grass that hadn't been mowed in a while. The old blue-and-white farmhouse had been elegant once, before someone cracked it open like a rib cage. One whole side was roofed with tarps, the siding torn away to let a march of pale studs mark out a planned addition. The overall impression was that of a shipwreck, tarp-sails luffing in the breeze.

Meredith pulled up to the front steps and got out. She leaned down into the car. "I'll go grab the shoes."

"Should I come in?" I didn't want to make her uncomfortable, but I was curious to see where she and Aiden came from. "I'm gonna need to try them on, right?"

Meredith hesitated so long I thought she might say no, then shrugged. "Yeah, okay."

I followed her up to the front door, where stacks of two-by-fours crowded a porch made for swings. The topmost pieces were gray and splintering, a layer of pine needles making it clear nobody had touched them in a while.

Inside, family photos lined the entryway. It was startling to see Meredith and Aiden in the same pictures, his arm draped over her shoulders. Two worlds colliding.

A man's voice called from another room. "Meredith?"

"Just grabbing some stuff!" She led me quickly toward the stairs, grit scraping the hardwood beneath our shoes. As we passed an open doorway, I saw a stocky man with Meredith's thick black hair sitting in a brown leather recliner, a beer in one hand and the case on the floor beside him. The TV in front of him was dark.

He looked up and saw me, eyes widening. "Oh! Hi there."

"Hi." I gave an awkward wave.

Meredith stopped with one foot on the stairs, then pulled herself back around with an effort. "Dad, this is Cara."

"Hi, Cara." Meredith's dad's smile cut through deep lines to make him look shockingly like Aiden. "What time is it? Shouldn't you be at school?"

"Half day," I explained.

"Right, right." He nodded, then seemed to notice his beer, setting it down out of view. "So, what are you two up to?"

"Gonna drive over to Redmond and have lunch at the mall." Meredith lied like river rock, smooth and cool. "Maybe see a movie."

"Great." Mr. Reyes's smile looked genuine but strained, stretched tight over a variety pack of emotions.

"I'll be home for dinner," Meredith said, and tugged me up the stairs.

"Nice to meet you!" I called over my shoulder.

Floorboards creaked as we walked down the hall. Open doors showed a cramped office with stacks of unopened mail, plus an old-school bathroom with purple tile. At the end of the hall, two doors faced each other. Stickers plastered the one on the right, including a black-and-red crow I now recognized as the Darkhearts logo, thanks to Aiden.

As Meredith turned away, I considered what it must be like to have the room across from his. To be constantly confronted by that closed door.

Then she opened her own door, and all thoughts of Aiden vanished.

I wasn't the neatest person, but my dirty clothes at least fell *near* the hamper. Meredith's layer of floor clothes was deep enough to grow crops in—archaeologists could probably date artifacts by where they appeared in the strata. Rising up from this fabric sea were an unmade bed, a desk with a laptop, and a set of adjustable dumbbells. Two lumps of rock-shaped plastic hung from nails over the closet, next to a poster of a woman dangling from a cliff with the words CLIMB LIKE A GIRL.

Meredith kicked her way through to the closet and began digging around. I stood awkwardly in the doorway, trying to take it all in. A pair of blue bikini-cut panties jumped out at me from the floor, and I jerked my gaze away.

Over by the bed, a short bookcase packed with records supported a turntable. In my imagination, Meredith lay on that bed in just a T-shirt and those underwear, hair splayed out across her pillow, staring at the ceiling as old records played. I wanted to crawl into the picture with her.

But the dust and pile of dirty plates on the turntable's clear plastic case said that if such a scene had ever happened, it had been a while ago.

"Here." Meredith held out a pair of neon-green shoes with smooth black soles. "Try these on."

I picked my way carefully over to the desk chair—the bed felt too intimate—and took off my sneakers.

"No socks," Meredith said.

I paused, climbing shoe halfway to my foot. "I'll get them all sweaty."

Meredith just looked at me.

Blushing, feeling like I was taking off a lot more than my socks, I quickly stripped them off and crammed my feet into the shoes.

"They're really tight," I said.

"That's good." Before I could register what was happening, Meredith knelt in front of me, grabbing my foot gently but firmly. She squeezed the toes, feeling around the sides, then looked up into my eyes. "You want them as tight as possible."

I was *definitely* sweating now. *It's just your foot,* I reminded myself. But the way she held it, so casually in control, probing softly at the edges . . .

Stop, I commanded. *You want her to think you've got a foot fetish?* Hell, *did* I have a foot fetish? I hadn't thought so, but I'd also never had Meredith up in my toes before. All I knew was that I simultaneously needed her to let go of my foot and wanted her to keep holding it forever.

She continued watching me. Desperately, I said, "Why'd you lie to your dad?"

She frowned and let go. "They're all paranoid now." She nodded to my foot. "You'll want your regular shoes to start."

"Right." I slipped back out of the borrowed shoes, keenly aware that the last feet in them had been Meredith's, naked against the rubber and mesh.

She led me back downstairs, through the silent house. My house was plenty quiet when Mom and Dad were at work, but this was different. There were three of us here, yet it echoed with absence. A home with a hole.

Coming down off the porch, I was struck by the huge maple rising up out of the yard. Cradled in its massive limbs, a truly epic tree fort reached for the sky—four separate platforms, the topmost with a plywood roof and enclosing railing.

I walked past the car to the tree's base, fingers rising to touch the weathered ladder boards nailed to the trunk. "Did you build this?"

"Yeah." Meredith stood with hands in pockets, a faint breeze carrying individual strands of her hair aloft. "Me and Aiden."

"It looks crazy professional."

A muscle twitched in her jaw. She seemed to be fighting the words as she said, "Our parents were always remodeling. There was plenty of scrap."

"I would have *killed* for a tree house like this." I leaned into the words, needing her to feel the praise. "You guys must have been popular."

Meredith shook her head. "Nobody else was allowed up there." A little sideways smile broke through her wall. "*We* weren't allowed up there, either, but after the second grounding, our parents gave up. We spent a lot of summers in there, just the two of us, reading comics and playing Switch."

"That sounds really nice."

"It was." Her lips compressed as she stared up at the old wood.

Amazing how her face could say so much with so little. Had I really thought she was cold the first time I met her? It seemed so obvious now that her detachment was a shield—a paper-thin bandage over a gaping wound. Here was a girl who loved like a hurricane, her silence a desperate attempt to avoid being swept away.

It hurt to see it. I could only imagine how Aiden must be feeling, now and for the whole past year, forced to watch silently. I turned back to the tree, letting my hand drift sideways across its bole, feeling the wrinkled bark.

From behind me, Meredith blurted, "We put him here."

"What?" I turned.

"His ashes." Her hand went to her chest, clutching the little crystal pendant she always wore—and for the first time, I understood that it didn't just *match* Aiden's, it *was* Aiden's.

She didn't meet my eyes. "Mom and Dad—they wanted to scatter him somewhere nicer. Puget Sound, or a mountaintop, or something. But that wasn't him." She looked up at the tree house. "*This* was him." She swallowed. "Or at least, it was *us*."

Her voice wobbled, and I felt an answering burn in my own throat—that invisible hand that clamps down around your neck, saying *I will* not *cry, goddammit.* I could see it in the set of her jaw, the lowered brows—sandbags against the rising flood.

I wished there was something I could say to break through that dam. To drain the sadness inside her. But who was I? Whatever plans Aiden might concoct, there was only one person who could fill the chalk outline in Meredith's heart.

But if I couldn't help, I could at least bear witness.

"You miss him." Stupid. Obvious.

She kept her eyes on the fort, tongue tucked pugnaciously under her upper lip. She looked like she had when she'd stared down Brandon—like she was preparing to take a swing at someone. When she spoke, it wasn't to me.

"I should have been there."

I looked to the fort, then back to her. "Where? The factory?"

"We always explored together. I could have dug him out. Or maybe I would've been the one who fell." Her tone took it for granted that that would have been better.

"*Mer . . .*" Aiden's pained rasp broke through his promised silence.

"It's not your fault," I said softly.

"Of *course* it's my fault!" She looked down at me at last, and the rage in her eyes shoved me backward. "I was pissed at him for dragging me to yet another fucking party—another chance to stand in the corner watching everyone adore him. I was sick of his advice, sick of his plans, sick of him always trying to make me *into* him— and sick of *me* always fucking *failing* at it. So when he wanted to explore the factory, I told him I was done being his sidekick. That he should fuck off and leave me alone." Her hands were out of her pockets, knotted into fists. "I didn't think he'd go without me." But even as the words left her mouth, she was shaking her head fiercely. "*That's not true!* I didn't think about him at *all*. Only how *I* felt."

I took a cautious step forward, hand out and low, as if approaching a growling dog. "That sounds like *his* fault."

"What, because he did what I said?" She sneered. "I told him to fuck off, and he did." She smacked a fist into her chest. "That was *my* pride." Another hit. "*Me.*"

"*Bullshit!*" Aiden yelled. "*None of this is her fault!*"

"*Stop,*" I snapped, not knowing who I was talking to.

Meredith drew back her fist to hit herself again.

I leaned in and grabbed her wrist.

We both went still, staring at our joined hands. Then Meredith looked back up at me, and her eyes were so hard I let go instantly, palms rising in apology.

I wished I could just make the two of them talk—prove to Meredith that Aiden didn't hold her responsible. But trying to force the issue now was too dangerous—it could ruin everything if Aiden didn't cooperate. And maybe even if he did.

Meredith's fist lowered, but not all the way, floating in front of her.

"If Aiden were here," I said carefully, "do you think he'd blame you?"

Her eyes stayed flat. "Does it matter?"

"Of course it matters!" I snapped. "You didn't make him go to the factory. That was him."

"Yeah?" She scowled. "Well, he's dead." She looked down at the ground. "And I'm still here."

Her hair hung down in her face, drawing a curtain between us. Above, maple leaves rustled, the decaying fort swaying and creaking in the breeze.

I took a deep breath, then stepped forward and touched her arm again.

"Maybe it doesn't matter whose fault it is," I improvised. "If it's not your fault, then you've got nothing to feel guilty about. And if it *was* your fault, then you can make it up to him by not beating yourself up about it. Because if he cared about you as much as you say, he wouldn't want this."

She snorted. "A year later, and everything's still about what *he* wants."

Without letting myself think about it, I slid my hand down her arm. The nylon of her jacket ran smooth against my palm. Then skin. My fingers touched hers.

She jerked—just like Sophia. I flinched, already seeing the scene play out.

But her hand didn't pull away. Startled eyes met mine.

"So don't make it about him," I murmured.

She searched my face, eyes gleaming with emotions too large to be set free. They circled like sharks in an aquarium, the shine of unshed tears the safety glass between us.

She lived on the other side, in a world I'd never understand: a frigid realm whose pressure would crush me. We were fundamentally alien to each other.

Yet her fingers curled up to meet mine. They moved slowly, softly, waiting for the anemone-like recoil—the drawing back that said it wasn't like that.

Then they were turning, sliding between my own, holding my hand with quiet authority.

I looked down at them, then up at her. The glass between us cracked in a sideways smile.

"You're good at this," she said.

"I'm good at lots of things," I quipped, my breeziness betrayed by the quaver in my voice.

"Oh yeah?" Her smile widened. "Like what?"

"Guess you'll just have to find out."

She nodded slowly, eyes not leaving mine. "Maybe I will."

She turned and pulled me back toward the car, not letting go of my hand. I followed, marveling at the weight of her arm, the newfound bridge between us.

Just like Aiden wanted.

Suddenly I felt dirty. I fought the urge to pull my hand back— not because I didn't want to hold hers, but because *she* shouldn't be holding *mine*.

Meredith had let down her guard. Trusted me enough to show me a glimpse of what she was going through. And here I was with a secret of my own—one that should by all rights be *hers*— following me around, whispering in my ear. Even now, I could feel his invisible eyes on us.

Her hand in mine—that was real.

But I'd also lied to her. Because she was right: while this was about us, it was also still all about Aiden.

We reached the car and she let go, but not before shooting me another of those new, softer smiles. The one that said she might be broken glass, but she wasn't going to cut me.

I wanted that smile. Wanted to curl up inside it. More than that, I wanted to return it—to strip away my armor and let her see underneath.

But I couldn't, because Aiden. Because I owed him. And not just for his help with ghost hunting—for getting me *here*. To this moment, with this girl who was the strangest, most exciting thing to happen to me in . . . ever. He'd told the truth: Meredith was special, and whatever this thing growing between us was, it was *good*. I wanted to hold her callused hand. I wanted to open her up, to brace against her and hold her wide, to keep seeing the fierce, loyal, terrifyingly beautiful creature that lived inside her.

I didn't want to lie to her.

But it was too late to stop now.

I smiled back and got in the car.

17

WE PULLED OFF onto a wide dirt shoulder, half a dozen cars already lined up at the trailhead.

"Shove anything you don't wanna carry under the seat," Meredith said.

I did my best to hide my laptop beneath other school stuff, leaving only my water bottle and jacket in my backpack.

Meredith popped the trunk and hauled out a gray pack as large and dirty as a baby elephant. It hit the ground with a thump I felt through my shoes.

"Jesus!" I reached down and grabbed the top handle, but it was like lifting cement. "You, uh, want me to carry some of this?" I was used to hauling around half a dozen textbooks, but my JanSport was nothing next to this monster.

"I've got it." She shrugged it easily up onto her back and nodded toward the trail. "Ready?"

The hike started like all trails in the Cascades, which is to say: up. We switchbacked through a twilight-deep forest, the thick trunks of second-growth conifers dwarfed by the giant stumps of those who ruled before them. We crossed streams on rocks and skirted mud pits churned by human, dog, and deer. My legs burned, confused by the departure from my normal biking, but fortunately my lungs didn't know the difference, allowing me to maintain a veneer of nonchalance. Aiden had said Meredith didn't get out hiking anymore, but you'd never have known from the way she carried Dumbo piggyback up the mountain.

After maybe a mile, the forest opened up onto the flat gravel of an old railroad bed. A slabby gray cliff spread out to either side of us, dotted by ledges of moss and grass. Well off to our left, another group was already climbing, their bodies colorful patches on the rock.

Meredith dropped her pack to the scree at the cliff's foot, then shucked her poof. Beneath, she wore a stretchy blue tank top that was ambitious for the temperature, even after the exertion of the hike. Nipples popped, daring me to look. I kept my eyes moving, never lingering long enough to get caught.

She opened the bag. "Ready for your first climb?"

"Absolutely not." It wasn't quite a joke.

"It's easier than you think." She hauled out a tarp and laid it flat, then began unpacking coils of multicolored rope and strange bits of gear—short braided straps with metal clips on either end. She pulled out something that looked like a tool belt tied to two smaller belts and handed it to me.

"Harness." She pulled out another in a different color. "Here, watch me." She stepped through the two smaller loops, then drew the main belt up over her hips. She pulled the straps tight around her waist and legs, then doubled them back through their buckles.

I attempted to follow suit.

"Here." She stepped close and knelt down in front of me again. I stood perfectly still as she adjusted the leg loops, loosening them and pulling them higher up my thighs. "Your legs are bigger than mine."

I looked away, blushing.

"I mean, you've got quads," she corrected, glancing up anxiously. "All that biking, right?"

"Yeah."

"That's awesome. I've got wimpy legs." Which was obviously false, but she clearly thought she'd offended me. And okay, I didn't *love* people commenting on my big thighs, even if I was proud of what they could do. But that wasn't why I'd looked away.

It was the sight of her on her knees in front of me, looking up, sunlight glinting off her cheeks and catching in her dark lashes. The feel of her hands moving confidently along the thin polyester covering my inner thighs. She slid fingers beneath the loops, pressing into me as she checked the fit, and I stared straight out over her head, trying to breathe normally.

An eternity later, she stood. "All right, you're good."

She had no idea. I did my best to dig a deep hole in my brain and bury the memory of her hands in it, not to be exhumed until I was safely alone.

"Now you check me," Meredith said. "Just make sure all the buckles are doubled back. I know I'm good, but it's just the thing you do."

She pointed to the various straps, and I managed to confirm that they were, indeed, as they should be. Also that they were pointedly framing her business district, which was definitely *not* what I should be thinking about right now.

She slid a band off her wrist and tied her hair back—something I'd never seen her do before. It looked good on her. Sporty. Confident.

"I need to climb first and set the rope." She clipped tools to her harness, then bent over to do something complicated with a metal anchor someone had screwed into the bottom of the cliff.

"What should I do?" I asked.

"Just hang out. I'll be quick."

Then she was off, speeding up the wall like a gecko, rope trailing behind her in two lines. Chalk from a pouch on her belt left little white splotches where she gripped the rock. Every six feet or so she stopped and clipped a strap onto one of her rope tails and another anchor set in the rock, running the rope through them like connect-the-dots.

Each movement was smooth and precise. Within moments I had to crane my head back to see her, her hands seeking out knobs and cracks, toes seeming to catch on nothing at all.

It was graceful. Timeless. Like watching an angel ascend to

Heaven under her own power. Through the half-moon cutouts of her shirt, the bare skin of her back knotted and dimpled with muscle. Swooping lines stood out on her arms, tendons popping on the backs of her hands. Below the hems of her capris, smooth calves bulged, and I had no choice but to imagine how they would feel under my hands, the softness of them turning abruptly to iron as I made her flex . . .

Except, wait—hadn't she spent the last year totally depressed? With hair as dark as hers, those calves should have been the Black Forest. What depressed girl shaved her legs? *I* sure as hell wouldn't have bothered.

Which meant maybe she'd shaved them for this.

For *me*.

A frantic alarm from my engine room let me know we were swamped and going down. Awooga. SOS. Abandon ship.

"Impressive, huh?"

Aiden's voice made me jump.

"Feels good to see her climb again." He sounded halfway between braggy and weepy. *"This . . . this is the* real *Meredith. How she's supposed to be."*

"Quiet," I hissed. I didn't want to think about him right now. This was *my* moment—mine and Meredith's—and I didn't want to share it. "You're not here, remember?"

"I know, just . . . good job, all right? You're crushing this."

"Go!"

Above us, Meredith paused, hanging easily in space, and shook her tail of black hair. Since when were ponytails this hot, anyway? I'd always seen them as the universal sign for *I haven't showered recently.* But on Meredith, it just seemed so . . . grabbable.

At last she reached the top of the cliff face and clipped into two short chains anchored to the rock, sitting back in her harness. She looked down and gave me a thumbs-up.

"See?" she called. "Easy."

"Yeah," I yelled back, "if you're fucking *Spider-Man!*"

She grinned, then set to doing something complicated with the rope. I contented myself with watching the show. Holly would be happy to know that I'd finally had a genuine religious experience, even if it was only in the way Meredith's harness emphasized her butt, like a jewel in a setting.

God, I was such a little perv today. But there was no harm in appreciating, right?

"Okay," she called. "Coming down. Stand back."

She kicked off, rappelling back down like a *Mission: Impossible* character, unclipping anchors as she went. As she touched down, I shook my head. "That was amazing."

"Thanks." She glowed with equal parts exertion and happiness, rock dust clinging to streaks of sweat.

She bent and dug into her pack, pulling out the spare climbing shoes. "Your turn."

In all the excitement of watching her transform into a goddess, I'd completely forgotten why we were here. I held up my hands. "I . . . don't think that's a great idea."

"Wrong." She came closer, shoes extended like a poisonous snake she wanted me to pet. "This wall's only as hard as you make it—you can grab whatever holds feel good. If you can climb a ladder, you can climb this."

I eyed the shoes warily. "I dunno . . ."

"I do." She smiled wide. "I believe in you."

Well, shit. What was I supposed to say to that?

I changed shoes quickly, sweating feet sticky against the tight rubber. When I was wedged in and laced up, I stood.

Meredith stepped forward with the rope, tying a complex knot and threading it through my harness before tying several more and handing me a bucket-style bike helmet. She produced another piece of gear that looked like a chrome pig nose. "This is so I can belay you." She threaded the free tail of the rope through, then clipped it all to her harness and stepped backward. "If you fall, I'll catch you. Like this." She held her right hand out to the side and sat down suddenly, half swinging. The rope jerked, almost lifting me off my feet.

"Always make sure the rope goes through your belayer's carabiner—not just the belay device—and that it's all locked off." She stood and directed my attention to her harness. "Go ahead and check me. See how the rope goes through both?" She pointed to the heavy metal clip binding the rope to her harness.

"Yeah."

"Squeeze it."

I reached forward and gingerly groped her carabiner's gate. It clicked but refused to open.

"All right, now you're ready to climb."

"That's an overstatement."

Meredith grinned. "Just remember: I've got you."

I looked past her to the wall, and to the rope trailing up, up, up. "Oh Jesus."

"Hey," she said gently, and touched my arm. The contact crackled along my bare skin like static, widening my eyes. Then it was gone, leaving only a tingle and traces of chalk.

She grabbed the rope a foot above my harness. "If you get scared, just say 'take,' and I'll pull the rope tight." She yanked hard, pulling me in close, harness holding me firmly by hips and thighs. "Just to remind you I'm here."

As if I needed a reminder. The nearness of our bodies, the ease with which she dragged me around . . .

"If you think you're gonna fall, or you want to let go and just hang, say 'falling' and wait for me to say 'fall on.'" She gave the rope another tug. "You're safe either way, it's just good practice."

My laugh came out panicked. "I'm not gonna *let go*." I'd be lucky if I could pry my fingers free long enough to reach a second hand-hold. Letting go was no longer in my vocabulary. Elsa from *Frozen* could fuck right off. If I were Jack from *Titanic*, I'd have been on that floating door in a second, pushing Rose off by her face.

"You might be surprised. Fingers get tired quick your first time." Meredith stepped back and nodded to the wall. "When you're ready, you say 'on belay,' and I say 'belay on.' Then you say 'climbing' and I say 'climb on,' and you know you're good to go." She spread her feet, one hand on the rope above her, the other holding its tail out to the side. Every pose this girl struck made her look like She-Ra. "Go for it."

I faced the wall and repeated the call-and-response, thankful my voice stayed level. Then I reached up and grabbed a likely-looking outcropping. The stone felt rough and cold.

I pulled. As with every time I'd tried to climb the rope in PE, absolutely nothing happened.

"Use your legs," Meredith advised. "You don't have to muscle up on your arms. Just use them for balance and focus on your feet. Find a foothold and just . . . stand up."

I tried again. This time I managed to find a solid hold just above my right knee, the toe of my borrowed shoe catching it firmly. I took a breath and stepped up, rising off the ground. Then I found another for my left foot.

"There you go!" Meredith said. "Now move your hands up."

I climbed. Slowly the ground retreated beneath me.

"Oh shit oh shit . . ." I murmured.

"Don't look down," Meredith instructed. "Look up. Follow the rope. Where you're going, not where you've been."

"You sound like my mom's podcasts," I grumbled.

Objectively speaking, climbing was hot garbage. Years of biking as my only exercise had done nothing for my wobbly jellyfish arms, and my sense of balance was a late-stage Jenga tower. It felt like my center of gravity was a foot behind my ass, the same butt that propelled me up hills now determined to peel me off the wall like a screaming slice of lunch meat.

And yet . . . the longer I did it, the easier it got. While my arms were weak, it felt good to be using all of my limbs. The stone felt solid under my hands, and there was a primal, simian satisfaction in dragging myself up it, some evolutionary echo from before we'd come down from the trees. Somewhere, deep inside, my body knew how to do this.

And then I looked down.

Meredith was a tiny speck below me. My brain knew I couldn't possibly be as high as it looked—I'd watched Meredith climb this whole route just minutes ago. Yet my stomach insisted the ground was a thousand feet away, the vertigo drawing me down toward a splattery death.

Fuck my monkey ancestors. They'd descended from the trees precisely so that they'd *never have to do this again.*

I screwed my eyes shut, plastering myself against the wall.

"I can't do this!" I shouted.

"Sure you can!" Meredith shouted back.

"I need to come down!" But it was a pointless statement. I couldn't have pried my hands loose from the rock with a crowbar.

"No, you don't." Meredith's voice stayed calm and steady. "You made it that far."

My knees and elbows shook, suddenly terrifyingly weak, threatening to give way at any moment. "I'm too high!"

"You're totally safe." I felt the tug against my harness as she drew the rope taut. "I've got you, remember?"

"Chill," Aiden whispered in my ear. *"Don't ruin this."*

"Fuck you!" I ground my face into the dirty stone, not knowing which of them I was swearing at and not really caring. "I'm not *like* you, all right? I'm not a fucking *action hero*! So just get me down! *Please!*" I was breathing rabbit-fast, only my scrunched eyelids preventing tears from falling.

"Cara." Meredith's tone remained absolutely level. She wasn't even yelling—just a firm, even voice that carried up the rock. She pulled harder on the rope, taking most of my weight. "Cara, *I've got you.* I could haul you up the wall on my own. But I don't need to, because *you can do this.*"

Sweat flooded out from between my toes, which was the absolute stupidest response to heights. What the fuck, evolution? Somebody's worried about slipping and falling to their death, and your response is to *make their feet slippery*? Absolute proof that intelligent design is bullshit. I'd have to remember to tell Holly. Assuming I survived.

"My fucking *toes* are sweating!" I protested.

"I believe in you," Meredith pressed.

"That makes one of us!" But it was hard to snap back with her words lodged in my chest. I opened my eyes.

The wall was still there, the rope still holding me.

And it wasn't like I could stay here forever.

"Fuuuuuck," I moaned, and reached up for another handhold.

"Yes!" Meredith shouted. "Send it!"

"Fuck fuck fuckity frig . . ." Slowly, keeping my eyes fixed firmly above me, I climbed. Every knuckle and toe ached with the strain, but still I gained ground.

And suddenly I was looking at chains. I'd reached the top of the route.

"Nicely done!" Meredith called.

"Oh my god!" Triumph and exhaustion warred inside me, turning my whole body watery. I clutched the chains, taking a shuddering breath. "Now what?" I yelled.

"Now you let go."

"WHAT?!" My bladder informed me that we really should have gone to the bathroom at school. And then stayed there.

"Just sit back in the harness," Meredith called, as if the words weren't utter batshit.

My entire body returned to cat-hanging-from-the-curtains mode. "No no no no . . ."

"Climbing down is harder than climbing up," Meredith noted. "Just let me lower you."

"Nope." I closed my eyes again.

"Cara. Look at me."

"I thought I wasn't supposed to look down!"

"Look at me."

Reluctantly, I opened my eyes, peering down over my shoulder.

A million miles below, Meredith looked back up. Even across that distance, her eyes bored into mine. She stood easy, hands on the rope, posture radiating confidence. Her face was serene—no trace of anxiety, no embarrassment at my meltdown.

"You're doing great." Despite the obvious evidence to the contrary, she sounded like she actually meant it. "Now it's my turn. I need you to trust me."

Those eyes expanded to blot out the rest of the world. Dark pools waiting to catch me.

Fuck.

"Take!" I shouted.

Her grin bloomed huge and soft. "Gotcha!"

I inhaled deep, feeling the cold sweat covering my bare skin. My whole body shivered as I called out, "Falling!"

"Fall on!"

I closed my eyes.

And let go.

There was one terrifying, vomit-inducing, foxhole-conversion moment of drop, every nerve in my body aflame with the knowledge that it was about to check out for good. My internal organs got together and mutinied, declaring that my brain was clearly unfit to lead if *this* was the sort of decision it was making.

And then I was hanging, the harness holding me securely, hands clutching the rope. My feet bounced against the wall, keeping me from swinging back into it.

"Perfect!" Meredith yelled. "Just like that!"

Foot by foot, she lowered me down. Weirdly, now that I'd actually let go of the rock, the fear was gone. I could look out and appreciate the trees blanketing the slope, the other climbers farther down. It was like as soon as I'd let go, my body had decided we were dead, and was now content to sit back and enjoy the afterlife.

I reached the ground. My limbs shook with adrenaline, equal parts triumph and that feeling of having almost been hit by a car.

"Congratulations," Meredith said. "You're officially Spider-Man."

"Oh my fucking *god*!" I threw my arms around her, hauling her almost off her feet. The metal lump of her belay device ground painfully against my pubic bone, but I didn't let go, shaking her like a dog with a toy. "You *asshole*! I almost peed myself!"

Meredith's arms went tentatively around me as well, patting awkwardly. "As the person standing beneath you, I'm really glad you didn't."

I hugged her tighter, her ear a cold comma against my cheek. Her hair still smelled like coconut and lime, but now blended with the dry rasp of rope and rock dust.

"Thank you," I whispered.

"That was all you." She relaxed into me, hands sliding across my sweaty back. Even being gentle, I could feel the strength in those arms, the solidity of them. Her chest pressed insistently against mine as she took a breath, expanding into me.

Slowly, like a wave receding, her arms slid free, parting us a step as she reached down to untie the rope from my harness. I watched her clever fingers, long and sure, easily unraveling the knot between us.

"I'm amazed you can still do that," I said. "My fingers are totally dead."

"Yeah?"

Too quick for me to process, she reached down and grabbed both of my hands, bringing them together between hers and rubbing.

"The rock's cold," she said. "Your hands are freezing."

She pulled my fingers to her mouth and breathed on them, hands cupping, trapping the heat of her against my skin. Clasped like a prayer.

Her eyes met mine, soft and questioning.

"Better?" she asked.

"Better," I breathed.

And I stepped forward and kissed her.

She didn't move. Everywhere we touched, her body stood frozen in shock, our joined hands clutched primly against her chest like a painting of a saint. Once again, I was certain I'd misjudged. *Oh fuck oh no oh please*—

And then she was kissing me back, lips parting, hands releasing and sliding up my arms to drag me closer. She tasted like her lip balm, sweet and sharp. She was surprisingly tentative, her lips moving slowly and gently.

I'd kissed guys before—both times ill-advised, always a slobbery mess. This was nothing like that. *She* was nothing like that. She was smooth and solid and I wanted to drown in her, to burrow inside her and hold her down and be buried alive under the warm weight of her and—

I moaned and tightened my arms, crushing her against me. She gave a startled laugh, right into my mouth, and I broke away long enough to glare. "What?"

"Just you." She grinned, shaking her head. "You're an extremely surprising person."

"You don't even know," I grumbled.

She kissed me again, more confidently now, her hands trailing down to my waist.

"I don't," she murmured into my neck. "But I want to."

We kept kissing, her thumbs coming around to grab me gently, tracing the points of my hips. I shivered beneath her touch.

She was slow. She was gentle.

She was making me *painfully* horny. If the muscles in my No-No Zone clenched any tighter, I was going to achieve nuclear fusion.

My hand spidered up her back to her ponytail. I ran fingers through its strands, shockingly thick and cool, then grabbed the base and gently pulled.

She gasped, her whole body jerking so hard I let go, stumbling a half step backward. Air rushed into the channel opened between us.

"Too much?" I asked.

"No." Meredith blushed furiously, chest heaving. Forget the hike—*now* she was out of breath. She gave a smile that was fifty percent mortification. "No. *Good.*"

My soul left my body at that smile. I reached forward and grabbed the front of her harness, pulling her roughly against me again.

"*Take,*" I murmured.

She laughed and wrapped me up, trailing a line of tiny kisses across my jaw to my ear. Her breath on my neck set every hair standing at attention as she whispered, *"Gotcha."*

This girl. I grabbed the sides of her face and pulled her lips back to mine, closing my eyes and feeling her smile with my own. My hands scraped down across her back. Searching for holds.

Falling, I thought.

18

AFTER THAT, CLIMBING suddenly seemed a lot less interesting. We sat pressed together against the base of the wall, holding hands with my arm wound around hers like a vine. Chalk dust made her fingers weirdly dry, seeming to grip my skin, keeping me from sliding away. Not that I wanted to.

We took a break from kissing to watch paragliders twirl and soar out over the valley, their chutes gentle arcs of color.

"They look like candy," Meredith observed.

"Or toenail clippings," I said.

She laughed and butted me with her shoulder.

"What? Tell me that's not the best description of that shape."

"Try. Harder." But she was grinning.

I snuck a kiss. "Would you ever do that? Paragliding?"

She shook her head. "No way."

"Really?" I glanced meaningfully up at the wall.

"Climbing's different—the rock isn't going anywhere. That—" She gestured out at the gliders. "One wrong breeze . . ."

I took the opportunity of her pointing to nestle in under her arm. She draped it easily across my shoulder, as solid and secure as stone. "I think they're both terrifying."

She looked down at me and smiled again. "Terrifying can be fun."

As if she wasn't proof of that herself. I still couldn't quite believe we were here, wrapped around each other like this. But I said,

"Sure—when you're watching horror movies. Climbing is like get-ting chased by a fucking *shark*."

"You get used to it."

"But *why*?"

Meredith looked away again, considering. In profile, she looked like a queen stamped on some ancient coin: the pointed chin, the gentle slope of her nose. I buried my own prodigious proboscis in the side of her neck.

I liked that she took the time to really think about things. To be honest, I was always in such a rush to respond that I just said the first thing in my head, always looking for that snappy comeback. But Meredith was comfortable saying nothing. Making you wait.

I'd have thought that would be infuriating. But in a world where most people were just waiting to talk, Meredith listened with her whole body, curving toward you like a satellite dish. And with her arm around my shoulders, fingers trailing softly across the bare skin beneath my sleeve, I was in no hurry.

"I think it's the freedom," she said at last. "When I'm up on a pitch, it's just me. There's nobody to compete with, nobody to com-pare to. Just me versus the route. I like solving the puzzle. It makes me feel capable. Strong."

"You *are* strong." I squeezed her bicep.

"So are you." She pulled back a little to see me. "What about you? Why do you bike all the time?"

"Same, I guess?" Then, firmer: "I like having something I'm good at."

"You're good at more than that." The suggestiveness of her smirk stole my breath away. How was this robot girl allowed to smile like that? I felt my face reddening and diverted before I embarrassed myself further.

"Do you climb at gyms, too? I've heard people talk about one in Redmond."

She made a face. "The bouldering place? Pffft—the point of climbing is to *climb*." She inhaled deeply. "Besides. This is my favorite smell."

"What—sweat?" I laughed, but actually, her sweat smelled amazing. Even here in her armpit, it had none of the stank of a locker room, or that funk that gets into polyester workout clothes no matter how many times you wash them. Her sweat smelled warm and slightly sour—almost citrusy—but also thick and spicy, like cumin. I wanted to rub my face in it like an animal, marking myself with her scent.

Twenty minutes into kissing Meredith, and I was already sniffing her armpits. Good lord.

Meredith laughed. "No! I mean this." She waved a hand at the valley. "Rock dust and that dry sun-on-pine-needles smell. It's like breathing summer."

I raised an eyebrow, leaning back to make sure she saw. "Are you always this poetic? Or only about rocks?"

She shoved me playfully. "Shut up!"

"Never." But I leaned back into her, softening my tone. "I like that you like this."

"Do *you*?" Her voice went suddenly tentative.

"Do I what? Like huffing trees?"

"Like this."

I was beginning to get the sense that Meredith only had two modes: brick wall and utter sincerity. You either got nothing or you got everything, like drinking from a fire hydrant. It made her a perfect straight man, and a lifetime of habit told me to tease her more. But the look in her eyes said she was genuinely anxious.

"Yeah, Meredith. I like this."

I felt her relax, ribs softening.

"Me too."

Still, I couldn't let her get off *that* easily. "You sure took your sweet-ass time deciding."

"*Me?*"

"Yes, you!" I elbowed her in the side. "I had to practically bribe you to get you to hang out with me!" I smiled to show I was kidding, though now that I'd said it, I realized a part of me still rankled.

"I didn't know you liked me!"

"I *asked you out*! How was that not a clue?"

"I don't know!" Meredith's shoulders hunched.

"Repeatedly," I pressed, enjoying the way she flushed.

"I don't *know!*" Meredith threw up her arms.

On the wall, her confidence had been *painfully* sexy. The way she'd literally held my life in her hands, calmly talking me through my panic, calling the shots but taking care of me . . . At the time, it had been terrifying, but now my body throbbed at the memory. Yet I decided I liked this flustered version just as much.

"You just appeared out of nowhere!" she said. "It didn't make sense! Why would you ask me out?"

I leaned in and kissed her, biting lightly at her lip. "Because you're hot as fuck?" It hadn't been the reason then, but it sure was now.

She kissed me back. I squeezed her hard, enjoying the pit-bull solidity of her torso. "I'm glad that seeing me almost vomit in fear finally got your attention."

"I've *been* paying attention!"

"Since when?" It suddenly seemed very important to know.

Meredith thought about it.

Did I say I liked that? I take it back—waiting was totally unacceptable when the question was about *me.*

At last, she said, "Since I picked you up for the concert."

"Wait—when you *picked me up*?" I remembered that interaction all too well.

She bunched her lips to the side—half smirk, half embarrassment. "You had those pants with the laces."

"You wouldn't even *talk* to me!" Her blank expression was seared into my memory. "You looked at me like I was . . . I dunno, an Amazon package you needed to deliver!"

"I was playing it cool."

"You were playing it *dead!*" I jabbed my fingers into the flesh beneath her ribs. "You douche nozzle! I was so self-conscious!"

She squeaked in a decidedly un-Meredith way and caught my wrists in climber-strong hands, holding them just short of tickling range with an ease that was as appealing as it was frustrating. "It's not my fault! You made me nervous. Besides, what did *you* have to be self-conscious about?"

"I thought you thought I was overdressed or something!"

"I thought you were the hottest girl I'd ever been that close to."

She said it simply—a statement of fact, like the capital of Arkansas, or the atomic number of helium. The casual sincerity lit me up like Christmas lights. I stopped trying to tickle her.

"Good answer," I conceded. "Bullshit, but a good answer."

"It's not bullshit! You're gorgeous!"

"Yeah, if you like parrots." I pointed at my nose. "I'm Toucan Sam over here."

"*I'd* follow your nose." Meredith grinned and pecked my beak. "Besides, the shape is more like a koala's."

"Oh, *that's* an improvement."

"Koalas are cute!" Her smile softened. "Seriously, though. It fits you. It's . . . dramatic."

"Are you calling me a drama queen?"

"Are you saying you're not?"

"You're not making it better." Though in truth, she was.

She laughed in exasperation. "Oh my god, Cara! I love your nose!"

"No, you don't."

"Yes," she said firmly. "I do." And she leaned forward and—with a noise like *glomph*—took my entire nose into her mouth.

"Gahhhh!" I jerked backward, wiping away saliva. "Gross!"

Meredith looked pleased with herself, to a degree normally only achieved by cats. "Nothing about you is gross."

"False." But the words still flared hot in my chest. Unwilling to lose an argument, even to the sexiest girl on the planet, I said, "One time I threw up SpaghettiOs at the zoo. The lady running the reptile house thought I was vomiting blood and tried to take me to the hospital."

"Okay," Meredith conceded with a sideways nod, "I agree. You're gross." She leaned in and gave my cheek a long, wet lick, like a dog. In my ear, she whispered, *"But I wanna be gross together."*

"*That's* your best pickup line?" But the words came out shaky, my body pulsing in time with my racing heart.

The kissing resumed. It started soft, but built like a song, getting harder and more urgent. At some point, Meredith turned and swung a leg over mine, straddling my hips and taking my face in both hands. The knobby rock of the wall pressed into my back, held there by the soft weight of her, gravel digging into my palms. Everything inside me ached, straining for more.

Then voices.

Meredith jerked, leaping off me with a guilty smile just as a group of climbers came up off the trail. The lead guy waved.

"Hey," he called. "You starting or finishing?"

Maybe both, I thought wildly. Good lord, Meredith was hot.

She looked to me. "You wanna climb again?"

I laughed, a little crazed. "I think I'm good for a while. Like, maybe the next century."

"But you were having so much *fun*." She prodded me teasingly in the side. Then she jumped to her feet and turned to the guy. "Just let me clean the route."

Belayed by one of the other climbers, Meredith scampered back up the cliff, then repacked the gear. I gave them space, moving a little way down the wall in an attempt to walk off the blush in my cheeks and the buzz in my stomach.

"*Good thing those other climbers showed up*," Aiden noted cheerfully. "*I was starting to worry you'd get her pregnant.*"

I twitched like an electrocuted trout. Despite everything, the distraction of kissing Meredith had somehow been enough to again make me forget he was watching. Now the knowledge of what he'd just seen flamed my cheeks. "Shut up," I hissed.

"*Hey, no shade—here I'd been thinking you might be shy. You gonna bill her dental insurance for that cleaning?*" He was clearly enjoying my discomfort.

"No talking," I reminded him.

"*Relax, she's talking to those dudes. Your secret's safe.*"

My secret. My stomach twisted, post-makeout adrenaline turning bitter.

I didn't want a secret—didn't want Aiden here at all. Why couldn't I just have this moment? Why did everything have to be so convoluted? I didn't know which I resented more: Aiden or myself.

I opened my mouth to tell Aiden to ghost off, but before I could, he said, *"Whoa—that feels weird."*

My anger stalled. "What does?"

"I don't know." He sounded strained, a little dreamy. *"It's like—"*

The words cut off.

"Like what?" My voice was too loud. I stepped behind an outcropping, out of view. "Aiden?" I whispered.

Silence.

A breeze whistled past along the rock wall. In the forest, trees swayed, their boles creaking ominously.

My stomach went cold.

"Aiden?"

19

WE WERE PARTWAY back down the trail when his voice returned. *"Well! That was weird!"*

"Aiden?" I stumbled and almost ate shit on a tree root.

Meredith turned to look back at me. "What?"

Shit. "I said 'it's late,'" I improvised. "I should probably get home."

Meredith gave me a confused, disappointed look—it was still early afternoon—but said only, "Okay."

I smiled, trying my best to seem normal. Inside, my intestines were knotted as tightly as the climbing rope.

"Aw, don't break up the party because of me!" Aiden said. As if it weren't *way* too late for that.

Back in the car, Meredith snuck concerned glances over at me. "You okay?"

"Yeah, totally. I'm great." But all I could think about was Aiden. We'd been together for several weeks now, and he'd never just been . . . *gone* like that. The possibility that he could suddenly disappear was terrifying, and the fact that I couldn't even ask him what the hell had happened had me popping my knuckles like bubble wrap.

"If this was . . ." Meredith faltered, then started again. "I mean, if this is too fast—"

That got me out of my head. I grabbed her hand, lacing my fingers through hers. "It's not. I'm just processing." I did a robot voice. *"Processing! Please hold!"*

Her shoulders relaxed, and she gave me that half smile. "So we're good?"

I brought the back of her hand to my lips and kissed it. "I think 'good' is a bit of an understatement, don't you?"

Back in my driveway, I managed to surface out of my worries long enough to give her a proper goodbye kiss. A part of me screamed that I should be crawling across the center console, dragging her into the back seat for some classic 1950s makeouts, but nothing overrides a lady boner like blind panic. I gave a tug on her collar and a smile that hopefully looked realer than it felt, then slipped out and ran back to my house.

As soon as the door closed behind me, I shouted, "What the *fuck* was that?!"

"A wildly successful date?" Aiden ventured.

"You know what I mean!" I flung my fleece onto the floor.

"Honestly?" he said. *"No idea. One second I was talking to you, and then I got that weird balloon-expanding feeling from when I died. Then everything just . . . blinked out. Or more like blinked* on—*like when you're in a dark room and then somebody turns on a light and blinds you. It only felt like a second, but when the light vanished, you were already hiking. Like I'd skipped ahead in a video."*

"And that's never happened before?"

"Never." He finally started to sound uncomfortable. *"What do you think it means?"*

I pulled out my phone and texted Holly.

"It means we've got a lot of work to do."

☙

"—aaaaaand we're back," Aiden announced.

"Time!" I called.

From her seat on my bed, Holly checked her phone. "Seventeen minutes."

One minute longer than last time. *Shit.* I entered it into my spreadsheet.

"The intervals could still be random," Holly offered gently. "You've only got a couple of data points."

But my clenching gut knew better. "The disappearances are getting longer. If he continues decaying at a linear rate, at maybe five blinkouts a day . . ." I tapped furiously at my phone calculator—then jerked, flinging it aside as if it were red-hot. "Fifty-five *days*?!"

"*If* the decay is linear," Holly soothed. "He could have more time."

"Or he could have *less*!" I leapt up off the carpet. "I haven't even figured out how to prove he *exists*, and he's going to disappear completely in *two months*?"

"*Why yes, I do have some feelings about the situation,*" Aiden deadpanned. "*Thanks so much for asking.*"

Holly chewed on her pen cap. "This doesn't make sense."

"I *know*!" I paced around the room, waving my arms. "What the *fuck*, universe?!"

She frowned. "No, I mean—he's been around for a year, right? So why's the countdown only starting now?"

Oh.

I froze.

"Cara?"

In all my panic about Aiden, I hadn't filled Holly in on the date.

"I, um . . ." My cheeks heated. "I kind of kissed Meredith . . . ?"

"*What?!*" Holly spasmed, bouncing all the way off the bed, dragging half the comforter with her like an ineffective parachute.

"*You didn't* kind of *kiss her*," Aiden observed. "*You kissed her like her tonsils were the antidote. Full-on end-of-movie kissing. Which, I mean—nice work. Eight out of ten from the judges' panel. Though you might want to ramp back the tongue.*"

"How could you not *tell* me?!" Holly scrambled back up onto the bed, grabbing my hand in both of hers. "Ohmygosh, Cara! I'm so happy for you! I mean—*should* I be happy for you?" Her expression leapt from excited to concerned.

Maybe it made me a bad friend, but in my heart, I hadn't known exactly what reaction to expect from Holly. She was the literal definition of supportive, but still . . .

I squeezed her hand. "Be happy."

"*Eeeeee!*" She squealed and hugged me, vibrating happily.

"Okay, okay!" I laughed and shoved her gently off.

She switched to hugging my pillow. "I want to know *everything*! Leave no detail out!"

"Later," I promised. "After we figure out what's going on with Aiden."

"What's to figure out?" She waved the pillow. "His whole deal is that he can't pass on until his sister's happy again, right? It sounds like you made her happy. So now that's starting."

It sounded so obvious when she put it that way. I flailed at the air. "But it's not supposed to happen *yet!*"

"*Don't look so disappointed.*" Aiden's good cheer sounded a little forced. "*This is just proof that we're on the right track—getting closer to completing the mission.*"

"Yeah, *your* mission," I snapped. "What about *my* mission?"

"*You sure seemed on a mission earlier. A bold expedition to the bottom of my sister's panties.*"

I reddened. "You know what? Feel free to disappear again anytime."

Holly watched, eyes darting back and forth between me and the empty point in space toward which I was addressing my fury. She placed a consoling hand on my elbow. "Cara, you knew he wasn't going to stick around forever."

"Yeah, but—" But what? I'd assumed Aiden would probably go wherever spirits normally went after he completed his unfinished business, but I'd figured helping Meredith would take time. You didn't cure somebody's depression with one makeout session. And I hadn't even taken Meredith to prom yet, which was our whole deal.

But prom was just Aiden's idea—when it came right down to it, we had no idea what the universe considered happy enough to put his ghost to rest.

Which meant it was time to quit fucking around and pull out the big guns.

I stepped up onto the bed, mattress creaking. Bracing one hand atop Holly's head, I leaned over her and plucked a picture frame down off the wall.

"What're you doing?" Holly asked.

I swiveled the little tabs and pulled the backing off, then withdrew the business card from the corner of the glass.

I'd been doing my best to document Aiden's existence on my own, but I'd barely scratched the surface. I couldn't afford to let him slip away without leaving me some bulletproof evidence.

I bounced down off the bed and into my computer chair, then opened my email.

To: himself@carsonkeene.com
Subject:

I hesitated, trying "Investigation Lead" and "Evidence of Paranormal Activity" before settling on simply "Ghost Found."

Dear Mr. Keene,

Hello! My name is Cara Weaver, and I'm a huge fan. I'm also a fellow ghost hunter with my own YouTube channel, *Caranormal Activity.*

I cringed, just as I had when Dad had told him—except worse, because now it was me. Telling Carson Keene you were a ghost hunter was like telling Jimi Hendrix you were a guitarist. But humility wasn't an option here. And hey—I'd actually *found* a ghost.

We met several years ago, at your signing at the Elliot Bay Book Company. You gave me your card and said if I ever needed advice, I should contact you.

I paused again, but there was no point beating around the bush. Trying to sound as professional as possible, I typed:

I'm writing now because I've established contact with a ghost. He's the spirit of a local boy who died here in Stossel, WA. While he can speak to me, he appears unable to manifest visibly, physically affect the world, or speak to anyone else.

I know how that sounds, but I've confirmed his existence via a series of tests involving him observing random outcomes (dice rolls, etc.) that I'd have no way of knowing and then reporting the results to me on camera. A video of one such test is attached.

Obviously, videos can be faked. I promise that mine aren't, but I realize that doesn't carry much weight.

That's why I'm hoping we can work together. In addition to valuing your input on experiment design, I believe that if we could publicize our findings together via your channel, it would reach a lot more people, and your credibility could bring in more scientists and other ghost hunters to help convince the general public.

The only catch is that we need to act quickly. The ghost appears to be losing his grasp on our world, and may only last a few more weeks.

Typing that line made my chest ache. I blinked hard and continued.

So if you're willing, we should meet as soon as possible so that you can observe the phenomena for yourself.

"*Not* too *soon*," Aiden noted. "*Prom first.*"

"We can't wait until *prom*!" If he'd had a neck, I'd have been throttling it like Homer Simpson. "I haven't even *proposed* yet, and you're already shorting out like a goddamn busted lightbulb!"

"*Relax. You've got plenty of time. And I won't leave until I've held up my end of the deal, I promise.*"

"You *can't* promise that! You don't know how any of this works!"

"*Hey, which of us is the ghost here? I knew it was my unfinished business with Meredith keeping me here, didn't I? And now that same feeling says I can't go 'poof' while I've still got unfinished business with you. It'll be fine—we can meet with your dude afterward. But right now, we need to keep your eye on the ball.*"

I shook my head. "That's way too flimsy. We've gotta get moving on this *now*."

"*The deal's the deal,*" he shot back. "*No telling anyone else until after prom.*"

"Why are you being such an asshole?!"

"*Hey! Bring it down a notch, Chicken Little. First off: prom is only, like, two weeks away. If this guy's really a celebrity, what are the odds he even responds before then? And second—are you telling me that if your hero shows up to make you famous, you're really gonna have your head in the game about prom? You think Mer won't notice?*"

He . . . wasn't wrong. I ground my palms into my eye sockets, then typed.

> For complicated reasons, I can't meet until Sunday, June 2nd or later.
>
> Thank you for your time.
>
> Sincerely,
>
> Cara Weaver

I sat back and reread it, then had Holly read it.

"It's good," she said. "Polite, but to the point."

"It doesn't make me seem bonkers?"

"It's a bonkers situation."

I closed my eyes, gave a single strangled scream, and clicked send.

The email disappeared. I slumped in my chair.

"There you go," Holly said. "It's in God's hands now—or at least Carson Keene's. You've done everything you can."

"Yeah." There was one more idea slowly surfacing from the depths of my brain, but it was better if Holly didn't know. And I knew Aiden would demand we focus on the prom proposal first.

As if on cue, he said, "*All right, fam! Promposal time—these props aren't gonna assemble themselves.*"

I turned to Holly. "Are you and Elvis ready for Saturday?"

"We're good." She hesitated, no doubt wondering if her role in my not-entirely-aboveboard courtship was putting her on God's naughty list. Then she set her shoulders and smiled. "It really *is* a romantic idea."

"Of course it is," Aiden preened. *"You're working with the best, babies!"*

Classic Aiden—the ego not even death could deflate. But as usual, it was delivered with that little extra flip of his voice, the flamboyant over-the-topness that invited you to smirk along with him. Cocky, but warm. A tone that said you were on the same team, and that all the faith he had in himself, he had in you as well.

I was going to miss that.

The realization hit me like a truck, clipping my tire and sending me spinning. My irritation transmuted into a sudden wave of grief.

Because for all that Aiden might piss me off, being here like this—me, him, and Holly—felt *right.* He was one of us. He was *mine*—my friend. I'd never had many, yet here he was: scheming, joking, arguing. Maybe he hadn't chosen me, but that hadn't stopped him from telling me his secrets and listening to mine.

And now he was going to disappear. Just like Holly. The injustice of it lodged in my throat like unchewed bread.

"Cara?" Holly watched me with concern.

"Yeah," I croaked, and turned back to my laptop, opening the planning document. "Prom time. Let's do this."

Inside me, another clock began counting down.

20

"IT'LL BE FINE," I said, meaning *it had better be fine.*

"*Famous last words,*" Aiden shot back.

"You would know." I locked my bike to the fence, shirt steaming and clinging from my midnight ride, then reached into my backpack and pulled out my Maglite. The factory in the dark was even creepier than during the day, its threatening appendages revealed piece by piece in the flashlight's beam.

"*Seriously, Cara. This is sketchy as hell.*"

"Yeah? Well, you aren't leaving me a lot of choice." I was still pissed at him for making me wait to meet with Carson, but more than that—I was scared. It was shocking how much his voice had faded since yesterday's kiss. Even when he wasn't blinked out—absences that continued to lengthen at unpredictable intervals—he no longer sounded like he was in my ear. More like a voice on the phone. An audible reminder of our time slipping away. "Ghosts are usually tied to the location of their death—it's probably why you feel that pull toward it. If there's anywhere you can affect the world, it's gotta be here, and we *need* some sort of physical phenomena—something that'll show on camera."

"*So you're gonna go alone into a place that already killed somebody.*"

"I'm a ghost hunter—*everywhere* I go already killed somebody." I gestured with the flashlight. "Left?"

"*Left.*"

I skirted around the side of the mill, away from the Phallus Palace.

As we went, I pulled out my phone and sent the text I'd already written.

Went back to the mill. Please don't be mad. If I haven't texted again in 3 hours, tell someone.

Holly would hate it, of course. But I couldn't afford to worry about that. This was for my future—something she'd already opted out of. And by the time she woke up, she'd already have a follow-up message saying I was home safe.

Hopefully.

The building we wanted rose up like a lopsided ziggurat. There was no path I could see, and the grass whispered against my pants, fletched seed darts burrowing into my socks. As I came around the rusted hulk of a silo, my flashlight caught the door.

And the giant plywood rectangle covering it.

"No no *no!*" I ran forward, light catching bright lines of police tape. "You said it was still open!"

"I didn't know they'd boarded it up!"

"I thought you *lived* here!"

"No, I'm pulled here when I'm not paying attention. I spend as much time elsewhere as possible. And I don't use doors anymore."

The plywood was thick, nailed deep into the jamb. I grabbed the edges and hauled uselessly, splinters digging into my fingers. *"Fuck!"*

"Shit. I'm sorry, Cara."

"There's gotta be another way in." I shined my light around, but found nothing.

"Hold on, I'll check."

There was never any physical sensation to his leaving, but in the silence that followed, I felt suddenly exposed.

"Aiden?" The word slipped out. I hated how needy it sounded, and forced myself to be relieved when he didn't answer. I'd been prepared for the possibility that he might blink out while we were here, requiring me to sit and wait for him, but now that I was actually alone in the dark . . .

"Okay," he said a few minutes later. *"I checked it out."*

"And . . . ?!"

"They boarded up all the doors and windows on the ground floor. The whole building."

"Fuuuuuuuuuuuck." I banged my head against the plywood and immediately regretted it. "Why didn't I bring a crowbar?"

"Because you're not an idiot? Entering is one thing, breaking is a whole different crime."

"So what am I supposed to do?" I felt dangerously close to tears, which just made me madder.

"This was just one idea. We can try something else."

"There *is* nothing else!" Aiden had died *here*. He was pulled *here*. This was our best shot. I walked back out and turned, playing my flashlight across the building.

"Maybe it doesn't have to be the exact spot. Maybe this is close enough."

My light caught on a neighboring building that had burned and partially collapsed against our target, bricks sloughing off in a landslide. The mess rose halfway to our building's first-floor roof.

"You said they boarded up everything on the ground floor?"

"Yeah . . . ?"

"Great." I ran to the pile and began climbing. Debris shifted with a grinding sound.

"Did I ever mention how I died under a pile of rubble?"

"If we were the sort of people who had good ideas, neither of us would be here right now." I switched to my headlamp to leave both hands free, clicking on the red-light setting to preserve my night vision.

Rubble slid ominously underfoot as I crabbed my way up the pile, each shift making my breath catch. At the top, I straightened carefully and grabbed the roof. Pulling hard, I jumped, managing to get my eyes above the edge.

Across a flat metal roof, a glassless window yawned.

"Bingo."

"Yeah, okay. If you can get up there."

"So give me a boost already."

Arms quivering, I lowered myself carefully back down, then

began piling up broken bricks, stacking them at the highest point. When it was several feet tall, I straightened. "Ta-da! Instant step-ladder."

"Or a Jenga tower."

I stepped carefully up onto my creation, reminding myself anxiously that if I could climb a cliff with Meredith, I could manage a few feet of building. Bracing my hands against the roof edge, I jumped, leaning forward and squirming ahead as if hauling myself out of a pool. When I'd safely beached myself, I sat up, spreading my arms belligerently. "Ta-*da*."

"Okay, I'm impressed," Aiden admitted.

"About time." I stood.

"Listen," he said seriously. *"If we're gonna do this, you gotta promise you'll listen to me, okay? I was pretty good at urbex, and it still killed me. If I say something's too dangerous, you pull out."*

"That's what she said."

"Come on, Cara—you need *me, remember?"*

As if I could forget. I sighed. "Fine."

"Thanks." He sounded genuinely relieved. *"Now hold on, let me check the roof."*

I waited, feeling simultaneously absurd and majestic, standing on an abandoned building with the wind tugging at my ponytail. If not for the dorky headlamp, I might have been a cutscene from a video game.

"Okay, supports look good, but stay on the edges—the areas over the walls will be the sturdiest. Once we're inside, stick to concrete—don't put your foot on anything unless you can see what's under it. And don't walk beneath anything that might collapse. If something smells weird or you're kicking up dust, put on your mask. And whatever you do, don't run—not even if a cop shows up. Running makes everything worse, and getting caught is better than falling. Got it?"

"Sir, yes, sir!" I snapped off a mocking salute.

"Better. All right, let's go."

I picked my way carefully around to the window. Inside was a wide concrete room with several dark hallways leading onward into the rest of the second floor. Stagnant water pooled beneath the windows, their edges abstract watercolors of pollen and mosquito larvae.

"Which way?"

"Center one? Maybe?"

My footsteps echoed off bare walls. The graffiti up here was of a higher quality, bubble-lettered tags and cartoon avatars interspersed with the names and dates of previous explorers.

Partway down the corridor, the concrete ended abruptly in open space, the floor falling away in a straight-edged drop-off. Maybe five feet across the gap, the hallway resumed again, continuing onward. I stuck my head out and saw that the split continued to either side and above us as well, rising up to a third story lost in shadow.

"What the hell? Who puts a friggin' *moat* in the middle of a hallway?"

"Maybe they used it to haul up logs or something?"

"Thanks a lot, The Past." I backtracked, turning into the other passages in search of an alternate route.

Each time, hallways ended in boxy rooms of blank and dirty concrete. I poked my head out windows, but the first-floor roof that had gotten me up failed to wrap around, leaving only a long drop to cracked pavement. A narrow concrete staircase that led to the ground floor had been boarded up from the other side. I gave it a kick, thinking the old doorframe might fall apart, but it held firm.

I returned to the broken hallway and knelt, peering down over the edge. The drop to the floor below couldn't have been more than fifteen feet, but in the red light of my headlamp it may as well have been a crack to Hell.

"Rope time?" Aiden suggested.

"I was afraid you'd say that." I dug into my pack and pulled out a coil of thick, plasticky rope harvested from one of Dad's survival bins. Actually *climbing* a rope was completely out of the question, but I figured if I tied big enough knots, even my wimpy arms could use it like a ladder.

There was only one problem. "Where do we tie it?"

"Um." Aiden hesitated, and I knew what he was seeing: blank concrete walls, without any convenient pipes or outcroppings. *"The windows?"* he said at last. *"You can run it out through one of them and then back in through another. Loop around the whole wall."*

That sounded sturdy enough. I went back out to the main room and did as he suggested . . .

. . . and found that the rope now ended partway down the hallway.

"That's all the rope you brought?" Aiden sounded incredulous.

"I wasn't planning to climb Rainier! Why didn't you tell me to bring more?"

"It's your *rope! How was I supposed to know how long it was?"*

"Whatever." I began pulling it in, hand over hand. "Maybe we can loop it around a support in one of the other rooms."

But it was no use. Each time, my rope proved woefully inadequate.

"Fuck." No wonder Meredith's climbing pack had been so big. I squatted back down at the edge of the gap.

This was it—the end of the line. Do not pass Ghost, do not collect a new life of fame and acclaim. Just ordinary Cara Weaver.

Or Scarf Girl. Maybe forever.

Unless . . .

Absolutely not, I told myself. *We're going to go home and send Holly a string of apology emojis and figure out something else.*

But my mouth had other ideas.

"I could jump it."

"Oh my god, Cara." Aiden sounded terminally exasperated.

"It's not that wide."

"It's not about how wide *it is! It's about how far you'll* fall *if you fuck it up!"*

My stomach agreed with him—violently—but pride forced some heat back into my voice. "So I won't fuck it up."

"Jesus Christ! Why are you both like this?"

For a second, I wasn't sure what he meant. Then I remembered the story of Meredith on the roof.

Suddenly I was awash in guilt. Here Aiden had already watched his sister smash herself to bits—had *himself* been smashed to bits in this very building—and now I was threatening to do my own dramatic reenactment.

But I was so close now, and time was running out. I might not get another chance.

I peered down over the edge, knees jellifying and skin prickling into goose bumps. Objectively speaking, this was a million times stupider than rock climbing.

But worse—it was *exactly* the sort of thing Aiden had asked me not to do.

And I'd promised.

Through gritted teeth, I asked, "Are you telling me to go home?"

A snort. *"Would you listen if I did?"*

I bit my cheek. Slowly, I nodded.

"Really?" He made no effort to hide his skepticism.

"Yes, okay?!" My hands balled into fists, and I squeezed my eyes shut, unsure whether I was frustrated or relieved. "I *said* I'd listen to you. If you say go home, we go home."

"Huh." He sounded surprised, but pleasantly so.

I waited for the hammer to fall. When nothing came, I cracked an eye. *"Are* you saying go home?"

He made a low, conflicted hum. Then, as if it physically pained him, he groaned a drawn-out *". . . No."*

"No?"

He sighed. *"Look, I should say yes. But as happy as I am that you're actually listening to me for once . . . I was always trying to tell Meredith what to do, and look where it got us. So yeah, it's risky. If the red flag I'm waving were any bigger, I'd be a fucking bullfighter. But . . . it's your call."*

Now it was my turn to be surprised. "Thanks," I said, and meant it.

"No problem."

Another pause, longer this time.

"You're still gonna jump it, aren't you?"

"Yeah, probably."

Another snort, this one with a tinge of admiration. *"Do me a favor and don't make me regret it, okay?"*

"I'll try."

He exhaled heavily. *"Honestly, as long as you don't biff it, you should make it across easy. I've seen what your legs can do."*

The compliment nestled into my chest, spreading soft wings. "I appreciate the pep talk."

"Hey—no guts, no glory, right? If I can't wave you off, I can at least be a cheerleader."

"Cheerleader, huh?" I smiled wider. "Gonna wear some spankies with 'Cara' written across the butt?"

"You know it! I'm shaking my pom-poms for you, baby!"

"Too far. Put your pom-pom away."

"Nope, too late now—Cheer Mode activated! Two-four-six-eight, clear the gap or meet your fate!"

"Good lord."

"No, wait—I've got a better one! 'Cara, Cara, she's our gal, if she can't do it, FUCK!'"

I snort-laughed. "Now *that's* encouragement!"

"I'm supportive and honest!"

It was ridiculous, but it really did make me feel better. When it came to moral support, he might not be Holly—but Holly would never have agreed to this. I could get used to having a friend a little less addicted to responsible choices.

I took one last look down into the gap, then stood and clicked my headlamp to its brightest setting. Harsh LED white lit up the concrete like a found-footage horror film.

I backed up a few steps. Then a few more. My good friend Foot Sweat was back, chilling the gaps between my toes. My muscles trembled.

"Hey," Aiden said. *"You've got this."* His voice had lost its banter, replacing it with warm confidence.

No, not just confidence—*faith.*

Aiden *believed* in me.

I put my head down and ran.

My feet slapped loudly on the concrete, the gap bounding toward me like a tiger in the bobbing light. I hit the edge, launched myself into the air—

—and touched down neatly on the opposite side, stumbling a few steps before catching myself on the wall.

"Oh thank god!" Aiden gasped.

"Hey!" I pushed myself upright, flapping my hands to shake out the jitters. "I thought you believed in me!"

"I do!" Aiden protested. *"That doesn't mean I can't also be scared shitless!"*

His worry felt almost as good as his faith. "Aww, Aiden," I teased. "I didn't know you cared."

"I care deeply about you. Specifically, your ability to press play on my shows every night."

"Wow."

"But seriously—I like talking to you."

I made a face. "Cara Weaver: better than another year alone!"

"That's not what I mean." His voice went suddenly urgent and earnest. *"I mean even before I died—it's rare to find someone you can talk to about* real *shit, you know? That was always just Meredith for me."*

I crossed my arms. "I thought you were supposed to be *great* at talking. The whole reason I agreed to listen to you is that you were Mr. Steal-Your-Girl."

"I was!" he insisted. *"I could pull girls all day—I'm the undisputed king of game. But once I got them . . . I dunno. Nobody ever wanted to go deep. It was all movies, makeouts, or awkward silences."*

"So you're saying silence is an option?" But I felt a flush of pride.

"See? You even give me shit like Meredith."

"And you like that?"

"In moderation." But I could hear his smile.

"In that case, I've been compiling a detailed list of all your flaws. Do you want them alphabetical, or just freestyle?"

He huffed a laugh. *"Whatever. I'm just glad you didn't mash your potatoes, all right?"*

We continued onward through a section of factory that might

have been workshops or offices: rusted pipes that now carried only tetanus, old documents papier-mâchéd to the floor by time and damp. Another staircase led up to a third story.

At the far end, a catwalk leaned out over an industrial cavern, the concrete floor below dropping down into big squared-off bays. Giant rusting tanks lined the walls.

The deepest of the pits was a mess of boards and debris. Above it, a jagged hole loomed in the high ceiling, wooden bones sagging downward.

"That's where it happened," Aiden said.

"Jesus." It looked like half the third story had collapsed. My first thought was that Meredith was wrong—there was nothing she could have done for Aiden if she'd been here, except die alongside him. Their fight had probably saved her life. I wondered if he ever considered that angle.

"Yeah. It looked totally solid—there was even graffiti from people who'd been there before." He sighed. *"But everything's safe till it's not."*

I took an open-air concrete staircase down to the factory floor. With nothing to fence off or board up, some cops had affixed an absurd X of yellow police tape over the last pit. As if anyone would need reminding that something horrible had happened here.

The pit had a ladder inset in the side, and I climbed down, rusted rungs leaving blood-brown stripes across my palms. At the bottom, I stood, taking in the haystack mound of broken wood and twisted metal.

"Welp," Aiden said, too lightly. *"Here we are. Home sweet home."*

21

"COZY, HUH? I'VE *been meaning to spruce up the place—put up some posters, maybe get some curtains."* Aiden tried for a joking tone, but I could hear the strain beneath it. *"Pull up some rubble, make yourself comfortable."*

"Aiden . . ." There was an indentation in the side of the pile, the clean-sawed edges of beams, and I knew without asking that it was where the first responders had dug his body free. The removed sections lay piled loosely in the corner.

"I know." He sounded tired. *"But we're here. What experiments did you want to run?"*

"Right." The clock was ticking. I tore my gaze away from the wreckage—blander than I'd imagined and somehow the worse for it—and began pulling things out of my pack, staging them on the ground.

The pit was even darker than the rest of the factory, moonlight from the windows having to reflect again and again to make it down to us. It was like being inside some great beast, awash in the amniotic red of my headlamp. I got my camera set up on its tripod, where it could record a wide master shot to go with close-ups from my phone, and propped my flashlight up on a fallen chunk of flooring.

"We need physical, reproducible phenomena," I said, zeroing out Dad's kitchen scale. "Movement, sound—*some*thing."

We started running all the tests we'd done before. I watched the scale and panned around with the thermal scope. Scanned the radio static. Held my hands on the talking board's planchette, waiting for the spirit to move me. I zoomed in on the single cotton ball I'd placed under a clear plastic cup, in hopes of showing that any movement wasn't the result of strings or air currents.

Each time, the result was the same.

"Nothing." I sat down hard on the rubble pile, realizing too late the gruesome disrespect, yet too defeated to bother moving. "We made it all the way here, and we've still got fucking *nothing*."

"Hey, the night's not over yet." Aiden's voice was noticeably stronger here—that much of my theory, at least, had proven correct. *"Let's just do some more tests."*

"Those *were* all the tests! Everything I've been able to think of, and we still don't have anything that *looks* like anything!" Wetness on my cheeks announced that I'd officially lost the war for composure. I hid my face in my hands, realizing with an unhappy snort that in addition to Aiden watching, the camera was still filming. Maybe I could post it on my channel: exclusive footage of the exact moment my dreams died.

"Dude. Hey. You'll think of something." Aiden's voice dropped low, a purr of reassurance. *"You always do. It's, like, your thing."* He laughed gently. *"You're the most stubborn person I know."*

Something tingled faintly against the skin of my arm, just below the sleeve of my T-shirt. I slapped reflexively at it, then checked my hand for the telltale blood spot of a glutted mosquito. It came away dry.

But the tingle was still there.

My heart started to pound.

"Aiden?"

"Yeah?"

I almost didn't dare say it out loud. But I had to know. I took a slow, shuddering breath.

"Are you touching my arm?"

Immediately, the feeling vanished. *"Sorry!"* Then: *"Wait—you felt that?!"*

"Oh my god." My lungs couldn't remember how to inflate. "Aiden. Do it again."

"*Okay . . .*"

The feeling returned. It was almost impossibly gentle—less a touch than a buzzing, like static electricity that's gathered but not yet sparked. I was reminded of my mom's friend who did "energy work"—how she'd hold her hand so close to your cheek that you could feel what she called her aura, but which I was pretty sure was just body heat. While all animals had bioelectric fields—platypuses could even use them to sense prey—the idea that a human could sense and manipulate them was probably bullshit.

But ghosts?

"Holy *fuck*." I scrambled to dig my phone out of my pocket with shaking hands, activating the flashlight and record functions.

"*I don't get it,*" Aiden grumbled. "*Why couldn't I touch you before? And if I can touch* you *here, why can't I touch anything else?*"

I thought fast. "You're pulled to three points, right? Me, Meredith, and this place. Maybe we're like amplifiers—on our own, we can only sense so much, but if you put two of us together, the effect gets stronger." My eyes widened. "If we brought Meredith here—"

"*No!*" The word came hard and sharp. "*You're* never *bringing Meredith here. Got it?*"

"But if we had all three—"

"*Are you out of your* fucking *mind?! I died* here, *Cara. How do you think that would make her feel?*"

Irritation flashed through me—followed quickly by shame. Aiden was right. Meredith was my girlfriend . . . or something like that, anyway. It should have at least *occurred* to me to consider her feelings.

"Whatever," I snapped. "It doesn't matter. We don't need her. Here." I held out my palm. "Can you touch my hand?"

This time the feeling was so slight that I couldn't be sure I wasn't imagining it. "Are you doing it?"

"*Yeah, but it doesn't feel like anything. There's no resistance, my hand just passes through. Same as your arm.*"

"So why's it not as strong?" My mind raced. "Maybe my hands are too rough." I held out my arm, switching the phone camera to macro mode and moving in until it could focus on every little hair. "Try my arm again."

I felt the tingle immediately. It was light, halfway between a breeze and the brush of the softest possible fluff. And cold—like a photo negative of the heat from a hand just about to touch you.

And there, on the screen—one tiny section of arm hairs stood up, waving in the air.

It's working. I'd forgotten about catching my breath. Air wasn't a priority. All my attention was on that little spot on my forearm.

"Can you—" My mouth was a desert. I swallowed and tried again. "Can you move it?"

"Like this?" His touch slid side to side.

On the camera, the ripple of hair followed.

"Oh *shit.*" I almost sobbed with relief. This was real. This was *proof.*

The motion paused. *"Should I stop?"*

"No!" The word escaped as a gasp.

"You're shaking."

He was right. My whole body was vibrating with adrenaline and relief. "Just cold," I evaded. Then my brain spasmed again. "Cold!"

"What?"

I hunched over and grabbed the thermal scope from its case, holding it up against my phone's lens. After a moment's adjustment, my arm came into frame, blazing hot beneath the cooler sleeve of my shirt. "Touch me again!"

"That's what they all say." But again I felt the ghost of his hand on me, sweeping like a static charge across every hair.

On the screen, a patch of my arm changed color, going cool in a slow path.

A shadow in the shape of a hand.

Now a sob did break free, exploding from my lungs. I doubled over, curling protectively around the scope.

"Cara!" Aiden sounded panicked.

"We did it." I felt more tears on my cheeks, but this time I didn't care. "Oh fuck. We did it." I made myself sit up and smile. "We've got video proof."

"Yeah." Aiden's enthusiasm sounded a little forced.

I looked down at my phone, which was still recording, and hit the stop button. "Christ." I laughed shakily, scrubbing my wrist quickly across my cheeks.

I had it. The thing I'd been trying for since I was thirteen years old, something not even Carson Keene had managed: clear footage of a ghost. And it wasn't even a random clip that someone could write off as a hoax or camera artifact. It was completely predictable. Controllable. *Reproducible.*

With this one night, I'd pulled ghost hunting out of pseudo-science and into the real thing. And more than that: for the first time since getting that rejection letter, I had a future—one better than any college campus. Relief effervesced inside me like shaken soda, leaving my body limp.

I sat there, still half in the hole dug by Aiden's body, struggling to get a grasp on both the situation and my galloping heart.

"Cara?" Aiden asked.

I took a slow breath.

"This," I announced carefully, "changes everything."

22

HOLLY GAVE ME the stink eye over the top of her straw. "You could have *died*, Cara."

"That's why you've got an Apology Milkshake."

"I thought it was a *Bribe* Milkshake."

"That, too."

"Efficient," Elvis noted.

"*Cheap,*" Holly corrected.

I checked the time on my phone. "You two should get into position, in case she gets here early. Remember: we need to see if Meredith's an amplifier too, but *discreetly*. She can't know anything's up."

Holly crossed her arms. "You really think you can buy my morals with a milkshake."

"When it's Oreo?"

Holly glared but sucked on the straw, round cheeks inverting.

"Besides," I continued, "it's for *science*."

Elvis raised an eyebrow. "You know how many historical villains have said that, right?"

"Elvis, come on—how can you not want to know how this all works?"

A low blow, hitting him right in the engineer, but he kept his own arms folded in a mirror of Holly, serious expression at odds with the over-the-top '80s headband and way-too-short jogging shorts.

"Back me up here, Aiden," I pleaded.

"I mean . . . he's got a point?"

I cast my eyes to the sky in frustration. How was it that I'd only gotten three hours of sleep after last night's factory expedition, yet somehow *I* was the only one capable of seeing things clearly? "Look, we can hash out the ethics later, but right now, I need to run these experiments."

Holly sighed. "I *should* be finishing our chem take-home—but sure, by all means, let's do the tests we're *not* getting graded on." She shook her head. "Honestly, Cara. Where would you be without us?"

The words lanced through me, stinging and enraging in equal measure. She could only say things like that because she still didn't get it. Even with the weirdness of Aiden, this was all so familiar—her and Elvis, the milkshake, the banter. We'd been here a thousand times.

And soon we'd never be here again.

I wanted to scream, to shake her, to tie them both up so they'd have no choice but to stay with me forever. Instead, I said, "Will you please just go?"

Holly gave one more loud slurp of protest, then passed the sweating paper cup to Elvis. Together, they turned and disappeared down the path.

"Finally!" Aiden groused. *"Meredith could show up any minute!"*

I checked the time on my phone. "You worry too much."

"And you don't worry enough. Elvis is right—this is dangerous."

"Hey, *you* wanted dates. *I* need data. This gets us both."

"You've already got data! If people don't believe the factory videos, why would they believe any from this?"

"They don't *have* to believe. The videos are just to get experts intrigued enough to meet with us, so they can watch you do your magic tricks in person. And the factory is a totally different situation—we have literally *no* idea what you'll be able to do if Meredith and I combine amplification powers. Maybe the effect will be even stronger." And more replicable—it would be a lot easier to get Meredith into a lab than to convince a bunch of scientists to trespass into a condemned factory. Not that easier meant *easy*, but figuring out how to convince Meredith to help with my new career—and not, you know, hate me forever—was a problem for another day.

"I still don't like you involving Meredith," Aiden grumbled. *"If you screw this up and hurt her—"*

"Simmer down, Papa Bear. I've got as much to lose here as you do."

"I'm not worried about me, *you dingleberry! Meredith's sensitive!"*

I snorted.

"She is*! You think you grow a shell that hard if you don't feel every barb?"* I could practically hear him shaking his head. *"Do you know how many times I've had to coax her out of her room with nachos and* But I'm a Cheerleader *after somebody made a stupid joke at a party? She can't just brush shit off the way you can."*

As if that was what I did. But his description of Meredith's vulnerable underbelly made me feel simultaneously slimy and smitten. "It'll be fine," I said, with more confidence than I felt. "Also— what's *But I'm a Cheerleader*?"

Aiden made a shocked noise. *"Are you* sure *you're queer?"*

I glared at the air. "Are you an expert in that now, too?"

"Mer always said that Clea DuVall was—" He cut off as Meredith's car pulled into the lot. *"Shit, okay. Here we go."*

I smiled wide, walking toward the car as Meredith emerged. She slid off oversized aviators, the coolly casual motion making my stomach clench, and not with nerves.

"Hey!" Aiden squawked. *"Those are mine!"*

"Shh," I hissed, barely opening my mouth.

A string of drainage ponds defended the Waterbrook housing development against the Snoqualmie's annual flooding. To keep homebuyers at the bottom of the hill from thinking too hard about that threat, developers had turned the ponds into a park, adding a manicured trail and meticulous landscaping—the kind where every shrub has a little Latin name tag. After-work exercisers in largely unwarranted spandex hustled past brigades of stroller moms sipping iced chai.

Meredith regarded it all skeptically, doing her now-familiar movie-star lean on the open door. "The ponds, huh?"

I gave my brightest smile. "I know how much you love the great outdoors."

Meredith smirked, sunglasses dangling insolently. "Cara. This is not the great outdoors."

I gestured. "What? There's water. There's nature."

"There's a guy leaf blowing the trail. I'm pretty sure there's Wi-Fi. This isn't wilderness—it's a strip mall for plants."

My shoulders hunched. "Yeah, well—"

She moved out from behind her door, bumping my hip with hers and letting the smirk widen into a proper I'm-messing-with-you grin. "It's great."

That smile. I still hadn't gotten used to the way it appeared out of nowhere, like the sun peeking through sucker holes on a cloudy day.

"Good," I said, face warming. "Because I'm *way* too broke to have concerts be our go-to activity."

"Fine by me." She patted the car door. "I don't think my nerves can take driving Bloodbath into the city again this soon."

I blinked. "You called him Bloodbath."

She shrugged. "That's his name, right?"

Did I say warm? My face was *ablaze*.

I led her out of the parking lot and down the trail, its too-clean gravel crunching beneath our feet. At the first big bend, the corpse of an ancient tree had been allowed to remain where it had fallen, jutting artfully out into the water and creating a pier for sunbathing turtles.

I hopped up on it and began walking out toward the end, first normally, then turning sideways as the trunk narrowed.

Meredith followed, no questions asked—and goddamn if *that* wasn't attractive, too. Also convenient. When I'd made it as far out as I dared on the slippery bark, I stopped, looking around at the panorama of water gleaming in the afternoon sun, the people scurrying like multicolored ants along the trail.

"Nice, right?" I tried to sound casual and failed spectacularly.

"Yeah."

We stood in silence, taking it in.

A silence that continued to stretch.

Come on, I thought, using all my willpower not to reach into my pocket.

Meredith seemed to pick up on my nervous energy. Or maybe it was just the fact that we'd been standing on a log in a pond for longer than one customarily stands on a log in a pond. She risked a look over at me. "Are we . . . waiting for something?"

My pocket chirped.

Game time. I took a deep breath.

"Yeah," I said.

And I reached over and took her hand.

Meredith looked down at our interwoven fingers, then up at me, curious.

"I wanted to bring you here, to the most visible part of the park"—I nodded to the view around us—"so that everyone can see me holding hands with my girlfriend."

If Meredith's grin had been a sunbeam, her smile was a supernova, carving into those smooth cheeks. I felt my knees go weak, which maybe isn't the best physiological response when you're balanced above a pond full of highway runoff. I grinned back goofily.

Meredith squeezed my hand. "Girlfriend, huh?"

My stomach buzzed like a hive of bees, unsure if they wanted to sting or make honey. "I mean, if that's—if that's what you want us to be?"

This time her squeeze carried all the strength of her climber's grip. Like my hand was the only thing holding her above the drop.

"Yeah," she said.

One word, but it might as well have been a match to a Cara-shaped pool of kerosene. The rest of the world boiled away, consumed by the heat of her palm—the slightly longer fingers, the unfamiliar calluses. The way her fingertips curled around mine, hooking in, was completely intoxicating.

Almost enough to miss the sudden touch of cold along my arm.

For a moment, it actually failed to register—and then a different thrill shot through me.

Aiden. His fingers moved, raising the tiny hairs, the same way they had in the factory.

I'd been right—Meredith *was* an amplifier. I didn't need the factory—just contact with her. Possibilities shot through me: the two of us on tour together, in labs and news studios, holding hands as Aiden crushed skeptics' objections. The applause flooding over us.

Us.

I blinked, refocusing on Meredith's eyes once more. Happy. Trusting. Folded up in a smile, thinking my rush of excitement was about me and her. The way it *should* have been.

Guilt flooded in. No, not guilt—anger. At myself. Because Meredith didn't even know it, but she'd been right, back in that conversation below the tree house. This *should* be about just the two of us. I'd just asked this badass girl to be my girlfriend, and she'd said *yes*. How dare Past Me ruin this perfect memory for Future Me? What kind of asshole was I, anyway?

I hadn't lied. We *were* out here because I wanted us to be visible to everyone.

But more specifically, I wanted us to be visible to Holly where she crouched in the bushes recording, the glint of the thermal scope barely visible through marsh grass.

Meredith sensed my sudden change in mood and pulled back, loosening her grip.

"We don't have to," she said. "I mean—"

"No!" I grabbed tighter as Aiden's hand continued drawing patterns along my forearm. God, I was gross. "I want to."

Meredith just watched me, eyebrows angled with concern. I took a breath.

"I want to," I repeated. A ghostly finger trailed up my bicep. "We're *good*," I said firmly, hoping Aiden got the message.

In my pocket, my phone chirped twice more—Holly's tone. I

breathed a sigh of relief as Aiden's hand retreated, and managed to give Meredith a genuine smile. "This is just . . . very new."

Meredith's face softened, and she squeezed my hand again.

I nodded toward shore, and we shimmied back sideways, neither willing to let go of the other's hand.

Back on the path, things felt more . . . well, not *normal*. There was nothing *normal* about walking hand in hand with Meredith. It was impossible to be casual when every neuron of my brain not dedicated to the plan was freaking out at the way our bare forearms brushed against each other. It didn't matter that I was already gripping her hand like a goddamned eagle talon—I wanted *more* skin contact. I wanted us molded to each other, her elbow in mine, until the drifting continents of our bodies reformed Pangaea.

Meredith laughed.

"What?" I asked.

She smiled. "Just you."

I stuck my tongue out at her.

"Charming."

"Charming enough for *you*." I squeezed her hand.

"Apparently."

She was so beautiful—eyes crinkled, elven ears holding back that cascade of glossy black hair. Her hand felt made for mine, two interlocking puzzle pieces. It should have been a perfect moment.

But I still couldn't forget that the *other* reason for holding her hand was to make skin contact for the experiments, to better combine our Aiden-amplification abilities. I'd taken her love of rom-com gestures and created one that simultaneously made her feel special and got me the data I needed.

Killing two birds with one stone should have felt great.

Instead, it just felt like killing birds.

I was trying to figure out what to say next when I caught sight of familiar shapes over her shoulder. "Hey!" I chirped, a little too brightly. "Look who it is!"

Holly and Elvis came jogging along the path toward us. For all that Elvis had gone overboard with the 1980s Jazzercise look, it did the job of making the big headphones and the retro radio on his belt look like an aesthetic choice.

Holly popped out her earbuds. "Hey, you two!"

Again, I felt Meredith pull away slightly, her hand loosening as if to ask *Is this still okay?*

I grabbed on tighter. "Hey, guys! What're you up to?" As if their outfits left any question.

"Oh, just out for a run." Holly forced a smile at me, and I hoped Meredith didn't know her well enough yet to see through it.

Elvis shot me a significant glance, then bent over and began scrolling the dial on his radio, headphones still on. As he did, the world erupted into noise.

"ELVIS!" Aiden shouted. *"ELVIS! ELVIS! ELVIS! ELVIS!"*

I tried not to squint against the sudden onslaught. Aiden was definitely louder now, with my hand in Meredith's, just as he'd been at the factory. I watched Meredith anxiously in my peripheral vision, willing my body to stay loose even as every nerve fiber bent toward her like a flower.

This was it—the most dangerous moment. We'd proven Meredith was an amplifier, but there was still no way to know exactly how that might affect things. Maybe it would make Aiden strong enough for Elvis's radio to pick up his voice. But if the combination of our powers allowed *Meredith* to hear him, even faintly, I'd need to scramble to make her think she was imagining things, to keep from blowing up the whole plan.

But Meredith just nodded politely. "Cool."

"If by 'cool' you mean 'abhorrent and deviant.'" My voice seemed too loud, but it was hard to tell what a normal volume was with a ghost screaming in my ear. "*Some* of us go *walking,* like *civilized* people."

"I see that." Holly looked pointedly down at our clasped hands, then gave Meredith a smile that was almost genuine. In a teasing voice, she asked, "So, Meredith . . . how's it going? Anything new?"

To my shock, Meredith actually blushed, looking away and grinning self-consciously. It was positively adorable, and I found myself wishing Aiden would stop bellowing and let me enjoy it properly.

I let Holly monologue—a prearranged story about hijinks on an orchestra field trip—until Elvis made eye contact again. He gave a little headshake.

"All right, well, we don't want to interrupt," I interrupted, waving at the trail. "Carry on with your couple's torture session."

"Running isn't *that* bad," Holly said.

"If it didn't suck, they wouldn't have to make you do it in PE." I pulled Meredith along with me down the path.

Meredith looked back over her shoulder at their retreating forms. "Please never take me running as a date."

The disgust in her voice warmed my heart, but I replied, "Says the girl who dangled me off a cliff."

She turned back and grinned. "You loved it."

"I loved the after-party." I bumped my hip into hers, shoving her halfway off the path, then pulled her back and nodded in the direction Holly and Elvis had gone. "But yeah—agreed. Running is for masochists. But I guess they gotta burn off that courtship-couple energy somehow."

Meredith frowned. "Courtship couple?"

"That's what Holly calls it. They're saving their first kiss for marriage."

Her jaw dropped. "They don't even *kiss*?"

"I know, right?" I shrugged. "It's wild even by Catholic standards, but Holly loves a challenge. Calls it her 'Everest.'"

"And Elvis is into it?"

"Probably not. But he's into Holly, so . . ."

Meredith breathed out, impressed. "Jesus."

"Precisely."

She laughed and shook her head. "Could *you* do that?"

I took a step away and gestured to myself with my free hand. "And deprive my girlfriend of all *this*?"

Meredith continued shaking her head at my ego, but yanked me back sharply, making me stumble into her. My adrenals surged at the contact. Her face was so close . . . it would be so easy to just angle my chin up . . .

"Honestly, I'm amazed they haven't spontaneously combusted," I said hastily, scrambling to keep from doing the same. "But their plan is to get married next summer."

"Wow."

"Yeah."

We crossed one of the outflow streams, shoes clanking on the bridge's bowed metal grating. Meredith paused, leaning back with her elbows draped over the railing. "You think you'll get married someday?"

"Um. Maybe?" That sounded better than *hopefully* and a lot better than *please God don't let me die alone with a dozen cats and a Chris Hemsworth body pillow.* "You?"

"I'd like to." Her face twisted in a faraway expression that wasn't quite a smile.

I squeezed her hand. "What's that look?"

"Nothing." She glanced away, embarrassed. "I just—Aiden and I argued about it, one time."

I jumped a little at his name, but managed to ask, "About marriage?"

She snorted, now smiling a little for real. "You don't know how many ways there are to be wrong until you've been Aiden's little sister."

I could almost hear the sound of Aiden restraining himself. "What was the argument?"

She looked out at the water. "I mean, I don't think we even actually disagreed. He just liked to argue. I wanted to rewind and watch the wedding scene from *Crazy Rich Asians* again, and he poked me, like"—she made a face—"'Why would anyone even *want* a wedding? Isn't it more romantic if staying together is a choice, not a contract?'"

Aiden playing devil's advocate? I could see that. "What'd you say?"

"I said 'Spoken like a cishet guy who's never had to fight for it.'" She smirked, then sobered. "And, like—yeah, okay, I get his point. But also . . . fuck it, you know?" She ran her free hand through her hair. "Life's hard. If you're lucky enough to find somebody you actually want to spend it with, fucking *celebrate* that shit. Maybe weddings are cliché bullshit. But they make us cry for a reason."

"Totally." I wondered what Meredith would look like getting married. Would she go traditional? Some strapless dress dripping down her like melted ice cream? Or would she butch it up, slim and devastating in a white tux?

Jesus, what was I even *thinking*? *Holly* was the one who wanted marriage and kids and the full Americana sampler platter. All I'd ever wanted was *away*—away from high school, away from Stossel, away from most everybody I'd ever known.

But maybe not away from Meredith.

She tilted her head back and stared up at the sky, jacket falling open to frame her white T-shirt. A spring breeze tugged at her hair, pulling it across her face in long calligraphy strokes. Arms spread out like she owned the world. Or at least this corner of it. *My* corner of it.

"The only times everybody gets together to talk about how great you are," she murmured, "are weddings and funerals. And at one of those, you're dead."

Dead. Right. I blinked hard—*focus, Cara.*

"Come on." I pulled Meredith across the bridge and down into a grassy patch full of dandelions in various stages of seeding. Oh-so casually, I snatched at several of the puffs, until I had a handful of white fluff. Then I held my hand out flat, watching for the agreed-upon counterclockwise swirl that would mean our amplification was letting Aiden affect the physical world.

Instead, the breeze caught it, scattering tiny parachute seeds out across the pond.

Shit. I grabbed another handful, this time shielding it with my body.

I realized Meredith was watching me, one eyebrow cocked curiously.

So much for casual. "I, uh, like dandelions." That earned a ghostly snort from Aiden. Well, at least I knew he hadn't blinked out.

"Dandelions?" Meredith's other eyebrow rose to match.

"I just think they're neat." Great, now I was the Marge Simpson potato meme. I took a last glance at the unmoving fluff, then blew it away and let go of Meredith's hand long enough to slip free of my backpack. "Hey, let's try something." I reached inside and pulled out the last test.

If Meredith's eyebrows rose any higher, they were going to become a hairband. "A Ouija board?"

"I thought, since we didn't find any ghosts in the graveyard, we could try again."

"Now?" Meredith frowned. "Did somebody die here?" I could literally see her body curling inward at the reminder of Aiden.

"No! I mean—I don't think so? I just . . . thought it would be fun." It sounded flimsy even to my own ears, but I wasn't going to let this opportunity go without squeezing in every test I could. I set the board down and pulled out the planchette.

"Okay . . ." Meredith was still frowning. The expression twisted my lungs like a side stitch.

"Here." I grabbed her hand and pulled it down to cover mine on the planchette.

That brought a smile back, if not quite as strong. Great—let her think this was just another elaborate excuse for hand-holding. I rushed past the guilt. "Just rest your hands on mine. Don't try to push. Let it move on its own."

She stacked her other hand on top. For a moment, nothing happened.

Then, ever so slowly, the pointer began to drift.

Yes! Come on, Aiden . . .

Meredith's eyes went wide.

"Just stay relaxed!" I yelped, doing a terrible job of it myself.

The planchette drifted upward, coming to rest briefly on the letter D before looping up and around to K, then down to either U or V.

Meredith frowned. "It's not spelling anything."

"That's okay." In order to make sure I couldn't subconsciously influence the experiment, I'd had Elvis pick a code and write it down for Aiden without telling me. I wouldn't put it past him to choose a bunch of random letters.

"No, really," Aiden whispered. *"It's not me."*

The planchette slid off the board without bothering with goodbye.

Meredith looked over apologetically. "Sorry."

"Don't be." I squeezed her hands.

"You're not disappointed?" Her lip twisted upward, more nervous than smirk.

The expression melted me. Here I was, yet again being a total weirdo on our dates, and *she* was worried about *me*? I let go of the planchette and flipped my bottom hand around, cupping hers and squeezing.

"Meredith," I said, expression grave. "Do you seriously think I could be disappointed right now?"

Once more, the clouds on her face parted. Relief flooded through me, and in its wake I realized how thoroughly soaked my armpits were. The sudden rush of victory and embarrassment was too much, and I couldn't help laughing.

To my surprise, Meredith laughed as well. And was it just me, or did she sound as relieved as I did? Suddenly it occurred to me that as nervous as I was about all this, it was still only our first date since the kiss at the climbing wall. Maybe she'd worried I'd freak out.

As if *that* were the thing making this situation weird. The idea only made me laugh harder. We collapsed into each other, giggling without knowing exactly why.

Yet underneath the laughter, something still poked at me, like a pine needle in a sock. Because while Meredith was laughing with me—was it really *with* me, if she didn't know the truth? Did anything happening right now count when I was keeping a secret?

Don't be stupid, I told myself. *Everybody has secrets.* What mattered was that I'd done it: Everything had gone exactly as planned. I had my data. Meredith was charmed. Total victory, all around.

As long as I didn't look too closely.

So stop looking, dummy. Just enjoy yourself for once.

Meredith turned toward me. This close, our noses almost touched, her dark eyes gleaming with reflected afternoon light. She cocked her head. "What are you thinking about?"

Don't look too closely.

I shook my head slowly.

"Nothing important."

And I lifted my lips to hers.

23

"TRY THIS ONE." Holly tossed a sweater at me, then disappeared back inside her closet.

I sighed and held it up. For all that Holly was a fashion queen in her own way, "fuzzy" was not a style we shared. I stuck it in the Goodwill pile. "Are we done yet?"

"As if. You've been putting this off ever since Aiden showed up. I need to start making decisions." She reappeared, still in her jogging wear from the park, holding a stripey knit top up against her chest. "Keep or throw?"

"Keep."

She looked down at it dubiously. "Really?"

Yes, I wanted to say, *because you wore it on my birthday last year, when we went to the roller rink and you laughed so hard that grape soda came out your nose, and the idea of you giving it away is another reminder that you won't be here for my* next *birthday.* But what I said was, "It makes your boobs look bigger."

"*Whoa, hey, what? Boobs? If you need an impartial judge, I volunteer as tribute. I'm a preeminent scholar in the field of mammary appreciation.*"

". . . and Aiden has rejoined the conversation," I noted dryly.

Holly rolled her eyes, but returned the shirt to the closet.

I turned back to my laptop, which still had the scope video up on the screen. I hit the space bar, playing it again. Though the little heat blobs of me and Meredith were pixelated with artificial zoom, the flickering cold blotch of Aiden was unmistakable behind me, solidifying into icy blue as it touched my arm.

This was even better than the factory. His spirit was more clearly defined—a definite boy shape. And it was out in public, in the middle of the water, where everything would be harder to fake. Visions of me and Carson danced through my mind, in labs or on stages presenting our research to important people. Scientists. The president. Hank and John Green. We just—

A shirt caught me in the side of the head.

"Hey!" I pulled it off my face and looked over to where Holly stood in the closet doorway, hands on hips.

"Are you gonna help or what?"

"I *am* helping!"

"No, you're watching that stupid video again."

My hackles rose. Here I was, watching Holly downsize her wardrobe in preparation for moving, my heart being ripped from my chest with every donated skirt, and *I* was the bad friend? "Sorry," I snarked, "I was distracted by proof of the supernatural. But by all means, let's focus on whether you'll need a second Hello Kitty hoodie at Bible college."

Holly's eyes widened—then narrowed. "You've only *got* that video because I helped you. We've been focused on your stuff for weeks, but I ask you for help with one thing, and suddenly it's too boring for you?"

"Your words, not mine." I was trolling, and I knew it, but seriously—could she not see how much this sucked for me? In addition to being another reminder of her leaving, she might as well have thrown her acceptance letter in my face instead of a horse camp T-shirt. (*Catholic* horse camp, of course—can't have good Christian girls riding unsaved horses.) Holly's room had always been a safe haven, but now every potato-shaped animal plushy sawed across my nerves like a cheese grater.

Holly crossed her arms. "I *lied* for you."

"Acting isn't lying. We've been over this."

"Yeah? Well, maybe I don't want to anymore."

The words shot through me like a bolt of lightning. "What?"

"Maybe I don't want to help you sneak around behind Meredith's back."

"Thaaaaaaat's not good." Aiden might as well have been voicing my own thoughts.

"Whoa. Hey. Slow down." I rose to my knees, hands up in surrender. "Look, I'm sorry I got snippy. I'll help, I promise." I picked up the shirt she'd thrown. "This one? The pink is great on you, but it's a little young-looking for college unless you're gonna go full Lolita. Put away childish things, right?"

But Holly wasn't distracted. "I mean it, Cara."

"Okay, fine! We've run all the tests I've got anyway. That part is done. All I need your help with now is the promposal, and you're done, I swear."

Holly looked away.

"Do something!" Aiden demanded.

Panic swelled inside me. "Holly. Hol." I knee-walked over, grabbing her hands. "We've already got the whole plan. I can't do this without you."

Holly bit her lip. "It just feels gross."

This was bad. Forget about my own frustration—I *needed* Holly.

"Counterpoint:" I argued, squeezing her hands. "It literally *can't* be gross. It's theologically impossible."

A transparent appeal to her hobbyhorse, but Holly perked up like cat ears at a can opener. "How?"

"Think about it: Aiden's only here by the grace of God, right? He's basically Meredith's guardian angel."

"I'm angelic as fuck," Aiden agreed, at the same time Holly said, "We don't know that."

I waved away both comments. "He's a dead relative. That's *classic* guardian angel material. And if he *is* her guardian angel, then whatever he does *has* to be God's plan, right? Which makes us helping him part of the plan as well."

Holly shook her head, but at least she didn't look angry anymore.

"You're totally ignoring free will—his and ours. What if this is all a test?"

"What if it is? If there's a decent chance he was literally *sent by God to help her,* then even if we can't be totally sure, don't we have an obligation to assist?"

"You can play that game either direction, though. Maybe God sent him to us so that we can change his mind."

"And maybe God sent him because *I fucking need this!*" I snapped. "What happened to 'God's got time for you, Cara'?" Holly scowled, but I rushed on before she could say anything, softening my voice. "Look—maybe you're right. But if there's no way to be *sure,* we might as well trust Aiden when he says he knows why he's here, right? Especially after all he's suffered." I saw the reminder of Aiden's lonely year dig into Holly's pudding-soft heart, and went for the kill. "Plus, true or false: Meredith's gonna love the promposal."

Holly's Grumpy Cat frown remained, but she was too honest to deny it. "True."

"Then regardless of what's going on with Aiden—how could making her happy be wrong?" I squeezed again. "Please, Hol. I need you. *We* need you."

Holly held out for one more second, then sighed. "Fine. But no more experiments—just a kick-A proposal, then a fun prom. A *normal* one. No ghost stuff."

"I promise," I said. An easy one to make, given that it had always been the plan.

Holly tugged me forward. "Now help me figure out my boot situation."

I followed Holly gratefully into the closet, squatting down beside her as she studied her shoe rack with the intensity of a bomb squad. It felt good to be next to her, but there was also a distance there. A crack that I knew would just keep widening, until she was too far away to see.

"*That was close,*" Aiden breathed.

It didn't matter. I had everything I needed to get everyone what *they* needed: Aiden would get to fulfill his mission. Meredith would get swept off her feet. And I'd get to have a future—one that wouldn't end as sad and empty as Holly's closet. Was that really so much to ask? After all I'd been through—all I was *about* to go through, with Holly leaving—hadn't I earned that?

My own words expanded like a balloon inside the enclosed space, jamming up against every shirt and dress, pressing into me.

How could that be wrong?

24

"WHERE ARE WE going this time?"

I half closed my eyes, doing my best to look mysterious. "You'll see."

Meredith tapped the steering wheel. "Most people like a little more direction when they're going fifty-five."

"Good thing you're not most people."

She grinned, and I fell so hard into that smile that I almost missed our turn after all. "Right! Here!"

Tires chirped and threw gravel as we tore into the Bear Mountain parking lot. It was afternoon on a Saturday, and cars packed every spot, spilling out to line the road in a parade of Subarus and roof racks. We waited for an old couple dressed like a prescription-drug commercial in matching Patagonia jackets to get into their car, then swooped in to take their spot.

"Voilà!" I gestured toward the looming wall of trees. "I *dare* you to say this isn't the great outdoors."

Meredith smirked. "We're going hiking?"

"Nah, I'm just really into vault toilets—I think it's that thump the poop makes when it hits the bottom."

Aiden groaned, but at least he didn't comment—I may not have been able to bar him from watching this time, given how important it was to him, but I'd made it *exceedingly* clear that any distractions risked blowing the whole plan.

Meredith shook her head. "You say the most romantic things."

"It's a talent." I unlocked my phone and sent a one-word text, then pocketed it and popped my door.

Meredith followed me out. "I didn't bring a pack."

"I've got it handled."

She eyed my own baglessness—half-skeptical, half-intrigued.

I hooked her arm with mine. "Come on."

I led her over to the trailhead, where a covered sign mapped the snarl of hiking trails spiderwebbing the grandiosely named hill. I made a show of consulting it. "The Coyote Creek Spur sounds good, don't you think?"

". . . Sure?"

"Great!" I bowed, sweeping out an arm. "After you."

"Right." Her suspicious look intensified, but she moved obligingly past me.

Our shoes drummed against dark earth packed tight. Overhead, maples rustled, carving the sunlight into slips and slices. There must have been hundreds of people tromping this mountain, but right here there was nothing but the calls of birds, the background hum of the highway, and the distant barks of excited dogs.

We rounded a bend in the trail, and Meredith jerked to a stop so quickly that I would have run into her if I hadn't been expecting it.

"What." The word was a laugh and a demand.

"What is it?" I asked innocently.

Ahead, leaning against a tree, stood a thrift-store wizard. A ratty gray bathrobe wrapped his body, while a Halloween witch's hat tilted precariously back on his head, making room for the non-negotiable rockabilly quiff. The only part of his outfit that *didn't* look old and moth-eaten was the fake gray beard, because who wants to wear a used beard? His staff still bore several awkward protrusions where twigs had been hastily snapped off.

"Hail, travelers!" he called in a ridiculous accent. "Come—listen to my tale!"

Meredith laughed again, incredulously.

"You stand in the presence of Elvisium the Mysterious!" the wizard announced. "Master of the arcane! Sage of the lost arts! Behold!"

He flung a hand toward the ground, which erupted in bangs and sparks. *"Magic!"*

"Such power!" I marveled.

"Oh my god." Meredith tried to sound derisive, but she was grinning from ear to ear. "If you have to yell 'magic' when you do it . . ."

"Come, come!" Elvis beckoned with his staff.

We approached. Elvis waggled eyebrows penciled to thick peaks.

"You seem like hearty adventurers," he crooned creakily. "Will you accept my mystical quest?"

Meredith wrinkled her nose. "Is that supposed to be a British accent?"

"It's a wizard accent!" Elvis protested.

"You sound like Mr. Burns married Mrs. Doubtfire," I admitted.

"Magic!" he yelled, and threw another handful of Pop-Its at our feet.

"Hey!" I jumped back.

"Only the boldest explorers will complete this quest and uncover their heart's great desire!" Elvis reached into his robe and pulled out a rolled scroll. He held it out to Meredith. "Do you accept?"

She glanced at me, then took it, unrolling it to reveal a hand-drawn treasure map, its edges ripped and burned, the paper lined and stained with age. (Or by being crumpled and dipped in tea.)

"Oh wow," I said. "Is that this tree?" I pointed to the big tree that marked the starting point, a dotted line leading away from it.

Meredith's face twitched through several expressions I couldn't quite read before arriving at a half smirk. She shook her head as if she couldn't believe any of this.

"And now," Elvis announced, "I vanish!" He pulled one side of the robe up across his face like a cartoon vampire, then turned and scampered toward the bushes. At their edge, he turned back and threw down more Pop-Its. *"Magic!"* Then he disappeared into the woods, high-stepping to keep his robe from snagging on the underbrush.

"You guys are ridiculous," Meredith said.

"Hey, I'm just out for a hike. I'm not responsible for wizards with speech impediments." I nodded to the map. "We should probably follow that, though."

"Right." She darted in and kissed me. "Never keep a quest waiting, right?" Her voice wobbled faintly with emotion, and I knew I was killing it.

The map led us along the trail, through several intersecting paths. Each time, a drawing of some obvious feature—a big rock, a log bridge, a waterfall—indicated which way to go.

At the bleached corpse of a Volkswagen Beetle, Meredith paused. "The line ends over there." She pointed into the brush where a faint game trail was visible.

"Well, we're explorers, right?"

Meredith gave me another of those vaguely disbelieving looks, then stepped off the trail, ducking under branches.

Cedar sprays grabbed at our clothes and I ducked low, staying in Meredith's wake. She rubbed at her face. "Letting me clear the spider webs, I see."

"There's chivalry, and then there's spiders. Just keep doing what you're doing."

The screen of trees gave way to a small clearing. Beneath a sprawling oak, a clear plastic Tupperware hung at head height, strung up with shiny red ribbon.

"Whaaaaaaat the eff," Meredith moaned happily.

"Careful. You're starting to sound like Holly."

Meredith stepped forward and pulled down the Tupperware. She popped the lid, and her eyes went round. "A *maple bar*?"

"Man, this quest seems made for you."

She turned toward me, confusion overriding her excitement. "How'd you know these are my favorite?"

Shit. Meredith and I had never gotten donuts together—never even discussed them.

"Guess it's more magic," I dodged. "Anyway, who doesn't love maple bars? Hey, is there anything else in that box?"

Still eyeing me like a mall cop, she turned slowly back to the box.

"A compass?" She pulled out a little watch-sized compass—another of Dad's survivalist stocking stuffers. "What are we supposed to do with this?"

"Dunno. But I know what to do with donuts."

She withdrew the single maple bar, staring at it as if it might start talking, then held it out toward me. "You want half?"

"Nah, I'm good. You go for it."

She didn't need to be told twice. She bit in, and her suspicion melted into a look bordering on orgasmic.

"*Fuck,*" she moaned, setting all sorts of machinery buzzing inside me.

"That wizard knows his shit, huh?"

"Right. The wizard." She gave me another look, skeptical but pleased, and took another bite. "You know, you—mmph!"

Her cheeks bulged, brows lowering in confusion as she reached into her mouth and pulled out a tiny cylinder sheathed in plastic wrap.

"Whoa!" I exclaimed. "Another clue!"

Meredith swallowed, then set the rest of the pastry back in the Tupperware. She unrolled the plastic wrap, then the slip of paper it protected.

"*Elves and bears, two hundred paces,*" she read.

"Weird," I deadpanned. "So is that a warning, or . . . ?"

Meredith's face went blank, eyes distant. Then: "It's directions. Elves and bears—both live at the North Pole. We need to go north."

"Damn." I was legitimately impressed. "You're good at this."

"No." She shook her head and gave me a little smile. "*You're* good at this."

She stepped in close and kissed me again, slower and deeper this time. She tasted like sugar and syrup. I pressed closer as our stomachs made contact, my arms going around her, feeling the ripple of her ribs, the suggestive ridge of a bra strap. Hidden geographies.

My mouth opened wider, breathing her in. She slid a hand down my back, curling under the edge of my shirt and against my bare skin, running torturously along the waistband of my pants, lighting fires wherever it touched.

How could this be all I'd ever wanted, and I'd never known? I lifted a hand, brushing strands of hair behind the delicate curve of her ear—and who would have thought an *ear* could be sexy? My lips slid over and down her neck, rooting into crew-neck cotton for her collarbone—

Then she was peeling herself away, and it was like gravity yanking me backward off the climbing wall all over again. But she just grinned, cheeks flushed, and held the clue up between us.

"Can't keep the wizard waiting."

"He's a wizard," I said, breathless. "He's got, like, *millennia.*" But I collected the Tupperware and the ribbon while she finished the maple bar in two enormous bites. She consulted the compass.

"North." She pointed off through the trees. "Help me count?"

We measured our steps. At a hundred and ninety-three, another scroll hung from a tree branch, ribbon glittering like a forgotten Christmas ornament. Meredith unrolled it eagerly.

"There is a house in New Orleans, three hundred paces." This time she didn't even have to think, just pointed. "'House of the Rising Sun.' The sun rises in the east."

We tromped through a relatively brush-free section, the needle-covered ground spongy, until we intersected a proper hiking trail, a new clue folded into an origami ninja star and tied up with more ribbon. Meredith unfolded it.

"Austin music festival, seventy-five paces." She grinned. "South by Southwest. Your wizard goes to concerts."

"Hey, I told you, he's not *my* wizard. And wouldn't you, if you had"—I wiggled my fingers and mimicked Elvis's wizard voice— *"magic?!"*

She grabbed my collar and pulled me in close for a kiss. As we broke away, she murmured, "There's a lot of things I'd do."

"Um," I managed, but she'd already turned and begun counting her steps.

The trail emerged into a clear-cut overlooking the valley, old enough for grass to grow up between the stumps and mounds of dried branches. Just off the trail, a red-and-white tablecloth had been draped over a stump, pinned down by a set of binoculars, two bottles of soda, and a bag of Maui onion potato chips. Small logs had been pulled up on either side to form seats.

Holly and Elvis stood by the picnic, wearing hiking boots beneath their formal best, Elvis still rocking the fake beard. Holly held her violin and Elvis an acoustic guitar. As we stepped into view, they began playing.

Meredith stood with mouth dropped open. Then her brows quirked, head tilting slightly as she recognized the song. "Is that Sly Gaze?"

"'Lay It Down,'" I confirmed—the top track off her favorite album, rearranged into a sentimental acoustic version.

"This is amazing," she breathed.

"I only work with the best." I offered my arm like a Victorian gentleman. "Shall we?"

I led us up to the table, seating her on one of the logs as if pulling out her chair at a fancy restaurant. Holly and Elvis backed away, still playing.

Meredith's expression was unreadable: a smile, but one that looked almost like it hurt—a bunch of emotions mixed together, like combining fountain drinks into a graveyard. "I can't believe you did all this for me."

"Believe it." I held out the binoculars. "One last thing."

She took them, then followed my sideways nod.

Thanks to the clear-cut, a section of highway was visible here—a very *specific* section, with a very specific boulder. One that now had three new words, in fresh red paint.

MEREDITH REYES: PROM?

Her entire body froze, fingers going white around the binoculars. A moment passed. Then two.

"Do you see it?" I prompted.

Her chest hitched in a ragged breath. I realized the binoculars were shaking, eyepieces jammed into her sockets, just as the first tear leaked out from beneath them.

"Meredith?"

She doubled over and began to sob.

25

"MEREDITH?" SUDDENLY I couldn't breathe, either. She looked gut-shot, arms wrapped around her stomach. Two red circles rimmed her eyes where the binoculars had pressed.

"Don't just sit there!" Aiden yelled. *"Talk to her!"*

I looked to Holly and Elvis for help, but they stood wide-eyed, silent instruments still held in playing position.

"Meredith," I repeated dumbly, as if her name might call her back from whatever storm had taken her. I leaned across the stump table and closed my hand gently on her arm.

"I'm sorry," she husked, raw and hollow. "I'm sorry, I'm sorry—"

"Hey—no." I moved so I was squatting beside her log, hand resting on her back. Each breath heaved like something tearing itself apart. "What's wrong?"

"Nothing," she gasped.

"Right," I joked gently. "This is just the effect I have on girls."

She shook her head, not looking at me. "It's not you. This is—this is all amazing. It's just me, I just . . ." She shook her head again, harder, then sat upright with a jerk, as if bucking someone off her back. She scrubbed angrily at her eyes with her palms.

I risked reaching up and pulling one of them away by the wrist. "You just what?"

She looked away, wiping her nose. "When we were little . . . Aiden used to draw me treasure maps, with these little rhyming clues. He'd pretend he'd found them in the attic, or the woods.

He'd follow along with me, acting surprised, and eventually we'd find some treasure he'd buried. It was how our whole exploration thing started."

I felt sick.

"*Shit,*" Aiden added weakly.

"I thought I was fine, that I could roll with it, but then I saw how you painted the rock, and it reminded me of painting it with him and his friends, and it's so stupid, but it just hit me . . ." She twisted her wrist around to hold my hand. "I'm sorry."

"Stop saying that. You have nothing to be sorry for. *I'm* sorry."

"*No.*" She squeezed painfully hard, turning at last to look fiercely into my eyes. "You couldn't have known."

Except that of course I could have. I'd let Aiden plan the fucking proposal. When he'd said she liked puzzle hunts, I hadn't questioned it. Plenty of people were into that sort of thing. But the maps, the clues, knowing her favorite kind of donut—what kind of idiot was I to not realize that having his fingerprints all over this, his vaunted "inside intel," might bite us in the ass? Even the one idea I'd contributed—painting the rock—had ties to him.

Meredith crying, snotting onto the back of her hand—this was all my fault. Someone call a janitor, because I was officially garbage.

Meredith must have seen it on my face, because she yanked on my wrist. I overbalanced and had to put my free hand down to catch myself, old bark and pine needles digging into my palm.

"This is *my* shit." Meredith thrust her head forward like a hawk. "You made me the most amazing proposal ever. *I'm* the one who's fucking it up." She looked away. "I always think I'm over it. I can drive his car, walk past his bedroom every day, and be fine. But then I'll . . . I'll see the fucking *gas station* we went to, or somebody wearing the same shoes, and it's like this wave just hits me, and I can't breathe, and I just—I—" She squeezed her eyes shut. "It doesn't even make *sense!*"

Now it was my turn to pull on her hand. "Of course it does."

"It's been a *year.*"

"Some things don't get better."

She collapsed into my arms. I knelt awkwardly on shards of bark, the remains of a thousand trees whose own lives had been cut short. Why these trees and not others? There was no reason.

"*Tell her*—" Aiden began, then hesitated, clearly at a loss. "*Tell her that . . .*"

I glared out over the crown of her hair and gave my head a single shake. He went mercifully silent.

Meredith's body shook, jerking beneath my hands in silent little dying-animal gasps. I held as tight as I dared, trying to take her weight onto me. But of course that was impossible. Nobody could carry this for her.

But I wanted to. Wanted that, and more. Because for all that it hurt to see her so wounded, it also felt *right*—to have her pressed against me like this. It seemed gross and shameful that any part of me could enjoy this, but there was no denying the feel of her body against mine, the intimacy of it. It wasn't sexual—or at least not *just* sexual—it was that this was *her.* Showing me what she kept locked away, so raw and real.

If she had to cry, I wanted it to be on my shoulder. Did that make me a bad girlfriend, or a good one?

At last, her breathing steadied. I felt it in the whisk of her exhalations, cool across the damp she'd left on my neck. I breathed deep, matching her rhythm and pulling it slower still, and tried to find the right words.

There weren't any. I gave up and spoke anyway.

"I know nothing I can say will help," I murmured into her hair. "But you don't have to pretend to be okay. Not with me."

She pulled back, slipping free of my arms until she was just holding my hand again.

She studied me, gaze still so intense. A streak of dirt slashed across one cheekbone, like eye black on a football player. Her eyelids were puffy, her face mottled and blotchy. It was impossible not to notice the blob of snot clinging just inside her left nostril. It was not, by any stretch of the imagination, a good look.

So why did I feel like my heart was going to explode? I wanted to crack open my ribs and tuck her safely inside. Hide her from the world.

She nodded once, decisively.

"Yes."

I squinted. "What?"

A familiar smirk twisted up her dirty cheek. "Yes, I'll go to prom with you."

"Oh!" I blinked. "Uh . . . awesome?"

"I mean, how could I not," she continued, "after you got down on one knee to propose?"

I realized I was, in fact, crouched like Prince Charming. I laughed and attempted to get to my feet, but she dragged me off-balance and into her lap. I twisted around so that I was seated on her thighs, and she pulled my head down and kissed me. Her mouth was thick and wet, her cheeks glazed and slightly sticky with tears.

It was amazing.

After a breathless moment, I realized Holly and Elvis were still standing there, pointedly not watching. I broke reluctantly away, sitting up with my arms around Meredith's neck, hers laced around my waist.

Meredith smiled. "Not exactly how you imagined this going, huh?"

I shrugged. "It could have been worse."

She scoffed. *"How?"*

I leaned forward until our lips almost touched, took a slow, pointed inhalation of her breath, and murmured, "You could have already eaten those onion chips."

26

THE FOUR OF us walked back through the forest together. As we reached the trailhead, Holly grabbed my arm. "Can I talk to you for a sec?"

"Sure . . . ?"

She pulled me all the way across the parking lot and out of sight behind the green-roofed outhouse. The smell of shit and hand sanitizer drifted lazily down from the chimney.

"Well, *this* is a lovely spot," I observed.

"What the *h*, Cara?" Holly's voice was a furious hiss, cheeks pinned down in a scowl.

"What?" I stepped back in surprise.

"Is Aiden here?" she demanded.

"*Yes . . . ?*" Aiden sounded as confused as I felt. I nodded.

"Good. Because you need to tell her about him. Right now."

"*What?*" Aiden squawked. "*No!*"

Holly gestured to the air around us. "Can't you two see what you're doing to her?!"

"*I'm* not doing anything!" I protested. "It's not my fault he died!"

"But you could *help*." She crossed her arms. "And you're not."

"I *can't*! I promised Aiden I wouldn't tell without permission. You want me to break my promise? How does that fit with the Holly Pham School of Ethics?"

Holly bit her lip. "Sometimes you have to. For the greater good."

"*What* greater good? Meredith was *already* sad about Aiden. *We* didn't do that, and it's not going away. So now you want me to make *Aiden* sad as well? Deny him his *literal* dying wish, just so you don't have to feel awkward?"

"Yeah!" Aiden agreed. *"Don't be selfish!"*

Holly looked uncomfortable, but she still had her head set low between her shoulders. Bulldozer Mode. "It's not right," she insisted. "She deserves to know." She brightened suddenly. "Wait—*I* didn't promise anything! *I* could tell her!"

"The hell you can!" Aiden snapped.

I held up my hands. "Holly, come on."

"Either you can tell her, or I can."

"And Meredith's gonna take your word for it?" Aiden's tone sizzled with acid. *"Because I'm sure as hell not helping you fuck up our plan. Cara, tell Joan of Arc to enjoy sounding crazy—I'm sure that'll make Meredith feel* way *better."*

I relayed a diplomatic translation.

"I can show her the videos," Holly shot back, glaring around at the empty air. "Of the experiments."

"Because two-dollar magic dice and a blob in the air are definitely *proof of her dead brother. Hey, maybe you can hook her up with a Nigerian prince while you're at it—I hear he's rich, he just needs your bank account number."*

"Fucking hell." I put my hands over my face. "Everybody just *shut up* for a second!"

To my surprise, they did.

I took a breath.

What did I even want out of this? Keeping things secret was Aiden's obsession, not mine. Telling Meredith about him . . . well, it probably wouldn't go *well*, but if I could get him on board, at least I wouldn't seem like a total nutjob. And I was going to have to tell her eventually—preferably before I published my findings, especially if I wanted any chance of her helping me amplify him for Carson and the rest of the world. Plus—she *would* want to know, right? Holly wasn't wrong about that. So maybe telling her *would* be the right thing.

But it would also be messy. And I couldn't afford mess right now. Between our new relationship, the prom plan, and trying to get all the proof I could before the Carson meeting, there were just too many plates in the air.

I lowered my hands.

"Aiden," I said. "She's right. Meredith deserves to know."

"*She* deserves *to be* happy," Aiden snapped back, "*which is* not *the same thing. And what about what* I *deserve? Trying to fulfill my earthly mission, remember?*"

I thought fast. "Maybe we can have both. Prom is in two weeks—let's just keep it quiet until then, okay? We can tell her afterward."

"*Are you even listening?*" Aiden growled. Holly looked equally put out.

"Holly, come *on.*" I pulled her to the corner of the outhouse, making her look out with me toward the cars. Meredith stood with Elvis, laughing as he took pictures of her in his wizard beard.

"She's *happy*, Hol. As happy as she can be. And today aside, she's finally not thinking about Aiden all the time." I dragged us both back out of sight. "Let her have this."

Holly still looked reluctant, but I could tell I'd gotten through. I waited her out.

"You'll tell her right after?" she asked.

"The very next day," I promised. Not that I had any idea how to handle that particular conversation, but one mess at a time.

"And Aiden agrees?"

"*Aiden feels like he hasn't been consulted!*"

"I'm consulting you now," I said. "Come on, dude—don't you want her to know you came back for her? Wouldn't *you* want to know, if the situation were reversed?"

There was a petulant pause. Then: "*Fine. But nothing until after prom.*"

"Great. It's settled." I angled my eyes pointedly at the outhouse wall. "Now can we *please* go somewhere that doesn't smell like a microwaved turd?"

Holly still looked disgruntled, but she snorted. "How do you even know what that smells like?"

We walked back toward the others. As we approached, Meredith turned, and even from across the parking lot the heat of her smile was enough to make me stumble. She was almost too bright to look at, glowing like my mom's full-spectrum SAD lamp. I felt her in my skin, and knew what I'd said to Holly had been true: there was no way I could risk this, this fragile happiness perched like a baby bird on the edge of the nest.

I drew close, and she reached out with one arm, tucking me possessively into her side. The wave of pleasure that flooded through me at the gesture, at the feel of her body through rough denim, was almost enough to wipe my mind clean.

But only almost. Because even as I reveled in that feeling, rolling in it like warm sand at the beach, I could see how precious it was—and how finite.

This thing we were right now, Meredith and I—it was *good*. It was simple, at least on her side. But how would she feel once she knew I'd been holding out on her? How would I feel in her place?

This moment, the press of her against me, was sunset on a Sunday, the last gummy bear in the bag: the blast of sweetness that means it's almost over.

27

FOUR DAYS LATER, Meredith pulled us halfway off a Forest Service road and parked. I opened my door and evaluated the waist-deep ditch beneath it. Ahead, two muddy ruts clawed up the hill into thick woods.

"More climbing?" She hadn't asked me to dress for it. Had not, in fact, told me anything except that she was taking me somewhere after school.

"Not exactly." Meredith grinned. She had one baby molar that had staunchly refused to fall, just to the right of her upper right canine. You couldn't see it when she was giving her cool smirk, but when she smiled—a *real* smile, wild and inviting—it threw things just slightly off-kilter. I'd read somewhere that mosques were always built with one deliberately misplaced tile, as a reminder that only Allah is perfect. That was Meredith's baby tooth: the imperfection that snaps the masterpiece into focus.

I realized I was staring and blushed, bending down to check my shoelaces. "So what are we doing?"

"It's not a surprise if I tell you." Meredith popped her door. "You were so amazing with the prom proposal, I wanted to show you something secret. Something nobody else gets to see."

I flushed red-hot, fingers fumbling. *Down, girl. She doesn't mean it like that.* Unless maybe she did? I stalled until I could look up again without embarrassing myself, then crawled out through Meredith's door after her, bringing only a leftover apple from lunch.

Unlike the active logging roads we'd passed, with their big yellow swing gates, this one was blocked by concrete barricade pieces, indicating that whoever had built the road was well and truly done with it. Meredith followed a muddy footpath between the blocks, then up over the trunk of a fallen tree.

I stuck close, enjoying the way the thin tech fabric of her hiking pants hugged her butt, tight enough to trace the slanting curve of her underwear. I knew panty lines were supposed to be unattractive, but I'd never understood it—they were a reminder of the underwear beneath someone's clothes. How could that *not* be hot? Same with whale tails, when a thong rode up above the waistband of someone's pants. They were all the butt equivalent of nipping out: something that was embarrassing when it happened to *you*, but delightfully distracting on everyone else.

I yanked my mind back out of Meredith's gutter as the trail widened, allowing us to walk side by side.

Meredith seemed to breathe easier in the woods, her body subtly uncoiling, as if straightening out of a perpetual defensive crouch. She walked with the air of someone who knew exactly where she was going. Somebody who was finally comfortable.

Unlike me. As much as I was enjoying spending time with Meredith, there was never a moment when my brain wasn't also silently screaming that I ought to be doing more with Aiden. More tests. More videos explaining what I'd learned. More research on who to contact if Carson Keene didn't come through for me. All set against the burning fuse of Aiden's accelerating blinkouts. It didn't matter that I was well past scraping the bottom of my idea barrel for experiments, or that prom was only a little over a week away—there had to be *something* useful I could do. How was I supposed to enjoy a walk in the woods when my entire life teetered on a pile of unknowns and finger crossing? I could feel the anxiety constantly threatening to leak out—into my interactions with Meredith, which was an absolute no-go, and my conversations with Aiden and Holly, both of which had been getting steadily more strained.

The whole situation made me want to lie down in the trail and take a nap. If only—

"What are you *doing*?" Meredith was looking over at me in fascinated horror.

"What?" I looked down at myself in confusion, finding only the half-eaten apple in my hand.

"You eat the *core*?!"

"Oh. Yeah." I held it out to show her. "If you eat from the bottom instead of the sides, you can eat the whole thing, like the core's not even there. My mom taught me."

"Is your mom a *horse*?" But Meredith was smiling, shaking her head.

The road ended in a circular clearing. On one side, an old washing machine leaned up against a gravelly embankment, its white skin pocked with rust-brown bullet holes. A familiar collection of beer cans and food wrappers blanketed the furrowed grass.

"This isn't what I wanted to show you," Meredith said quickly, frowning down at a bulging trash bag someone had hauled all the way out here just to dump. "Why are people such garbage?"

"That's kind of the universal question, isn't it?" I made my way across ridges of half-hardened mud to the old washing machine. "My dad's always taking me shooting in places like this."

Meredith's eyes widened. "You shoot guns?"

"Yeah . . . ?" I pretended to study the washing machine, watching her out of the corner of my eye. You never knew how people were gonna react to guns.

But Meredith just looked curious. "What kind?"

I shrugged. "Pistols. Shotguns. His AK."

"You shoot *assault rifles*?" *Now* Meredith looked properly shocked.

"I mean, not *plural*." I held my hands up. "We're not, like, militia cosplayers. But Dad has this whole thing about how if only right-wing folks have guns, there'll be nobody to fight back when they go all *Handmaid's Tale*."

"Do you think that'll actually happen?"

"Probably not?" I wandered back over, kicking a half-crushed Rainier can. "But like you said, people are garbage. If we were a normal country, I'd say we should get rid of *all* the guns. But since apparently we can't . . . maybe this is the next best thing?"

Meredith studied me. "So you're half horse, half queer commando."

I laughed. "I guess? Dad definitely subscribes to the Sarah Connor School of Child-Rearing. Mom's a little more normal, but only barely. Our last vacation was to a goat farm, so we could learn how to shear and weave."

Meredith grinned. "That sounds *adorable.*"

"Dude, no—goats are disgusting. The males smell *terrible.*"

"So just like humans, then."

"*Worse.* You know how the males attract mates? They *pee on their own faces.*"

"Kinky." But Meredith's smile faded. "At least your family does stuff." She inclined her head. "Over here."

At the far end of the clearing, the road shrank to nothing, the only sign of its passage a swath of younger, skinnier trees. I followed Meredith into the brush, stuffing my hands into my pockets to keep them clear of nettles.

"We went on climbing trips," Meredith said suddenly.

"What?" It took me a moment to recatch the thread.

"My family." She didn't look back at me, just kept walking. "Everybody would get home on Friday night and we'd drive out to Vantage, or the Pinnacles, or Castle Rock. Mom and Dad would sleep in the back of the truck, and Aiden and I would share a tent. We'd always get grocery store donuts on the way, so that the next morning we could wake up early and climb before things got crowded."

I didn't know what to say, but it seemed important to keep her talking. "Sounds nice."

She gazed up into the canopy. "Even after Aiden's water polo started eating our weekends, we'd still go whenever we could." She shook her head. "Now Mom works all the time, and even when she's home, it's like she's not really there. Dad doesn't even do that. He's theoretically freelancing, but . . ." She shrugged.

"I'm sorry."

Her shoulders just bobbed again.

Ahead, the trees finally thinned, quaking leaves twisting and flashing like fishing lures against the clear blue of the sky. At last Meredith turned, reaching back for my hand. "*This* is what I wanted to show you."

We stepped out into the wide meadow of a power-line cut. Knee-high grass stretched off into the distance, carving a straight line across rolling hills. With their vaguely humanoid shapes, the transmission lines resembled giant robots, marching up the nameless slope behind us, lines humming and clicking with current. Farther on, the brown line of a dirt access road wound between their feet, but up here the steep slope had apparently made it too much hassle.

"Wow," I breathed.

Meredith smiled a little. "I know we're not really that far, but when I'm out here, it feels like there's nobody for a thousand miles. Just me and the mountains." She stared out at the wilderness, face taking on a faraway look. "My Fortress of Solitude."

"Like Superman."

She looked over in surprise. "You like Superman?"

"I like Henry Cavill in spandex."

She made a face. "Gross. Also, he's old enough to be your dad."

"And he can be my daddy anytime."

"Ew!"

"Jealous?" I leaned over and bit her shoulder.

She laughed. Still holding my hand, she towed me over to the base of one of the towers, where a flattish rock offered a commanding view out over the valley. We sat, squeezed together at arm and hip and thigh.

"It's even better at night. You can see so many satellites." She tilted her head back, offering me that perfect profile, the smooth and naked expanse of her throat. "Do you know what the ISS does with its sewage?"

"Now who says romantic things?"

"Just playing to my audience."

I snorted. "Touché. Umm . . . do they throw it out an airlock?"

"Yup." She smirked, still staring at the sky. "They fire it back toward Earth and let it burn up in the atmosphere. Somewhere out there, someone's wishing on a shooting star that's actually a flaming bag of human shit."

"Seems appropriate." The ten percent of my brain that wasn't currently memorizing the pressure of her body against mine scrambled for something to keep the conversation going. "Do you come out here a lot?"

"When I need to think." Her smirk fell away. "Or when I need to stop thinking." She reached into a pocket and pulled out the little pen-pipe, converting and packing it.

"Where do you get that, anyway?"

"One of Aiden's friends." She held it out to me. "You want some? I can light it for you."

I reddened. There had been something deeply sexy about her lighting it for me last time, in a classic-movie, Humphrey Bogart sort of way. The casual confidence, the reach of her hand toward my face.

But I shook my head. "I don't think I actually like smoking. It burns my throat."

"Yeah, this pipe's kind of harsh. Have you ever shotgunned it?"

"I don't know what that is."

Her knowing smile should have felt condescending, but the intimacy of it was too appealing. "I'll show you."

She held the pipe to her lips, pursing them softly around it in a way that pulled the crackling hum of the transmission lines deep into my core. She breathed in slowly—then turned and cupped her hand around my chin and cheek, pressing her mouth to mine. My lips opened with hers.

Then she was breathing into me. The smoke was warm but no longer hot, softened by her lungs, filling my mouth with the taste of fire. I felt the pressure of her breath and inhaled, taking her into me, feeling her billowing slide down my throat and into my lungs.

She broke away, watching. I exhaled slowly, smoke curling up dragon-like from my nostrils.

"Better?" she asked.

"Much." I slid a hand beneath her hair, to the smooth skin at the back of her neck. It still seemed impossible that I was allowed to do this. "But I think we can improve it."

I pulled her close, and we kissed again. My hand slipped down her back, snaking under the hem of her jacket, and then—like jumping off a bridge—up under her shirt. When she made no move to stop me, my hand rose, sliding along the firm, muscled plane of her back, the stegosaurus knobs of her spine. She moaned softly into my mouth as I reached the raised line of her bra clasp and traced along its bottom edge, feeling the scalloped ripple of her rib cage.

Her own hands went around my waist, the pipe abandoned and forgotten. They climbed my sides, thumbs pressing authoritatively on the front of each rib, hesitating just below the wire of my bra.

I made an impatient noise. She laughed softly into my mouth, relieved, and then her hands rose, thumbs making little circles along the padded cups.

There was no room on the rock. It dug painfully into my hip as I turned and twisted, trying to bring more of us into contact. With a frustrated growl, I rolled off it, pulling her down on top of me. She laughed in surprise and delight as we hit the ground. Stalks of long grass stabbed stiffly into bare skin where my shirt had ridden up, but it didn't matter, because Meredith pressing down on me was everything. She covered me like a blanket, squashed against me in one long perfect curve, and I dragged her face down and kissed her ferociously, predatorially. Her hands followed the grass up under my shirt, grabbing at my sides again, fingernails sharp little crescents of pleasure.

Then her knee slipped between my thighs, and the world electrified. Some distant part of my brain registered the ridiculous sound of artificial fabrics sliding against each other—the *zip zip zip* like somebody running in snow pants. But the rest of me was completely absorbed in the soft weight of her holding me down, *possessing* me. My fingers scrabbled along her back, hooking under her bra like a safety handle and holding on for dear life as her kisses moved hungrily down my neck.

"Ohhhhh my god . . ." Meredith breathed shakily into my ear, and the reverence in her voice—the *awe*—demanded more. I rolled her over so we were side by side and lifted my shirt up, popping my bra hooks and yanking the cups awkwardly up without taking it all the way off, savoring the way her eyes went wide. My hand found her leg, sliding up the inside of her thigh.

"Yeah?" I murmured.

In response, she kissed me hard and grabbed my wrist, dragging it up to the waistband of her pants.

This wasn't happening. I knew my life, and there was no possible way that it could involve Meredith rubbing my hand insistently against her stomach, panting into my mouth. But she squeezed my hand again, making an impatient little whine.

In a daze, I slid beneath underwear elastic, feeling the cool smoothness of her skin give way to a wiry tangle of hair . . .

. . . and only hair. I felt around, trying to make it seem sexy rather than incompetent, but her pants—still zipped and buttoned—trapped my wrist painfully. I shifted, trying to find a better angle, but my fingers still found nothing but dense curls.

I was fucking it up. My hand was in Meredith Reyes's pants, and I was *fucking it up.*

And then, at last—farther down than seemed possible—I found what I was looking for. Meredith's breath stuttered like a failing engine.

I did my best to replicate what I liked myself, but it was surprisingly difficult—the angles all wrong, my arm squashed between us and everything bending the wrong way.

But it must have been enough, because Meredith stopped breathing. Her back arched, thighs squeezing together and grinding my knuckles mercilessly.

"*Heugh!*" She inhaled hugely and went limp. I withdrew my mangled hand.

"Kiss me," she whispered, shivering with aftershocks. "Kiss me kiss me kiss me—"

As if she had to ask.

⌇

Afterward, we lay there in the grass, rocks and thorns digging into our backs. One of Meredith's cheeks was entirely coated with red-brown dust.

At last, she spoke.

"Holy cats."

My laugh burst out of me like a gunshot, so loud it should have sent birds flying from the trees. "My entire body is buzzing," I said. The rough ground beneath me could have been a cloud. "I feel like I'm floating."

Meredith grinned hugely. "You're welcome."

I shot her a fake-skeptical glance. "It *could* be the weed."

"Madam!" She pushed up into a sitting position, one hand going to her chest in mock outrage.

"Uh-huh." I stretched up and kissed her, then shuffled my bra back down into something approaching a normal configuration. I attempted to get to my feet, and the clearing spun around me, like my brain was sloshing inside my skull. "Whoa."

Meredith grabbed my arm. "Okay, maybe it's a *little* bit the weed."

"I'm good."

Another grin. "Only good?"

"What, you want a parade?" I grinned back, and managed to sit down on the rock without embarrassing myself. My fingers were sticky, and I turned away and made a show of scrubbing at my face as an excuse to sneak a sniff. Meredith smelled like me, but also different—musky, sharp, a little onion-y.

She moved up next to me, wrapping an arm around my waist and lacing her fingers through mine. "So, um." After everything we'd just done, her sudden shyness was adorable. "Have you ever done that before?"

"No."

"Not even with a guy?"

"Nope." I squeezed her hand.

"Boldly going where no man's gone before." Her eyes glittered happily. "I should've brought a flag."

"Oh my god—stop talking." I kissed her hard, biting her lip playfully. To make sure she knew I was kidding, I asked: "What about you?"

"No." She blushed. "I mean, nothing like that."

"Define 'like that.'"

She looked uncomfortable. "One of Aiden's friends made out with me on a dare at a party. But she was straight, and it was mostly just kissing. Nothing like . . . that."

A goofy smile pulled almost painfully at the corners of my mouth. "Well, apparently we're both prodigies. Because in the words of a wise lady . . . holy cats."

Meredith laughed, and any tension vanished. She leaned into me, and I wobbled a little on the rock.

That just made Meredith laugh harder. "You're really baked, aren't you?"

"I guess?" I blinked rapidly. The landscape was still beautiful, but it felt a little unreal now, like a painted backdrop for a movie. "You smoke this all the time?"

She shrugged. "You get used to it."

"But *why?*"

She bit her lip, giving it actual thought. "It lets me turn my brain off. Climbing is the only other thing that really does that." She gave me a sidelong grin. "Okay, maybe the only *other* other thing. But when my brain won't shut up, it's nice to be able to stop and just focus on the present."

"But the present sucks! I mean—not right *now,* obviously. *Now* is great. But in general."

"Only if you think about it." She nuzzled into my neck. "If I can *stop* thinking . . . I can look out at the hills, feel the wind, and it doesn't matter what's happened or what's gonna happen." She squeezed my hand. "This can just be *this*."

"Huh." I was so used to being disillusioned, to constantly focusing on how much better it would be once I was out of Stossel. But right here, in this moment, I felt both completely drained and inflated like an inner tube. Meredith and the sun were warm against me. The air smelled clean. It was . . . peaceful.

Meredith felt me relax. "Nice, right?"

"Yeah." I propped my head up against hers, looking out over the hills, the sharp-edged path of the power-line cut.

It *did* feel good, sitting like this with her. We didn't even need to talk. I could imagine the two of us as rocks in this field, leaned up against each other for centuries, slowly wearing down together. The thought filled me with a soft glow.

"How do you think they maintain this place?" I asked. "I mean, it goes over cliffs and rivers. How do they keep the forest from moving back in?"

"Helicopter chainsaws," Meredith answered.

"Well, naturally," I deadpanned. "It's either that or tying the saws to bears, and it's way too hard to get the bears to go in a straight line." I turned toward her, passing the joke baton, but her face was totally straight. "Wait—serious?"

"Yeah. They have these giant chainsaws with like a dozen spinning blades that they dangle on ropes. Then they just fly along the edge of the tree line. There's videos on YouTube."

"Chainsaws. On ropes. Next to *power lines*." I shook my head. "How did humanity survive this long?"

"I don't know," she countered. "Doing risky shit is how we evolve, right? Even if it doesn't work out most of the time, people who take chances are the reason things change." She bumped her shoulder into mine. "Like you."

I blinked. "Me?"

"You asked me out when you didn't even know me. And when I fucked that up, you came back and did it *again*. And now here we are." She kissed my neck. "No guts, no glory."

The unwitting echo of Aiden's words from the paper mill kicked me in the chest, driving the air from my lungs.

Meredith felt it and pulled back, looking at me with concern. "What?"

I'd totally forgotten about Aiden—the deal, the deceptions. In an instant, the whole situation came rushing back, avalanching past my barriers.

"Cara?" Meredith frowned, searching my face. "Are you okay?"

Get it together, Cara. The plan was the plan, and whatever damage I'd caused was already coming. No way out but through.

"I'm fine." I shook my head. "Just not used to weed. My skull feels like a balloon." Which was true.

"Okay." Meredith still looked concerned. She took my hand. "And this was okay?" Her free hand made an anxious gesture, incorporating both us and the patch of grass we'd flattened.

"Yes!" Which was a lie, but not in the way she meant. I smiled wide and told the safest part of the truth: "That was amazing. *You're* amazing." I squeezed her fingers, putting my forehead against hers. "You're always so careful, making sure I'm okay, but seriously—my legs are Jell-O. You're gonna have to carry me back to the car."

Meredith smiled, relaxing. "But then who'll carry me?"

"Guess we live here now."

I took all my guilty reservations and stomped them down, like packing a cartoon suitcase. I was *here*, with *Meredith*—my *girl-friend*. That was all that mattered right now.

My pocket vibrated. Without thinking, I pulled it out, glancing at the new email notification.

Keene, Carson
RE: Ghost Found

Hi, Cara! Thanks for reaching out, and I'm glad to see . . .

"Shit!" I tapped to open it.

"What?" Meredith asked.

"Oh, um—nothing. Just a sec." I turned slightly away, hiding the phone with my body as I read.

Hi, Cara!

Thanks for reaching out, and I'm glad to see you're still ghost hunting! The video you sent is intriguing.

I'd love to meet up the morning of the 2nd to observe your haunting in person and discuss the possibility of a joint investigation. Does that work for you? If so, please suggest a public place we can meet. (I know you might want to keep your findings confidential, but for my own protection I can only meet fans in public. Please bring a parent or guardian if you're underage, and regardless, make sure both you and they have signed the attached release form indicating your consent to be recorded.)

Looking forward to speaking further!

Best,

Carson

Oh my god. This was really happening.

Sunday the second was the morning after prom. Everything was moving so quickly. But that was what I'd asked for, wasn't it? With Aiden fading, the sooner the better, and I'd have fulfilled my side of the bargain the night before.

I remembered my promise to Holly, that Aiden and I would tell Meredith that day as well. Well, fine—get it all out at once. First Carson, then Meredith. A clean sweep. Of course I still didn't have the first clue how to have that conversation with Meredith, but I'd burn that bridge when I came to it.

Before I could lose my nerve—this was *Carson Keene*—I hit reply and typed, Sounds great! How about the Second Street Café at 11?

Send. The email zipped away, taking my breath with it. I stuck the phone back in my pocket.

And turned back to find Meredith watching me. Again.

"Who was that?"

"Just Holly." I struggled to keep my expression neutral. "Prom thing."

"Ah." Meredith's face didn't change. "Should *I* know about it?"

"No, it's just—about what we're gonna wear." The lies were coming easier now, each one pulling the next out with its weight, like the chain fountains we'd made in physics. "I wanna surprise you."

"You and surprises." But she could clearly tell something was off. Her expression drew inward, armor sliding down into place like the security gates at the mall.

Fuck. My head was still fuzzy from the weed, and I felt stupid and exposed. Exactly why had I thought smoking was a good idea? I tried for a jokey tone, tossing my hair imperiously. "I'm a woman of mystery."

"That's an understatement." Meredith smiled, but there was no baby tooth, that part of her tucked safely away again.

I shut up before I could do further damage and nestled in next to her, laying my head against hers so she couldn't see my face. There was another moment of awkward stiffness, and then she softened and put an arm around me. We sat and watched the power lines, which now seemed to be marching off toward some unknown apocalypse—an end they could see coming, but couldn't turn away from.

I hugged Meredith's waist. "This is nice."

"Yeah," she said.

Lie by lie, we built the wall between us.

28

I LEANED MY head against the passenger window in hopes that the vibrations transferring from glass to skull might drown out my thoughts. In the driver's seat, Dad sang along to Garth Brooks, to Aiden's delighted horror.

"I'm so sorry you have to live like this," he deadpanned. *"Is it genetic? Are doctors working on a cure?"* As usual, he'd decided to take my inability to talk as an invitation to practice his stand-up routine. But given his accelerating blinkouts, the monologuing was at least a comforting reminder that he was still here.

Unlike *some* people. Dress shopping was something I *should* have been doing with Holly, but she'd already acquired her own dress months ago, and was now busy all weekend with another of her church-group things.

Except that those were really just excuses. For all that she made a show of being supportive, Holly's disapproval of my subterfuge was wearing on us both. For the first time in my life, it felt easier to *not* be around her. Which was maybe convenient—a way to ease myself into a Holly-less future.

Not that *I* was exactly thrilled with me, either. Never mind that my logic was sound, and that it really *would* be worse to drop the Aiden bomb on Meredith before prom—I'd still just lost my virginity to her while lying my ass off. Everything I felt about her, everything she felt about me, was all built on a foundation of bullshit. I'd catfished her as bad as any Tinder troll.

And Aiden—despite the fact that I was giving him exactly what he wanted, I couldn't shake the growing feeling that I was doing *him* dirty, too. A deal was a deal, but somewhere along the way I'd started to actually *like* the guy—his obvious love for Meredith, his constant eagerness to talk or listen. Holly's black-and-white worldview might be grating, but even I had to admit that plotting to exploit your friends for fame and profit wasn't a great look.

I was using all of them. And the worst part was, I had no plans to stop.

Dad glanced over. "You're quiet this morning."

"Just planning my attack."

"Cara Weaver: Fashion Sniper." He pulled into a parking spot and killed the engine. "Do you want me to come with, or . . . ?"

Dad's idea of formalwear was a plaid flannel over his NO STEP ON SNEK shirt. "I think I've got it handled."

Dad slumped with relief. "Okay, great. Just text me when you're done, or if we need to venture farther afield."

"Thanks, Dad." I slid out my door and headed for the store.

"Goodwill?" Aiden's voice was incredulous. *"You're buying your prom dress at a* thrift store?"

I put my earbuds in so I could respond without drawing attention. "Consumerist much?"

"Thrift stores smell like old people and sadness."

Inside, the shop did, indeed, smell of cheap detergent and secondhand textiles, but my mood rose as I warmed to the argument. "That's why we drove to Redmond. We're a mile from Microsoft headquarters—I've seen loungewear here worth more than my laptop. There's gotta be *something* prom-worthy."

"So you're gonna dig through other people's rejects."

I am *other people's reject,* I thought. But I said only, "As opposed to spending three hundred bucks on a dress I'm gonna wear once? Absolutely." Mom had actually offered to pay for it—she was not-so-secretly thrilled that I was going to a school activity for once. But it was the principle of the thing. "I'll be damned if I'm gonna

drop that kind of money on a dance I don't even want to go to."
Though that wasn't entirely true, either: a part of me *was* a little
excited to get dressed up and go out with Meredith—and Holly
and Elvis—even if it would be more fun to go literally anywhere
else.

A frothy mass of seafoam ruffles marked the start of the fancy-
dress section. Aiden made a gagging noise. *"It looks like an over-
frosted cupcake."*

"I didn't say they were *all* winners."

I got to work combing through the racks. For all my big talk, a
lot of the dresses *were* garbage—puff-sleeved eighties nightmares
and shapeless fashion sacks. A rainbow of chiffon, satin, and or-
ganza slid past with the metallic *shnick* of hangers on pipe. I pulled
out a pink bridesmaid monstrosity with a skirt short enough to set
Holly's Bible on fire. "Who *wore* this?"

"Somebody who totally blew the groom at the rehearsal dinner."

"Definitely." I pulled out a velvet dress with a lace-up bust. "Oooh,
here we go."

"You'll be queen of the Ren faire."

I made a courtly curtsey. "Milady, wouldst thou do me the honor
of backing thine ass up?"

Aiden belly laughed, and I felt a now-familiar glow of triumph.
I grabbed a faux-buckskin hippie dress with a midriff cutout and
held it up. "You know what they say: you can never have too much
vaguely appropriative fringe."

"Ten dollars says someone has done mushrooms in that dress."

We continued on, critiquing dresses and making each other snicker.
Yet even as we bantered, the melancholy began to slide back in.

Because this thing we had—this easy invisible-friend compa-
nionship—was time limited. With Aiden's plan working and Meredith getting happier, there was no way to know exactly how much
longer he'd be around. And sure, he'd sworn he wouldn't vanish while
we still had unfinished business (though a paranoid part of me still
whispered that I had no way of knowing what God or the universe

would consider fulfilling our bargain). But even if I got enough evidence out of him to convince the world—*he* would still be gone.

It wasn't like I had a choice. His whole mission was a catch-22: If we followed through and I kept making Meredith happy, he'd disappear. But even if I intentionally blew everything up with Meredith—something I absolutely did *not* want to do—that would just end with *both* of them mad at me. There was literally no way to keep them both.

Aiden's voice jerked me out of my reverie. *"Only one rack left! So much for Operation Hand-Me-Down. Your quest to go to prom smelling like Bengay and mothballs is thwarted!"*

"Oh ye of little faith." I began riffling through the rack. "If we have to, we'll suck it up and hit one of the—*Hel*-loooo!" I pulled a dress free. "Look at *you*."

It was black, with leaf-shaped cutouts in the lace overlay, revealing more and more of the red fabric beneath as it descended until by the hem it was full crimson. Wide straps crossed the chest and back.

"It's a witch dress," Aiden noted.

"Damn straight." I double-checked the size—no way I was actually this lucky—then speed walked to the fitting rooms.

"Is it really a prom dress, though?"

"It is if I wear it to one." I pulled open the dressing room's slatted door. "Wait outside."

I shucked out of my clothes, then shimmied into the dress. For a second I was caught in the web of straps, arm trapped above me, one of the straps tight around my neck. *Guess this is how I die.* Then I got things sorted, and it slid down into place. I turned to look in the mirror.

The black straps turned my pale skin to freckled porcelain. The fabric hugged my chest and waist without bunching, looking sleek and dramatic. The skirt flared slightly in an A-line, ending just below my knee, and rose a perfect few inches as I twirled.

It was goth without being Halloween, sexy without being pornographic. The perfect answer to a bullshit institution like prom—

something that rejected the whole premise while simultaneously beating haters at their own game. Let them have their pastel pastries—I was a fucking femme fatale.

"Aiden," I whispered. "You can come in now."

I heard him before he spoke—the sharp drawing in of breath. He held it for a long moment, then let out a low *"Wow."*

The weight of that word, the way it seemed to drag the air from his nonexistent lungs, made me blush with pride. "You approve?"

"You look incredible."

"Yeah?" I turned slowly, showing him the crossing ladder of straps up my back, milking the moment.

"Hundred percent. Meredith's going to lose her mind." He sighed. *"I know you didn't want to go to prom, or do any of this, but seriously— you've been totally rocking it. It's gonna mean a lot to Meredith. And that means a lot to me."* His voice hung heavy with emotion. *"Thank you, Cara."*

The sudden sincerity stabbed through me. How was he always like this? One minute freestyling creative insults, the next so earnest that it left me feeling awkward and exposed. "You're welcome," I managed.

"Not just for prom, either." He blew out another breath, longer this time. *"Back when it was just me, in the factory, I would have been happy to move on into the light, or whatever. But now that I can talk to you, things feel . . .* important *again. Not just Meredith—everything. I have* fun *with you. And it sucks not knowing how much longer this'll last."* He laughed, a little strained. *"I guess that's always true, though, right? Even if I were alive, I could still get hit by a bus."*

"Or fall through a factory floor?"

He laughed. *"See what I mean? You're always roasting me."* His voice went wistful. *"Anyway. However much time I get . . . I'm really glad I get to spend it with you."*

My throat went tight. I looked back down at the dress in the mirror, blinking hard as the colors threatened to run together in the sudden blur of tears.

"Well," I said with forced lightness, digging beneath my armpit for the price tag, "stay away from any ghost busses, because we've still got plenty of work to do after prom. Your days as the world's most famous phantom are just beginning, baby."

I expected a return volley—some sort of joke or quip. Instead, there was a long pause, then a slow *". . . right."*

Something in his tone raised the hairs on the back of my neck. I met my own eyes in the mirror. "Aiden?"

He hesitated again, then let out an angry breath. *"There's something I should tell you."*

Alarm bells clanged in my head, anxieties sliding down fire poles as they raced to battle stations. "What are you talking about?"

"I don't—" He stopped. *"I just mean . . . I don't know how much longer I'm gonna be around."*

"You mean the blinkouts." Sweat glands in my armpits sprang to life, laying claim to the unpurchased dress. "We calculated that— you've still got lots of time. And I'm your new unfinished business, remember? You can't leave until we're done."

"I know, I'm just . . . not sure that's how this works."

"What do you mean, 'not how this works'?" I could feel the panic waters rising, threatening to close over my head. "What happened to your ghost instincts?"

"I kinda . . . made that part up. To reassure you."

"*Reassure* me?!" This wasn't happening. "It's not about *reassurance*! We made a fucking *deal*. You *have* to stay!"

"I want to! I just don't know if I actually can. *Ever since you and Meredith kissed, I've been able to feel things like . . . accelerating. Coming to a close. I don't think we have as much time as we thought."* He tried for an upbeat tone. *"But at least you've got the videos, right?"*

"Those aren't enough and you know it!" I was being way too loud. "I need *you*!" The lump in my throat said maybe that was true in more ways than one. "You *promised*!"

"I know." He sounded truly miserable. *"I'm sorry."*

"Sorry does *shit*! You're a fucking *liar*!"

"Hey, I don't know *what's gonna happen! Maybe your math is right*

and we've still got another month. Maybe I really won't leave until we're finished. I just wanted to be honest."

"Oh, *now* you wanna be honest! Now that we've wasted fucking *weeks* on prom shit, when we should have been doing so much more!" A horrifying thought arose. "The Carson meeting—you *knew* you were starting to disappear, but you still wouldn't let me schedule it until after prom!"

"Yeah." Aiden's voice had passed through guilty and into exhausted. *"I didn't want you to lose focus."*

The world seemed to go dim, the tinny thrift-store music receding into a distant whine.

And somewhere in the back of my head, a voice—my own, smug as a cat—whispered, *Here it is.*

Because this was what always happened, wasn't it? What a wiser part of me had been waiting for. Aiden, Sophia, all my other "friends" from before Scarf Girl—it was always the same. People cared about you right up until it was inconvenient. Until you didn't give them exactly what they wanted.

And then they betrayed you.

Familiar rage pumped through my veins, burning away the pain like a hot mug against a mosquito bite.

"You lied." My voice came out emotionless, ground down like a knife on a sharpener until it slid easily between ribs. "You lied to my face so that I'd follow your plan."

"Dude, come on! I just wanted what's best for Meredith."

What was best for Meredith—not *me*. Nobody ever worried about *me*. That was why I had to watch out for myself. Why I kept my distance from people. I'd let myself forget that with Aiden.

And look where it got me.

I bent over, angrily gathering up my clothes.

"Cara, please . . ." Aiden's hangdog whine scraped across my skin like poorly chewed fingernails. *"I don't—"* He broke off.

I pulled my jeans on under the dress. When he didn't continue, I turned to face the mirror, glaring at myself. "You don't *what*, Aiden?"

But there was no answer. He'd blinked out again.

"Of course." I yanked off the dress.

Just more proof that he was never really here for *me*.

Just another way to leave.

29

I OPENED THE door and slid inside before the truck had even rocked back on its wheels.

Dad looked surprised. "That was fast! You found a dress?"

"Yeah." I didn't look at him, just tossed the bag in the back seat and buckled in.

He cocked his head. "You don't seem excited."

"I am." I pulled out my phone and checked my email again. My panicked attempt to reschedule the Carson meeting glared out at me from the top of my inbox—along with his out-of-office auto-response.

"Right." Dad watched me in that neutral way he always got in moments like this. Where Mom's interrogations were courtroom drama, Dad just sat there like a bearded Buddha on casual Friday. "You wanna talk about it?"

"No."

"Okay."

When he still made no move to put the truck into gear, I leaned back against the headrest, staring at the upholstered ceiling. "People fucking suck."

Storm-cloud brows lowered as he looked toward the store. "Did someone in there do something?" He reached for his seat belt release.

"No!" I held out an arm to stop him. "Just . . . people in general. They all suck."

His frown slanted humorlessly up on one side. "You sound like your grandmother."

A little red-hot burst of satisfaction burned through my malaise. "Nana was a smart lady."

But Dad just looked sad. "She was paranoid."

Seeing that pity on his face stung, and I fired back with more venom than intended. "Says the guy with a garage full of guns and canned food."

He recoiled. "That's different."

"Sure." Dad didn't deserve my scorn—*he* wasn't the one I was pissed at—but I couldn't quite get control of my tone.

"It *is* different." Dad turned away, drumming his fingers on the steering wheel. "It's one thing to prepare for the worst, but if you start *expecting* the worst, it becomes a self-fulfilling prophecy. You expect everyone to screw you over, so you go on the offensive and shove everyone away."

"You say that like it's a bad thing."

"It *is* a bad thing." He ran a hand over what was left of his hair. "That's how you end up living alone in the woods at eighty-three, with no friends and no community."

I wanted to arch my back and hiss. Dad talking shit about Nana felt like he was attacking *me*. "Nana took care of herself! She didn't need anybody!"

"Right." Dad laughed bitterly. "Like how she didn't need a cardiologist to manage her arrhythmia. Or the time the pipes burst and she almost died of dehydration because she refused to call a plumber. She'd never let me hire anyone, and was too stubborn to move in with us, out of that *fucking* house." I saw the word twist up inside him, striking out like a snake. "Cara, being alone *killed* her."

My chest felt tight. "You told me she fell."

"She *did* fall." Dad gripped the molded rubber of the steering wheel, fingers going white. "And when she did, there was no one there."

The words kicked me in the gut. I'd always assumed it had been instant—had been too scared to ask for details. Would Nana still be alive if there'd been someone with her? If *I'd* still been there, instead of at school?

But the way Dad said it—like it was her own fault she'd died—pissed me off too much to let it go. I lifted my chin. "Nana made her choice."

"She sure did." Dad shook his head, face hard. "And she made it for the rest of us, too."

Silence fell, both of us staring out the windshield.

Then he sighed, deflating back into his usual teddy bear softness. He reached over and put a hand on my shoulder.

"I know you admire your grandmother, Cara. And she really was a remarkable woman. I'm glad you got so much time with her. But don't make her same mistakes, okay? Being self-sufficient is good, but it's like a go bag—you should only use it when you have to. Life's a whole lot better if you trust people. And that means you've gotta take risks—gotta give people the chance to surprise you." He smiled. "Your mom taught me that, a long time ago."

He clapped his hands as if knocking away dirt.

"*Any*way—my issues with my mother aren't the topic here, Dr. Freud. We were talking about what's bugging *you*."

I shrank back in my seat. "Nothing."

"Uh-huh."

He waited.

I waved toward the windshield. "So, are we gonna go, or . . . ?"

He tented his eyebrows. "I can do 'expectant pause' for as long as it takes."

"*Bluhhhh.*" I bounced my head backward off the headrest and covered my eyes, but there was no holding out on Dad when he was like this. At least if I got it out of the way now, before Aiden returned from his dressing room blinkout, I wouldn't have to deal with the added weirdness of him eavesdropping. "Things just got . . . *complicated* with a friend."

Talk about understatement. Aiden was a liar, Holly was peeved at me for not coming clean with Meredith, and Meredith—well, she wasn't pissed at me yet, but she probably would be shortly. All on top of the fact that each day of dating Meredith apparently brought Aiden one step closer to floating into the light and leaving me with nothing but a handful of sketchy videos.

Adding to my persecution, Dad started singing Avril Lavigne's "Complicated."

I glared out from between my fingers. *"Really?"*

He grinned. "Sorry. Complicated how?" Caterpillar eyebrows began waggling. "Is it . . . *romantic?*"

"I think we've reached the limits of your need-to-know here, Dad."

"But I'm a font of romantic wisdom!" He gestured to his flanneled torso. "I mean, look at me!"

"No comment."

"That's my point!" He raised a finger. "I'm a balding nerd who smells like a brewery, married to a hot lawyer who makes three times as much as me. From a Jane Austen perspective, I punch *way* above my weight. I'm a love *ninja!*"

I rolled my eyes, but his ridiculousness was working. "All right, Mr. Darcy. But I'm still gonna need you to ninja-vanish on this one."

"Okay, okay." He beamed, clearly proud to have dragged me partway out of my funk. "I'm just gonna say, though, that honesty is usually the best policy in these things."

I barked a laugh. "Since *when?* Have you *met* people?"

He held up his hands. "I know, I know, but trust me—even if it doesn't work, it's better to get stuff out in the open." He started the truck and shifted into reverse, turning to look through the back window. "Just be honest. Everything after that is up to them."

He kept talking, but whatever he might have said was drowned out by the pop of the cartoon lightbulb turning on over my head.

Because he was right—honesty *was* the solution to all my problems. Or at least, most of them. My brain darted from fact to fact like the math-lady meme, testing out connections.

Premise: Aiden's existence was tied to Meredith's happiness—as she got happier, his spirit got fainter. The blinkouts hadn't even started until the two of us kissed.

Up until now, that had seemed like a no-win situation. If I kept dating Meredith and making her happy, it meant completing Aiden's mission and losing him forever. And while I could always dump her in order to keep Aiden around, that would make *all* of us unhappy, not to mention remove any incentive for Aiden to help me. There were no good options.

But I'd been thinking too small. Because as far as we knew, whatever mysterious rules were governing this didn't care about prom, or dating—those were *Aiden's* obsessions. As far as we knew, the universe only cared about Meredith's *happiness.* Pulling her out of her depression was Aiden's unfinished business.

And if Meredith found out that Aiden's ghost was still here, only to have him immediately disappear because she was happy . . . well, that would be depressing, right? To lose him a second time, especially knowing that this time it was undeniably because of her, would make her deeply *un*happy.

Which would mean his mission would remain incomplete, and he couldn't move on.

It was almost stupidly elegant: the same paradox that had been driving me crazy, but turned on its head. As long as Meredith knew Aiden existed, he couldn't disappear without making her sad, which would undo all his work and perpetuate his unfinished business, thus keeping him here.

Which meant all I had to do to keep both my girlfriend *and* my ghost was tell Meredith the truth—or at least the part about Aiden existing. Hell, this would even make things better with Holly. She kept badgering me to be honest—so I would be.

Checkmate, God.

It wasn't perfect. I didn't *want* to make Meredith sad. But maybe she wouldn't have to actually *be* sad—maybe it was enough just to know that she *would* be devastated if Aiden's spirit passed on and left her again. Conditional depression. And as I'd told Holly, it wasn't like Meredith wasn't *already* sad about Aiden. Some wounds don't heal, you just bandage over them and keep going. And *I* wasn't abandoning her—the opposite, in fact. I'd be right there to help her through it, the same as I had been so far. We weren't losing anything but the lie.

Holly would hate that line of reasoning, of course. The idea of intentionally hurting somebody for personal gain was anathema to her.

Which is why I wouldn't explain the ramifications. All she needed to know was that I'd be telling the truth, just like she wanted. And Aiden—well, he'd already agreed we'd tell Meredith as soon as prom was over. If he hadn't done the math and realized that would trap him here indefinitely, that was on him.

And frankly, right at the moment, I didn't give a whole lot of shits *how* he felt. He'd made his priorities clear, and in doing so reminded me that I needed to look out for my own.

I unclenched my jaw and stretched out in the passenger seat.

"Thanks, Dad. That actually helps."

"It does?" Dad's eyebrows chased his hairline up his forehead.

I laughed. "The wise-sensei bit doesn't work if you look surprised."

He laughed with me and cranked the stereo, letting Alan Jackson extol the virtues of getting drunk on a riverbank. My heart felt lighter as we sang along.

At last, I had a plan. The weight of deception and anxiety that I'd been carrying since the start of this whole stupid deal slipped from my shoulders.

I wasn't cruel—I'd keep my promise and wait until after prom. Aiden still seemed to have some time, and I owed Meredith that much. One night of carefree fun, before things got, as Avril would say, *complicated.*

But after that . . .

After that, it was time to get what *I* wanted.

30

THE SCHOOL WEEK shot by in a haze, but at least I wasn't alone in my distraction: everyone was stretched thin between prom prep, random end-of-year spirit days, and finals studying (which I now cared about even less than most seniors—thanks, UW!). Even the teachers looked strung out, clawing their way toward the margarita-soaked parole of summer break.

In my case, the whirlwind was organizing my notes and videos for my meeting with Carson, who still hadn't responded to my request to reschedule. Every moment was spent racking my brain for additional experiments, broken only occasionally by the delightful distraction of Meredith.

Now, at last, it was prom night. Holly had me seated in my desk chair in front of my bedroom mirror, laptop open to tab upon tab of updo ideas.

"But my hair looks good *down*," I complained. "That's why I *do* it that way."

"It doesn't matter." Holly gathered my locks up in both hands. "It's the Rule of Fancy: whatever you normally do, do the opposite. If your hair's curly, straighten it. If it's straight, curl it. And if it's always *down*"—she tugged playfully but firmly—"you put it *up*."

I crossed my arms. "That's stupid."

"That's fashion. It's not about better or worse, it's about *different*—showing you put some effort into it. That's what makes it special."

"So the suffering's the point?"

"It really explains so *much,"* Aiden noted.

Holly snorted. "Don't be a baby. You're gonna look amazing."

She wasn't wrong. Several YouTube tutorials later, my hair was in a perfect braided chignon, shot through with black ribbon that matched my dress and made my red hair pop. Holly's hair we curled and pulled back on the sides, pinning it in a clasp so it tumbled loosely down over one shoulder.

For makeup, Holly made me help her do glittery smoky eyes, building up layer after layer until she had a totally glam orange ombre—sort of a Jules-from-*Euphoria* look. We finished it off with a set of false lashes.

"Is it too much?" she asked.

"It's gorgeous," I reassured her.

"Elvis is going to have an aneurysm," Aiden agreed. *"In his pants."*

I was still grumpy about Aiden being here for this, but Holly had insisted we let him stay for the appropriately clothed portions. Half the *point* of prom, she explained, was prepping with friends.

Which was fine for her. She and Aiden *were* friends—or at least pen pals, passing notes through me. I was a different story. Had Aiden ever *really* been my friend? Or were we always just two people using each other?

Holly waved a hand in front of my face. "Hey. You gonna put some lipstick on that pout?"

I blinked. "Huh?"

"You've been scowling at yourself in the mirror for, like, thirty seconds. You okay?"

"Yeah. Fine." I leaned in and resumed contouring, using two different colors of concealer to try and shrink my nose.

Holly gazed over my shoulder with her freshly Bowied eyes and sighed. "You know you're the only one who thinks you need to do that."

It should have been reassuring, Holly telling me that my nose was fine. But right now it just felt like another judgment. I pointed the concealer tube at her. "I don't criticize *your* makeup routine."

"I'm just saying, there's a difference between enhancing and hiding. If I was trying to look *different*—like, if I was trying to disguise my monolids or something—I'd want you to call me on it. You've gotta own your look."

"Owning my look means doing what I want with it," I shot back. "And what I *want* is a nose that doesn't make me look like a goddamn anteater."

"Your nose looks fine," Aiden said. *"It's strong."*

"I don't care what *you* think, either," I snapped.

"Okay," Aiden said, infuriatingly agreeable. *"But Meredith likes it, too. Remember rock climbing?"*

Against my will, I remembered that afternoon at the climbing wall—the way Meredith had leaned over and taken my whole stupid nose in her mouth. It had been more weird than sexy, but . . . fuck, it *had* been a relief.

Which was ridiculous. I was my own person, with my own opinions, and eighteen years of insecurity didn't just vanish because somebody thought you were cute.

But when I looked back in the mirror, my nose no longer seemed quite so overpowering.

Half an hour later, we were sitting on the floor, toes separated by wads of paper towel and the air thick with nail polish fumes, when my phone chirped. I looked down and saw a new email notification.

Keene, Carson
RE: Rescheduling
Hi, Cara—sorry I didn't get back to you sooner. Still on for 11 tomorrow?

"Shit!" I waved my hands around, fingers splayed, trying to dry the nails faster. I didn't dare pick my phone up off the carpet with the polish still wet, let alone try to type.

Holly looked over. "What?"

"Just a message from Carson." God, who could've imagined I'd ever be saying *that*? As if we were on a first-name basis. "About tomorrow."

"Right." Holly turned away, ostensibly checking herself in the mirror, but not before I caught her frown.

Well, screw her. Holly had the luxury of disapproving—her life was already perfect. She didn't *need* anything. I forced my irritation down and tried to remind myself that pretty soon *I* wouldn't need anything, either. Tonight might as well be a celebration of my impending fame.

Holly looked at her own phone. "Crud, I've gotta get home. Mom wants family pictures before Elvis shows up."

With the aid of a ballpoint pen, we managed to dig her car keys out of her bag without messing up her nails and gathered up her various implements of cosmetic torture. Then she was off, pulling out of the driveway with the steering wheel pinched between fingertips like the daintiest crab, leaving me alone with Aiden once more.

"*So,*" he ventured. "*This is it.*"

I let the words hang in icy silence. There'd been plenty of that since the thrift store.

"*. . . Maybe I should go check in on Meredith,*" he suggested.

"Good idea." Anything to get him out of here.

When I was sure he was gone, I slipped carefully into the dress, then into a pair of strappy black block-heeled sandals. My favorite sugar-skull-themed purse matched well enough, and everything that wasn't essential for the dance went into my backpack with the after-party supplies.

I realized I was missing my keys and ran downstairs. As I passed through the kitchen, Dad wolf whistled. "Look at you! Do a barrel roll!"

I twirled obligingly.

"Do you have everything you need?" Mom entered from the garage, wiping grease from her hands. "Phone charger? Safety pins?"

"Cash?" Dad reached for his wallet. "You can't depend on credit cards and phones for everything."

"Pretty sure the global financial network isn't gonna crash while I'm at prom." But I took the pair of twenties he held out.

"Pictures!" Mom held up her phone.

The doorbell rang right as we finished. Dad and I both started toward it, but Mom lunged sideways and flung out an arm, practically clotheslining us. "No way! Cara, run back upstairs so you can make your grand entrance. Brian, get your phone ready."

I rolled my eyes. "Mom, it's fine."

She gave me a look bordering on glare. "Cara Weaver, you did *not* get this dressed up just to answer the door like she's the dang *pizza guy.*"

I returned the look with interest, but headed back upstairs. From the hallway, I heard the door open, followed by my mother's bubbly entertaining-company voice. As the conversation stretched, I realized I'd been conned—trust my mother to figure out the perfect excuse to get Meredith alone. Mom might be excited about me dating, but that didn't mean she wouldn't still grill Meredith like a steak.

"I think Meredith's about to confess to planning 9/11," Aiden noted, startling me with his sudden reappearance. *"Your mom is sweating her hard."* He sounded delighted.

"Quiet," I snapped. "No talking tonight, for real. Silent observation *only.*"

"I know, I know . . ."

At last, Mom called out, "Cara! Meredith's here!"

Putting my shoulders back and involuntarily thinking of Aiden's dating shows, I swept imperiously around the corner and down the exposed staircase.

Meredith stood in the living room, hands held nervously behind her like a soldier at parade rest. The green sequins of her sheath dress glittered, leaving sculpted shoulders bare. Aiden's little crystal pendant hung down between the straps of her halter, drawing attention to the smooth skin between her collarbones. Her hair was a shiny black cascade, still parted down the center but now held up sweetly on one side with a silver barrette.

Her mouth opened slightly as her gaze followed me down the stairs. From the door to the kitchen, Mom caught my eye, shooting me a smirk.

I crossed the room, stopping a few feet in front of Meredith and panicking slightly. What was the proper greeting in this situation? I definitely wasn't going to kiss her in front of my parents. Should we hug?

Meredith clearly didn't have the answer, either, so we ended up standing there, watching each other slowly turn red. I gave an awkward little wave.

"You're taller," Meredith blurted, then blushed deeper.

"Heels do that." Three inches was a lot more than I was used to, and with her in flats, it was enough to show her from an entirely new angle. Her eyes seemed larger, her fierce cheekbones more delicate. Something about being taller pinged my protective instincts—which was ridiculous, considering how easily she could toss me over her shoulder. (And how much I maybe wanted her to.)

"You look great," she said, smiling anxiously.

My heart pounded. Who'd let all the air out of the room? "So do you," I managed.

"Oh! Um—" She pulled her hands out from behind her back, revealing a bouquet of yellow flowers tied with silver ribbon. "I picked you these."

I took them dazedly, trying to hide my confusion. "Dandelions?"

She shrugged self-consciously. "You said you liked them."

For a second, my mind was blank—and then I remembered the ponds, and the dandelion test. "Oh! Yeah."

The human body is a truly amazing thing. In that instant, my organs went two entirely different directions: My heart swelled and rose into my throat, because holy *shit,* how thoughtful was this girl to remember one offhand comment, then stop on her way to fucking *prom* to pick me yard weeds in a fancy dress? But at the same time, my stomach twisted and sank, because the comment she'd remembered had been a lie—another convenient cover for my endless scheming. The opposing emotions stretched me between them like a rubber band.

Mom broke the spell. "Picture time! You girls want me to get any with your phones?"

"Yes, please." Meredith unlocked hers and handed it over.

"I hope you're cool being on my mom's Insta," I said dryly, staggering back onto more solid ground.

From the background, Dad asked nobody in particular, "What about corsages? Do people not do that anymore?"

Approximately a hundred photos later—and with the bouquet safely deposited in the fanciest vase a dandelion had ever seen—Mom handed back our phones and patted my cheek. "All right, you are released. You girls have fun."

"Thanks, Mom."

"Nice to meet you both," Meredith said in a respectful tone I'd never heard from her before.

"Nice to meet *you*, Meredith." Mom's grin was entirely too knowing. "We look forward to seeing you again soon for that dinner."

"*Yes-okay-love-you-bye.*" I grabbed Meredith's hand and steered her out the door, scooping up my jacket and backpack on the way.

As we walked to the car, I said, "Sorry about my parents."

"They're nice." Meredith grinned lopsidedly. "Your mom's a little intense."

"Tell me about it."

Meredith stepped forward and opened my door for me. I raised an eyebrow. "So chivalrous."

"You wear a fancy dress, you get the fancy-dress treatment."

"Your dress is fancier." But I got into the car.

As she slid into the driver's seat, the sequined fabric of that dress dragged against the upholstery, pulling open the side slit to display one smooth leg all the way up to the thigh. The flash of bare skin drew my gaze like a magnet.

Meredith scootched around, tugging it closed in embarrassment. "I'm not really used to—"

Before she could say more, I launched myself at her, pulling her face to mine and kissing her like the world was ending. I didn't dare mess up her hair, no matter how much I wanted to ball my fist up in it, but instead slid my fingers down the back of her neck, from the tiny hairs at her nape across the rough scales of the halter and onto the naked plane of her back. My fingers spread out across bare skin, desperate to claim as much territory as possible.

There was an instant of surprise, and then she kissed me back just as fiercely, car keys falling with a jangle down between her seat and the center console as one hand slid around my side, the other rising to probe lightly at my chignon. She made a little mewling sound that blazed through me like a Roman candle.

"You like?" I purred.

"You look so *fucking* hot." Her words were a growl, teeth tugging at my lip. "I love your hair. It's so thick and tight."

"Note to self: Meredith likes my tight buns."

Meredith leaned back with a grin. "Bun intended."

"You're such a— Shit!" I jerked backward, laughing.

Her eyes went wide. "What?"

I nodded to the rearview mirror, and she turned to see our faces, lipstick hopelessly smeared, my crimson muddled in her pink. She laughed and wiped at her lips. "Caught!"

"It's like that ink they put in the fire alarms to mark who pulled them." I dug into my bag and came out with tissues, handing one to Meredith.

"God, I've got you on my *teeth* already." As if that weren't the sexiest thing she could possibly have said. She curled back her lip, rubbing the tissue along her incisors.

When we'd cleaned off the smudges and reapplied in our respective flip-down visor mirrors, Meredith gave me a suddenly shy look. "I've got something else for you."

"Really?" I turned back to face her fully.

"It's not a big deal," she said quickly. "Don't get excited."

I raised expectant eyebrows.

Meredith opened her clutch and pulled out two matching braids, handing one to me.

I ran my finger over the red, black, and green strands, feeling their pebbled texture. "You made us friendship bracelets?"

"I asked Holly about your dress colors. So I could combine them." She looked away. "It's totally sixth grade, I know. But—"

I slid across onto the center console, turning her face toward mine and stopping just short of ruining her lipstick again. My fingers slid up across her cheek.

"I love it," I whispered.

"Yeah?" She smiled in relief.

"Yeah." I leaned close and pressed my cheek softly against hers, breathing in her ear, then slid back and held out my hand. "Put it on me?"

Her eyes widened, but she gently tied the bracelet around my wrist, then let me do the same for her. My thumb bowed across violin-string tendons, resting on the soft beat of her pulse. Then we leaned back, grinning goofily at each other.

"Guess we're officially friends now," I said.

"Guess we are."

"What kind of friends are we talking here?" I teased. "Are there benefits? Is this an upgrade or a downgrade?"

She gave me a look that further challenged my already outmatched deodorant. "You'll just have to wait till the after-party to find out."

I blushed but laughed. "Hate to break it to you, but the after-party is going to be the most G-rated event you've ever attended. Holly's parents do *not* mess around."

She took my hand, lacing her fingers through mine. "Guess we'll have to take our time getting there, then."

My mouth went dry. "I can live with that." In the sense that I now maybe couldn't live *without* that. If this were an old-timey cartoon, steam would be shooting out the top of my dress. I wondered if I could convince Aiden to take a walk for that part of the evening . . . It would no doubt result in some choice commentary, but thankfully, so far he was maintaining his promised silence.

I glanced at the clock on the dash. "We'd better go. They're gonna be waiting for us."

Meredith reluctantly released my hand, and for the second time that day, I helped someone dig awkwardly for their keys.

Even when you added in nearby towns, Stossel didn't have many restaurants fancy enough for a prom dinner. Rich kids would no doubt be taking their parents' credit cards for a spin in downtown Seattle, while normal kids could either waste an hour driving to and from Redmond or pack into one of the valley's few local spots.

Castelvetrano was the latter—one of those upscale Italian places that serve pizza but look disappointed in you for ordering it. On normal weekends they catered to anniversary dinners and Microsofties weaving back from local wineries, but tonight the gravel lot was packed with soap-windowed trucks and dented minivans.

Holly and Elvis waited at the front desk, her in an elegant orange gown with a ruched skirt, him in a rented tux with a matching orange vest and tie.

"Damn," Meredith said appreciatively. "You two look great."

"Thanks! You too!" Holly gripped Elvis's arm and gazed up admiringly. "Couldn't he be the next James Bond?"

"It's about time we got a Bond with glasses," I agreed.

Elvis looked pleased, but only held up his phone. "They'll text when our table's ready. Wanna go down to the water?"

Part of Castelvetrano's charm was its wall of windows overlooking a bend in the river. Trails next to the parking lot led us down to a rocky beach already studded with dressed-up couples.

"Too bad the salmon aren't running," I observed. In a few months, diners would be able to watch salmon thrash their way upstream to spawn, tails slapping frantically as they rocketed like Jet Skis across the shallow riffles.

Holly made a face. "I don't get why people love watching that. It's sad."

"Why sad?" Meredith asked.

"Because they're on a suicide mission," I said. "Beating themselves to a pulp just so they can get laid before they die."

"Aren't we all," Meredith said. I laughed.

Elvis nodded toward a big rock at the water's edge. "Hey, let's climb up there and take a picture."

Holly frowned. "We'll get our clothes dirty."

"Wear it like you stole it. Come on, I'll lift you up. Cara can take the picture." He looked to me for confirmation, then grabbed Holly's hand and led her away, leaving me and Meredith alone again.

"You're both right," I acknowledged. "About the salmon. It *is* kind of depressingly metaphorical. All those fish torn up like zombies, trying to make something happen."

"Maybe." Meredith's hand slipped into mine. "But they also know what they want and go for it."

Her slow smile turned my stomach to jelly, but I managed to say, "Are you comparing my dating style to a rotting fish?"

She threw her head back and laughed, perfect shoulders bouncing. When she looked back down at me again, it was with that trademark tongue-behind-upper-lip scrutiny. But it didn't stop the corners of her mouth from curling up. "Do you know how amazing you are?"

I smiled back. "I . . . don't think I should answer that . . . ?"

She stepped closer. "This last year . . . it was like I wasn't even here. I didn't notice anything, didn't care about anything. Just kind of drifted through. Like a ghost."

The word made me twitch, but I did my best to cover it.

She slid closer still, pressing her bare arm against mine, trapping our clasped hands between us.

"When you came up to me at lunch, it was like pressing play on a paused movie. You brought me back."

Guilt, desire, and something softer brawled inside me, threatening to turn me inside out. I managed to smile. "Guess I really am a ghost hunter," I joked, cringing internally.

"Guess you are." She was so close now, her eyes huge and bright. Her flushed cheeks looked indescribably smooth. Slowly, deliberately, she leaned up and kissed me—just the barest whisper of skin. My brain fizzed, and I had the random thought that kisses like this might be proof of homeopathy—the less of it there was, the stronger it kicked.

She lingered, soft as the tuft of a dandelion seed, then withdrew just far enough to see both my eyes. My breath shook, and I knew she could feel it in every place our bodies touched.

"You're gonna get my lipstick on you again," I murmured.

"That's the plan." Her eyes crinkled, and she leaned close to whisper in my ear. "Wear it like you stole it."

Somebody called my name. Atop the big rock, Holly and Elvis waved to get our attention.

I shifted, breaking reluctantly away. "Hold that thought."

Meredith grinned and squeezed my hand.

"Don't worry. I do."

31

WE GOT A table next to the window, Holly making us all lean in for selfies. Around us, other teens in formalwear did the same, the few adults looking slightly shell-shocked at the chattering flock surrounding their candlelit dinners.

The menu was the sort of thing where everything was written twice—in swirling cursive Italian and grudging printed English—and it was better not to look at the prices. I decided to be adventurous and ordered the venison ravioli. Meredith opted for chili-garlic clams, and Holly went for the glazed duck with wild cherries.

Elvis got pizza.

"Mine is a man of simple tastes," Holly explained to Meredith.

"I'm a man of *conviction*," Elvis corrected. "Besides, if that other stuff was as good as pizza, people would eat it all the time. Pizza's ubiquity is proof of its supremacy. QED."

Nobody could really argue.

"This is so *fun!*" Holly reached across the table to grab my arm, and her smile was so earnest that I couldn't help but forgive all her guilt-tripping and anxiety. "Full-on double date!"

"We need those 1950s ice cream floats with the two straws," Meredith agreed. "Archie Comics–style."

"There'll be plenty of ice cream at the after-party," I said.

"I've got six different flavors," Holly announced proudly, "plus chips, popcorn, and ten different specialty root beers from that LDS root beer store, so we can do a tasting."

"Damn," Meredith said, impressed. "You don't mess around."

Holly beamed. "I am the ding-dang *queen* of slumber parties."

"It really *does* sound perfect," I admitted.

Elvis made a face. "You're not the one sleeping in a tent."

Despite the fact that Holly and Elvis were basically human purity rings, there was no way Holly's parents were letting them spend the night under the same roof. As a compromise, the three of us girls would sleep in the living room, while Elvis got his own tent in the backyard.

"You'll just be on the other side of the window," Holly told him.

"Like a prison spouse," I added helpfully.

"Or a zoo exhibit," Meredith chimed.

I did my best David Attenborough. "And here we have the rare teenage male, *Sweatius hornballius.*"

Meredith laughed, bright and brassy as a trombone, and my heart glowed incandescent.

Elvis rolled his eyes. "Says the girl who gets to sleep next to *her* date."

Which was true—for all that Holly abhorred lying, even she wasn't about to out us to her parents. As far as the Phams knew, we were just two dateless friends going to the dance together, a wholesome and frankly more believable situation than the truth.

I reached out and patted Elvis's shoulder dramatically. "No one said true love was easy. We'll give you a flashlight and everything."

"And I'll make us all pancakes in the morning," Holly said, squeezing his hand.

"See?" I said, overly casual. "You'll still get to eat Holly's cake."

Meredith snorted so hard she inhaled a clam, and Holly and Elvis both turned bright red as I slapped her back.

Holly was right—this *was* fun. In this moment, it was impossible to hold on to the stress that had been poisoning my last few weeks. Because this, right here, was everything I wanted: Meredith squeezed into the booth next to me, her leg bare against mine through the slit in her skirt. Holly and Elvis laughing and bantering. This was how it was *supposed* to be. My swollen heart still ached at the knowledge that we'd never be here again—that in a few months, everything would be different. But in the meantime, the night was ours for the taking, a river rushing toward unknown destinations. We—

"Cara!"

I blinked, trailing off in the middle of the story I'd been telling about my family's Great Lasagna Disaster.

"Cara?" Meredith echoed, looking concerned.

"Cara, we need to talk! Right now!"

I frowned, biting down on the inside of my cheek. Fucking Aiden—he'd *promised* not to interrupt. I ignored him. "So everybody's shouting, and Dad's running to get the hose, but he doesn't realize—"

"Goddammit, Cara, it's an emergency!"

I cut off again, grimacing as I slid out of the booth. "Hold on—I'll be right back."

"You're gonna pause *there*?" Elvis was incredulous. "What happened to the raccoon?!"

But I was already moving across the restaurant, around the corner into the little wood-paneled alcove hiding the bathroom doors. I yanked my phone from my purse as cover. "What?!"

"It's happening." Aiden's voice was even, but it was the smoothness of pond ice: thin and brittle.

"What's happening?"

"I'm, um . . . I think I'm dying?" The last word shook a little. *"For real this time."*

The ice broke, dropping me through into cold and darkness. My pulse throbbed in my ears. "How do you know?"

"I'm not sure—I just do. It's different from the other blinkouts. It feels like when I died—the world's getting all dark, like I'm looking out through the fabric of a T-shirt. But I can feel that light again, above me, pulling, and it's . . . strong." He grunted the word, like lifting a heavy weight. *"I don't know how much longer I can hold on."* He already sounded thinner, reverb-y, like someone receding down a long hallway.

"You *can't* go yet!" My heart beat ineffective wings against the cage of my ribs. "What about the deal?!"

"I know. I'm sorry." He sounded genuinely apologetic. *"I thought we'd have more time. But I guess this was all Meredith needed."*

"What about what *I* need? I need *you. Here.*" My throat was closing, allergic to this whole situation.

"I want to be."

"Then *stay.*" My voice was an angry hiss, but my eyes prickled treacherously, fear eating away all other feelings like the tide undermining a sandcastle.

Yes, things had been strained between us since the dressing room. But before then, the time we'd spent making jokes, talking late into the night—we'd *enjoyed* each other, goddammit! And as much as he'd pissed me off, what was his crime, exactly? Caring about his sister too much? Whatever we were to each other, it was totally unfair for the universe to drop him into my lap only to yank him away.

A girl in pink tulle exited the bathroom. One look at my face sent her scurrying.

"I'm trying." Aiden's voice sounded strained. I imagined him dangling over a cartoon cliff, clinging to a tiny plant. *"It's not working."*

"Then try fucking *harder.*"

"I'm sorry, Cara." His voice went ragged, quieter still. *"I just needed to say thank you again. For everything. Hanging out with you is the only thing since I died that's made me really happy, and—"*

"*No!*" I was shouting now, feeling tears running mascara-dark down my cheeks. "You don't get to make a fucking *exit speech*! You're *staying.*"

"Cara, I can't—"

"I know." I scrubbed at my eyes with my wrists, leaving dark smears. "But I can."

And I turned and sprinted back through the restaurant.

Heads turned as I dodged between tables, nearly knocking over a waiter carrying plates of fettuccini. As I reached our booth, everyone looked up in alarm.

"Cara?" Meredith asked, right as Holly gasped, "What's wrong?!"

My chest was heaving, and not from the run. Was I really doing this?

I put my palms on the table to steady myself.

"Meredith," I said carefully, "your brother's not dead."

"*Cara!*" Aiden howled. "*What the* fuck*?!*"

The whole room seemed to go silent. Eyes widened all around the table.

In a small voice that sounded totally unlike her, Meredith asked, ". . . what?"

"I mean, he *is* dead," I amended quickly, "but not *gone*. He's a ghost." I took a deep breath. "And I can talk to him."

Holly buried her face in her hands. "Effing H."

Expression drained from Meredith's face. "What are you talking about?"

I slid into the booth next to her, grabbing her forearm. "I know this sounds bonkers, but it's real, I promise. He's here with us now."

"*Really,* Cara?" Holly looked up at me, and the fury in her eyes was something I hadn't seen since the night we first met, with the youth group. "You're doing this *now*?"

"I don't have a choice!" I turned back to Meredith, gripping her arm as if I could physically push the belief into her. "He's *real*, Meredith. We went out to the factory a few weeks ago to do a video for my channel, and ever since, he's been following me around, talking to me." I pulled up one of the dice videos on my phone, then held it out. "Look."

"*This wasn't the deal!*" Aiden shouted, but his voice was already stronger—proof I'd made the right choice.

Meredith ignored the phone, turning instead to Holly and a shell-shocked Elvis. "You understand this?"

Holly's jaw looked tight enough to crack molars, but she nodded. "It's real. Your brother's a ghost."

"*Please.*" I shoved the phone into Meredith's hands. "Just watch the video."

This time she did. She played it once through, my voice narrating tinnily through the speakers. Then again.

She looked up at me. "You guessed the dice roll." Too flat to be either question or accusation.

"I didn't *guess*," I explained. "Aiden watched and told me the answers. We've done it dozens of times."

"My brother . . . talks to you." Still no reaction, just establishing facts.

"Yes! We don't know why I'm the only one who can hear him, but he's here and he loves you and—here, Aiden, help me out! Say something only you would say!"

"How about 'fuck' and 'you'?" Aiden spat. *"You* promised *you'd wait! You're ruining everything!"*

I bit back a scream of frustration. "Here," I said, scrolling rapidly through my phone again, "let me find one of the other videos."

Meredith's gaze sharpened. She sat up straighter and looked around, seeming to see the rest of the restaurant for the first time. All the teens who'd stopped eating, fancy Italian sodas forgotten and forks halfway to their lips as they watched the show at our table.

"Is this a prank?" she asked quietly.

"What?" I shrank back into the upholstery. "Of course not!"

"You sure?" The suspicion in her tone shredded my insides.

"Meredith!" Holly reached across the table, all giant puppy eyes. "We wouldn't do that! We're your *friends!*"

"Then *what?*" Meredith's expression finally softened, pleading with us to make this all make sense. "Why are you saying this?"

"Because it's *true.*" I dropped my phone and grabbed her hand again. "I don't know why Aiden's a ghost and other dead people aren't, but he is. He's here right now, and he needs our help." I stopped just short of saying *and he's being kind of a dick about it.* There were many angles of this relationship it seemed better not to get into just yet.

Meredith's stare swept back and forth across the three of us, taking in our earnest expressions. For several seconds, nobody spoke.

Then she murmured, "I don't believe this."

"I know." I squeezed her hand. "It's a lot to take in, but—"

"*No.*" She pulled free with a jerk. "I mean *I. Don't. Believe. This.*" She enunciated each word, punctuating every syllable as she looked around the table. "Are you even *listening* to yourselves?"

"That's why we've been doing these tests." I held up my phone. "So we can prove it. To the whole world. We've even got a famous ghost hunter from YouTube coming in to help us."

"YouTube." Something shifted in the flat planes of Meredith's face, the blankness that had been an empty page hardening to cement. "This is about your channel."

"No!" I protested. "I mean—okay, yes, in the beginning it was. But now we just want to help him. Help you *both*." Which wasn't entirely true, but I could feel the conversation spiraling out of control. "I didn't want to tell you like this, but Aiden's ghost is—"

"Ghosts. Aren't. *Real!*" Meredith yelled the last word directly into my face. The force of it seemed to shove her backward, deeper into the booth.

Away from me.

She shook her head, a look of grim understanding dawning. "*Jesus.* This has been it the whole time, hasn't it?" She snorted an angry laugh. "I always wondered why you picked me. Why would you ask me out? You'd never even talked to me. It all seemed so random. Except it wasn't random at all, was it?"

I squirmed, and she saw it. She seemed to curl inward, reverting back to that raven-haired terminator from the lunchroom.

"This whole time, it was about Aiden. You thought you'd hang around the girl with the dead brother, see if you could get something for your stupid channel. Some paranormal bullshit that would validate your obsession." Her lips pressed tight, chin wrinkling. "But since there isn't any, you decided to make your own. And then bust it out on prom night, because . . . drama?" She raised her eyebrows. "Making sure we'd all look good for the camera?"

"Meredith, please!" I held my phone out to her. "I can prove it's all real!"

"You can't, actually. Because it's not." She nodded calmly toward the open side of the booth. "Move."

"I don't—"

"Move." She kicked out under the table, connecting with my thigh and shoving me halfway off the padded bench. I stumbled to my feet, and she slid out past me.

"Wait!" I grabbed her arm as she stood, and she whirled so fast I let go, raising my hands defensively. "Please! Just hear me out."

"I've heard enough." She bit her upper lip as if deciding something, then leaned closer. Quietly, perfectly controlled, she said, "I don't know if you actually *believe* this shit, or if you're just an opportunist cashing in on other people's pain. But either way, I'm done."

And in a flash of green sequins, she was across the room and out the door.

32

I STOOD STUNNED for a moment—just long enough for everyone in the restaurant to get a good look at my epic failure—then ran after her.

...and promptly tripped over my stupid heels, almost face-planting into an old couple's shrimp risotto. I got back up and stumbled outside just in time to see Meredith's car peel out of the lot in a spray of gravel.

"Fuck!" I shouted.

"That's an understatement," Aiden observed acidly.

"I didn't hear *you* helping back there!" I wasn't sure who I was angrier at—him, or myself. The way Meredith had looked as she left...it hadn't been so much pained as *understanding,* as if everything were finally clicking into place. Here, at last, was the rejection she expected from the world.

I knew that feeling all too well. The idea that I'd made Meredith feel it too made me want to throw up.

I ran back inside, sliding into our booth.

"Cara! What the *fudge*?!" Holly's flushed scowl pulled her penciled brows down tight.

"That seemed *entirely* suboptimal," Elvis agreed.

"It's not my *fault*!" I grabbed for my composure—what was left of it—and lowered my voice, leaning in. "Aiden's dying! I mean, you know—*again*."

Holly's scowl evaporated. "He's disappearing for real? Right now?"

"Yes!" Apparently I'd been right that the universe didn't care about prom. I just hadn't expected to cross the Meredith Happiness Threshold so soon. "He called me away to say it was happening—that he was being pulled toward the light."

"Emphasis on 'was,'" Aiden snapped.

"So you're not feeling it now?" I tried to keep the hope out of my voice.

"Everything still feels kind of . . . wibbly. But no, I'm not going toward the light anymore. Congratulations—you fucking happy now?"

"Happy" was probably the last adjective I'd use at the moment, but at least that much of the plan had worked.

Holly cocked her head. "So you ran back and told Meredith? Why?"

Guilt tugged at my insides like a period cramp. "Because I didn't want him to disappear without her having a chance to say good-bye," I improvised.

Holly nodded, because of course that was exactly the sort of thought she would have had in my position.

Elvis, on the other hand, frowned. "You ran back here because he was fading. But now he's not?"

I shifted in my seat. "Seems like it."

"Because his mission isn't finished anymore." He watched me from behind those big glasses. Trust good ol' logical Elvis to go full *True Detective* and put the pieces together. "She isn't happy, and isn't going to prom."

"So he can't move on." I saw it click in Holly's face. She turned to me, ombre eyes squinted as if she couldn't quite understand what she was seeing. "Did you *know*? That telling her would stop him from passing on?"

My face flushed. "I mean, I thought it was *possible*. Who knows how any of this works?"

Holly sat back, shaking her head slowly. "Oh, Cara . . ."

The reproach burned like hot road tar. First Meredith, now Holly. I wanted to peel off my skin, or at least slump beneath the table.

Fortunately, Elvis saved me. With no particular indication of how he felt about my decisions, he asked, "So what happens now?"

"What *happens*?" I gaped theatrically at him. "I go *after* her, you idiot!" I angled my head to indicate Holly. "Hasn't she made you watch any rom-coms?"

Elvis shrugged. "I spend them thinking about video games."

"As is only fair," Holly acknowledged. She narrowed her eyes at me. "But does she *want* you to go after her?"

"It doesn't *matter* what she wants!" I realized how that sounded and added, "I mean—she's overwhelmed right now. It's a lot to take in. But we can't let her think we're lying to her!"

"You *have* been lying to her," Holly noted.

"But now we're not!" I realized people were still looking in our direction and forced my voice back under control. "We can't let her think we aren't really her friends, right?" Holly flinched, and I leaned into the opening. "You said it yourself. We've gotta convince her this is all real."

"Because you were doing so *well at that earlier,"* Aiden sniped.

"Because you wouldn't help!" Holly's eyes widened and I said quickly, "Not you—Aiden's being a dick."

"I'm not the one who wrecked everything!"

"Oh really?" I glared down at the table so I wouldn't look *as* deranged. "And exactly what choice did you leave me? I wasn't the one running out on my side of the deal. Now are you gonna help us, or what?"

"Why should I?" Aiden sulked. *"You already ruined prom so you could trap me here."*

I closed my eyes and clutched at the leather of the bench seat, trying to hold back a scream.

But to my surprise, it was Holly who answered.

"This is your fault, too, you know."

I opened my eyes.

Holly was addressing the empty air next to me. She sat perfectly straight, her expression of maternal disappointment more appropriate for a school principal than a girl in a prom dress. "If you'd let Cara tell Meredith about you earlier, instead of swearing her to secrecy and insisting on your convoluted scheme, Meredith could be having the fun prom you wanted. Instead, she's miserable. If you *really* care about her, you've got a responsibility to help us fix this."

Coming from Holly, the rebuke hit like a sledgehammer, and even just catching a sideways piece of it again made me feel like a dog who'd shat on the carpet. When Aiden spoke once more, all the fight had gone out of him.

"Yeah, okay. I'll help."

My breath rushed out in a whoosh. "*Thank* you!"

Holly nodded primly.

"So how do we do it? You already explained the situation to her."

This much, at least, I had managed to plan for.

"Give me a secret," I said. "Something only the two of you could possibly know."

"But nothing that would break any promises," Holly inserted. "Or that would embarrass Meredith."

I started to protest—feeding us inside information was why Aiden was *here*—but stopped, not daring to push her any further. And it wasn't like things had been going great my way.

"Fine," Aiden said, sounding grim. *"I've got one. It's not embarrassing. Not for her, anyway."*

"Perfect," I said. "Hit us."

He hesitated for so long I thought he might have blinked out, but then said, *"Bluetooth."*

I waited. When it was clear no more was coming, I said, "That's it? 'Bluetooth'?"

"Yeah. And no, I won't be elaborating."

I raised an eyebrow. "I need a secret, not a password. What if she asks for an explanation, but you're blinked out?"

"Guess you'll just have to take that chance. But trust me—that's plenty."

"Fine." I started to stand—then stopped halfway. I opened my mouth, but before I could ask, Holly sighed and said, "Yes, we can give you a ride."

Embarrassed gratitude warmed my cheeks. "Thanks."

"I'll get our check." Holly slid out and went to track down our waiter.

"How'll we find Meredith?" Elvis asked.

"Judging by the direction of the pull," Aiden said, *"I think she's headed back to our house."*

I explained. As Holly returned carrying a fancy leather bill case, I clapped my hands, trying to convince everyone I had the situation under control. Especially myself.

"All right, Aiden," I announced. "Let's take you home."

33

THE THREE AND a half of us drove most of the way to Meredith's house in grumpy silence, punctuated only by narrated directions from Aiden. Elvis sat in the back, clearly more than happy to distance himself from the tension bubbling between me and Holly. As we got close, however, it finally boiled over.

"I totally understand why you don't want Aiden to disappear," Holly said carefully. "But what if there's a reason it happened tonight?"

"We know the reason." I glared out at the passing trees. "It's prom. She was happy."

"Maybe," Holly allowed. "But also, tomorrow's your meeting with Carson—the start of your big ghost reveal. Doesn't that seem a little suspicious?"

My eyebrows shot up. I looked over. "You think Aiden's trying to sabotage our deal?"

"Hey!" Aiden protested, right as Holly said, "No! I don't think he's controlling it at all. But what if the timing means something else?"

"What—that God hates me? I already knew that."

"God doesn't hate you, Cara!" Holly gripped the wheel tightly, frowning. "Just . . . what *other* reasons might there be?"

Holly always went full Socratic method when she really wanted to moralize at you—rhetorical questions designed to make you say what she was thinking, so she didn't have to. It was deeply passive-aggressive, and right now I didn't have the spoons to deal with it.

"You've clearly got something in mind," I snapped. "So just say it already."

Holly bit her lower lip. "What if you're not *supposed* to reveal Aiden to everybody?"

"Says who? God?"

"Maybe," Holly replied, as if that were a reasonable answer.

"That's bullshit! If whoever's assigning hauntings didn't want me to tell the world, they could have had him haunt *literally* anybody else!"

"Maybe they should have," Aiden groused.

"Maybe it's not about him," Holly suggested. "Or not *just* about him. Maybe it's also about you. To teach you something."

"What—that people will take what they want and then fuck off? I already know that, thanks."

"Fucking hell!" Aiden moaned. *"Will you quit acting like I've got* any *control over this?"*

Holly grimaced, but managed to keep a grip on her Sunday school tone. "Maybe the point was for you to help without getting anything in return. To do the good deed for its own sake."

"And maybe it's because God's a perv who wants to watch two girls make out. See? I can play this game, too." I was tired of Holly's everything-happens-for-a-reason lecture, and even more tired of what it implied about me and my choices. "We've already been over this. Stop trying to make everything into some moral lesson. Turn here."

Holly signaled and slowed, turning carefully into the Reyeses' gravel drive. As she parked behind Meredith's car, she made one last attempt. "I'm just saying—what if you're *supposed* to let him go?"

"Life isn't a test, Hol." I released my seat belt. "There's no *supposed to*—no secret plan that'll make everything work out right. Only what we make happen for ourselves." I opened my door and stepped out. "Wait here."

⌣

For all my bravado, my gait faltered as I approached the porch, each footfall up the steps coming slower than the last, clunking hollowly on the old wood. At the door, I stopped, heart pounding like I'd just climbed Novelty Hill on a fixie.

"Aiden?" I whispered.

"What?" He still sounded pissed.

"Just checking." I knocked.

Silence. Then footsteps. The door cracked open to reveal Meredith's dad. He blinked owlishly at me, and I suddenly remembered that I was still in my prom gear.

"Hi, Mr. Reyes. Is Meredith here?"

Another blink. "Cara, right?"

"Yes, sir." I had no idea if Meredith's dad was a "sir" guy, but it never hurt.

He stared, clearly trying to figure out his role in whatever this situation was, then just as clearly decided it was none of his business. He opened the door wide. "She just went upstairs." The question of *why* hung in the air, not quite asked.

"Thanks." I scurried for the stairs, catching a glimpse of a dark-haired woman in the living room as I passed.

The hall was the same as I remembered it, but when I reached the end, the wrong door was cracked. Across from Meredith's room, Aiden's door hung ajar. I took a breath and pushed it open.

Aiden's room was a mirror of Meredith's own, its hardwood floor shockingly bare after Meredith's blizzard of dirty clothes. There were the sorts of things I'd expected: Sports medals on flag-colored ribbons. Printed-out photos of Aiden at water polo matches. A poster of a tiny helmeted explorer standing beneath the dome of a ruined cathedral.

Yet there were also surprises: A cubist bookshelf crammed with young adult romance novels. A homemade protest sign. A bureau mirror decorated in loopy cursive dry-erase marker, which made me realize I'd never actually seen Meredith's handwriting.

Everything was neat and tidy, the lines of the bed hospital straight. A carefully curated museum.

Meredith sat cross-legged in the middle of the floor, dress rumpled and knees poking out through the slits. She whirled as the door opened, and I caught a glimpse of the photo on her phone—Aiden as homecoming king.

"What are you doing?" she demanded.

"I just wanna talk." It felt like a gamble to step inside and close the door, but still safer than the possibility of one of her parents coming to investigate.

She scrubbed a wrist across each of her eyes and stood, expression locked down tight. "You've said enough."

"Maybe." I nodded to the picture on her phone. "But *he* hasn't. He says to tell you 'Bluetooth.'"

She stared at me, uncomprehending.

Fuck. "He said you'd know what it means." I tried not to let my panic show.

Her eyes widened in understanding, but then her face iced over again. "I don't know what you're talking about."

"I think you do," I pressed, not sure if I was bluffing or not.

"She totally does," Aiden agreed.

She crossed her arms.

I looked up to the ceiling. "Help me out here, Aiden. What the fuck does 'Bluetooth' mean?"

"No. No way. Tell her . . . tell her 'house speakers.'"

I did. Again, the twitch of an eyebrow, but her posture didn't change.

"Goddammit, Meredith, quit being a dick!"

"Will you quit whining and just tell me already?!" I snapped.

Aiden made a little closed-mouth scream noise, then said, *"Fine! So one night when I was fifteen, I was in the bathroom watching porn on my phone while everyone else made dinner—"*

I made a face. "I take it back. I don't want to know."

"Too late. So there I am, engaged in furious hand-to-gland combat, but for some reason I can't get my headphones to work. But whatever,

I've got a good imagination. So I finish up and come downstairs—only to realize that earlier I'd used my phone to stream music on the house speakers. And it was still synched."

My hand flew up to cover my mouth. "No."

"Yuuuuup. So the whole time I was in the bathroom, my phone was blasting the 'Anal Amateurs' subreddit directly into the kitchen. Where Meredith and my parents were cooking dinner."

Despite the seriousness of the situation, I burst out laughing. Meredith took a step back, either from the convincingness of my reaction or from being in the same room with a girl laughing at the voices in her head.

"I swore them all to secrecy," Aiden finished. *"Especially Meredith."*

I quickly repeated the story.

Meredith gripped her own arms so tightly that her fingers dug white, scalloped grooves in golden skin, but still she shook her head. From the way her lips twitched, I wasn't sure if the gesture was directed at me or at herself. "He must have told you."

"Yeah, just now."

"I mean *before*," she snarled.

"Why?" I spread my arms. "He didn't even *know* me before. Why would he tell his most embarrassing secret to some loser underclassman?"

"I don't know!" Her shout surprised us both, pushing us a step apart.

"Tell her about the time we explored the abandoned missile base in Redmond," Aiden said, getting into it now. *"The old flooded missile silos. That was where she told me she was gay, and I told her I already knew."*

I narrated as quickly as I could, trying to get out of the way and just be his voice. He started addressing her directly.

"When you were eight, we got one of those butterfly-hatching kits, and you named them Claudia, Cinnamon, and Alejandro. You love decorating Christmas cookies, even though you don't like eating them. We once got in a huge fight at Abuelita's house because you bought up all the ones and fives in Monopoly and refused to give change. You—"

"Stop!" Meredith doubled over, clutching her stomach, pum-

meled by the fire hose of memories. When she looked up, her eyes were streaming again. *"How?"*

"I don't know," I admitted. "But it's not a trick. He's *here*, Meredith. And he loves you." My own eyes started to water—mirror neurons: activate. I stepped closer. "He loves you *so much*, Meredith. Literally the first thing he wanted when he realized I could hear him was for me to get to know you. To make sure you were all right."

Despite the tears, her eyebrows still managed to rise. "And you thought the best way to do that was to ask me to *prom?*"

"Oh. Um." Awkward. "That was kind of . . . his idea?"

"Don't tell her that!" Aiden yelled.

"Right." Meredith straightened slowly, visibly pulling herself back under control. "Of course it was." She sniffed. "And what was in it for you?"

"Nothing!"

"Really?" Above black clouds of bleeding mascara, falcon eyes narrowed. "Because I shot you down *hard*, and you came back for more. You bought me a concert ticket with no reason to think I'd say yes. That's pretty fucking persistent for a Good Samaritan."

She had me pegged. The exposure made me angry.

"Fine," I admitted. "He agreed to help me prove ghosts are real. For my channel."

"Fucking hell," Aiden muttered. *"Are you* trying *to blow this?"*

Meredith looked like she'd expected it, but that it hurt anyway. She shook her head. "Classic Aiden. So sure I can't get a date on my own that he has to hire a fucking *supernatural escort service.*" A horrified look darted across her face. "Did—did he tell you to—" She stumbled over the words, and that moment of weakness seemed to make her angry enough to finish. "Is that why you fucked me?"

The profanity was deliberate—cold and cruel, taking our transcendent moment on the hillside and turning it dirty.

"What?!" I felt like she'd reached down my throat and scraped out my internal organs. "No!"

"Really?" Rage and shame chased each other across her face. "Because it sounds like the sort of thing he'd do. *Poor little Meredith,*

never hooked up with anybody. He used to say this stupid thing—"
She lowered her voice, dropping into a cartoonish yet surprisingly
recognizable impression. *"Boobs are the original antidepressant."*

"Shit." Aiden sounded embarrassed.

"I didn't agree to do anything but ask you to the dance." But now
I was pissed, too. "And screw you for even thinking that."

"Why *wouldn't* I? I don't *know* you, Cara!"

"Yes, you do!"

"Do I? You've been lying this whole time."

I threw up my arms. "Yeah, about *one* thing!"

"It's a pretty big thing." She did that staring-you-down, running-
her-tongue-beneath-her-upper-lip thing. To think I used to find
that hot . . .

I grabbed at my hair, ignoring the way it yanked on my chignon.
"Yes, *okay,* asking you to prom was his idea! And the concert, too.
But everything after that—fuck, everything from the moment we
got to the show—that was me! The *real* me. Because I *like* you,
Meredith! I like you a *lot.*"

She stuck out her chin. "And why should I believe you?"

"Because I'm being honest!" God, even with her looking at me
like I was shit on the sidewalk, she was *still* devastating in that
dress. "If I wasn't telling the truth now, why would I say all this
stuff that makes me look like a total asshole?" Which raised the
question: *Was* I a total asshole?

Meredith was fully in control again, working the problem like a
route up a rock. "So why now? Why tell me like *this,* in front of
everyone?"

"I didn't have a choice! He was fading—I didn't want him to
disappear before you two had a chance to talk." It wasn't *not* true.

"What do you— Wait, he *was* fading?" Those eyes missed nothing. "He's not now?"

"Yeah."

"Why?"

"I don't know!" But that wasn't good enough—I needed to stop
lying. Whether because Meredith deserved better, or just because

it wasn't working. "Okay, I don't know for *sure*," I amended. "But maybe it's because . . . because making sure you're happy is his unfinished business—the thing he has to do before he can move on. And now that you're unhappy again, he's stuck here."

"So it's *my* fault?" She looked simultaneously stricken and offended.

"No!" Aiden and I shouted together. I held out my hands, doing my best to fall on my sword. "It's mine! I'm sorry, I messed this all up. But I didn't want him to go before I told you the truth."

"You could have told me the truth at any point," she observed coldly.

"Would you have believed me?"

She flapped an angry hand. "I barely believe you now! But if you had him feeding you secrets like this, you could have done it any other night."

"But that wasn't the deal." I heard the shittiness of the words even as I said them.

"The deal." Her nostrils flared. "That's what I am to you."

"No! Not anymore!" I forced myself to step forward and grab one of her hands, holding it in both of mine. "Look, I don't know why this all happened this way. I don't know why I can hear him, when it could have been anyone else." I thought of Aiden's words in the dark that first night. Of Holly's words in the car. "But don't you think maybe it *means* something? Like, maybe we're *supposed* to be together?"

Meredith's eyes were black ice. With terrible, unstoppable deliberateness, she slowly pulled her hand away.

"All it means," she said quietly, "is that my brother thinks he knows what I need better than I do. As always. So much so that he got you to pretend to be my girlfriend."

"I'm not pretending!" I protested. "I *am* your girlfriend!"

She pursed her lips. "That's not up to you."

I blinked, pulling my head backward. "You're dumping me?"

"No, I *already* dumped you. Back at the restaurant." Her tone was a surgeon's scalpel. "But don't worry—it's not *really* dumping if we were never actually dating."

Oh god. "Meredith—"

"*Stop.*" A guillotine falling. "You need to leave now."

My voice rose, panicked and squeaky. "But don't you want to talk to Aiden?" It was a desperate move, and sounded like it.

But Meredith just snorted, scowl deepening. "Why?"

I couldn't process the word. "What?"

"I always knew he never believed in me." Her chin trembled, but her eyes burned. "Constantly hauling me around, convincing people to be nice to me, trying to make me more like *him.* This is just par for the course."

"*Meredith*—" Aiden started.

"But when I met you—" She swallowed, a delicate motion of her throat. "When I met *you,* I thought, okay—here at last is *one person* who isn't tolerating me because I'm Aiden's sister. *One person* I won over on my own. Who likes me for me." She shook her head angrily, hair whipping outward. "But it turns out it was *still* all about him. This whole time you were with me, *he* was the reason." A tear broke free of her lashes and slid down her cheek, carving a new channel in the delta of her mascara.

"That's not true!" Not the way she meant it, anyway. I didn't know what to do with my hands—shit, with my *anything.* I grabbed the sides of my head, as if I could hold the situation together that way.

"*Mer . . .*" Aiden sounded gutted. "*I'm so sorry. Cara, tell her—*"

"No!" I jerked sideways, snapping at the air. "*You* shut up!" I turned back to Meredith. "Meredith, I *love* being with you. I've never met anyone who makes me feel the way you do. I—I fucking *hate* school dances, but I was excited to go with you. With *you.* After that first date, I made Aiden promise to stay away whenever we were together, because I wanted you all to myself. All that stuff we talked about—that was *me.* That was *real.* And I just—fuck!" I flailed my arms, then began counting on my fingers. "You're smart, you're fun, you're strong, you're *kind of* a terrifying robot sometimes but in an *extremely* sexy way, and I wish I'd just told you the truth from the beginning, but I don't regret any of it, because all the hours I've spent with you were the first in five years that I wasn't thinking about escaping this *fucking* town." I spoke as quickly as I could, my words getting thinner and tighter until I reached the end and inhaled in a honking gasp.

Meredith's mouth turned up involuntarily at the undignified noise. I leapt on it, hands sliding together as if praying.

"Please," I begged. "You've gotta believe me." I cut myself off at last, lapsing into silence.

Meredith watched me, face the same blank mask as that first day in the lunchroom. At last, she spoke.

"I *do* believe you, Cara." Her words came slow, almost gentle. "But you're too late."

Her eyes searched the room for the brother who was and wasn't there.

"Get out. Both of you."

34

I RAN DOWN the stairs and out the door, outpacing confused looks from Meredith's parents.

"*Hold up,*" Aiden began, "*we need to—*"

"We don't need to do *shit*, Aiden. So for once in your life, please just shut the *fuck* up." My face burned furiously as I jerked open Van Morrison's door and piled in. "Let's go."

Holly's eyes went wide. "Meredith's not coming?"

"What do *you* think?" I cringed at the nastiness of my voice, but not quickly enough to choke it off.

Holly's face went all Sad Muppet. "I'm so sorry, Cara—"

I turned away, unable to face her pity. "Can you just drive, please?"

Holly put the minivan in gear. At the end of the driveway, she asked, "Where're we going?"

A good question. I put a hand over my eyes, distantly noting that I was probably smearing my makeup. As if that mattered now.

"Just take me home." I hated how brittle my voice sounded. But my insides were a car accident, and each word sawed at the lump in my throat.

Holly signaled obligingly and turned out onto the road.

Aiden scoffed. "*Are you seriously going to just—*"

"Not. A. Fucking. Word!" I shouted it directly at the ceiling, making Holly jump.

"*Hey! I'm not the one who fucked this up!*" But he went sulkily, mercifully silent.

The anger inside me thrashed and howled—at myself, but also at Meredith and Aiden. Because he was right—I *had* fucked this up. Had maybe been fucking it up since that first night. By some measures, I'd been fucking up my life since at least the eighth grade, if not the moment of my birth.

But so had Aiden—by dying, by treating Meredith like a sidekick, by coming up with this stupid plan. And Meredith, well, she no doubt had her share. That was what people *were*—a rolling cascade of fuckups that either broke them in half or polished them like rocks in a tumbler.

So yes, it was my fault. But it wasn't *just* my fault.

Yet somehow *I* was the one paying for all of it.

For several minutes, the car was quiet save for the voice of Holly's phone navigation. *You are on the fastest route home.*

Yeah, no shit, Siri.

Holly spoke first, as usual, her tone gentle. "You could still come to the dance with us."

I groaned.

"I know it's not what you wanted," she hurried on. "But we could still have fun, the three of us. And you're already dressed up."

I leaned my head against the cold window. "No."

"Or . . . we could skip the dance." She glanced in the rearview, making eye contact with Elvis. "Go straight to the after-party. Eat ice cream and binge old seasons of *Jet Lag* till we pass out."

Out of the corner of my eye, I could see what those words cost her. Holly lived for nights like this: a fairy-tale dance with her one true love, all gussied up and orchestrated down to the minute. But here she was, willing to throw it all away for me.

It should have been comforting, having a friend like that. Tonight, though, it was just another reminder of how soon she'd be gone. Because even if she hadn't left yet, she'd still already decided to abandon me. And what was one dance in the face of multiple years alone?

The more I thought about it, the more her willingness to sacrifice for my sake felt performative. Was it even really for me? Or was it just another way to remind herself what a great person she was? Hanging out with me was probably ideal for that, given the blinding contrast between us. *Holly* would never lie to her significant other. *Holly* would never give anyone reason to dump her, because *Holly* was a Disney princess who always did the right thing.

The unspoken accusation knotted hot and tight inside my chest.

"I just wanna be alone," I said.

She nodded, giving me space—once again, the perfect friend. My teeth itched.

We passed through the edge of town, close enough to the school to see it lit up against the encroaching night, parking lot already filling with cars. Red and silver balloons bobbed from the sign out front.

The silence congealed, growing tenser. Shifting in her seat, clearly reluctant but unable to resist opening the tragic worm-can that was conversation with me, Holly finally asked, "Is Meredith okay?"

I barked an angry laugh.

"What did you tell her?"

"Everything," I spat. "Just like you wanted."

Holly grimaced. "Well, that's good, at least."

The words stabbed through me, piercing whatever organ was responsible for self-control.

"*Is* it?" I turned sideways in my seat to glare at her. "Is it *really*, Hol? Exactly what about this looks good right now?" I knew I was lashing out, but had neither the strength nor, honestly, the desire to stop. Because wasn't this all a little bit *her* fault, too? Miss Honesty Is the Best Policy?

Holly frowned. "I know it didn't go how you wanted. But she deserved to know the truth."

"Oh, *hooray*! The *truth*!" I gestured to the idea with a big game-show smile. "The thing that makes *nobody* happy!"

Holly's face scrunched further. "If you hadn't waited so long, it might not have been so bad."

That little tinge of righteousness in her voice was a gift. Finally—

something I could push back against without her aikido-ing away from me.

"Right!" I snapped. "Because this is all definitely *my* fault. *My* fault a ghost with a hard-on for prom made me lie to his sister. That was *totally* my choice."

"Aiden's responsible for this, too," Holly dodged.

"But you still think it's my fault. Just say it."

Holly's lips went razor thin. "We all have to take responsibility for our choices."

"So the moral is that I deserve this."

"I didn't say that."

"I should absolutely have thrown away my whole future just to have a clean conscience. Thanks, Jiminy Cricket!"

Holly stared out the windshield, nostrils flaring. "I'm not gonna say I told you so—"

"If you have to say that, then you definitely are."

"Fine," Holly spat, catching fire at last. "I *did* tell you so." But she shook it out like a match, going soft again. "I'm not trying to make you feel worse, Cara. I'm just saying maybe there's a lesson here."

"Of course! A patented Holly Pham Teachable Moment!" I held up my phone. "Hold on, lemme record it for your channel."

Her face flushed, going darker in the lights of the dashboard. "I didn't mean it like that."

"But you *always* mean what you say, remember? Because you're so *honest* and *pure*! Just another reason why everyone loves you!" I was full-on yelling now.

"This isn't about me."

She was right, but it didn't matter. I wanted to fight, and she was here, and tonight that was good enough. Sometimes the whole world is a face that needs punching.

"No," I seethed, "because you never lie, never cheat, always the perfect little saint-in-training. Well, I'm sorry to *disappoint* you. Sorry you had to sacrifice being popular to hang out with the weird little *sinner* who fucks everything up. Maybe it can count as community service. Get you a better seat in Heaven."

Holly's mouth fell open. "Is *that* who you think I am?"

"If the shoe fits . . ." I was making it up as I went along, wanting only to make contact, to land a hit. Like they said in *Fight Club*: I wanted to destroy something beautiful. "You won't even swear! You're Captain-fucking-America. Everything seems so simple to you because you've always been perfect—perfect student, perfect Christian, perfect girlfriend. You applied to *one* college, and there was never a question, because you've never *not* succeeded at something you cared about."

"That's not true!" Holly snapped.

"Of course it is! *You* get everything you want. *I'm* the one who's always losing." I jabbed two fingers into my chest. "I just lost my girlfriend, and my only friends are about to ditch me for fucking *Bible college,* but all you wanna do is tell me how I deserve it." I flung my arms wide, knuckles rapping against windshield glass. "Well, guess what, Hol? You're right! I'm trash! Just like everybody else. Maybe if you *failed* once in a while, like a *normal* person, you'd understand that."

From the back, Elvis finally gathered the courage to lean forward between the seats. "Dude. Cara. You need to chill."

I rounded on him. "Chill like *you,* you mean? Letting Holly run your life, making all your decisions? Getting towed along behind her like an inner tube? Good luck with that. At least I got to *kiss* my girlfriend."

"That's *it*!" Holly yanked the wheel, tearing off the highway onto a side road and braking so hard onto the shoulder you could hear the tires digging furrows in the gravel.

The motion threw me around in my seat, and I glanced back at Elvis, whose face mirrored my shock.

Holly put the van in park, then twisted toward me.

"I've always told myself it's other people's fault you don't have more friends. That they're the ones who made you so defensive, and if they only got to know you, they'd see what a great person you are." She leaned forward, lips pinched so tight and high that they almost touched her nose. "But I was wrong. The way you've treated Aiden and Meredith, the way you're talking right now—you don't give a *shit* about anyone but yourself."

The fierceness in her tone knocked me back. Dazed, I went for the low-hanging observational fruit. "You swore."

"I did." She tilted her head. "See? I can break rules, too. I just *choose* not to, because I'm *trying* to be the best version of myself. Even when it's hard."

I staggered back to my conversational feet, putting up my gloves. "Well. Aren't *you* just the Second Coming?"

Holly's face contorted in disgust. "Really? *That's* what you're gonna say?"

I shrugged. "Guess I'm not the best version of myself tonight."

Holly shook her head again. "This is exactly what I'm talking about. You're always pushing people away. That way you never have to try." She sucked her teeth. "You think everything's *easy* for me? You're an angry little hermit crab, and I've been trying to pull you out of your shell since eighth grade. But instead, you've pulled me in with you." She waved at the mostly empty van. "Do you think I *like* never getting to bring anyone new to our lunch table? Never getting to go to parties together? To always have to weigh doing things with other people against *your* feelings of abandonment? It took you *months* to accept Elvis, and then only because I didn't give you a choice." She flicked a hand off the steering wheel, earning a tiny horn toot. "Do you have any idea how much *work* it takes to be your friend?"

My chest felt kicked in. I wanted to snap back, but couldn't get any air into my lungs.

She sat back and drew a deep breath, then huffed it out.

"But maybe you're right. Maybe I shouldn't be so uptight. Let myself do the wrong thing for once." She looked down at my phone. "How much battery do you have?"

The question startled me so much that I checked. "Fifty-six percent . . . ?"

"Good." She jerked her chin toward the door. "Get out."

"What?" How many times were people going to say that to me tonight?

"You heard me." Holly's bare shoulders lifted in an exaggerated Elmo shrug. "Out."

"Holly . . ." Elvis murmured.

"It's like two miles to my house!"

Holly's eyes were hard. "You'll make it."

"In *these* shoes?" God, how did it come to this?

That hit home. For a second, Holly looked uncertain. Then her face firmed again—the sort of righteous resolution I only ever saw deployed on my behalf.

"Text someone who cares," she said. "Because right now, that's not me."

This was worse than Meredith. At least there, I'd known it might be coming. From Holly, who'd been my sword and shield since that first night on a curb together, it felt like the whole world dropping out from under me.

But the thing about the ground crumbling beneath you is that by the time you realize you're falling, there are no good options left.

"Fine." I wrapped my jacket and my anger around myself and got out of the van.

Holly reached over and pulled the door closed. Taillights blinked on as she shifted, signaled, checked her mirrors and blind spot—

—and drove off down the road.

35

I WATCHED THE taillights recede.

"*Well,*" Aiden drawled, "*that was sure something.*"

I ignored him, mind tumbling over itself.

How exactly had this happened? I couldn't remember everything I'd said, only the way it had felt. It had seemed *necessary.* A release of poisonous pressure, like venting a nuclear reactor before it could melt down.

But now all I could see was Holly's face. As with Meredith, it wasn't the hurt, or the disappointment, but the resignation. The *acceptance.*

Holly Pham—queen of redemption, the female Mr. Rogers, she of the boundless belief—had finally lost faith in me.

The wind blew cold across my bare legs. I hugged my jacket tighter.

In the distance, brake lights flared.

My heart lurched, scrambling up into my throat as the minivan executed a textbook three-point turn and drove back toward me. My limbs went loose, and I almost sat down right there in the gravel.

Because Holly *hadn't* abandoned me. I'd said the worst things I could, pushed her harder than anyone should, and she'd still come back. Turned the other cheek and forgiven me, like the good person she was. I'd been wrong to mock her for it.

Because forgiving is what friends do. And Holly was the best one I'd ever had. My eyes burned with shame and gratitude.

The van slowed, then stopped in the middle of the road. The driver's side window rolled down, revealing Holly's anxious face. "Hey."

Amazing that I could ever have doubted her. I gave a sheepish smile. "Hey."

From inside the van came a snapping sound, and then she was reaching out the window, tossing something. I caught it before even recognizing it.

A fat green glowstick, straight out of the van's emergency kit. The kind you'd set out for visibility if you broke down at night.

"Safety first," she explained.

And drove away.

36

THE BIKE TRAIL cut a railroad-straight path through farms and wetlands. Headlights strobed across it as cars whooshed by on the highway, rising and falling in pitch. In the quiet gaps between, the night filled with croaking frogs and the rustle of rodents helping themselves at the U-Pick strawberry fields.

I walked fast, heels crunching on gravel. I could have called my parents, but explaining the situation—even halfway—sounded more exhausting than walking home. Not that I loved being alone in the dark.

But of course, I wasn't alone.

"You really do have a way with people," Aiden observed.

"Fuck off."

"See what I mean? Total charmer."

"I don't wanna talk right now."

"Well, tough shit, princess, because I do." His voice lost any hint of humor. *"I honestly can't even process how badly you've fucked this up. Like, there's dented-the-car-level fuckup, and then there's drove-a-bus-full-of-orphans-off-a-cliff, and lemme tell ya, you just* flew *through that guardrail."*

"What was I supposed to do?! Just let you disappear?"

"Yes!" Aiden howled. *"Don't you get it? We don't get another shot at this!"*

"We had a deal," I spat back.

"And that's still all that matters, huh? You don't care what happens to me, or to Meredith, as long as you get your proof."

"I can care about both."

"Can you, though?" A snort. *"God, I'm such an idiot."*

"At least we agree on something."

"Holly's right—you really don't *care about either of us. So maybe it's good that this all fell apart. I can see now that you don't deserve Meredith. Not if you're willing to hurt her like this."*

"Oh, *fuck* you, Aiden!" I stopped in the middle of the trail, spinning around as if I might find him behind me. "I never wanted to play manic pixie dream girl in your stupid rom-com! If you wanted to fix Meredith's problems, you should have haunted a fucking *therapist*. This whole secret dating scheme was *your* idea!"

"Yeah, it was." His anger cracked, and I could hear the fear beneath it. *"And you blew it."*

"You blew it first by getting your dumb ass killed. If her problems are anybody's fault, they're *yours*."

The silence of a direct hit. I clenched my fists in victory.

"I know," he said finally, voice brittle. *"And I'm sorry the timing didn't work exactly like we agreed, but this was my chance at redemption—at actually helping Meredith, and making this all mean something. And you threw it away. For what? So I can ride around doing card tricks for you?"*

Now I was the one with nothing to say.

"So now Meredith's even worse off than she was, and I'm still stuck here. Only now I know it's all pointless." He sounded close to tears.

At long last, my brain—which had apparently abandoned ship somewhere in Meredith's driveway—finally caught up, smacking me on the back of the head and reminding me, *You need him, dumbass.*

I forced my voice to soften. "It's not pointless. Meredith just needs time to process." My own thoughts raced. "Look, you're still here, right? That must mean there's still a chance to complete your mission."

"You don't know that."

"You don't know it's *not* that." Maybe not the strongest logic, but work with what you've got. "We'll figure something out. And in the meantime, we can introduce you to the world and cover your side of the deal so that when Meredith *is* happy again, you can move on with a clean conscience. Everybody wins." By the end of my speech, I actually half believed it.

But Aiden just laughed.

"My side of the deal?" His voice was ragged. *"The deal is* over, *Cara."*

"It doesn't have to be."

"I think it does." He sighed. *"Maybe I ruined Meredith's life, but you ruined my afterlife. So, thanks but no thanks. I'm out."*

"What do you mean, 'out'?!"

But there was no response.

"Aiden?"

The night air blew through me.

"Fuck!" I kicked the ground, scraping my bare toes and sending an arc of gravel blooping into the marsh.

So here it was at last: no ghost, no girlfriend, no best friend. Totally and completely alone. The night felt like a deep-sea trench—dark and cold, the crushing weight settling in my chest and making it hard to breathe.

They were right to be mad at me. *I* was mad at me. But also: *fuck* them. I'd *tried* to fix things. I'd apologized. I'd chased Meredith back to her damn house trying to explain, and all three of them had judged me without trial. Exactly *one thing* went wrong, and they kicked me to the curb—in Holly's case, literally.

For them to give up on me like that—that wasn't friendship. That wasn't *love.* Love was unconditional. It was helping someone bury bodies, standing by them even when they screwed up. Anything less was just another fucking *deal*—a contract to help everyone pretend they weren't alone.

If they weren't with me now . . . it meant they'd never really been with me at all.

The thought turned my bones soft, making me want to crumple

up into a ball. Maybe I could just lie down here and never get up. *If a Cara falls in the forest, does anyone care?*

Nana had understood. Whatever Dad said, she'd known other people were a liability—that making your happiness contingent on theirs was asking to be hurt. So while everyone else was impaling themselves on each other's jagged edges, she'd taken *responsibility*. She'd dug a moat around herself, for everyone's safety. She'd been totally unencumbered, and thus capable of anything.

And now I was, too.

The thought kept my eyes dry. But it didn't pump the water from my lungs.

I turned to continue my midnight march—only to stumble again, heel turning beneath me and dumping me hard onto the gravel. Rocks bit into my bare knees.

"Fucking *heels!*" I grabbed the offending shoe and chucked it as hard as I could. There was a rustle and a splash as it disappeared into the tall grass.

Right. Because that *definitely* improved my situation.

I found myself waiting for Aiden to call me out, automatically readying my riposte. But the only commentary was the chorus of horny frogs.

Fuck this. Fuck *all* of this. I dug into my purse for my phone, realizing as I did so that my after-party bag was still in Van Morrison. But a missing nightguard was the least of my problems right now.

I unlocked the screen, already planning what to say to my parents to prevent as much conversation as possible.

And saw the notification for the email from earlier, still bright and unanswered.

Still on for 11 tomorrow?

Carson Keene. Our meeting.

And just like that, I realized I didn't need any of them. Not Holly, with her self-righteous guilt trips. Not Meredith, with her complicated baggage. Not even Aiden, with his stupid deals.

Sure, it would have been better to have Aiden working with me. I'd promised Carson a chance to interact with a real ghost, and of course I'd *like* to be able to replicate our experiments. But I still had dozens of videos, including all the footage from the factory and the ponds. That was better than most ghost hunters ever got. And I was still the only person Aiden could talk to. Considering how lonely he'd been in the year before he met me, how long could he *really* stay away? The dude couldn't even change a channel on his own.

I didn't *need* him—I *owned* him.

For the first time, I didn't have to worry. I didn't have to feel guilty, or hold back, or live by someone else's standards. Like Meredith had said in the car that first night—I could be whoever I wanted to be, right now. The last shackles binding me to this town—this *life*—had fallen away.

And I had Carson Keene. With him on my side, the runway was finally clear. All that was left was to take off.

I might not have friends.

But I could still have fame.

Sitting with one shoe on in the middle of a dark swamp, I opened the message and typed back.

Absolutely. See you then.

37

THE SECOND STREET Café was a classic diner: the kind of place where waitresses called you "hon" regardless of age and football players regularly challenged each other to finish twelve-egg omelets. Cracked red vinyl seats squeaked under the weight of the usual post-church rush.

Yet today, there was an additional crowd. They straggled in in pajama pants and last night's tuxes, eyes bloodshot and hair tied up in messy buns. They squashed hip to hip into booths, laughing with the giddiness of having been up all night or clutching coffees with the theatrical moans of the proudly hungover. Neighboring tables called back and forth to each other, clique boundaries temporarily suspended.

I watched the flock of them, chattering and brightly colored, and couldn't help but think of Holly. Had she and Elvis gone to the dance? Had her parents let him stay over without the buffer of other girls? I imagined the four of us in this booth: Meredith's head on my shoulder as she struggled to stay awake, me razzing Holly and Elvis for splitting a breakfast milkshake. Telling ourselves the story of prom, already enshrining the night in our shared mythology.

Instead, I was alone in an empty booth. That should have made me mad, the way it had last night—cursing them all with every step of my long hike home, before crashing into bed in my muddy dress. But now, with sun streaming in through the windows and

Queen's "Don't Stop Me Now" on the jukebox, I just felt tired. A fire can only burn so long before it turns to ash.

Screw it. I hoped Holly and Elvis had still managed to have a fun prom night without me. They deserved it. And Meredith—I hoped she wasn't too broken up. While my own wounds still stung, I could admit now that I'd done most of the damage. Never mind that I hadn't *meant* to hurt any of them.

But what was done was done. Nothing to do but forge on alone.

"Anything else, hon?" The waitress looked meaningfully down at the hash browns I'd been pushing around, the solitary plate out of place on a table built for sharing.

"No thanks. I'm waiting for someone."

"Right." She gave me a hooded look that was equal parts pity and exasperation, but moved on.

A paper straw wrapper flew between tables, eliciting another storm of laughter.

Then the door chimed open . . . and there he was.

He looked straight out of one of his videos—dark jeans and a blue blazer over a red Pizza John shirt. Yet at the same time, he also looked subtly different: cheeks a little heavier, blond hair a little thinner. I was suddenly aware that, despite his boyish charm, he was basically my dad's age. Also, for some reason he was wearing extra-chunky black glasses, their lenses slowly transitioning from dark to clear as he looked around the restaurant.

It felt surreal to see him in this environment—as if every head should be turning, cameras flashing as people rushed to get his autograph. Yet nobody seemed to notice him.

His gaze lit on me, and I waved. My own outfit choice had been grueling: something sharp, adult, flashy enough for a future You-Tube celebrity, but not so sexy that he'd think I was flirting with him. Never mind the fact that he was Carson Keene and I was nobody—I needed him to take me seriously as a colleague. I'd settled on a bright, summery dress, topping it with my trademark moto jacket for branding purposes and to keep from showing too much skin.

He raised his chin in acknowledgment and picked his way over to my table, then held out his hand. "Cara Weaver?"

"Hi. Yeah." Did you stand up to shake hands? But there wasn't a lot of room in the aisle. I shook, trying not to fangirl—*I was touching Carson Keene*—and he slid into the booth opposite me.

"Thanks for coming," I said.

"My pleasure." He nodded to my plate. "Any good?"

"Oh, uh . . . yeah?" I felt suddenly self-conscious about my ketchup-y swamp of potato shreds, and laughed awkwardly. "Any hash browns are good hash browns, right?"

"They're all good spuds, Bront."

It was the sort of meme my dad would reference, but I laughed anyway.

"So just as a reminder, this is all being recorded." He reached up and tapped the side of his glasses, which I saw now had a tiny embedded lens.

"You want to publish *this*?" I didn't know whether the thought was thrilling or terrifying.

"No no—I wouldn't spring that on you. It's just something I do when meeting privately with fans, to make sure there's no"—he waved vaguely—"misunderstandings. That still cool?"

"Yeah, sure." It was a little creepy, but I wasn't stupid: I might not be a minor anymore—barely—but I was still some rando, and he was a full-on celebrity whose career could be ruined by any hint of #MeToo. Of course he was paranoid.

"Okay, great." He folded his hands. "So! Tell me about this ghost."

I took a shaky breath, trying to figure out where to start. "So, uh, there's this factory . . ."

I laid out the story: finding Aiden, his mission to help Meredith recover from his death, all my different experiments trying to verify his existence. I did my best to dance around the whole dating angle, saying only that I'd agreed to help him pull his sister out of her funk. As I talked, I pulled up the best video clips on my phone, playing him the thermal camera recordings from the factory and the ponds, the bruise-colored blob that was the closest thing Aiden had to a physical manifestation.

Carson listened carefully, interrupting only to ask clarifying questions or order coffee from the waitress. The intensity of his focus was disconcerting, but it actually made it easier to keep talking—the way he soaked up every detail drew the story out of me like a magnet.

When at last I finished, stopping just short of the previous night's prom disaster, he passed the phone back—and there was that Video Carson smile, warm as a heat lamp.

"Congratulations, Cara. You might really have something here."

Lightning ran through my veins, threatening to melt me into a puddle of twitching goo. This must be what it felt like to be Pikachu. I held myself together enough to say, "You think?"

"Absolutely."

This was it: the moment I'd been waiting for. The whole world felt fuzzy and indistinct, which was exactly wrong because I wanted to *save* this memory, to engrave it into my brain so I'd never forget.

His eyes traveled a brief circuit through the empty air around me. "This is a great start. But—and please don't take this the wrong way—these videos would take about ten minutes to fake in Premiere. You said in your email that Aiden follows you around. Can we try the dice thing right now?" He pulled out his own phone, its case branded with the *Ghoul Scout* logo. "I've got a random number generator app."

"So, um . . ." I'd known it was coming, but it still didn't make it any easier to say the next part. "He's . . . actually not here right now."

"He's not." Carson frowned, voice flattening, and I could see him walking back his estimation of the situation. Of *me*.

"I know what you're thinking," I said quickly. "But the videos aren't staged, I swear! It's just . . ." I groaned and shoved a hand in my hair. "It's complicated."

The way he crossed his arms was a dagger in my heart, but he said, "Try me."

So I told him the rest, warts and all: the dates, prom, Aiden storming out on me. I tried to end on a high note, pointing out how the failure meant Aiden couldn't pass on yet, but it sounded feeble and desperate to my own ears.

Carson took it all in carefully. When I finished, he said, "I see. That *does* complicate things."

"I know." I couldn't meet his eyes.

"But hey." He softened, reaching out and tapping my elbow. "It's not the end of the world. We can still salvage this."

I looked up. "Yeah?"

"If you're right that your ghost can't move on or talk to anyone else, then we've just gotta wait him out. Find something else you can offer him in exchange for cooperation. And like you said, you disrupting his unfinished business is perfect—now you've got him trapped here indefinitely." He grinned. "We've got all the time we need to do this right."

Trapped. The ugliness of that word rasped like a nail file. But wasn't that exactly what I wanted? Aiden here, forever?

I nodded.

"I've got a fan in the physics department at UW," Carson continued. "Once you've got the ghost working for you again, we can get him into a lab and see about examining him in other spectrums. Observe him under more controlled conditions, see how he responds to different stimuli." He inclined his head respectfully. "And replicate your original experiments, of course."

Controlled conditions. Different stimuli. As if Aiden were some new strain of bacteria we were poking and prodding. Zap the lab rat to see what it does. "Of course."

"We can release the same videos on both our channels, if you want." Carson's tone suggested he was being generous. "Or you can just guest on mine." He took a sip of coffee, then gestured with the cup. "I checked out your channel, you know. There's some good stuff there. You just need eyes on it."

Once upon a time, those words would have had me so far

over the moon I'd have burned up on reentry. But now I just felt queasy. "Thanks."

"I especially like the whole Masked Exorcist bit. A hook like that is everything for branding. The worst thing you can be on the internet is boring."

I imagined what Holly would say if she heard me like this, calmly discussing how to bottle Aiden up. "Um, we probably won't be able to get her back on."

"You think?" He raised a surprised eyebrow, then shrugged. "Well, maybe that's for the best. Funny gets clicks, but from here on out you'll want people to take you seriously." His mug traced little circles in the air. "Either way, your numbers are gonna *explode,* so get ready. You'll wanna make sure you're set up to properly monetize the . . ."

His words faded out, and I was once again floating inside myself somewhere, watching through the windows of my eyes as he prattled on, using the syrup jug and jam tubs to represent different components of our release strategy. My future, reduced to makeshift pieces on a greasy game board.

Maybe he was right. Maybe I *could* strong-arm Aiden into doing more experiments with us. Wasn't that exactly what I'd thought last night? Force him into it by withholding my help, my conversation— doling out access to the world in exchange for tricks. Like a prisoner working for cigarettes. A dog performing for treats.

My stomach cramped.

I was so close to my dream. But was this really how I wanted to get there?

I interrupted Carson. "What if we just used the videos?"

He blinked, as if unused to being cut off. "Sorry?"

"What if we just published the videos we've got? No more Aiden experiments."

His brow furrowed. "Why would we do that?" He shook his head. "Those videos are a start, but they're not gonna get us the attention we need. They're suggestive, but they're not *proof.*"

"I just don't think Aiden's gonna wanna help us."

"So make him." He said it so lightly, grinning that famous smile. "Don't worry, you'll figure it out." He raised his mug in a salute. "I believe in you."

Meredith, on the climbing wall.

I believe in you.

Suddenly it was all I could do to keep my hash browns from coming back up. I shrank back into the cigarette-scarred seat. "I'm . . . not sure I wanna do this."

Carson's mug froze in midair. "Excuse me?"

"I'm sorry." I moved to slide out of the booth. "I shouldn't have wasted your—"

"Whoa whoa *whoa.*" Carson's hand shot out, blocking my exit. A microsecond later he seemed to notice what he'd done and yanked it back just as quickly, holding it as far away from me as possible. "Just hold up a sec! Let's talk about this."

The way was clear—but he was still Carson Keene. That gravity was enough to keep me in my seat. "I don't wanna use Aiden against his will."

"So don't! Convince him! *Negotiate!*" Carson leaned in, eyes huge and blue. "Cara, I *want* to believe you—and if you're being honest with me, then the two of us are poised to become the most famous ghost hunters of all time!"

It was everything I'd ever wanted to hear. Everything I'd whispered to myself before falling asleep at night.

But I still couldn't meet his eyes.

He saw it and shifted gears. "But forget about that for a second. This is the most important scientific discovery since . . . shit, maybe just the most important discovery, *period.* What happens after we die is *the* question." He flapped a hand emphatically. "I know your ghost is all butthurt right now, but even if he doesn't come around—are you really gonna let *one dude* stand in the way of *the future of human knowledge?*" He shook his head, trademark hair flopping. "This is bigger than him. Bigger than *all* of us."

He was right. Objectively correct. The world deserved the truth.

And yet no matter how I turned it, how many angles I observed it from, one fact kept bubbling up:

I didn't *care*.

Yes, people deserved to know. But I didn't like *people*. I liked Aiden, and Meredith, and Holly.

I'd never get famous unless I published. But so what? Why did I care more about the opinions of random strangers than the people I loved—the people who, until I'd screwed them over, loved me *back*? I'd always told myself all I needed was a few ride-or-die friends, and everyone else could go to hell. Yet here I was, sacrificing those same friends for the faceless masses.

If the only way to win was by hurting the people I cared about, what was the fucking point?

I knew my friends. And they wouldn't want this.

Which meant maybe *I* didn't want this.

"I'm sorry," I said. "I can't."

Carson steepled his hands, projecting thoughtful sincerity.

"I know this is hard," he said. "Nobody wants to be a jerk. But it's our *job*, Cara. An investigator does whatever it takes to reveal the truth." He jabbed the table with a fingertip. *"Whatever. It. Takes."*

I looked at him, stretched out over the table, elbow slowly absorbing syrup where it rubbed up against the pitcher, and it was like I was seeing two overlapping images.

One was Carson Keene from the internet, the man I'd idolized since childhood. Driven. Unflinching. *Famous.*

But now there was another as well: An aging influencer desperate for validation. A man who'd drive two hours on a Sunday to team up with a random teenager. A man who'd sacrifice every friendship, enslave a dead kid, and call it idealism.

The life I'd always wanted seemed suddenly small and sad.

"Everyone who ever dismissed us," Carson pressed, "everyone who called us cranks and pseudoscientists—we can prove them wrong, once and for all. Because we're *right*, Cara." His hands balled into fists. "We're *right*."

I stood and dug into my pocket, dropping one of Dad's emergency twenties onto the table. Hearing his voice in my head. *You gotta give people the chance to surprise you.*

I looked down at Carson, hair askew, creeper glasses recording.

"We *are* right," I said softly. "But it's not worth it."

38

MY QUADS SCREAMED as I hauled myself up the last stretch of trail. Leaves slapped at my face, and then I pushed through into sunlight.

Meredith sat on the hillside, arms across her knees. The yellowed grass lapped halfway up her body, folding her into the landscape. She stared out at the transmission lines with such intensity that it felt blasphemous to intrude.

She turned at the sound. "What're you doing here?"

"What do you think?"

She started to respond, then paused, blinking at my bedraggled state, the bike helmet bumping against my hip. "Did you *bike* all the way out here?"

"Obviously?" I gestured to the sweat patches spreading from my pits. "I'm nervous, but I'm not *this* nervous." I bent over, catching my breath. "I tried your house first. This was the only other place I could think to look." I straightened again, massaging the stitch in my side. "Couldn't you have chosen a Fortress of Solitude somewhere *flat*?"

An expression that might have been impressed flickered across her face, but she smothered it in the cradle. "Whatever you came to say, I don't want to hear it."

"Are you sure?" I held out my hands, palms up. "Because I've been writing my speech the whole way here, and it starts with, 'You're totally right, I'm a self-centered asshole.'"

Her face gave nothing away—but she didn't tell me to leave, either. I sank down on my haunches, still well away from her, grass waving between us like an anime samurai duel.

"I'm sorry, Meredith. I'm sorry I didn't tell you everything from the start. I'm sorry I lied, and that I was so focused on finally finding a ghost that I let it override everything else. It was selfish, and stupid. You trusted me, and I let you down."

Still she said nothing.

"But there was one thing I never lied about." I locked eyes with her, meeting her stare for stare. "I never lied about liking you. Ever since that first night, watching you dance at the concert, I haven't been able to stop thinking about you. I haven't *wanted* to." I shook my head. "Everything I said back at your house is true. You're the most intimidating girl I've ever met, in the best possible way. And I know I don't deserve you, but I *want* to. I wanna be the person you thought I was." I grimaced. "I like that version better."

At last, Meredith spoke.

"I do, too," she said. "Too bad she's not real."

"But she *could* be." My chest contracted—a snarl of barbed wire pulled tight. I wrapped a blade of grass around my finger. "All this time, I thought I was looking for a ghost. But really, I was just looking for a way to feel comfortable in my own life. You do that to me, Meredith. When I'm with you, I don't need anything else."

Meredith snorted. "Can you even hear how this is still all about you?"

"I know, but that means it's also about *you*. Because we're the *same*, Meredith." I leaned forward, kneeling on the stony ground. "We've both built these giant defensive walls because we've given up on people ever seeing us for who we want to be. But you shouldn't hide, because you're *amazing*. I wanna make you feel that. I wanna spend every day forcing you to confront what a complete and utter *badass* you are, until you see yourself the way *I* see you. When you feel like a nobody, I wanna be there to prove you wrong. I wanna be in your corner, and I fucking *need* you in mine."

I held up my wrist, displaying the woven colors of the bracelet she'd made.

"I know we started for the wrong reasons. But I'm here now for the right ones."

I made myself stop, my heart pounding into the silence. I wanted to say more—to somehow convey the way it felt to sit next to her on a sun-warmed rock, to lie side by side in the dirt or ride shotgun with her through an endless beat of streetlights. But I'd said things the best I could, and more wouldn't help.

Her gaze slid slowly from the bracelet up to my face. "You done?"

Those eyes. My hope shattered like a dropped mug.

Only one thing left to say, then.

"Not quite." I took a deep breath, forcing down the despair building like thunderclouds inside my chest. "Because even if you can't forgive me—I don't want to be the thing that stands between you and Aiden. He came back for you, Meredith. Even if you don't want to talk to me, you should talk to *him*."

Meredith grimaced. Her eyes flashed with her own storm of emotions—the fury, but also the longing. In that gaze was every self-recrimination, every night spent lying awake, cursing Aiden. Cursing herself.

She turned it away, out toward the hills.

"Don't come here again."

My lungs felt clamped shut. "Meredith—"

Her voice broke. "Just go."

Her anger I could take, but not this. Hadn't I hurt her enough already? *Fucking know when you're done, Cara.*

I stood.

"Okay." I dug into my pocket and pulled out the thumb drive, then stepped closer and held it out.

She looked over at it, then up at me.

"It's all the evidence," I explained. "Of Aiden. Videos, mostly."

Slowly, as if her hand were moving against her will, she reached out and took it.

"I didn't keep any backups."

Her eyes shot wide, then narrowed. "Why?"

I shrugged, trying not to show the effort it took. "Because you're the one he came back for."

Still she looked suspicious. "What am I supposed to do with it?"

"Whatever you want." I turned away so I didn't have to keep seeing that wary expression. "Watch it, publish it, throw it in the bushes—it's yours."

I walked away, feeling her eyes like a knife between my shoulder blades. At the tree line, I paused, still not daring to look back.

"I don't know if people will believe it's proof of ghosts," I said. "But it's proof he loves you."

Then I slipped between the branches.

39

MY BODY FELT like a lightning-struck tree, thin skin wrapped around a blackened hollow. Yet as much as I hurt, I also felt lighter. Like I might float up off the ground.

It was over—all the lying and maneuvering and conflicting loyalties. I'd made my deal with Aiden in hopes of becoming the person I'd always wanted to be. But I'd met that person now. And I didn't like her very much.

Whatever Meredith chose to do with the videos, it wasn't any of my business. Maybe it never really had been. The bond tying her and Aiden together—it belonged to them, not to me. Whatever choice she made, I hoped it brought her comfort.

Because I'd made mine. I'd chosen Meredith. Whether she chose me back or not.

I could live with that.

Behind me, sticks cracked.

I turned just as Meredith came barreling through the leaves. She stopped short, glaring. A huntress framed in green.

"Did you really not keep any of the videos?" she demanded.

I nodded.

She crossed her arms, watching me.

It was so much of who she was, that stare: Piercing and evaluating. Weighing my heart like Anubis, finding every crack, every inconsistency, every area where I should have been better. If she hated me, at least it was because she knew me now. Meredith looked inside you and gave you the love you deserved.

She nodded sharply. "Fine."

I blinked. "'Fine' what?"

"You get another chance."

My brain stuttered, failing to process. The little beach ball spun. "You—"

She stalked forward, grabbed me by my sweaty collar, and mashed her lips against mine. The roughness of it—the scrape of salty fabric against the back of my neck, the power in her body as she pulled me to her—made it real. I made a noise that could have been either laugh or sob.

Just as abruptly, she broke off and pushed me back far enough to look into my eyes.

"And if you *ever* lie to me again," she said, still looking furious, "I'm gonna haul you up a climbing wall and leave you there."

I grinned. "Deal."

Carefully, watching her face the whole way, I leaned in to kiss her again.

It was not an all-is-forgiven kiss. Even as she pressed against me, I could feel her holding back, keeping me at a distance. There was a heaviness there, a weariness. She might have unlocked the castle gate, but her walls were back up, and all the stronger for having been proven justified. There was no telling how long it might take to wear them down a second time.

But she was giving me the chance to try.

We broke apart again. I ran a hand down her cheek. "I'm almost afraid to ask, but . . . why'd you change your mind?"

Meredith frowned, then loosed a shaky sigh.

"Because you're right. You're a self-centered asshole, Cara. You hurt me. A lot. And the worst part is, you'll probably do it again."

I waited.

So did she.

"Uh . . ." I ventured.

"But." She tugged on my collar again, and at last the corner of

her mouth turned up. "You're also the only girl who's ever made me want to deal with her bullshit."

I smiled weakly. "Hooray . . . ?"

She pushed me back a foot, creating space between us. "After Aiden, I tried to stay away from everybody. So nobody else could ever hurt me like that." She shook her head. "But it doesn't work. You can't keep the bad stuff out—you just lock it in with you." Her eyes were still so fierce. "So *yeah*, I'm pissed at you. But being pissed doesn't *get* me anything. Giving up on you now wouldn't make me hurt any less. It'd just cost me all the good parts of being with you."

"So you're saying there are good parts."

She snorted. "You do *not* want to go fishing for compliments right now." She gave me a little shake. "But you see me for who I am. And you keep coming back." The smallest smile. "That's worth some hurt."

All my hopes crowded into my throat, like cartoon characters stuck in a doorway. "I *am* persistent."

She made a face. "It's your best and worst quality."

I slid my hand up her forearms, cupping her elbows. "I thought that was my sparkling wit."

"Pfffffft." But she darted in to kiss me again. And in the touch of her lips, I could feel how this might go: each kiss a little softer, a little easier. Something inside me released with a sigh.

I ran my cheek against hers, so achingly smooth, then leaned back. "So . . . we're good?"

"No." She shook her head. "We're good *and* bad. We're fucking *messy*." She gripped my arms, thumbs digging into me. "But we're here, and we're dealing with it. Together."

"Together," I agreed, and leaned my forehead against hers.

We stood like that, encased in a bubble of rustling emerald. Outside lurked a world that would cut us up and stitch us back together. Beyond this moment would be another, and another. Some would be magical. Some would be safe. And some would take more from us than we could imagine.

But that was life. There was no opting out. We were both just standing in a river, waiting to see what the water carried to us, and what it carried away.

But we could choose who we stood next to.

My hand slipped down into hers. Strong fingers wrapped around mine, holding me in place. An anchor against the current.

I closed my eyes and breathed her in.

And in my ear, a faint voice whispered:

"Perfect. No notes."

40

VAN MORRISON CRUNCHED to a stop. Holly shifted into park, but didn't cut the engine.

"Thanks for the ride," I said.

"No problem." She turned and gave me Concerned Mom eyes. "You good?"

God, Holly. Let it never be said that she didn't walk her talk. She'd barely even made me grovel before forgiving me, especially after she heard what I'd done with the evidence. I didn't deserve a friend like her.

But I was trying. Because I could see now that Nana had been wrong.

Other people weren't the problem.

Other people were the point.

"I think so." I drummed my hands on the dashboard. "Thanks for . . . you know. Not hating me."

She cocked her head. "Contrary to popular belief, you are not, actually, all that hateable."

"Popular belief, huh?"

She grinned. "Yeah, but eff those people."

I threw my head back and laughed. "You are going *hard* today, lady. I mean, who'd ever have thought I'd see Holly Pham cut class?"

"It's only two periods. I can still make it before AP History." A glance at the stereo's clock gave lie to her chill demeanor. "Help me with filming tonight?"

"Of course." With my channel going on indefinite hiatus, I'd have plenty of time to help Holly with hers. "Lemme guess: This one's on forgiveness?"

She made a face. "I was thinking the perils of self-righteousness."

I shrugged. "It's not self-righteous if you're right."

"See, this is *exactly* why people need a video."

I reached over and grabbed her hand.

"Seriously, Hol—I really am sorry. For everything. You're the best friend anyone ever had."

"Glad we're in agreement there." But her face softened, and she shook our clasped hands gently. "You know you can never lose me, right?"

I hunched defensively. "I know."

"And you can always come visit."

"At *Bible college*? That place'll catch fire the second I walk through the doors."

"Then we'll hang out on the quad." Her other hand went to cover mine, puppy eyes in full effect. "And I'll call you every day."

"Holly." I dropped the banter and gripped her back like the lifeline she was. "I'll be okay. And I want this for you."

"Really?" She looked so desperately hopeful—not just for herself, but for me as well. Because that's who Holly was: the person who believed in you so hard that maybe *you* started to believe, too.

"Really." I smiled. "*One* of us has to change the world, right?"

She grinned back, eyes brimming, and pulled me in for a hug. It was awkward, seat-belt-strangled, and I never wanted to let go.

But maybe I didn't have to. Just because someone's leaving doesn't mean they're leaving *you*.

She pulled back, blinking rapidly, and nodded toward the door. "Go. Help them say goodbye."

I got out. Holly waved and drove off.

When I turned around, Meredith was standing on her porch. Morning sun filled the valley, climbing the stairs and slanting a honey-warm glow that left her half illuminated, half in shadow. I stood paralyzed by the dichotomy of her.

Then she stepped toward me, into the light.

"I could have picked you up," she noted.

"It's okay. Holly wanted to help." I approached and took her hand, then walked us slowly to the big tree. Up among the weathered remnants of the fort, a murmuration of starlings filled the air with bright chatter. They sounded like sunrise.

I turned to face Meredith, taking her other hand as well. "Ready?"

"Absolutely not." She tried to smile and only got halfway there. "Let's do it."

I took a deep breath. "Aiden?"

"I'm here." His voice was the faintest I'd ever heard it. *"Hey, Meredith."*

I repeated the words, closing my eyes to try to take myself out of the equation.

"Hey, Aiden." Meredith's voice wobbled.

Yesterday, in Meredith's secret meadow, the three of us had talked for hours: Meredith holding my hand to feel the faint electrical tingle of Aiden's hug. Lying with her head in my lap as the two of them relived their shared memories. It had felt weird, being the connection between them. But it had also felt good. To wipe the tears from her cheeks. To feel the two of them laughing—one from the outside, one from the inside.

They'd decided not to tell their parents. Aiden didn't feel like he could handle it, didn't think there was enough left of him to make it through the whole process again. Maybe one day Meredith would tell them the story. But for today, he'd agreed to hold on until their mom went to work and their dad left to run errands so that the three of us could be alone here, in this place.

Aiden had come back for Meredith.

So she would see him off.

She took a shaky breath, hands trembling. "I hated you, you know. For going without me."

"I know."

"But I hated myself even more." Her hands gripped mine as if clinging to a wall. "For making you go."

"You didn't make me do anything."

"But I *wanted* to." The pain in her voice made me open my eyes, only to see that she'd squeezed hers shut. "I *wanted* you to leave me alone. To stop always trying to orchestrate my life. I was mad, and I was jealous, and I was sick of always being your project—the plus-one you dragged along to parties and things."

"But you wanted *that stuff!"*

"Yeah, for *myself*!" She pointed at her chest. "I wanted it to be *mine*—for people to want *me* there, not tolerate me because they wanted *you*." She shook her head, chin doing most of the moving. "It wasn't just that everybody thought of me as just your kid sister. It was that *you* thought of me that way, too."

"I never thought of you as 'just' anything." Aiden's voice wobbled. *"You're my favorite person. I just wanted . . . wanted the world to see you the same way I do. But I fucked it up. And I've kept fucking it up, trying to control your life."* A ragged breath, voice rising in pitch. *"I'm so sorry, Mer."*

"I'm sorry, too."

"You have nothing to apologize for. I'm the one who was wrong. About everything. But especially about you." He laughed once, explosively, like someone getting the Heimlich maneuver. *"You don't need my help, Mer. You never did."* Then, in something closer to his usual bantering tone, he said, *"I mean, come on. You made it through the worst thing anyone can experience—losing* me.*"*

That earned a genuine laugh from Meredith.

"And now here you are, stronger than ever, and with an awesome girlfriend to boot. I'm proud of you, Meredith." His voice turned earnest. *"Can you forgive me?"*

Meredith's lips quivered, but turned up on one side.

"Of course I do, dumbass."

"Thank you." The words came out in a whoosh, and in his relief I heard the question beneath the question.

Because if Meredith could forgive him—then she could forgive herself, too.

"I wish you could stay," Meredith said.

"I know. But I had my time. I just couldn't go until I knew you'd be okay."

A tear escaped down Meredith's cheek, and she wiped it away. "I'll be fine."

"I know." I could hear his smile. *"I just needed you to know it."*

She rolled her eyes, sniffing. "Still with the mind games."

"Hey, what're big brothers for?"

Everybody went silent.

"So," Aiden said at last. *"I guess this is it."* He tried to sound confident. *"Thanks for the assist, Cara."*

"My pleasure." And then, because I couldn't help it: "What's it feel like?"

Aiden laughed. *"Still investigating, huh?"* His voice went dreamy. *"Don't worry. It's like I told you before—it's the easiest thing in the world. Like you're in a warm ocean, and you can just let go and . . . float."*

"Sounds nice."

"You know, I really think it is." He sounded peaceful. *"But you'll see for yourself someday. No rush, okay?"*

"We'll take our time," I said dryly.

"Good call." His voice grew fainter. *"All right, here we go."*

Meredith squeezed my hands painfully tight. "Love you, Aiden."

"Love you, too." He gave a long sigh of relaxation. *"Later, sis. See you on the other side."*

I can't tell you exactly what it felt like. Aiden had always been just a voice inside my head, with no physical sensation. But I still felt him leave. One minute he was there, and the next . . .

Meredith saw it in my face. "Is he . . . ?"

I nodded.

She folded forward into me. We were both crying, but they weren't sad tears, or happy ones. Just release.

It was like Aiden had said: sometimes, at the end of something, all that's left is to let go.

⌐

An eternity later, Meredith pulled back. Her eyes were red, but her smile was real. She darted forward and kissed me, mouth thick and phlegmy and perfect.

"Thank you," she whispered.

"Thank *you.*"

We leaned into each other, balancing. A cathedral dome held together by its own immense weight.

Into that space, I whispered, "You okay?"

She shook her head slightly, hair scratching faintly against my forehead. "Not really." Then, with another tentative smile—"But also . . . maybe?"

I knew what she meant. I rubbed my nose against hers. "Should we go?"

"One sec."

She broke away, then turned to the tree and began to climb—smooth, feline movements, limbs graceful and body weightless. At the top, she stepped off onto the highest platform. Reaching back under her hair, she untied Aiden's crystal pendant, then tied it around a branch and climbed back down.

At the bottom, she took one last look up at where the necklace hung, almost invisible. Just another sparkle among rustling green and brilliant blue.

Then she turned and hooked a hand around my waist, pulling me close. When she kissed me, it was with the slow, lazy warmth of something just beginning.

"Okay," she said when we finally broke apart. "*Now* we can go."

"Are you sure?" I grinned, a little dazed. "Maybe we should run that test again. Just to verify results."

"Dork." But she reached up and cupped my cheek. "Come on."

Hand in hand, we turned and walked back toward the house.

Behind us, the cloud of starlings rose and took flight, dissolving into the endless summer sky.

Acknowledgments

First off, thank you to my indefatigable agent, Josh Adams, and the Adams Literary team—for helping turn a dream into a career, and for constantly reassuring me that everything is in fact fine and normal.

Thank you to my editor, Sara Goodman, for both believing in this book and letting me know where it was only half-cooked—this story would be very different without her keen insight. Thanks as well to assistant editor Vanessa Aguirre for keeping all the plates spinning smoothly.

Have you ever watched the credits scroll at the end of a movie and wondered why books don't have the same thing? Me too—so here are a bunch more folks who deserve both recognition and my deepest thanks for helping bring this book from my head to yours:

Publisher: Eileen Rothschild

Managing editor: Eric Meyer

Production editor: Cassie Gutman

Production manager: Chris Leonowicz

Copy editor: Shawna Hampton

Proofreader: Susannah Noel

Authenticity editor: Teresa Tran

Jacket designer: Kerri Resnick

Designer: Jonathan Bennett

Cover artist: Sivan Karim

Marketing: Alexis Neuville and Brant Janeway

Publicity: Kelly South

Sales: Rebecca Schmidt, Sofrina Hinton, Jennifer Edwards, Jennifer Golding, Jaime Bode, Natalia Becerra, Julia Metzger, D'Kela Duncan, and Isaac Loewen

Creative services: Britt Saghi, Kim Ludlam, Tom Thompson, and Dylan Helstien

To everyone else at Wednesday, St. Martin's, Random House Audio, and all my foreign publishers—thank you from the bottom of my heart. A particular shout-out is owed to Chloe Sackur and the Andersen Press team in the UK, who read an early draft, asked hopefully, "Is it going to get shorter . . . ?," and bought it anyway when the answer was no.

My beta readers make all my books better, and this one is no exception. Thank you to Jessica Blat, Katie Groeneveld, Kat "I don't know this character until I know her shoes" Tewson, and Emily "realistic female arousal consultant" Childs. Special thanks as well to Chris Wolfe for convincing me to write the book when I'd abandoned it after two chapters, telling me it was fine to have exactly one chapter from Aiden's point of view. (It wasn't, but it got me moving again.)

Thank you to my families, both the Lafond Clan and the Arnolds, for always having my back. Thank you also to the many friends who prop me up and remind me what really matters: to Wabi, to the Screamin' Hole, to Mooncastle and Fafnir and the Brides of the Lizard God and Zefram the Warp Corgi . . . The list goes on and on, and my life would be so much smaller without each and every one of you.

Finally, thank you to my wife, Margo, who remains the best person I've ever known. Love you, babe.